FIGHT AND FLIGHT

FIGHT AND FLIGHT

SCOTT MEYER

ROCKET HAT  INDUSTRIES

Published by Rocket Hat Industries

ISBN-13: 978-0-9862399-7-7
ISBN-10: 0-9862399-7-6

Cover design by Eric Constantino

The following is intended to be a fun, comedic sci-fi/fantasy novel. Any similarity between the events described and how reality actually works is purely coincidental.

1.

"The eight of us have been killed a combined total of sixty-seven times," Jeff said. "This strikes me as a problem."

A youngish man in a silver sequined robe raised his hand.

"I'm not a school teacher, Martin. If you have a question, you can just ask."

Martin glanced around at his friends, wearing their wizard robes and hats, seated in a cluster of chairs in Jeff's home: a small, unassuming blue hut that, thanks to a magical portal he'd created and a much larger hut out in the woods, appeared to be bigger on the inside than it was on the outside. Jeff stood at the front of the room, addressing them.

Martin said, "Sorry. The whole thing just kinda gave me a Hogwarts vibe."

"That's fine."

"Anyway, I don't have a question so much as a statement. None of us is dead."

"Yes, well, when I say we were killed sixty-seven times, what I mean is that we were nearly killed sixty-seven times, and were only saved by the use of magic or dumb luck."

"Then why not say that?"

"I wanted an opening line that was a real grabber. Something to get your attention before I show you the chart."

Gary raised his hand. The loose sleeve of his black robe slid down to reveal a thin bare arm, as the Dokken T-shirt he wore beneath it had short sleeves. The pale skin of his arm almost matched the bleached white bone that made up his skeletal artificial leg. "I have two questions. One is: Aren't we all here for movie night? The other is: What chart?"

Jeff sighed. "Yes. We are here for movie night. After we discuss the boring business of all of us nearly dying a whole bunch of times, we'll move on to the vital task of watching an old movie."

A black man in a purple robe asked, "What are we watching?"

Jeff said, "Thanks for not raising your hand, Tyler. We're watching *Mad Max: Fury Road.*"

Gary said, "Mad Max! Good! Mel Gibson's the coolest!"

Martin said, "Yeah, you're from 1992, aren't you?"

"Yes. So?"

"So, enjoy enjoying Mel Gibson while you can."

Jeff said, "As for your second question: *What chart?* The chart I haven't shown you yet because I only just got my first sentence out before I got sidetracked."

Jeff waved his magic wand and said, "*Montri la* diagram." An easel holding a large chart appeared next to him. The left side of the chart had a list of the names of the wizards present. Along the top Jeff had listed every event in which one or more of the wizards had nearly been killed, using shorthand titles like "Orcs," "Giant Squid," and "Mud Elemental." A grid full of check marks illustrated which wizards had nearly been killed by each danger. The wizards were silent for a moment while they read and absorbed the information.

Jeff said, "I only included peril that we've faced after finding the file, discovering that the world is a computer program, and coming back here to Medieval England to pose as wizards. Whatever trouble some of you might have gotten into to make you decide to come here is your own business."

Brit the Younger adjusted her glasses, peering across the room at the chart. "Huh. That's funny. I would have assumed that Martin had nearly been killed the most, but Phillip just edges him out."

"Yes," Phillip said, stroking his beard. "But I'd have you know that all of the attempts on my life have happened since I met Martin."

Martin said, "Jeff, I have to object. You say that Phillip nearly killed me in our first duel. That's just not true."

Gwen shook her head, then brushed her light brown bangs out of her eyes and said, "No, Martin, but the villagers thought he killed you, and let's face it, he could have if he'd wanted to."

"Easily," Phillip said.

Tyler said, "I see what you're getting at, Jeff. That's not a great safety record. But, I mean, we *are* time-traveling wizards. Shouldn't we expect a certain amount of danger?"

"Yes, That's my point. We should expect danger, but we don't. That's why we keep getting caught with our pants down."

"We wear robes," Gary said.

"Yes, Gary. Now shut up. My point is that we need to be more prepared. We need to develop real means of defending ourselves and make sure that we have practice using them."

Gary said, "Well, yeah, obviously. That's why I created the Kato Protocol."

"Yes," Jeff said, "But I'm afraid that while having wizards just randomly attack each other without warning has been good for a few laughs, it hasn't really added to our tactical readiness."

"*Tactical readiness.* You've been hanging around with Roy too much."

"No, the rest of you haven't been hanging around with me enough." Roy was an older man from an earlier time, with a crew cut so precise and severe it had become a way of life.

Gary asked, "You wanna hang out with me sometime?"

Roy said, "I do not."

Gary shook his head and waved his hands. "Whatever. Look, the point is, the Kato Protocol is in place so that we'll be ready for attacks and develop offensive weapons, and I think it's succeeded."

Roy said, "That's because you've mistaken jumpiness for vigilance, and you're using the wrong meaning of the word *offensive*. We want *offensive* as in *the opposite of defensive*. Not *offensive* as in *it offends people*. Like your inventions: the fart bomb, the helium-voice spell, and the commando ray."

Martin said, "I've been meaning to ask you: How <u>did</u> you make a ray that caused people's underwear to disappear?"

Gary smiled. "It was a happy accident. I was working on a wedgie ray and it malfunctioned."

Brit said, "Look, Jeff, you're right to be concerned. But if you're this worried about it, why not do what we women did with Atlantis? Create a new place for yourselves somewhere far away that will be safe, instead of living among all these primitive villagers."

Jeff said, "Two reasons. One: if you look at the chart, you'll see that the vast majority of the things that have threatened our lives have come from other magic users, not the locals. Two: if you look closely at your own row on the chart, you'll see that more than half the times you've nearly been killed took place in Atlantis."

Roy nodded. "It's impossible to create a safe place for people to go, because it becomes unsafe when people go there."

Jeff said, "I don't understand why you aren't taking this more seriously. We've all nearly been killed multiple times. Gary lost a leg. I had my powers stripped away, then got dropped off of a cliff! You almost weren't able to hop back in time and save me. This is serious. Our lives are at stake."

"Yeah," Martin said, "But while you point out that we've nearly died sixty-seven times, I'd remind you that we figured out a way to save ourselves sixty-seven times. We always think of something."

Phillip said, "Yes, but Jeff has a point. It would be smart of us to try to think of something in advance, instead of waiting for things to go wrong. What do you have in mind, Jeff?"

"I propose that we each develop a weaponized macro, a spell that will be a useful weapon. Something that has real teeth. Then, when they're done, we'll share them with each other."

"And who do we test them on?" Tyler asked. "The locals? Each other?"

"We'll test them and practice using them in regularly scheduled organized skirmishes against some sort of artificial opposing army that we'll create. That way we won't have to pull our punches."

Gary said, "That actually sounds like fun."

Phillip said, "All right. Let's put it to a vote. All in favor of enacting Jeff's plan, raise your hand."

Everybody raised a hand.

"And everybody in favor of having Jeff create the opposition army, raise your hand."

Everybody raised their hands but Jeff.

Jeff said, "Wait one minute! This was my idea! Why do I get the hardest job?"

Roy said, "Because you suggested it. You never worked in a corporate environment, did you?"

"But why do I have to do it alone? I won't have time to work on a weapon of my own."

Martin said, "Are you kidding? Jeff, if you do this right, you'll have the best weapon of any of us. You'll have an entire army you can summon and command any time you need it, and it can be any kind of army you want."

Jeff said, "Oh, that's . . ." He paused, thinking, then continued. "A really good point. Any suggestions?"

Gary said, "Yeah! You should—"

"Does anyone but Gary have any suggestions?"

"Oh, come on! That's not nice. I'm going to be fighting whatever you come up with, too, and of all of us, I'm the one who's been hurt the worst. If anything, my opinions should count double."

Tyler said, "I have a suggestion, Jeff."

"Yes, Tyler?"

Gary said, "Man, what a rip-off!"

Tyler said, "I suggest we hear Gary's suggestion."

The other wizards groaned.

Gary said, "Thanks Ty."

"Thank me by making a good suggestion that isn't a waste of our time."

"Right. Jeff, I think you should make an army of women."

The wizards groaned again, louder.

Tyler shook his head. "You just couldn't do it, could you? It just wasn't in you."

"Why?" Brit the Younger demanded. "Why would Jeff make an army of artificial women?"

Gary said, "Why wouldn't he?"

Brit asked, "Did you miss the part where he said we're going to be fighting whatever it is he makes?"

Gary said, "No, I didn't miss that. That's what I have in mind. He could make, what do you call them, Valkyries. The big, tough women with the spears and helmets with wings on them. They'd be a challenge to fight. Brit, you have to admit that women are just as capable of fighting as men."

Gwen said, "He's right, Brit. You, specifically, do have to admit that."

Brit narrowed her eyes to slits. "Yeah, I suppose I do. So you're suggesting that Jeff make an army of tough female warriors for us to train against."

Gary said, "Yeah."

"And they'll be strong?"

"There's no point in doing it if they aren't"

"And fierce?"

"I wouldn't have it any other way."

"I suppose I can get behind that."

Phillip leaned over, put his hand on Brit's shoulder, and said, "I'd hold off on endorsing his plan just yet. Gary, what would these female warriors look like?"

"Like tough female fighters."

Everyone sat silently, waiting for Gary to say more.

"They'd have great big swords, and battle-axes. And they'd be wearing armor."

Still, nobody spoke.

"Like shiny metal bikinis."

Brit let out a frustrated grunt. Phillip said, "There it is."

Martin said, "You're picturing them riding on giant tigers and wolves, aren't you?"

Gary pointed at Martin. "Totally! See Martin gets it."

Gwen said, "You want us to train against an army that looks like it was airbrushed on the side of a van."

Phillip said, "Gary's a necromancer. His entire life looks like it's airbrushed on the side of a van."

Gary said, "All right, fine! So you don't want the army of Valkyries. Whatever. I don't hear any of you making any suggestions."

Tyler said, "It should be period appropriate. No jet fighters or anything. It needs to blend in with this time."

"Valkyries. They'd fit this time perfectly," Gary muttered.

Gwen said, "And it should look formidable. Whatever it is, just looking at it should scare you."

"Valkyries look formidable," Gary grumbled.

Roy added, "And the enemy should be resourceful and adaptable. It should change its tactics in reaction to ours."

"Valkyries are adaptable," Gary insisted.

"Really?" Brit asked. "How so? In what way, Gary, would you say that Valkyries adaptable?"

"Well, it seems to me that I've seen pictures where they're in a snowy setting and they're wearing a fur bikini instead of metal. That's something."

"Yeah, that's something all right," Brit scowled.

Jeff said, "Okay, this isn't getting us anywhere. I'll give it some thought, and I'll try to come up with something that addresses all of your requests."

Phillip said, "Very good."

Jeff said, "Except Gary's, of course."

Phillip said, "Very good indeed!"

Two months later . . .

Martin glanced back over his shoulder. The dragon was still gaining.

"That's right," Martin muttered. "Come to papa."

He heard Phillip's disembodied voice in his ear. "Martin, a dragon's closing in on you. It's a follower. Martin, do you read?"

Martin touched the tips of his left thumb and ring finger, the wizard equivalent of the push-to-talk button on a walkie-talkie.

"I read," he replied, and instantly regretted it. He wore goggles that made seeing while flying at speed easier, but they did nothing to help talking while flying at speed. His cheeks puffed full of air like a small, fleshy parachute. He felt a tendril of drool flow across his jawline and down the side of his neck.

"I read you," Martin repeated, more clearly. "It's only gaining because I'm letting it. I can fly much faster than this, thanks to my brilliant innovation."

Phillip said, "Martin, wearing goggles to keep the wind out of your eyes doesn't qualify as a brilliant innovation."

"You didn't think of it."

"I didn't have to, Martin. I thought of using long-range homing missiles. That's why I was able to take my dragon out at a range of two nautical miles. Now I'm free to act as a spotter and warn you that a dragon is closing on you!"

"I'm trying out a move," Martin said, hoping it would get Phillip off his back.

"Well unless that move is called *getting bitten in half by a dragon*, you might want to—oop!" Phillip interrupted himself, sputtered for half a second, then shouted, "Martin, hard left! Now!"

Martin tilted his staff violently to the left and executed a sharp, diving turn. He looked down past his feet and saw a dark shape arcing through the empty space where he would have been, had he not been warned. Martin allowed himself to fall into a dive, still watching the fast-moving object. It was Gary. He could tell by the black hair, robe, and hat, and the fact that his left leg beneath the knee appeared to be that of a skeleton.

Gary held his own staff with one hand and grasped a loose, tangled rope with the other. The rope led to another dragon, which turned and spun in an effort to figure out where its quarry had gone. Gary swung about in the dragon's wake like a water-skier who had fallen but hadn't yet realized that he should let go of the towrope.

Martin heard Gwen ask, "Again with the Spider-Man web?"

"We were told to come up with a power we could use in a fight," Gary shouted, more from the exertion of maintaining his grip than from anger or fear. "I've got something new, too, but I still say the webs are a legitimate power that I can use in battle. I don't see why everyone gives me a hard time about it."

Martin leveled off, zipping along about fifty feet above the forest canopy. He heard Tyler say, "Because it lacks any originality. You just copied from Spider-Man."

"No wizard's ever copied Spider-Man before," Gary shouted. "That's original-ish!"

"It makes no sense for a wizard to shoot webs," Tyler yelled.

"So nobody'll expect it," Gary said. "Besides, I'm a necromancer! I'm all about spooky and creepy. Spiders are spooky and creepy. It fits."

Brit the Younger said, "He's got a point, actually," but Martin had stopped paying attention to the voices in his ear. His evasive maneuvers had left him below and in front of his dragon. Martin slowed, looked up and to the rear, and saw exactly what he hoped he'd see: the dragon, with its wings folded down against its body, diving directly toward him.

Martin watched the dragon approach, its gaping mouth looking like an open garbage can, only painted red and surrounded by a ring of assorted kitchen knives. Martin judged the dragon's speed, predicted its trajectory, and when he thought the moment was right, he triggered his macro.

As the dragon closed in on his position, Martin's silver robe and hat glowed with a grid pattern of silver light. Then Martin exploded into a cloud of swirling silver boxes, which multiplied as the dragon flew through them. The boxes converged and re-formed into a thirty-foot tall copy of Martin constructed from floating silver blocks, like living, glowing LEGOs.

Maneuvering the giant silver body was like trying to move in five ski suits plus boxing gloves, but he managed to grab the dragon by the shoulders and hang on to the beast's back.

The dragons were all the same size, roughly forty feet from tooth to tail if they stretched out straight, but of course they seldom did. The whole point of having a whiplike tail and a snakelike neck is to bend them, and the dragons did so constantly as they flew. Heads the size of barrels weaved through the wind, leading bodies the size of hatchback cars, armed with two powerful rear legs that ended in claws that could grasp a full-grown man, all supported by immense leathery wings. They were large enough to seem terrifyingly strong, yet thin and graceful enough to look utterly incapable of carrying a thirty-foot-tall man made of silver bricks.

Despite supporting another creature almost its same size, the dragon did not look alarmed. It continued to fly, gaining altitude and scanning the sky as if trying to figure out where Martin had gone.

Gary said, "And you pick on me for having no originality."

"I invented this macro myself," Martin grunted.

"Yeah, a long time ago."

"I'm using it differently now."

"You're using it to grab and hang on. How imaginative."

"And I'm using it to tell you to shut up."

Martin let go of his staff, freeing his other hand to hold on to the dragon. The giant silver-block representation of the staff fell, spinning to the forest below. At one time losing his staff would have robbed Martin of all his powers, but the wizards fixed that weakness first thing when they finally got serious about defending themselves.

The dragon tried to gain altitude. Martin tried to keep his grip. He saw Gwen streaking through the sky with another dragon following behind. Nearby, Brit the Younger flew slowly while an attacking dragon closed in from the side, what they referred to as a *flanker*.

From the way she flew, Martin could tell that Brit saw the dragon. From the way the dragon flew, Martin could tell that it saw Brit. Then, from the way its trajectory changed, Martin could tell that it saw that there were suddenly two Brits. Then there were four of her, then eight. Soon the dragon was surrounded by identical reddish-brown-haired women wearing horn-rimmed glasses and dark blue robes, wielding magic wands.

The dragon spun in the airborne cloud of Brits, not knowing which Brit to attack first. All of the Brits pointed in the same direction, moving in unison. Martin nearly followed their fingers to see what they were pointing at, but then one of the Brits, whose finger just happened to be pointing at the dragon, shot a ray that caused the monster to lose consciousness and fall from the sky.

All of the Brits collapsed back into one. Martin turned his attention to his own dragon. With his gigantic left hand, he grabbed a handful of the beast's neck, then he pulled himself forward and brought his immense right fist down into the back of the dragon's head. Its neck bowed slightly, reacting to the downward pressure, but otherwise the dragon took no notice of him, which Martin found more than a little insulting. He pounded on the creature's head several times, with all of his might, to no effect.

"Stupid dragon," Martin said. "I'm wailing on the back of its skull and it doesn't even know I'm here."

"Ugh, noted," Jeff's disembodied voice said. "Try, uh, try hitting it in the side of the head. That should be more vulnerable."

Gary shouted, "Or you could try this!" Martin turned to look. Gary stood on the back of a dragon holding two spiderwebs as if they were reins. He raised his staff into the air, and shouted: "*Fumo ĉarego!*" The staff transformed into an Uzi submachine gun.

"A gun?" Martin said. "You're a wizard, man! You're supposed to have style! Where's the style in just shooting it with a gun?"

"Asked the guy punching his dragon in the head." Gary leaned to the side, having learned from Martin's mistake, and fired a burst toward the dragon's temple. The dragon went limp and dropped like a stone. Gary hovered in the air, watching it fall.

Martin punched the dragon in the side of the head. It finally noticed Martin and spun violently, trying to shake him off or maneuver him so its hind legs could slash at him. Martin hooked an arm around the dragon's neck and swung around its circumference like a poorly weighted hula hoop. He slid forward and found himself hanging just below the dragon's head. The dragon barely seemed to notice him. Martin let go with one hand, balled his giant silver fist, and hit the dragon in the eye as hard as he could.

The dragon didn't look injured in any way, but it instantly went limp and spiraled to the treetops below. Martin let go and floated in place, watching the dragon fall and listening to Gary's sarcastic slow clap.

"So stylish," Gary said. "So elegant. Without a doubt the most refined eyeball punching I have ever witnessed."

Martin looked past Gary to a lone dragon flying in the distance, searching for an opportunity to attack.

Martin said, "I'm glad you're paying attention, Gary. Keep watching. I'll show you what teamwork looks like." Martin, still a blocky silver behemoth, streaked past Gary. In the past the wizards had needed a staff or wand in order to fly, another weakness they had chosen to rectify. Martin flew with great speed and seized the lone dragon by the throat.

As the two lumbering figures pinwheeled through the air, the dragon said, "What the hell, man?" in Tyler's voice.

Martin moaned, "Oh, that's right. Shape-shifter."

"That's right," Tyler the Dragon said. "Shape-shifter. I've only been working on this morphing protocol for weeks. You helped me write the code!"

"We're fighting dragons! If you turn into a dragon, what do you expect me to do?"

"I'd appreciate it if you'd let go of my throat, for one thing."

In the background, Gary stopped laughing long enough to yell, "Go team!"

Martin knew that he didn't really have Tyler by the throat. He had a projected copy of whatever dragon Tyler targeted when he triggered the spell, by the throat. Tyler was suspended inside the dragon, in control and quite safe, just like Martin inside his own giant façade.

Martin let go. Giant Martin and Tyler the Dragon hung in midair.

"Thanks," Tyler said, sarcastically.

A dragon flew in, a blur of momentum, and barreled into Tyler, knocking him out of Martin's field of view.

Martin said, "You're welcome." He turned to Gary, who kept laughing. "You saw that dragon coming."

"Yup."

"And you didn't warn Tyler."

"No. I didn't warn you either."

"Yeah, I noticed. And what about you, Phillip? Where were you?"

"Watching Gwen," Phillip said, quickly. "There's three of you idiots against one dragon while she's on her own with two followers on her tail."

Martin and Gary wheeled around and saw her in the distance, a small speck in a charcoal-gray robe with a light brown pixie cut, pursued by two larger, more menacing green specks with huge wings and teeth. Behind the dragons they could make out another dark blue speck: Brit. She had noticed Gwen's situation on her own while they were bickering. Martin and Gary flew, closing the distance between them and Gwen as quickly as they could.

"Hold on, Gwen," Martin said. "Help's coming."

"Don't." Gwen said. "Stay back."

"It's cool. We're happy to help."

"I don't need help. I've got this. Just give me room, all of you."

Martin and Gary both stopped dead. Brit altered course to meet up with them.

"Okay," Brit said. "We're clear."

As the three of them watched, the hem of Gwen's robe lengthened, billowing out behind her like a cape. It continued growing, folding and flapping hypnotically. The mass of charcoal-gray fabric drew to a point where it emanated from Gwen, but easily measured thousands of square meters at the rear, where the dragons attempted to fly through it, and became hopelessly entangled.

Gwen disconnected from her immense train. The fabric began to constrict and withdraw, collapsing in on the dragons until they both fell to the ground, helplessly encased in a tight fabric envelope.

"See, Gary," Martin said. "That's the kind of thing we're looking for. That has style."

"Thank you," Gwen said, flying over to the other three wizards as they hung motionless. "Although, turning into a giant silver golem and grappling with the dragons does have a certain epic quality."

Martin smiled and bowed.

"And . . . ?" Gary said expectantly.

"And shooting the dragon with a gun is just brutish and stupid."

"Yeah, it is," Brit agreed.

Phillip's voice cut in. "There'll be plenty of time for all of us to make fun of Gary later, and we will, but there's still a dragon in play."

Martin said, "Tyler's on top of it."

Phillip said, "Only about half the time. He could use some help."

In the distance they saw two dragons locked in combat, seemingly at a stalemate. Without a word, they all set out to intercept them.

"Tyler," Gwen said, "in the future, you might want to turn into something stronger than your opponent—not exactly as strong."

Tyler grunted. "Hindsight."

"Hold on, Tyler," Martin said. "We're almost to you."

Roy said, "Negative! Clear the area. Inbound."

Tyler moaned.

Back in his original time, Roy worked as an engineer at the Lockheed Skunk Works, and his approach to the dragon problem reflected that. The wizards stopped well clear of Tyler and the other dragon, who were grappling and slashing viciously at each other in a clear blue sky above an emerald-green pasture, dotted with sheep like tiny cotton balls. Their dragon battles had never drifted this far from the starting point before, but then this one dragged on a bit, through no fault of the dragons.

"There," Brit said, and pointed to a distant white line that quickly became surprisingly close. Tyler changed from a dragon back into his human form, a stocky black man in a purple robe and hat, and tried to put as much distance between himself and the dragon as he could, but he had very little time.

Roy moved with so much speed the air itself seemed damaged by it. He flew behind a transparent cone-shaped shield that he produced via magic. It pulled him along by two handles and protected him from wind and damage. It had the opposite effect on the first dragon it hit, which was destroyed on contact.

This time he knifed through the exact spot where the dragon had been hovering, but at the last possible second, it leapt two of its own wingspans to the left in a manner impossible for a creature its size.

Roy was long gone before the deafening crack of the sonic boom had dissipated, replaced by the voices of wizards, mostly whining that what the dragon had done was cheap and unfair. They all converged and defeated the dragon with no difficulty, then drifted over to Tyler, who had actually been closer to Roy's flight path than the dragon Roy targeted in the first place.

Gwen asked, "You okay, Tyler?"

"If none of you tries to help me anymore, I might live."

Roy decelerated and looped around to rejoin his friends. His contrail formed a large circle in the sky. "Tyler's fine. We're all pretty much indestructible, or I wouldn't have passed Mach One that close to any of you."

"And I'm glad you did," Phillip said, ascending from his high vantage point. "It looked really cool from up there, and Tyler needed the help. At any rate, the battle's over. Time for notes."

They all descended to the pasture, landing roughly at the exact spot where Tyler's dead dragon would have, if it hadn't dissolved before hitting the ground.

Once they had all touched down, Martin deactivated his macro, changing from a shining silver giant back into the slightly less attention-grabbing form of a young man of average height and weight with short black hair, wearing a shining silver robe and matching hat. He held up his hand and said, "*Martelo de Thor.*" They heard a distant rustling in the woods, then Martin's staff flew out of the forest, across the pasture, and into his hand.

"I swear you deliberately lose your staff, just so you can do that," Gwen said.

"And you're right," Martin said.

Jeff materialized.

Gary gestured toward Jeff and bellowed, "Behold, The Dragoneer reveals himself!"

"I've told you, I'd prefer to be called *The Dragon Master.*"

"And I told you, that's not going to happen."

"Yes, Jeff," Phillip said. "I'm afraid The Dragoneer has stuck. If it's any consolation, the Jeep Wagoneer was a fine vehicle. Anyway, let's start by talking about what went well. My missiles and Roy's hypersonic ram both worked, as did the Multi-Brit, but I think it's clear that the standout was Gwen's macro."

Everyone agreed. Gwen thanked them, muttering about how there were still improvements to be made.

"Always," Phillip said. "Which brings us to what went wrong. We'll start small. Gary, your gun is stupid. Please, at least dress it up to look magical. Make it look like a demon skull and have the bullets glow an eerie green. Something, okay?"

Gary said, "I accept your note."

"Also, I don't like your spiderwebs, but I agree with Brit that you actually made a case for them fitting your milieu, so well-done you. Martin, you had difficulty downing your dragon, but that's not really your fault. It's part of a larger issue we'll come to in a moment.

"Tyler, perhaps it would be instructive if you told us what you think went wrong with your macro."

"Like Gwen said, I should probably turn into something stronger than the thing I'm fighting. Also, I realized that dragons, even these dragons"—he glared at Jeff as he said this—"have more experience fighting as dragons than I do, so I should probably choose a few creatures to turn into, and practice fighting as them."

"An excellent idea. Sadly, that brings us to the problem we end all of these sessions on—the quality of the opposition."

Jeff looked at his feet. "Before you all tee off on me, there are a couple of things I have to say. First, lacking though my training dragons are, and I admit they are, just getting them to this point has been really difficult. I don't think you appreciate how hard my job is here. You each just have to develop one or two powers. I have to construct a synthetic creature from scratch that can hold its own against all of those powers at the same time."

Tyler raised an eyebrow and asked, "Really, from scratch?"

"Okay," Jeff admitted. "Not totally from scratch. I grabbed the dragon models and animations from a special effects house that worked on *Game of Thrones*, but the behavioral algorithms, the AI, the attacks, and the integrated seating positions and riding algorithm are all me."

"Yes," Roy said, "but who told you to waste time making the dragons rideable in the first place?"

Tyler said, "I did. Sorry. It's just . . . dragons! Someone's gotta ride 'em eventually. Right?"

"The point is," Jeff said, "I've done a lot of work on the dragons, and none of it has been easy. Especially since they're supposed to fight a coordinated pack of indestructible, overpowered wizards who adapt their tactics every time. Remember the first battle, where you just had rays automatically target and obliterate them as soon as the battle started?"

"Yes," Phillip said. "And we agreed that wasn't fair to you. That's why we allowed you to make them invisible to the auto-targeting algorithm."

"Then the next battle you just trapped them in an invisible force-field box so they couldn't move."

"They're called *exclusion fields,* and then we allowed you to make the dragons immune to all exclusion fields after that."

"You can call them *exclusion fields* all you want, but I'm calling them force fields from now on, for the same reason the rest of you are calling me The Dragoneer."

Brit the Younger said, "And, for the record, I took out my dragon today by putting an airtight force field around its head until it passed out."

"Isn't that kind of cruel?" Gwen asked.

Brit said, "The dragon wanted to eat me. Besides, it's not like it's a real animal."

Jeff said, "The point is, how could I have predicted that? And how am I supposed to defend the dragons from it next time, let alone have them fight back effectively when you've also made me fix their fire breath and talons so they don't actually hurt anything?"

Martin said, "The fire, the teeth, and the claws don't damage anything, but they do still hurt. Any chance of getting the pain simulation turned down?"

"No. Sorry. I know you don't like the pain, but that's the point. Without the pain, we could just let them slap us around all day with no consequences."

"Jeff, I'm just saying, the dragons are meant to be sparring partners. We want them to be challenging, but not dangerous. It's understood that if one of your dragons breathes fire on us or slashes us across the throat or gut we're out of the fight."

"Is that understood?" Jeff asked.

"Yes," Gary said.

Martin added, "Now that we've made it clear to Gary that it's important to follow the rules, and that crossed fingers are not legally binding, it is."

"Look, Jeff," said Phillip, "we all appreciate that there are serious balance issues, and that you're doing your best. We're willing to work with you on this, but Martin beat the hell out of that dragon, and it didn't even notice. I think making the dragon's scaly back tougher than its belly is fair, it just can't be impervious to damage."

"Why not? We're training for battle here. What if we have to face a foe that's impervious to all damage?"

"If we're fighting something we can't damage, then we're doomed. Nobody needs practice being doomed."

"Least of all us," Gwen said. "We have a natural talent for it."

Jeff held up his hands as a signal of surrender. "I admit, that was a mistake. I can dial up the sensitivity of the back region. No problem. It'll be done in time for the next fight."

"Good, but that wasn't the real problem today," Roy said.

Like the other wizards, Roy had stumbled across a data file that proved reality was actually a computer program. By manipulating the file's various entries, it allowed him to do seemingly magical things, like flying, and traveling back in time

Unlike the other wizards, Roy found the file on a room-sized corporate mainframe in the early nineteen seventies, by which time he was already middle-aged. Thus, he was older than the others, and from an earlier, less *enlightened* time. One could tell from looking at his outfit—a trench coat and fedora modified to work as a wizard robe and hat, his iron-gray crew cut, his staff, which was the bridge cue from the pool table at his favorite dive bar—and his manner of speaking, which tended to be bracingly direct.

"Can you explain to me how, aerodynamically, a dragon could hover, then move sideways over a hundred feet in less than a second?"

Jeff shrugged. "You all said you wanted the dragons to be less predictable."

Brit said, "And we do. I'm sorry, Jeff, but they only attack one of three different ways. One either comes straight at you like it's trying to play chicken, gets behind you and chases you, or comes at you from the side."

"Yeah," Martin said. "We aren't calling out *front, flank,* or *follow* at the beginning of every battle because we like alliteration."

"Well, not *just* because we like alliteration," Gwen said.

"But listen to yourselves," Jeff said. "They attack from the front, the back, or the side. I'm sorry to tell you this, but if you count above and below as sides, which the dragons do, then there are no other choices. There are only three physical dimensions. I only have those three options, unless I have the dragons attack you in the past, which I could do!"

Phillip placed a hand on Jeff's shoulder. "You're right. You're right. I'm sorry. We don't mean to gang up on you. The problem isn't that they attack from specific directions, it's that once a dragon starts attacking one of us from that direction, it only attacks us from that direction, and always in the same way."

"But they choose their plan of attack at random."

"Yes, but once they've chosen, they behave predictably."

"Which is why I thought the evasive maneuvers I added would be welcome."

Tyler said, "But a dragon wouldn't be able to hover and lurch sideways like that. We need the dragons to be unpredictable, Jeff, but we also need their actions to be things we could reasonably anticipate."

"You're asking me to make them predictably unpredictable."

"That's what we need," Phillip said. "Can you do it?"

"It's possible. Anything's possible. I just have no idea how."

"Well, you don't have to get it done today."

"Yeah," Gary said. "The next battle isn't until next week."

As the meeting broke up and the wizards went their separate ways, Phillip and Brit the Younger left together, as did Martin and Gwen. Tyler turned to Gary and said, "I'm gonna go get some food. You in?"

Gary said yes. Tyler asked Jeff and Roy if they wanted to come along. Jeff said no. Roy glanced at his dejected friend and told the other two to go on without them.

Tyler said, "Suit yourself. What do you feel like, Gary? Say, what happened to your staff?"

All of the wizards used either a staff or a wand, often personalized in some way. Tyler's staff had a Rolls-Royce hood ornament for its headpiece. Jeff's usually had dolls of the four members of KISS lashed to it but, as Tyler noticed, today there were only three dolls.

Gary looked at the staff and said, "Oh, yeah, I lost Gene Simmons. I haven't replaced him yet."

Tyler said, "I've got time. I'll help you look for it."

"No, I know where it is, and it's lost. I'd just rather get a new one."

"That's silly. If you know where it is let's just go get it."

Jeff bit his lip, grimaced, then said, "Okay, look. I was sitting in the latrine, the big communal one in Leadchurch, playing with the Gene Simmons doll, which I do when I'm bored, and I dropped him. He's gone. Understand?"

When Tyler finished laughing, he said, "Yeah, I understand. Man, leave it to you."

"Oh, shut up. It could have happened to anybody."

"No, Gary, you were sitting in a communal latrine, playing with a KISS doll. I would never do either of those things, and I'd certainly never ever do them at the same time."

"Well I guess that's what makes you and me different."

"No, it's what makes you different."

Tyler and Gary dematerialized, taking their argument elsewhere, leaving Roy and Jeff alone in the pasture. "Don't worry about it, kid," Roy said, "They all know what you're trying to do is hard."

Jeff shook his head. "My repeated failure keeps reminding them."

"Ah, don't be that way. You can figure it out, but you won't do it by feeling sorry for yourself. Look, why don't we go to your workshop. You can show me what you've done so far. Maybe a fresh set of eyes on the problem will help. I'm pretty much done with my weapon macro.

I want to reshape my nose cone to maximize the shockwave, but that's just fine-tuning. I have plenty of time to help."

"Thanks, Roy, but this is my job. Like you said, I'll figure it out. I just need to work the problem. Something'll come to me."

Roy understood. "You wanna get some dinner? I'm headed to the Rotted Stump." The Rotted Stump was the town of Leadchurch's local tavern and inn.

"No thanks," Jeff said. "You do realize that you're the only wizard that actually likes eating there, don't you?

"Yeah. That's just because I'm the only wizard the other people who eat there like, but if you're with me, everyone should be nice enough."

"I need to take some time and run through what happened in the battle while it's fresh in my mind."

"Suit yourself, kid. Don't drive yourself crazy over it. That won't help either."

Roy clapped Jeff on the back, then teleported away, leaving Jeff alone. He considered going home. Then he considered going for a quick flight to clear his mind. Finally, he sat on a clean patch of grass right there in the pasture and watched the sheep ignore him.

3.

Bishop Galbraith stood outside the lead church, his church, admiring how the late afternoon sun utterly failed to glint off the church's lead siding and shingles.

He heard a young female voice behind him say, "Good morning, Your Excellency."

Bishop Galbraith turned around to see an eleven-year-old girl with bright, energetic eyes, wearing dull, tired clothes. A wiry gray dog stood by her feet, wagging its tail so vigorously, it was having to bend at the waist to put enough force into it.

"Good morning to you, Honor," Bishop Galbraith said. He glanced down at the wiggling dog. "What brings you and Runt to town?"

"Sonny needed to go to the market to buy supplies."

"I see. Smart lad. Catch them late in the day when they'd rather unload their wares for cheap than carry them home for the night."

Bishop Galbraith started walking slowly toward a small door near the rear of the church. He had tarnished silver hair and deep frown lines, but he was not so old that his mobility was affected. He didn't walk slowly because he was forced to. He walked slowly to force others to.

Honor followed the bishop. Runt followed Honor, running in a zigzagging pattern behind her.

"Tell me," the bishop said, "has Sonny mentioned whether the merchants are treating him fairly?"

"He hasn't said they don't. Why?"

Galbraith thought, *Because I warned them if I heard any talk about a merchant mistreating Sonny, everyone would be talking about how I mistreated that merchant.*

"No reason, Honor."

"I don't want to bother you, Your Excellency. I just wanted to give you our tithe." Honor reached into the rough burlap bag slung around her shoulder and produced a small bundle wrapped in cloth. "It's mutton. I hope it will do."

Bishop Galbraith took the bundle. "You always say that you hope the mutton will do, and we always accept it. I've never seen someone so apologetic about giving to the church."

Honor looked at the ground. "I figured you'd rather have coin, or gold, instead of just meat."

"Young lady, do you know what we do with the coins and gold that get tithed to the church?"

"Give it to the less fortunate?"

Bishop Galbraith thought, *Less fortunate? This girl, whose sixteen-year-old brother is raising her on his own while they tend to their sheep, is ashamed that she can only give me food to help those less fortunate.*

He said, "We use part of the tithes to assist the needy, but we don't give them money directly. We buy them the things they need, because merchants tend to give the church a fairer price. One thing everyone needs is food. You giving me mutton actually saves me the trouble of going out and buying it."

"So you don't mind if we tithe with goods instead of money?"

"Not at all. In fact, when you and your brother bring in mutton, I'm inclined to say it counts double, so feel free to tithe half as often."

A male voice said, "Does that go for everyone?"

Galbraith heard the voice off to his left, and noted that the breeze was blowing in from his right, which is why this particular parishioner had managed to sneak up on him.

The bishop turned to face the man. "No, Hubert, it does not."

Hubert was gaunt and filthy. It was hard to describe him further. His hair, clothes, and skin were all filth colored. He nodded and smiled at Honor with filth-colored teeth, then continued his conversation with Bishop Galbraith. "Don't be so hasty, Father. You'd be surprised at some of the things I find in the course of my work."

"You're a dung sifter, Hubert. Some of the things you find might surprise me, but the vast majority of it would not."

"Often I find things that are quite valuable."

"*Were* quite valuable, Hubert. You find things that were quite valuable once. No, in your case, I ask that you tithe in money."

Hubert smiled and bowed slightly. "I had to try, Your Excellency, but I understand. Money it is."

"Not money you found," Galbraith added. "In fact, you can tithe half as often as long as you give me your word that you'll only donate money you were given as change or were paid directly by another person. Now if you'll excuse us, I need to bring this young lady inside."

Galbraith took two quick steps to a small lead door set into the side of the church. He opened it and ushered Honor inside. Runt paused at the threshold for an instant, but Galbraith gently encouraged her to enter with his foot.

After the lead door swung shut with a dull *whump*, Honor asked, "Why did you need to bring me inside?"

Bishop Galbraith said, "Because I needed to come inside to get away from him, and I wouldn't have felt right about leaving you behind."

Bishop Galbraith led Honor and Runt around a corner, through a door, and into the church's kitchen. Nuns in flour-dusted habits and stained aprons fussed and tinkered in an atmosphere heavy with smoke and steam. "This," the bishop said, "is where the food we purchase for the poor is prepared."

The bishop called out, "Sister Flora. Young Honor has donated some of her and her brother's wonderful mutton."

He held up the bundle Honor had given him. Sister Flora swept forward to take the meat from the bishop. "Oh, isn't that nice. Thank you so much, Honor. I assume you'd like it prepared as usual, Your Excellency."

"However you think is best, Sister Flora. The kitchen is your area of expertise, not mine."

"And would you like it, and the rest of your dinner, served in your quarters as usual, Your Excellency?"

Galbraith chuckled and looked at Honor. "There's been some misunderstanding, Sister Flora. Honor donates her mutton for the poor."

Sister Flora said, "I know she does."

Bishop Galbraith laughed, as did the nun, who looked down at Honor, then jumped as if someone had jabbed her with something sharp. "Bishop Galbraith," she said, "you know you can't bring a dog in the kitchen. It's not clean!"

"Sister Flora, I'm sure it's all right. If you had your way I wouldn't be allowed in the kitchen."

"That's right, and for the same reason."

"Relax, Sister Flora. We're just passing through." He turned to Honor and asked, "Where are you off to next?"

"Back to the market to meet up with Sonny."

"Excellent. Would you mind if I walked with you? I'm headed to the Rotted Stump to hear informal confessions."

Honor asked, "You hear confessions in a tavern?"

Sister Flora said, "*Informal confessions* is just what His Excellency calls it when some guilty soul buys him a drink."

The bishop shrugged. "Those who want to buy a drink for a clergyman usually feel bad about something. When I accept their generosity it makes them feel better. It's an important duty I perform for the good of my flock."

Honor asked, "When you accept their drink, does that mean their sins are forgiven?"

"Absolutely not," Bishop Galbraith said. "If anything they're probably making matters worse. The Lord detests taking shortcuts."

The bishop said farewell to the nuns and left the kitchen. Honor started to follow, but after the bishop had turned his back, Sister Flora handed her a hunk of bread. Honor took it and started to thank her, but the nun put a finger to her lips and winked. Another nun threw a bit of meat to Runt, who leapt to catch it in midair. Honor silently mouthed the words *thank you,* but Sister Flora nodded her head toward the bishop's direction and made a shooing motion with her hands. Honor and Runt ran to catch up with the bishop, who was already holding open the door to the outside.

After they had walked for a while in silence, Bishop Galbraith asked, "Sonny doesn't mind you walking around town unaccompanied?"

"No. As long as I steer clear of Kludge and his boys, I'm pretty safe."

The bishop looked down at Honor and smirked when he saw the bread in her hands. His smirk faded when Honor let out a little yelp of alarm. He looked up, and saw a bearded man in light blue robes and a pointed hat holding a wooden staff, and a woman in a dark blue robe and hat and horn-rimmed glasses materializing in the street in front of them. The bishop's smile came back, stronger than before.

The man said, "Bishop Galbraith, good to see you."

"Phillip."

"I believe you've met my friend, Brit."

"Indeed. Good day, Brit. Have either of you met Honor and Runt?"

Phillip bowed theatrically to Honor, and then also to Runt. "Good to meet you, Honor. Runt." Phillip opened the door to his shop, a two-story building with a window full of dusty trinkets, dried, dead animals, and small bottles full of smaller dead animals and trinkets. He invited the bishop and Honor in. Honor was relieved when the bishop said, "No thank you."

As she and the bishop continued to walk, Honor said, "You're friends with a wizard, Your Excellency?"

"Yes," Bishop Galbraith said. "Phillip has helped me more than once."

"I see."

After a few silent steps, Honor asked, "Do you know why that witch wears a mask?"

Galbraith said, "She's not a witch. She's a lady wizard."

"Is there a difference?"

"Witches and warlocks use magic and are in league with the devil. Wizards use magic, but as near as I can tell, Phillip doesn't even believe that the devil exists."

"Oh. Sorry. Do you know why she wears that mask? It looks like it might be carved from wood. It's too thin to keep anyone from knowing who she is, and the little windows it holds in front of her face make her eyes look bigger than they should."

Bishop Galbraith said, "I don't know. We could go back and ask."

Honor said, "No," a little too quickly.

Galbraith asked, "Tell me, Honor, what do you think of wizards?"

"Father never much liked them."

"Yes, but I didn't ask what he thought of them. I asked what you think of them."

"They're strange."

"That's true."

"I don't trust them."

Galbraith laughed. "I don't trust them either."

"But you said that one is your friend."

"Yes, he is. I don't trust wizards, but I do trust my friend Phillip. Just like I don't trust people, but I do trust my friend Honor. Do you see what I mean?"

Honor said, "Yes, I think I do. But . . . Your Excellency, I've seen wizards do some strange things in the sky out near our place."

Galbraith snorted. "I've seen them do strange things in the middle of town. Girl, you don't know much about wizards, so it's wise of you to be cautious. It would also be wise of you to learn more about one or two of them. I can tell you that Phillip has used his powers to help many people. Did your parents ever tell you that the parishioners of the lead church used to suffer terrible pain in their knees, elbows, bellies, and heads? Phillip stopped that. Said he put a spell of containment or something on the lead siding. I don't understand it, but it worked. If you ever get the chance, I say strike up a conversation with Phillip. You'll either learn that you like him or you'll learn that you don't. Either one of those is good to know."

4.

One week later, after another battle with The Dragoneer, and his pets had wound down and the last dragons had been dispatched, Martin said, "That was not fun."

Jeff said, "I disagree."

Gary said, "Your stupid dragons still ended up dead, Jeff."

"True, but it was a lot harder to kill them this time."

Phillip said, "I can't argue with that. Okay everyone, let's regroup and discuss what just happened. Please come back to my position."

Jeff said, "Why don't we meet by the cage instead?"

Phillip asked, "What cage?"

"Look down, at the clearing. I think you'll see it."

"Oh, yeah, I see it. Okay everyone, meet up by the cage."

The clearing, a broad, flat meadow was bounded by thick, dense forest. A raging torrent of a river curved around like a moat, through the woods and along nearly half of the clearing's perimeter. On the other half, the woods concealed steep, impassable hills and cliffs, dense thickets of thorn bushes, and large patches of harmless-looking, rash-inducing vegetation. The nearest civilization was a lone sheep pasture more than two miles away. The wizards knew this clearing well. They could gather there knowing that the prying eyes of the local inhabitants could not see them. Which was a good thing, because right now more than half of it was taken up by a huge, domed cage containing seven dragons.

Seven wizards stood outside the cage, watching the dragons, who simply stood around, occasionally taking a few steps, or lying down, or standing back up. One ate some grass. Neither the cage nor the dragons had been there before, and none of them could figure out why they were there now.

Jeff appeared, looked at the caged dragons for a moment, then turned to his friends and said, "I'm sure you all have questions."

Phillip said, "Yes, I do. Gary, why were you tardy for the fight today?"

"*Tardy*. What is this, junior high?"

"You're a time traveler," Tyler said. "How do you manage to always be late?"

"With effort. Come on, think about it. Nobody wants to be the first person at a party. It's weird and awkward and boring. You have to wait for everyone else to get there. I avoid all that by not showing up until I'm pretty sure everyone else is here already. That way I never have to waste my time waiting for anybody else."

"So you avoid an uncomfortable experience by forcing it on everybody else," Martin said.

"Somebody's gotta turn up first. I just let everyone else do it. It's not like you don't get anything out of it. You all get to spend a few minutes feeling superior to me."

"And we do," said Roy.

"That doesn't bother you?" Gwen asked.

"It might, if I were here to see it, but I never am. Another reason to show up late."

Brit said, "Everybody, this is pointless. We're never going to talk Gary into being on time, and even if we do, our reward will just be spending more time with Gary."

The wizards grumbled agreement and lapsed into a silence.

Jeff said, "I figured you'd all want to know why I'm keeping dragons around when you aren't fighting them, and why they were so much harder to kill this time."

Roy said, "They were harder to kill because instead of attacking us they just took off running."

Martin said, "Flying."

Gwen said, "Fleeing would be the best word, I think."

Roy said, "Yeah, fine, whatever. They took off fleeing. They fled. The only reason it was harder was that we had to chase them down. It took me twenty minutes to finally get mine."

"Yeah," Brit said. "We're supposed to be training to defend ourselves. Chasing and attacking something that's trying to get away is the opposite of self-defense."

"A valid criticism," Jeff said, "but you have to admit, they fled and dodged in a realistic yet unpredictable way."

Roy said, "That's true."

Jeff asked, "Don't you want to know why I'm keeping the dragons around when you aren't fighting them, and why they were so much harder to kill this time?"

Phillip said, "Oh, we do, but you're obviously dying to tell us, so there's really no reason for us to ask. If it makes it easier, I'll take the bait. Jeff, why are you keeping the dragons around when we aren't fighting them, and why were they harder to kill this time?"

Jeff said, "The two questions are deeply related."

Martin said, "Yeah, we kinda figured. You wanna get to it, please?"

Jeff said, "The dragons aren't real animals. When they spawn at the beginning of a fight, they aren't being born. Their code exists. I'm just activating it. And, when you defeat them, you aren't killing them. They're not alive. They're just empty, animated, scary-looking shells. Preprogrammed puppets. The only reason any of your spells worked at all is that I watch you all attack the dragons and make them react on the fly."

"We know," Brit said. "We're all computer programmers. We wouldn't be here if we weren't. The question is, why are they in this cage, and why did they run, I'm sorry, *flee* from us?"

Jeff said, "I'm getting to that. When you *kill* them, they don't die. They just disappear, right? They aren't destroyed. All this time I've just been moving them somewhere you can't see them. It's an old game programming trick. You think they're gone for good, but really they've just gone away. Then I'd deactivate them after the match was done. When I programmed the last iteration, I had them teleport into the cage here when you beat them."

"Okay," Phillip said, "that explains why the dragons are here, wandering around in a cage. Now would you like to tell us why they're suddenly so much harder to kill?"

Jeff looked at Phillip, then he looked at the other wizards, then he looked at the dragons, then, finally, he turned back to Phillip and explained, "Because I improved them."

Phillip thought a moment and said, "Fair enough. That is your job in this, I suppose."

Brit asked, "Is it because they're persistent? Because you gave them some memory, and now, since the dragons exist continually, they are able to remember and learn from their experiences in a way the temporary ones couldn't?"

Jeff said, "Maybe. Sure. Yeah, that, what Brit said."

"Or," Tyler said, "did you just alter random bits of their programming through trial and error to change their behavior, and you're keeping them around between fights because you like the idea of having pet dragons?"

Roy said, "Hold on, now, Jeff's an engineer. He wouldn't have changed random stuff and relied on trial and error. He'd have changed very specific things, methodically applying trial and error."

"And what's wrong with wanting a pet dragon?" Jeff added. "They're so cool, and we're wizards. What's the point of having me make dragons if I can't keep them?"

Gwen said, "You've already named them, haven't you?"

Jeff started to deny it, but admitted. "This one here is Preston. That one's James. The red-faced one's Wilson, and that one at the back there with the bluish wings is Lucy."

Phillip said, "I don't know, Jeff. This seems like weird for weirdness's sake. It'll just freak out the locals."

Jeff said, "I'd like to point out that Gary lives in a cave shaped like a skull, Brit lives in the same town as a future version of herself, and Martin's front parlor contains a statue of Grimace."

Martin said, "Not just Grimace. There are other statues. Optimus Prime. The Stig. Boba Fett."

"And I don't live in the same town as Brit the Elder," Brit said. "She lives in the same town as me!"

Phillip said, "Despite their cogent arguments, I concede that you have a point, Jeff."

"Thanks. Besides, they're perfectly safe. Heck, I'm going to have to spend the next week trying to figure out how to coax them into attacking you at all instead of just fleeing."

5.

Honor sat in the pasture, tending to the sheep.

This morning, *tending to the sheep* meant sitting with her back against a tree on a pleasant, if overcast, day, watching the sheep eat and Runt play in the tall grass.

Blackie and Harry, the two larger dogs that Sonny, and their father before him, had officially recognized as sheepdogs, stood near the sheep, watching their every move, freeing Honor to simply glance at the sheep occasionally and listen for the dogs' barking.

Runt sat with her head in Honor's lap. Honor scratched behind Runt's ears absent-mindedly. Runt wagged her tail and pushed her head up harder into Honor's scratching fingers.

Honor reached into her pocket and pulled out a bit of folded cloth that, when opened, revealed something she might have mistaken for a large rock, if she hadn't made it herself out of oats.

She broke off a piece of her scone, grimacing from the effort needed. She gave the piece to Runt, and smiled as the dog crunched it up and swallowed it. "Glad you like it," Honor said. "The sheep do, too. I know Momma's were better."

Honor looked at the working dogs and the sheep just in time to see one of the sheep vanish. She blinked, rubbed her eyes, and looked again, clearly seeing the empty space where the sheep was not.

Honor stood up and walked to the spot where the sheep had been standing. She counted the remaining sheep. She ended up one sheep short, exactly as she expected.

The sheep disappeared, she thought. *This has to be magic. Either a wizard took my sheep, or the sheep learned magic on its own, which I doubt.*

She looked to the horizon, out over the forest, where she'd occasionally seen the wizards, far off in the distance, doing weird, inexplicable things in the sky. She saw red light reflecting off of the bottoms of the clouds. *Bishop Galbraith said I should get to know the wizards better. Asking them why they took my sheep and why they've got a bonfire going is as good a chance as any.*

She turned to Blackie and Harry and said, "Keep an eye on the flock. I'll be right back." She knew it was just for show. Blackie and Harry would keep an eye on the flock no matter what she said. She looked down at Runt and said, "You stay here." This was also for show. Runt would follow her no matter what she said.

Honor looked at the reddish flashes on the clouds again to get a clear fix on the wizards' location, then set off into the forest. Runt followed without hesitation.

The conventional wisdom among adults was that the woods were impassable, but Honor didn't know the meaning of the word, one of the few real advantages of being mostly illiterate.

"Runt, the wizards seem to be to the west, beyond the thickest, darkest part of the woods. We could go around to the north, but that part of the forest is full of those tall plants with the white flowers and spotted leaves. You know, the ones that make you feel like you're on fire. We could go around to the south, but that's where the river is, and the riverbank will crumble away and drop us in the rapids with no warning. No, we're going to have to go through the heart of the forest."

She looked down at Runt, whose tail was wagging because she didn't understand a word Honor had said.

"I agree," Honor said. "This is a nice chance to see what's there."

She mostly saw hills and thorns.

The hills were steep, but she had strong legs and plenty of time, so that didn't bother her. There were places where the bushes were so thick that she had to climb over them, carefully choosing each foot and handhold, carrying Runt along with her in a sack on her back. In other places the gaps between the thorn bushes were so narrow that only Runt could squeeze through. The little dog would stand on the other side of the obstacle, waiting for Honor to clamber over the bushes and catch up.

Honor heard the wizard long before she saw him. Or, more accurately, she heard the things that were with the wizard. Occasional loud animal roars at first then, as she drew closer, snorts and grunts between the roars. Then she started seeing flashes of orange light filtering through the woods. When she heard a man's voice and the braying of the sheep he had stolen, she knew she was getting close.

Runt had walked along beside her since they passed the thorn barrier, but Honor thought it would be good to hide from the wizard, at least until she knew what he was up to, and she certainly didn't want Runt running out to him, looking to get her belly rubbed. Honor picked the dog up, put her back in the sack with her head sticking out, and slung the dog over her back. Runt peeked out over Honor's shoulder like a second head, seeing everything Honor saw, and occasionally licking Honor's ear, just to remind her she was there.

Honor crept closer to the edge of the woods, moving slowly because she didn't want to be seen, and because she couldn't believe what she saw.

It was a cage, larger than any building in town. She thought the church would fit inside with room to spare. It was the most impressive and, in its way, the most terrifying thing she'd ever seen, save for what was *in* the cage.

They were dragons. She'd never seen a dragon before, but she knew that they were dragons. Even for a novice, dragons were pretty easy to identify. Looking at them, listening to them roar, feeling the radiated heat as they breathed fire at one another, watching them eat grass from the floor of their cage, she had no doubt in her mind that these were dragons.

Between her and the dragon cage she saw a pen, also made of metal, somehow spun like thread and woven in a loose but regular diamond pattern, supported by metal posts. Normally it would have been a marvel to her, but with the cage and the dragons in the background, it paled in comparison.

In the pen, a male wizard in dark gray robes chased the stolen ewe. It ran around the outer edge of the pen while the wizard ran behind, shouting, "Come on! Come on! Fight me! I won't really hurt you, but you gotta show some backbone."

The sheep reached the corner and turned to face the wizard, who stood toward the middle of the pen, spreading his arms to take up more space. If the sheep made a break for it, he'd only need to lurch in that direction to block her escape.

"All right," the wizard panted, severely out of breath. "You're cornered. You can't run. Now, come at me, bro!"

The terrified ewe took two quick steps to her right, then darted hard to her left while the wizard leapt to block the route she did not take. The wizard lost his footing and fell to the dirt while the sheep ran past him in the unguarded space and retreated to the far corner of the pen. The wizard rolled over to look at the sheep and shouted, "Coward!"

Bishop Galbraith had told Honor, "I don't trust wizards. I trust my friend Phillip."

This wizard isn't Phillip, she thought, *and I don't trust him one bit. He means to feed my ewe to his dragons.* Honor bit her lip in anger and concentration. *I could wait until his back is turned and rush him. I might knock him over into the mud. Then, he'd be angry. An angry full-grown man, with magical powers and hungry dragons to feed. What do I have? Runt, and a couple of scones in my bag. So all I have to fight him off with is more dragon food. No, I have to go tell Sonny. Then we'll go tell the bishop. Then he'll talk to his friend, Phillip, and we'll see if he's really worthy of the bishop's friendship. It's not a good plan, but I might not get eaten in it, so it's the best plan I have.*

Honor turned her back on the wizard and his dragons and plunged back into the forest.

Jeff rose to his feet and approached the sheep. "Come on. I'm not that tough. You can totally take me. I won't even fight back." He put his hands behind his back, to appear harmless. "I'm not really going to hurt you, I just need you to make some kind of attempt to fight me. Something—a bite, a kick, anything."

He took another step toward the sheep, which feinted to one side, then darted to the other again. Jeff fell for it again, literally. He rolled over on his back, looked at the sky, and said, "This is why nobody ever says *as brave as a sheep.*"

He sat up and shook his head. "I'm going to have to rethink this whole thing. I've got another five days. There's still time." He smiled at the sheep and told it, "Sorry for the inconvenience."

He extended a hand, muttered some words in Esperanto, and the sheep disappeared, returning to where it had come from. Then he muttered some more Esperanto, and disappeared as well.

Hiking to where the wizard had his dragons and her ewe, Honor had walked through unfamiliar territory, driven by curiosity. Hiking back, she covered now-familiar territory, driven by righteous anger, so she made much better time.

Honor and Runt emerged from the woods exactly where she'd entered a few hours earlier. Harry and Blackie were still standing guard over the flock, just as she'd left them. She decided to count the sheep one more time before going to Sonny, just in case the wizard had stolen another while she walked back.

She counted three times, and got the same answer each time. There were exactly as many sheep as there were supposed to be, as if the wizard had never stolen a sheep at all. She chalked this up to magical trickery, but it would make it harder to convince her brother and the bishop that a sheep had been stolen.

She couldn't let the fact that the wizard had somehow covered up his crime stop her from trying to get justice. He stole her sheep. Then he abused her sheep before feeding it to his dragons. Now he was using his sorcery to cover it up somehow. Of course, she hadn't seen him feed the sheep to the dragons, and now had no evidence that he'd even taken the sheep in the first place, but just because his crimes were confusing and well hidden didn't make them any less wrong. She knew what she knew, and right now she knew that she needed to warn the adults. Even if they didn't listen, or didn't believe her, and things went horribly wrong, they could never claim she hadn't tried.

Honor called to Blackie and Harry and, together with Runt, the four of them herded the sheep toward the holding pen and the farmhouse, where Sonny was tending to the rams.

6.

A new day arrived in Atlantis, in its usual idiosyncratic manner.

On land, or the surface of the sea, dawn starts as a glowing sliver of orange on the horizon that slowly grows until the sun is fully exposed and the land is bathed with light.

But Atlantis was built on the inside curve of a gigantic bowl, which floated in the Mediterranean, all but its rim submerged below the water line. So sunrise presented in Atlantis as a diffuse orange glow in the sky followed by a thin line of direct sunlight along the inside edge of the city's western rim. Every day in Atlantis started in a pleasant haze of adequate but scattered light, which made for cooler temperatures and less severe hangovers.

As the bright line of daylight starting slowly oozing its way down the wall of western Atlantis, Brit the Younger and Phillip were just sitting down to breakfast.

The two of them had not moved in together, because they didn't have to move. They were wizards, and had the option of simply creating two permanent portals leading from Phillip's rustic hut on the edge of Leadchurch, and his office and '80s-themed game room in the middle of Leadchurch proper, directly into the living room of Brit's tastefully decorated minimalist apartment in Atlantis, two thousand miles away and nearly fifteen hundred years earlier in time. This arrangement gave them each the illusion of independence, along with a combined two-bedroom, three-bathroom home with ocean and pastoral views, in a convenient downtown location (in two different towns), with generous entertainment space, a home office, a garage, and a mind-bendingly confusing time-zone shift that served as a constant source of conversation.

They took their meals at Brit's, because she had a nice table, dishes, flatware, and Nik, a devoted servant who made meals that were healthier and more aesthetically presented than the food Phillip prepared with his stew pot or magically pulled out of his hat.

They were both picking over their last few bites of breakfast when they heard quiet knocking and anguished shouting in the distance. Phillip and Brit both rose to their feet. Nik stepped in from the kitchen. All three of them listened to the sounds for a moment, then Phillip and Brit approached the two portals to Phillip's time. They both opened the rustic wooden doors and stuck their heads into the portals, then pulled their heads back out. Phillip said, "I've got the shouting."

Brit said, "I've got the knocking."

Phillip said, "I'll go see what the shouting's about."

Brit crowded past Phillip and darted into the door he had checked. "No way! The shouting sounds much more interesting. I'll take it; you take the knocking."

Nik said, "And I'll do the dishes."

"Good, we have a plan. Now, break!" Brit closed the door behind her, leaving Phillip no choice but to enter the door she had checked, the one with the quiet knocking.

Phillip emerged from the portal in the room above his office. He quickly but carefully walked around the early '80s bachelor-pad décor, the vintage GORF machine, and his pride and joy, the immaculate Pontiac Fiero. He nearly ran down the stairs, through his séance room, and into his front office—a small space stuffed with mysterious looking powders, salves, and curios, none of which served any purpose beyond looking mysterious. As he approached the door, the knocking remained quiet but took on a more urgent tone through its rapid delivery and shaky cadence.

Phillip opened the door, said, "Yes Hubert, what can I—" then stepped out into the street.

Hubert, his eyes wide with panic, lurched behind Phillip into the open door to the shop, ducked around the side of the door frame for cover, and whispered, "Master wizard, sir, we have a problem."

Phillip said, "Yes," shutting down any further explanation. He knew all too well what he was looking at, but for the moment he had no idea what to do about it.

He heard the high-pitched warbling tone that told him another wizard wanted to communicate with him. He lifted his left hand as if he were examining a bowling ball just before trying to make a seven-ten split. In the empty space above his hand, he saw a ghostly image of a letter *B* that rotated and morphed into a letter *T*, then a letter *Y*. He answered the call, and heard Brit the Younger's voice.

"Phil, I'm at your hut. I think you'd better see this."

Phillip said, "I can see it."

One of the few advantages of having your town get overrun by a small herd of dragons is that dragons are large enough to see, even from a distance.

Many miles away, Martin sat in his warehouse, at his table alone, eating his breakfast while talking with Gwen, who was not there. Instead, a real-time image of her head floated over Martin's table so that they could make eye contact and talk like civilized adults while they ate their respective breakfasts. Mostly they talked about where they might go for lunch. Gwen, like almost all female wizards, lived in Atlantis. Martin lived in Camelot, which sounded just as exotic as

Atlantis until you learned that Camelot was just London, renamed by a wizard named Jimmy during a bout of temporary megalomania.

"Let's just go to the café here near my place," Gwen said.

"We always go there. I'm tired of it." Martin pulled a bottle of syrup out of his hat and poured it on his waffles.

"Do you eat waffles for breakfast every day?"

"Yup."

"Why? You can pull anything you want out of your hat."

"Exactly. I can have anything I want, so I make waffles every day. There's no better way to start the day than with fresh, hot waffles, slathered in butter, with syrup squeezed from a plastic bottle shaped like an old lady, just as nature intended."

"Why not just create the waffles pre-syruped? You'd save a step."

"Tried it. If my hands shake, even a little bit, I end up with a sticky hat."

"Whatever. Look, let's just go to the café. We always go there because it's always good."

"Well, maybe I'm tired of good."

"So you'd rather eat somewhere you know will be bad?"

"I'm not saying that. It's just . . . it might be nice to eat somewhere here in Camelondon."

"So you do want to eat somewhere you know will be bad. Martin, food in Atlantis is made to modern standards. Food in Medieval England, not so much."

"Gwen, we can eat here without eating here *now*. We're time travelers. Let's act like it. How about I take you to lunch in London in the mid-sixties? Piccadilly Circus at the height of the mod scene. It'll be like living in the first five minutes of an Austin Powers movie."

Gwen thought for a moment, then said, "That may be the best idea you've ever had. I'll need to find something appropriate to wear."

"What about me?"

"Your silver robe should fit right in."

The wavering tone that denoted someone calling them sounded. Martin looked at the image of Gwen and saw a second, smaller image of Phillip's face, looking angry, which meant it was urgent. Martin warned Gwen, then conferenced Phillip in.

Martin said, "Hey, Phillip. You've got Gwen and I. What's up?"

Phillip said, "It's *Gwen and me,* and we've got a problem! Many problems. Big problems! Many big problems! I need one of you to call the gang and get them all to come to Leadchurch. We need help!"

Gwen said, "Well, I'll have to make the calls, because Martin's probably already there with you by now."

Martin said, "Hey, Phillip."

Phillip turned to his right and saw Martin standing next to him, in front of his shop in Leadchurch.

Gwen asked, "What's going on there? Everyone's going to ask when I call them."

Martin said, "Dragons! The town is overrun with dragons!"

There were two dragons in the street in front of Phillip's shop. They didn't seem angry, or even upset. If anything, they seemed curious. One peered through windows and poked its head under awnings. The other walked down the street slowly, moseying really, looking at the buildings as it went. The dragons walked on all fours, but the front two of the four had been adapted into wings instead of legs. This gave the dragons' gait a clumsy, labored quality.

The dragons were calm and quiet. The people, on the other hand, were terrified and quiet. They huddled in corners, hid behind barrels and wagons, anything large enough to block the dragons' view. As soon as a dragon turned its back, the people behind it would silently dart into the nearest open door.

Most of the buildings were only one or two stories tall, so the dragons poked up above the rooftops. Martin could see two more dragons from where he stood. He glanced out toward the edge of town and saw Brit the Younger hovering above the rooftops. She looked right at him and gave an exaggerated confused shrug.

Gwen remained sitting in her home in Atlantis, and could think a little more rationally than the others. "Why didn't you call Jeff first?"

Martin said, "She's got a point."

Phillip gritted his teeth. "Right. I'll call Jeff. Please call everyone else, then come here. Hopefully by then we'll have a plan."

Gwen hung up. Martin said, "This is something, isn't it?"

"Yes," Phillip said. "It's safe to say that this situation definitely qualifies as being, as you say, *something*."

Phillip called Jeff. After a moment of ringing Jeff's logo, a simple picture of Jeff's face, clearly taken himself just to have something to use as a logo, appeared. A sleepy voice said, "Hello?"

Phillip said, "Dragons, Jeff! Downtown Leadchurch is overrun by dragons! Your dragons!"

Jeff no longer sounded sleepy. "What? No way!"

"I'm afraid so."

"No, there's no way they could have escaped."

"They must have."

"Are you sure they're dragons? Have you seen them yourself?"

"I'm looking at them right now."

"Well, they must have gotten out, I guess. I'll go take a look at the pen."

Martin rolled his eyes and Phillip shook his head while they waited for Jeff to confirm what they already knew.

Jeff shouted, "No way! You say my dragons are there with you?"

"Yes," Phillip said. "I assume they are not in your pen."

After a heavy silence, Jeff said, "I'll be right there."

"Yes, I expect you will." Phillip turned to Martin and said, "Jeff'll be right here."

Jeff materialized, looked up at the dragons, who were still peacefully exploring the street, and shouted, "No way!"

Phillip turned to Martin and said, "Jeff's here."

Martin asked, "How'd they escape?"

Jeff said, "We can discuss that later. Right now we should just concentrate on getting the dragons out of here."

Martin nodded and said, "I'll take that to mean *I don't know*."

Roy appeared, looked alarmed, then asked Jeff what went wrong. Tyler appeared, and followed the same procedure as Roy. Gary turned up last, and just giggled while pointing, first at the dragons, then at Jeff, then at the frightened locals.

Gwen arrived last, having called everyone else before rushing to the scene herself, and they discussed their options.

Martin said, "What's the big deal? Jeff, just zap them back to their cage."

Phillip said, "No, don't. We mustn't give the locals the idea that we're too powerful. We want them to respect us, not be terrified of us. Also, if Jeff banishes the dragons like he's flipping a light switch, they might get the idea he created the threat to begin with."

"Yeah," Jeff nearly shouted. "Yeah, that's a bad move. I won't do that!"

"Fine," Gary said. "So we kill the dragons right here and Jeff makes more. One second, I'll get my machine guns."

Gwen said, "No, don't. These people are on edge already. We don't want to cause a panic. I say we shoo the dragons out of town, then deal with them away from any spectators."

"Gwen's right," Roy said. "Heck, running away is all these dragons are good for anyway."

Jeff said, "Hey, that's not fair."

Brit said, "Isn't it?" She took three steps toward the nearest dragon, which sent it flying into the sky.

They watched to see what direction it flew, but the dragon circled, not seeming to feel threatened, or at least not threatened enough to want to stray too far from the other dragons.

"Okay," Phillip said. "That worked a treat. I say we roust the other dragons, then when they're in the air we chase them off and eliminate them away from town. Agreed?"

Everyone agreed, in a noncommittal sort of way. As they split up to walk through the streets and startle the dragons, Gary said, "Okay, Jeff, how many dragons were there total?"

Jeff said, "It doesn't matter. The dragons that are here are here. We can do a census later, okay?"

The wizards fanned out, walking cautiously, street by street. They knew that the dragons couldn't actually harm them, or anyone. They were computer-generated puppets. They looked and felt real, but their claws would go right through you like a painful ghost, and their fiery breath felt blisteringly hot, but would not cause burns. The chief danger was that one of the dragons would panic and step on someone, or accidentally knock a wall over on them. The wizards' caution was mostly caused by a psychological response to the dragons' intimidating size, the palpable fear of the citizens who watched from the buildings all around them, and Jeff muttering, "Slowly. Be careful," over the battle comm.

A second dragon took to the air, followed by a third and a fourth. They made good progress until Gwen called out, "Hey, Jeff, why did you give this one horns?"

"What?" Jeff said, in that gasping, hoarse voice that people make when they attempt to shout a whisper. "What do you mean, horns?"

"Yeah," Roy shouted. "What do you mean?"

Gwen said, "This one's got big, curved horns."

The wizards converged on Gwen's location, and sure enough, they saw a large, light gray dragon with two impressive, spiraling horns sprouting from its head.

"Why'd you give this one horns?" Tyler asked, as Jeff joined the group.

"Yeah," Roy asked. "Why, Jeff?"

Jeff moaned, "Oh, no way."

"It's really cool. That's reason enough," Martin said, walking slowly toward the horned dragon.

Jeff said, "Martin, hang back a second."

Martin said, "Why? They can't hurt us."

Roy looked at Jeff and said, "He's right, isn't he?"

Jeff said, "Yeah! Of course! I think."

Martin drew closer. In the sky above the town, the four dragons that had already been shooed circled. The horned dragon watched Martin approach, and slowly lowered its head.

"See," Martin said. "I think it wants me to pet it! I'll chase it off."

Martin ran two steps, an act which sent the previous dragons flying. The horned dragon chose instead to charge directly at Martin, ramming him with its wrecking-ball-sized head and massive horns, pushing him backward until they both struck the side of a house. Martin's torso provided a cushion that prevented the dragon's massive head from striking the wall, but all of the dragon's force carried through him, and still did quite a bit of damage.

Martin let out a pained cough.

Jeff shouted indistinct, alarmed vowel sounds, as if he needed to speak but was at a loss for words.

Roy offered, "No way?"

"I know, right?" Gary said. "Now it attacks."

Jeff ran forward. Martin crouched on the ground in front of the wall, which now bore a Martin-shaped dent. The dragon backed up several steps, lowered its head again, and was about to ram again when Jeff leapt between the dragon and Martin, and used his wand to emit a blinding flash of light. The dragon reared back, confused.

"Martin," Jeff shouted. "Do your thing!"

"What?" Martin asked.

"Be big! Grow up! Get swole! I don't know what you call it, just do it now!"

"You want me to trigger my macro?"

The dragon shook its head vigorously, then regained its bearings and lowered its head, preparing to ram both Martin and Jeff in one run.

"Yes! That! Now!"

Martin did as he was asked, quickly dissolving into a cloud of silver boxes that exploded outward, swirled around in a large cloud, then coalesced into a new, silver Martin that stood thirty feet tall. The dragon looked up from its ramming stance, realized that it now faced a much larger adversary than before, and chose to flee. It soared into the air and joined the other four dragons flying circles in the sky high above the city.

Tyler looked up at the dragons and said, "Let's see. If Jeff made seven, and we've accounted for five, that means there are two still lurking around."

"Yes," Roy said. "If. I'm curious, Jeff, why don't you just delete the dragons?"

"I can't."

"Can't because you there's a good reason not to, or can't because it's not possible?"

Brit moaned. Phillip asked, "What are you getting at, Roy?"

"These aren't the dragons Jeff made. They're still safe and sound in that geodesic dome you made for them, aren't they?"

Jeff said, "I made these dragons, too. Just not deliberately. The ones I made deliberately are back in the cage."

Phillip said, "Jeff, you're telling us that you created extra dragons, by accident?"

Gary said, "It happens."

Roy said, "No, it doesn't, or at least it shouldn't. What happened, Jeff? Did you cut some corner? Take a little shortcut, did you?"

"What I did isn't important right now."

Brit said, "It's very important, just not quite as important as the small herd of dragons circling over town."

"Will it remain a small herd, Jeff?" Roy asked.

"I hope so."

Brit said, "That's not a good answer."

"No matter," Phillip said. "Right now these dragons are our problem, and luckily, I have a way to deal with them." Phillip lifted his staff above his head and flew into the sky above town.

"Does he have a way to deal with them, Jeff?" Roy asked.

"I hope so."

Brit scowled and said, "That's still not a good answer."

Phillip gained altitude until he drew level with the dragons. He found the one with the horns— the largest and most aggressive dragon. He intended to deal with it first. Phillip prepared his missile spell, locked the targeting system onto the horned dragon, and fired.

There was no actual, physical, missile. Just a ball of bright, pulsing light that tracked its target using the aiming algorithm from a video game. The pulse of light streaked through the sky. The horned dragon saw it coming and turned in an effort to evade. The missile struck the dragon in the side and exploded with an artificially generated blinding flash and the all-too-real force of several sticks of dynamite—enough power to reduce a car to a smoking ruin.

The dragon was shoved off course but suffered no damage.

Brit rounded angrily on Jeff. "Why?"

"They aren't real," Jeff explained, miserably. "They're not real animals. They're non-player characters. Avatars. Simulations. Unless they're programmed to react to something, they won't. Shooting one with a weapon they aren't programmed for and hoping it'll kill them is like insulting a mannequin and hoping to hurt its feelings."

"Didn't you program them to be killed by missiles?" Tyler asked.

"No, I didn't. I haven't done any custom programming on these dragons. I didn't know these dragons existed, and even with the other dragons, half of the time I had to just watch what you guys did and decide whether or not to count it as a knockout and trigger the kill animation."

"Well then what are you waiting for?" Gary asked. "Kill these off already."

Roy said, "He can't."

Jeff shook his head. "I don't have any direct interface with these dragons."

"Why not?" Tyler asked.

"Because he didn't create them," Roy said. "He has no idea how they came to exist. That means that he doesn't know where their entries are in the file, and his control program doesn't have any hooks into their code. They're completely autonomous. Poorly programmed, but autonomous."

"Well, can't we just make them vanish anyway," Gary asked, "like we do with the cockroaches we find in our homes?"

Brit asked, "You do that?"

"You don't?"

"I don't have cockroaches in my home."

"Well aren't you fancy?!"

"Too risky," Roy said, straining his words through gritted teeth. "We don't know how they appeared, so we don't know what process they somehow got tied to. If we make them disappear we don't know what else might disappear along with them."

Gary said, "That sucks."

"I know it sucks," Jeff shouted. "I'm painfully aware that it sucks! I'll be happy to have an in-depth discussion about the suckage later, but right now we have dragons circling overhead, freaking out the locals!"

"They're not circling anymore," Martin said, shielding his eyes as he looked to the sky. "They're all chasing Phillip."

Phillip flew in large, lazy curves, just fast enough that the horned dragon couldn't quite catch him. It followed every move he made, and the other four dragons followed both of them.

As the wizards stood and watched the dragon's pursuit of Phillip, many of the citizens slowly began to peek their heads out of their hiding places, some lured by the relative quiet, others drawn by the sound of the wizards arguing.

Gwen asked, "Jeff, if these dragons aren't programmed to react to our weapon spells, is it possible that they also aren't programmed to *not* respond to our usual defensive spells?"

Jeff took a moment to decipher Gwen's double negative, then said, "I hope so."

Brit said, "We haven't had a lot of luck with that response today, but it's worth a try." She pressed her thumb and ring finger together to trigger the battle communications macro and said, "Phillip, there's a chance our defensive spells might work. Try throwing up an exclusion field behind you. Let's see if it stops them."

Phillip turned around to face the dragons and muttered "*Mura rapida,*" Esperanto for *quick wall,* to create an exclusion field, an invisible barrier through which no living thing aside from himself could pass. His speed dropped as he watched the horned dragon approach the invisible wall, reach it, and pass through it as if it weren't there.

Phillip waited a bit too long to continue fleeing; he couldn't see the invisible force field, so it took him an extra second to convince himself that it hadn't worked. When he finally got up to speed, the horned dragon was only a few yards behind him. He could have outrun the dragons easily, of course, or simply teleported away. He hadn't, because as long as the dragons kept chasing him, they were, to some extent, under his control. He could simply lead them around by the nose for as long as he wanted, unless something happened to upset the balance of power.

The horned dragon opened its jaws and exhaled a scorching jet of whitish-yellow flames, which fully enveloped Phillip.

The rest of the wizards had watched the entire sequence of events unfold. As Phillip's startled, pained yelp reached their ears, Martin asked, "Is this what it's like to watch me?"

"Usually," Gwen answered.

The dragon reached the end of its lung capacity. The fireball dissipated. Phillip was gone. The wizards were only puzzled for a moment before they heard coughing behind them.

Phillip had teleported out of the fireball and was standing behind them. The program that gave the wizards their powers also manipulated their entries in the repository file to make them impervious to physical damage, so none of them had any doubt that Phillip was all right.

Gary said, "Good thing the fire can't hurt you, eh?"

"Harm," Phillip coughed. "The fire didn't harm me. I assure you, it hurt quite a lot."

Tyler said, "Yeah, well, that's how Jeff programmed them. It hurts, but it's not real fire. It won't burn anything."

"Yeah," Jeff said. "That's right. I mean, Phillip, could you tell? It's the fake fire I programmed, not real fire, right?"

Phillip narrowed his eyes and asked Jeff, "Why are you asking me?"

"An excellent question," Brit said, "And one we'll have to table for now." She pointed to the dragons. They flew in a loose formation with the horned dragon in the lead. It seemed to have seen where Phillip went. It brought the others down the street toward the wizards at just above rooftop level, with great speed and ominous intent.

The knowledge that one has unnatural powers doesn't quite trump one's natural instincts. The wizards started running away from the dragons before taking to the air. As they ran, Gary asked, "Jeff, how'd you get them to act so lifelike?"

"By doing something stupid," Jeff said.

7.

Sonny and Honor were making great time.

Honor walked quickly because she needed to speak to Bishop Galbraith. She had to tell him what she'd seen in the woods: the wizard, the dragons, and the stolen sheep that seemed to reappear afterward. She had faith that the bishop would know what it all meant. Or, he'd know what to do. She never knew her grandfather, but she knew her father, and her father called Bishop Galbraith *Father*. That was close enough for her.

Sonny also needed to speak to Bishop Galbraith. His little sister had come back from grazing the sheep talking about wizards and dragons and needing to go see the bishop. Either something had happened out in the woods, she had seen things she didn't understand, and she needed help, or nothing had happened in the woods, she had seen things she didn't understand, and she needed help even more.

"We should have gone last night," Honor said.

Sonny said, "No, I told you. You needed your sleep."

"I didn't sleep anyway."

"Yeah, I know."

Runt ran circles around Honor and Sonny at first, excited by the change of routine, or maybe agitated by Honor's state of mind. Whatever the reason, Runt tired herself out pretty fast, and Honor ended up picking up the dog and carrying her.

Sonny said, "One good thing about setting out so early is that Kludge and his gang should still be asleep when we pass their camp."

Honor said, "Mm-hmm."

"The walk back might be dicey, but if we keep a distance and don't give them a reason to bother us, we should be fine. They're a rough lot, but they're lazy and they know we have little money, so we're more trouble than we're worth."

Honor chuckled and said, "Lazy Bastards."

"Honor! What have I told you about calling people that?"

"Not to, but that's what they call themselves. It's the name of their gang."

"Does Kludge and his gang doing something make it all right for you to do it, too?"

"No. I'm sorry."

"That's fine. An understandable mistake. As you say, they do call themselves that. We just have to be better than them."

Honor asked, "Why do they call themselves that?"

Sonny said, "I dunno. They think it sounds tough, I guess. Or maybe someone called them that and Kludge liked the sound of it. Either way, I think it's really only an accurate description of one or two of them."

Honor walked in the lead, carrying Runt. She rounded a bend in the road that allowed a clear view of Leadchurch in the distance. She looked at the town and thought, *It won't be hard to convince His Excellency that I saw dragons. All he has to do is look up and he'll see them himself!*

Sonny rounded the corner only steps behind her and stopped in his tracks when he saw the dragons flying in circles above the rooftops.

She wasn't making up stories, and she wasn't imagining things, he thought. *That's good news, I suppose.*

Honor said, "I told you we should have come last night."

Sonny said, "I'm not sure we should have come today."

Honor resumed walking. Runt barked and squirmed and struggled in her arms.

"Honor, see, even the dog knows we should stay back."

Runt broke free of Honor's grip, hit the ground, and started running straight toward town. Honor ran to chase Runt, and Sonny ran to chase both of them.

"What do you think you're going to do?"

"I'll tell them what I saw."

"You saw dragons! They know there are dragons! They can see that for themselves!"

"But they don't know a wizard is controlling them."

"You don't know that either!"

Honor's pace slowed. Sonny thought for a moment that he'd gotten through to her. He caught up to his sister and stopped. In the distance he saw Runt also stop, looking back over her shoulder at the two humans who were no longer chasing her.

Honor kept staring into the distant sky, watching the dragons. Sonny put a hand on her shoulder and said, "Look, you were right about what you saw, but that doesn't prove—"

"No," Honor barked, "You look!" She pointed into the sky. "I was right about what I saw, and that proves it!"

The tiny form of a person floated into the gray morning sky, leading the dragons. It had to be a wizard, though they were too far away to make out any details, or even identify the color of the wizard's robes. The wizard made some broad gesture toward the dragons, then turned and looked at them for a moment. One of the dragons belched a huge stream of fire, which enveloped the wizard, and when the fire had dissipated, the wizard had vanished. The dragons circled one last time, then flew in low along the rooftops of the town, the lead one breathing fire as it went. Sonny couldn't see what damage they were doing, but the round, roiling billows of flame made it easy to imagine.

"There, now you don't need to warn people about the wizards controlling the dragons. After seeing that, they'll know." Sonny looked at the empty spot where Honor had been standing, then looked ahead to see her sprinting toward town as fast as she could, Runt running just ahead of her.

The wizards ran in a group down the middle of the street. The dragons flew single file right at them, following the street's path. For a sick, giddy moment Martin thought, *This must be what it's like to be a bowling pin.*

Martin realized that his macro was still active. *Of course, I'm larger and more visible than all of the other pins combined,* he thought. *That seems like a bad thing.*

Then the lead dragon started blowing fire, and all thoughts of bowling left Martin's mind.

The wizards scattered in every conceivable direction, leaving the dragons at a loss as to which wizard they should follow. The dragons rose back into the sky to regroup.

The wizards had scattered around the general area, but were still able to talk, thanks to the battle comm.

Tyler shouted, "What have you done, Jeff?"

"I'm sorry! I'm sorry! I didn't plan any of this!"

Phillip cut in, "Tyler, we're all upset, but there'll be time enough to put a boot up Jeff's arse later."

Roy muttered, "I'm not so sure. I intend to take my time."

"We have bigger problems right now," Phillip said. "We have four dragons, which are impervious to all of our weapons, attacking the town. We have to get them out of here before something terrible happens."

Martin said, "Dragons are attacking the town! What do you mean, *before?*"

Gwen said, "He means that the dragons can't really damage anything. They cause pain, but that's it. One just blew a huge fireball all over a street lined with wooden huts and nothing caught fire. We don't even know if the big one ramming things will damage it. That wall might have only been dented because you were between it and the dragon."

"Exactly," Phillip said. "So far the only damage has been to our dignity and our respect for Jeff. But the longer this keeps up, the better the chances are that something genuinely bad will happen."

Brit said, "Sorry to say this, but I think it's already started happening."

The street had been deserted, but now they saw a tight cluster of six or seven men, all armed with swords, spears, and shields. The Leadchurch militia had arrived.

The horned dragon also seemed to notice the militia, and since a small group of men on the ground makes a much more tempting target then a spread-out bunch of hiding wizards, the dragons settled in for another strafing run.

The wizards all watched, some of them shouting as they did so, but they were at a loss as to how, or even if, they should intervene. They couldn't stop the dragons. The dragons couldn't injure the men. If the wizards took actions to stop the dragons from attacking the men, those measures probably wouldn't work, and might actually pose a hazard to the men they wanted to save.

The dragons flew in a straight line, and each attacked the same way in turn. They'd each lead with a massive jet of flame that splayed out before them like the beam of a motorcycle's headlight. Then, as the beast's head passed over the men, their sharp claws and lashing tail would come into play.

The men used their shields, which were made of metal, wood, or a combination of the two, to hold back the flames, which did not work. The fire completely enveloped them. The men, however, crouched behind shields with their eyes squeezed shut, so they didn't see the flames surrounding them. They felt intense heat and saw an orange glow through their eyelids, but simply assumed that since they survived without any noticeable burns, the shields had worked. Once the fire subsided, they had the claws to contend with, but the dragon's belly hung right above them, exposed and vulnerable. The men tried to use their shields to block the dragon's attack while they flailed with their swords and spears at the dragon's softest target.

The talons sliced through the shields and the men as if they weren't even there. Literally. The dragons' feet shoved the men about, but the sharp claws passed straight through them, leaving no marks—just a trail of stinging pain. The men swung their weapons as hard as they could, following through as the blades bounced off the passing dragons and were stopped, usually by the body of the man standing next to them.

The ghost pain from the talons and the genuine pain from their own swords led the warriors to assume that a toenail or two had gotten past the shields. When the last dragon flew past, the men had a moment to look at each other, and saw plenty of blood to reaffirm this belief.

One of the men said, "The dragons did their worst, but we're still standing, and we gave as good as we got!"

The men stopped groaning long enough to cheer at their courage.

Brit said, "They gave exactly the same as what they got, because they gave it to themselves."

The dragons came back for another run. The militia started groaning again, but they faced the dragons with their shields and readied their blades.

Roy said, "If this keeps up, those poor fools are going to kill themselves."

Phillip agreed but didn't waste time saying so. Instead, he flew into the air and said, "*Ĉi tiu iras al la dek unu.*" The Esperanto phrase triggered a macro of Gary's that amplified the speaker's voice to near-deafening proportions. Gary used it to make embarrassing noises at inopportune moments, but the other wizards often used it as a sort of public address system.

"Friends," Phillip said, "Lay down your weapons and find cover. Don't attack the dragons. You'll only hurt yourselves."

Runt easily outran both Honor and Sonny, because Runt had the advantage of not having to stop occasionally to wriggle free of the grip of her older brother, or of having to repeatedly grab her little sister. The only thing slowing Runt down was having to stop, turn around, and bark at her two human companions to hurry up.

They were nearly to the edge of town now, and Honor had just torn herself free of Sonny's grip for the umpteenth time when she heard the voice. She recognized it instantly as belonging to the wizard in blue, the one Bishop Galbraith considered a friend. He said, "Friends, lay down your weapons and find cover. Don't attack the dragons. You'll only hurt yourselves."

"See! He's telling them not to fight the dragons," Honor said. "That proves the wizards are behind this!"

Sonny grabbed her by the arm again and said, "Maybe, but that's even more reason to stay away from the whole thing!"

Honor kicked Sonny in the shin. He cried out in pain and let go. Honor took off like a shot, shouting, "I'm sorry, I'm sorry, but our neighbors are in trouble! I need to warn them!"

Sonny shouted, "Believe me, they know!"

The dragons swept down the street the opposite direction from the way they'd come before.

The militia had turned around and was ready for them.

The dragons flew over the men, bathing them in searing flames and slashing at them with their claws. The men hid behind their shields until the fire passed, then stabbed wildly with their weapons at the passing creatures' bellies as before. This time Martin saw arrows shoot in from the distance, striking the dragons in the flanks, bouncing off uselessly, and falling point first onto the heads of the swordsmen below. When the fifth dragon had passed, the men were badly bloodied and seemingly still unaware that their wounds were inflicted entirely by their own efforts.

Martin said, "They're killing themselves, and it's our fault."

"No," Gary said, "They're killing themselves, and it's Jeff's fault."

"I'm sorry, okay?!" Jeff shouted. "What do you want me to do, go throw myself between them and the dragon?"

Gwen said, "That wouldn't do any good."

"That doesn't mean I don't want it," Gary said. "It'd be really satisfying."

"This bickering isn't helping," Phillip shouted.

Gary said, "But it's also really satisfying."

Phillip barked, "Shut up! Does anybody have an idea how to stop this?"

Brit mumbled, "They seemed spooked by Martin as a giant. Beyond that, I dunno if it'll stop it, but I have something that might help." She floated in the air, swiping her finger back and forth in space. She and Gwen were citizens of Atlantis and had access to a different interface program. It still linked to the mysterious repository file, just like the program the Leadchurch wizards called *the shell,* but it had a different set of macros preprogrammed, and used a visual interface instead of verbal triggers.

Brit glanced up and saw that the dragons were turning around, lining up for another run. She quickly looked back to the menu of options only visible to her, muttering, "Don't look at the dragons, look at the macros. The dragons won't help you, Brit. The macros will. Don't . . . got it!"

She stabbed her finger at an option only she could see and pointed her other hand at the men with their shields raised. She spread her fingers, and a cone of shimmering white light spread out and bathed them. They took on a glow, which quickly flared, held its blinding intensity for three seconds, then subsided. The bright light seemed to spook the lead dragon into aborting its attack. He veered up and away. When the flash faded, the men were slumped on the ground, unconscious. They would have looked rather peaceful, if not for all of the armor, and weapons, and their various injuries.

Brit looked relieved. The militiamen lay where they had stood, ready to face the dragons again despite their wounds. She found it odd that she could be so deeply impressed with the valor they displayed while making a mistake.

Roy asked, "So you knocked them out?"

"Much more than that," Brit said, "But there's no time to explain now. Gwen, look up a macro called *Medevac-Experimental*. It's something Louiza and I've been working on. It's meant to stabilize injured people and send them to Atlantis."

Gwen said, "Where there's a real, modern doctor instead of a barber with a pet leech."

"Exactly. Everyone else, your job is to get these dragons out of here."

Everyone agreed, or at least nobody actively disagreed, so the wizards got to it. They all had their jobs to do, and the unspoken task of figuring out how to do it.

Sonny had given up on stopping Honor from running into harm's way, and now just hoped to be there to protect her from harm when she found it. Unfortunately, harm made itself easy to find.

They ran up a narrow side street, more of a footpath by modern standards, just wide enough for a single cart to traverse. The street emptied directly onto the main road, the one on which the militia confronted the dragons. In the distance, Sonny saw a wall of flames, followed by a dragon flying just above the roofline. Then he saw four more walls of flames, followed by four more dragons. As the last dragon passed, Honor reached the junction, ran out into the street, and stopped. She stood, bathed in orange light, watching the dragons with a look of amazement and horror on her face.

Runt caught up to Honor and jumped around her feet, yapping. Honor didn't seem to notice.

Sonny got to her a second later. He slid to a stop, grabbed Honor's arm, looked for some cover to throw her under and, in the process, glanced down the street himself.

The dragons flew in the distance, soaring up and to the left in an orderly line. On the ground, he saw a group of men, townsfolk Sonny recognized, though he knew few of their names. Men who lived in town and had clearly come out to defend their homes. They looked like they were taking a pretty bad beating, but he couldn't quite tell through the white glow of the spell a female wizard cast on them. Honor recognized the she-wizard as the one in the mask who seemed so friendly with the wizard leader, Phillip. The lady wizard floated in midair, shooting her magic from an extended hand. The light from her hand faded, but the men glowed brighter for a moment, before they stopped. After that they just lay on the dusty ground, unconscious or worse, while the she-wizard moved on to other nefarious things.

Sonny scanned the area behind them, saw an oxcart parked in front of a hut, and started toward it, dragging Honor as he went.

"She bewitched them," Honor shouted.

"I saw," Sonny said quietly.

"They were just defending their homes, and she bewitched them!"

"Yes, I saw."

"Then why aren't you upset?!"

"I am very upset, but I'm being quiet, because I don't want her to notice that we saw it! Now get under this cart and hush!"

"We need to find the bishop!"

"No, we need to hide from the dragons."

As he stuffed his struggling sister under the oxcart, Sonny noted that Runt had seen where they were going and was already under the cart, waiting for them.

The small don't survive long unless they learn when to avoid attention, Sonny thought as he dove under the cart next to his sister and her dog. *I hope Runt can somehow teach Honor that lesson. I sure seem to have failed at it.*

Brit and Gwen had a clearly defined task: to find the injured and hit them with Brit's medevac spell. It stood to reason that any fresh injured would be in the vicinity of the dragons, so they simply fell in behind the last dragon in line and kept their eyes open.

The rest of the wizards fanned out, flying above the rooftops, looking for the archers who had added their friendly fire to the previous attack.

Any hope that the dragons might just leave died when Gwen said, "The dragons are coming back for another run. They don't know the swordsmen are neutralized."

Martin, still in his giant form, hovered in midair and watched the dragons settling into the same flight pattern as before. The horned dragon in the lead opened its mouth, but stopped short of breathing fire. Martin waited, planning to rush the dragons when it would startle them most. He watched as the lead dragon cocked its head to the side and studied the unconscious men in the street as it approached. The dragon continued its trajectory, but it closed its mouth, swiveling its head from side to side looking for a new threat, rather than raining fire on the old threat.

Tyler obviously saw the dragon's behavior as well. "Maybe if nobody attacks them, they'll leave on their own."

As if on cue, Martin saw a flash of light in his peripheral vision. He spun in the air, and saw five men with bows standing in line near the large stone trough. The light came from the oil-soaked rags wrapped around their arrowheads, which they were hastily lighting with torches.

The urge to communicate shot through Martin's brain so quickly that the proper words couldn't keep up. "Arrow guys!" he said. "Arrow guys with fire!"

Most of the wizards figured out what Martin meant only in time to clarify what they were seeing. As the dragons drew even with the archers, five balls of flame flew in graceful arcs toward the horned dragon in the lead.

Martin attempted to throw up a barrier to stop the arrows, but he had too little time and too much adrenaline. The barrier went up just after the arrows had passed. Martin heard some shouting below, but the arrows monopolized his attention as they struck the dragon in the ribs, bounced off uselessly, and fell to the buildings and people below.

The lead dragon didn't seem to feel the arrows, but the sight of them spooked the four follower dragons. They scattered while their leader continued down the street.

Phillip's voice was still being amplified, and he knew it. "Flaming arrows against fire-breathing dragons? They won't do any good! You're just going to burn the town down!"

Martin looked down. He saw two more injured men, but Gwen would deal with that. He had to prevent more injuries, which would not be easy. At least one arrow had landed on the roof of a hut. In an instant Martin understood why people seldom fireproof an item by thatching it.

He never liked it when Phillip was right, and this time was worse than most.

Honor pressed in close to Sonny, holding Runt near. The buildings and the oxcart above them restricted their view, but they could see enough, and they heard plenty.

One of the wizards shouted, "Arrow guys! Arrow guys with fire!"

"He's warning the dragons," Honor muttered to Sonny, "or his friends so they can protect their dragons."

Across the street a door opened a sliver, and Bishop Galbraith poked his head out, looking up to see who yelled.

Honor shrieked, "Father! Father Galbraith!"

The bishop squinted across the street, then shouted, "Honor? Sonny? What are you doing here?!"

Honor cried, "I need to talk to you!" Before Sonny could stop her, she had run out from under the cart, into the middle of the street. He and Runt both clambered after her, shouting her name and yapping madly.

Galbraith flung open the door to the hut and dashed out to meet Honor. Behind him, a man, a woman, and a little boy crouched in the darkness. Galbraith grabbed Honor's arm and started to pull her back to the hut. Sonny and Runt were only a step or two behind and were more than ready to follow Honor and Galbraith into the building, but they all stopped when a shadow fell over them.

They looked up and saw an immense horned dragon gliding directly overhead, and the shimmering form of a wizard, made large and radiant by the power of his magic, doing nothing to interfere with the dragon in any way. Then several flaming arrows bounced off of the dragon and fell directly on top of Honor, Sonny, Runt, and Galbraith.

To Honor's lasting shame, she dropped to the ground and curled into a ball.

To Honor's lasting regret, Sonny and Bishop Galbraith both threw themselves over her.

She heard their grunts of exertion, and the bishop saying some very un-bishop-like things after his head and Sonny's head collided, making a sound like two rocks banging together. She heard both of them make pained noises, and felt them crawl off her. She rolled onto her back and crab walked backward several feet to get some distance. Galbraith had a flaming arrow sticking out of his leg. He beat at it furiously, trying to put out the fire and grunting under his breath as he repeatedly slapped himself at the site of a fresh arrow wound. Sonny had two flaming arrows protruding from his back. He made no effort to put the fire out. He spent all of his energy rising to a crawling position.

He asked Honor if she was hurt. She didn't answer. He told her to get under the cart. She didn't move. She felt a light tugging on her cloak and heard Runt whining through clenched teeth. Later, she would remember angrily that, in that moment, even Runt showed more intelligence than she had.

Father Galbraith barked, "Move girl! Under the cart, now!"

Less than a second later she was under the cart, but would never have any direct memory of how she got there. The bishop's tone of voice had managed to get through to her nervous system by going around the middleman of her conscious brain.

Honor heard the lead wizard, *the bishop's friend*, say, "Flaming arrows against fire-breathing dragons? They won't do any good! You're just going to burn the town down!"

Honor whispered, "He's taunting them!"

The flame from Galbraith's arrow had died, but tendrils of smoke still rose from the wound. He scuttled over to Sonny and attempted to beat out the flames on the boy's back. Sonny winced in pain and Galbraith slapped as furiously as he could until one of the female wizards, the one with the brown hair who sometimes worked as a tailor for the local farmers, flew by and cast a spell on them. Galbraith and Sonny froze in place, bathed in white light. Then the light flared and subsided. Sonny and the bishop both seemed to be asleep. Aside from breathing, neither of them moved.

Honor saw that the fire on Sonny's back was out, and the arrows were gone. She thought, *The wizards are trying to hide what they've done.*

Martin turned his attention back to the archers, and saw to his horror that they each had a fresh flaming arrow nocked and their bows drawn.

He yelled, "Stop, you idiots! It won't work! I've blocked your arrows anyway. Just go hide somewhere!"

The men didn't listen, instead aiming at a point somewhere off to Martin's left. The archer on the end shouted, and they all released their strings. The arrows flew gracefully for ten feet, then struck the invisible force field. They bounced up and over the backs of the archers, into the buildings behind them. Not one of them seemed to notice. The horned dragon, which landed on the roof of the hut opposite them and looked to be preparing to breathe fire on them, had their undivided attention.

The men dove for cover behind the stone trough. Giant Martin spun to face the dragon. He had little time to think, and instinctively resorted to the first menacing action most people learn. He made jazz hands at the dragon, and yelled "Booga-booga!"

The dragon seemed spooked by Martin's display, but instead of fleeing, it attacked. It bathed Martin, every building in sight, and the archers in fire, or at least tried to. The force field Martin had created to block the flaming arrows also blocked the dragon's flames, creating a flat wall of fire where there would have been a roiling, turbulent cloud of it. Of course, the archers would never know that the force field saved them. They were hiding their faces for protection from the fire that wasn't hitting them.

The dragon blew its lungs out, then paused to inhale. One of the archers peeked out from behind the trough, looked at the dragon, then looked behind them.

Of course, behind them was another row of closely spaced huts with thatched roofs which, thanks to the deflected flaming arrows, were now smoldering.

The archer cried, "Much more of this, and the town will be destroyed!"

Martin agreed with this statement.

To Honor, it felt like she spent an eternity lying in the dirt, looking at Sonny and the bishop lying in the street, but in reality it took less than ten seconds for her to snap out of her shock. She scuttled out from under the cart. She grabbed Sonny by the feet and dragged him under. Then she did the same for Bishop Galbraith. They were both breathing, but completely unresponsive.

There, she thought. *I've made them as safe as I can. Now I have to make myself as safe as I can, because if either of them wakes up and finds out that I let myself get killed, they'll never let me hear the end of it.*

The town was in chaos. The dragons had landed and were spewing fire in every direction. The sky buzzed with flying wizards, who seemed to be either egging the dragons on or casting spells on innocent people like her brother and Bishop Galbraith.

She asked herself, *What building in this town is least apt to catch fire?* and immediately answered herself: *The lead church.*

She was unaware of lead's relatively low melting point.

Also, she thought, *it's God's house. If any place is going to be safe from the wizards, it'll be the church.*

She picked up Runt, muttered a quick apology to the two unconscious men she couldn't carry, and took off running for the church.

Honor's journey to the church felt like a trek through hell. She witnessed horrors, evil, and cruelty beyond anything her young mind had ever imagined.

Fire seemed to be everywhere. The dragons produced gigantic plumes of flame every time they exhaled. Few buildings seemed to be burning yet, but she feared they all would catch fire in time. She thought about her brother and the bishop lying helpless under the cart, and cursed herself for not being strong enough to carry even one of them. She clutched Runt even tighter and kept moving.

She saw a large dragon with curved ram-like horns, and the enormous silver wizard, shining with eerie magical light, making no move to stop the dragons, instead shouting insults at some men cowering behind a water trough. Further down the street, a smaller dragon blocked most of the road, spreading fire over as much of the area as possible. A wizard dressed all in black stood on the dragon's back, feet planted between its giant shoulders. There were countless strands of a stringy mass, like the webbing of an immense, unholy spider, extending from the back of the dragon's head to the wizard's white-knuckled fists. The wizard pulled on the strands with all of his might. Honor had been around animals all her life, and immediately recognized the webs, despite their unusual appearance, for what they were. *They're reins,* she thought. *He can steer the dragon, and aim its fire wherever he wants!* Honor came to a corner. She looked toward the church, and saw only one dragon and one wizard in her way. Many other people seemed to have the same idea, because there were many more citizens visible along this street than on the previous one, all moving toward the church.

She looked the other way, hoping to avoid being surprised from behind by a dragon, or a wizard. Unfortunately, she saw both.

The dragon perched on a building, snarling down into the street, where several bystanders cowered behind a wizard. He had red-and-purple-striped robes, and the darkest skin she had ever seen. She paused to watch, confused. For a moment, it almost looked as if the wizard wanted to protect the people. Then, in a scene that haunted her nightmares for years to come, the wizard turned into a dragon himself. The people behind him screamed, understandably. Honor turned away. *God knows what those two dragons are going to do,* she thought. *But I know I don't want to watch them do it.*

She ran for the church, despite the fact that it also meant running toward another dragon and another wizard, which she was beginning to think was even worse. She felt relieved when the wizard, an older man with a strange, dirt-colored robe and a hat with a wide brim, flew away, even though he did so with so much speed that she heard a crack and felt the wind he kicked up from far away.

The dragon seemed confused. The wizard was gone. The dragon's nostrils twitched. The beast inhaled, shook its head furiously, then singled one man out.

Honor immediately recognized Hubert, the dung sifter.

The dragon saw Hubert, and Hubert saw that the dragon saw him. As the beast reared its head, preparing to incinerate him, Hubert crouched, curled into a ball, and extended one hand, holding a small idol shaped vaguely like a person, modeled out of some brown material. Honor only got a brief glimpse of it before Hubert disappeared from view, completely engulfed in flame. Honor kept running.

She had made it past the awful scene and behind the dragon before it ran out of breath and the flames subsided. She didn't want to look, but did so in spite of herself when she heard Hubert laughing.

He stood in the same spot where she'd seen him last, completely unharmed, dancing for joy and holding his idol over his head, triumphantly.

In her confusion, Honor stopped and stared at Hubert, trying to make sense of what she saw. Runt barked, snapping Honor out of it just in time to see that the dragon had turned to face her, and was taking a deep breath.

"Little girl," Hubert shouted, "Catch!" He drew back his hand to throw the idol, but he never followed through. A beige streak, followed by a deafening boom and a powerful shock wave blew through, knocking Hubert off his feet and Honor and Runt back into the wall behind them.

Honor dropped Runt to steady herself. The dragon had vanished. *The wizard must have magicked it away, to where it could do more damage,* she thought.

Across the street, Hubert sat flat on his backside, looking dazed but still clutching his idol. Honor heard several staccato, insistent barks, and saw that Runt had run ahead toward the church and stopped, waiting for Honor to follow.

Hubert came to his senses and shouted, "I'm not hurt! I'm not hurt!"

Honor wanted to warn him about the she-wizard in dark blue robes and mask floating in the air above the building behind him. The she-wizard pointed a hand toward Hubert, as if preparing to cast a spell. She listened for a moment to him shouting that he was not hurt, shrugged, and withdrew her hand. Then the she-wizard winked at Honor, smiled, and flew away.

Honor ran as fast as she could all the way to the church. Runt ran ahead, yapping, as if telling everyone to stay out of Honor's way. They found the door held open by a nun who shouted to everyone within hearing range to get inside, where they would be safe. Runt stopped shy of the door, as always, but the nun reached down and pulled Runt inside as Honor dashed in.

Almost half of the town seemed to be sheltered by the church's lead cladding, and within the next few minutes, it seemed like the other half of the town joined them. While they were inside the church, the fire could not get to them, and the wizards would not dare try. Of course, thanks to the stained glass windows, all they could see of anything happening outside was the occasional red glow, but most of them were pretty sure they didn't want to see anything beyond that.

Martin tried to talk the archers out of shooting at the dragons again, but they didn't find his insults persuasive. They each nocked another arrow and hastily held them over the torch to light them, then dove back behind the trough while another thick blanket of fire rolled toward them.

Of course, the fire breath stopped at the force field. Martin took this as a victory. He couldn't stop the dragon from breathing fire, but he could stop the fire from hitting anyone. And, of course, the fire wouldn't actually injure a person if it did hit them, and, so far, none of the people he had helped in this manner acted grateful, or even noticed his assistance. But on a day like today, any victory seemed good.

"You can stand up," the giant floating image of Martin yelled. "I'm holding back the fire with my magic."

The men didn't stand, or even move. From behind the trough, one of them yelled, "Then why don't you use your magic to kill the dragon for us?"

"I can't. Sorry."

"Is your magic not strong enough?"

"I guess you could say that."

"Then we'll keep hiding, thanks."

The dragon ran out of breath. Martin clearly caused it distress, but it held its ground. The archers stood, aiming their arrows.

"It's a fire-breathing dragon," Martin said, floating down closer to the men. "Why do you think flaming arrows will hurt it?"

"Flaming arrows are better than regular arrows," one of the archers said.

"But fire won't hurt it!"

"Won't help it either, and there's still the arrow. PULL!"

Martin flew between the men and the dragon. "Guys, stop! I can't let you shoot those! You're just setting your own town on fire. The dragons are harmless."

The horned dragon behind Martin chose that moment to belch out another plume of fire, directly at his back. Martin's world reduced to two sensations: bright orange light and searing pain. He screamed in agony, surprise, and frustration at having his last statement so quickly and succinctly refuted.

The force field between himself and the archers remained in place, so he knew the archers were being spared this pain. When the flames died away, he saw that they had once again hidden behind the trough, this time with their flaming arrowheads sticking up like antennae.

The archers sprung to their feet, nocked their bows again, and took aim.

Their leader said, "Out of the way, wizard."

Martin said, "No!"

He had expected that they would wait for his next sentence, in which he'd explain yet again how what they were doing was counterproductive, but the leader said, "Suit yourself. Aim for between his legs, boys! Try to fire through the gap!"

Martin got out of the way, still shouting, "No, don't do it!"

Again, the men loosed their arrows in unison. Again, they only flew a short distance before they struck Martin's force field and bounced up and back, over the archers' heads. This time, instead of watching, Martin acted. He quickly threw up another force field, between the archers and the building behind them.

The force field successfully protected the already-smoldering building. Unfortunately, quicker than Martin could react, the arrows bounced off of it, and fell limply back down onto the very men who had fired them. Not every man got hit, but they all shouted at Martin as if they did. Martin apologized profusely until Gwen swooped by, medevaced the lot of them, shook her head at Martin, and moved on.

Martin shouted, "It wasn't *all* my fault!" Then he found himself again enveloped in flames from the horned dragon behind him.

Martin flew up, out of the fire and away from the dragon. He deactivated his macro, reducing again to his normal size. He took a second to survey the scene. He found far too much scene to survey quickly, and resorted to activating the battle comm and asking, "Phillip, what's going on?"

Phillip floated high above the town, coordinating. "Actually, it's a good time to make a general report. Pretty much the entire town has taken refuge in the church. My offensive power, Gary's, and Martin's seem pretty useless. The dragons aren't running from us anymore. Roy has successfully pushed one dragon out of town. Where are you now, Roy?"

"I think about twenty miles out to sea, but it's hard to tell. The flight path hasn't been straight. I can't hurt this thing, just push it around. Do we know how to kill them yet?"

Phillip said, "Jeff?"

"If I knew, I'd have said something when they first showed up."

"Right," Phillip said. "We'll all discuss that later. Tyler's also having some luck. He turned into a dragon, fought one of the real dragons, and if you look to the northeast, you'll see that he's now chasing it out of town."

"Actually, it's chasing me," Tyler said. "But anything that works is fine. I just hope this isn't a Pepé Le Pew situation."

"Indeed," Phillip said. "So, we have a house fire and three more dragons to get out of here. Ideas?"

Gary said, "They all followed the big one that likes Martin."

Martin said, "It's tried to kill me four times."

Gwen said, "Well, some of us aren't great at expressing our feelings."

"My point," Gary continued, "is that if we can get that one to go, the other two might follow."

Phillip said, "Yes! Then, even if Roy and Tyler's dragons return, they'll follow it. Good idea, Gary!"

As if wanting to prove Gary's point, the horned dragon had taken flight, and the two remaining dragons fell in behind it.

Gary said, "Thanks. Okay, so how do we get Horney to leave?"

"Please," Phillip said, "Don't call it that."

"But it's the only one with horns."

"That's just an excuse."

"Yeah, but it's a good one."

Martin said, "Giant me just made it aggressive. Flashes of light scared it off, but it came right back."

Brit said, "We're almost done with the wounded. I don't see anyone else out in the open. Maybe my macro would freak it out. Gwen, can you finish up without me?"

"Yeah, I just told some townsfolk that we're putting the wounded to sleep so they can rest and recuperate. Now I'm going to pop back to my time and buy some infrared goggles so I can see if any wounded are hiding from us."

Phillip said, "Sounds good. I say do it."

Gwen said, "I'm glad, because I already did. I left right after I said I was going to go. Spent a week, saw some family, bought some fabric. Anyway, I'll start the search."

Phillip said, "Good. Yes, do."

Gwen said, "I already have."

Brit said, "All right, intercepting Horney. So I try to get him out into the countryside, then what? We don't know how to kill them."

Martin said, "If we can really run them off, great. If not, we can do like Gwen did. Go away, figure out how to deal with them, and come back to this moment."

Brit flew quickly into the dragons' flight path. She set a collision course with the lead dragon and triggered her macro, suddenly becoming a swarm of Brits, all flying straight down the dragons' throats.

The horned dragon in the lead flew through the Brit cloud as if it didn't exist. The second, which flew behind and a bit to the side of the leader, had seen the Brit cloud approaching as well, and followed the horned dragon through.

The third dragon's view seemed to have been blocked by the two lead dragons. It panicked when it saw a cloud of countless fast-moving objects arcing around the other two dragons and into its path. It reared back, flapped its wings madly, dove, turned, and flew at top speed in the opposite direction, pursued by the Brits.

"Well done, love," Phillip said. "Think you can keep at it until the dragon's a few miles away?"

"No problem," Brit said.

"Good. That leaves us with two. The leader seems stubborn, but let me try something."

Martin landed in an abandoned street, and watched as a stream of Phillip's missiles streaked down from on high. They tore through the air in a constant dotted line, far more of them than ever could have come from a real plane, hitting the tail of the horned dragon and exploding at a sustained rate of three or four a second.

The horned dragon flew much faster. The second dragon also flew much faster, in the opposite direction. From its point of view, its fellow dragon disappeared, replaced by a deafening, sustained explosion. As the smaller dragon fled from the noise and the fire and the smoke, the line of missiles split. Halfway up the stream, the missiles stopped pursuing the horned dragon and instead targeted the rear of the smaller dragon. When the missiles started to make contact, the dragon made for the horizon at top speed.

"Okay," Phillip said, "I'll keep the pressure on this one."

Martin asked, "Why'd you switch targets to the other dragon? You left Gary and me with the biggest, meanest one, and now it's angry. I just answered my own question, didn't I?"

"Admirably," Phillip said. "Now get to it, that scary dragon isn't going to attack itself."

Martin gritted his teeth and shook his head. Past experience gave him reason to fear that Gary's assistance would make the task slightly harder than dealing with the dragon by himself.

"Gary, you got any ideas?" Martin turned and saw that Gary stood next to him in the middle of the road, holding Uzi submachine guns in both hands. Martin barely had time to cover his ears before Gary started firing them both at the dragon as it flew above the town, hundreds of yards away.

It seemed Gary had worked some programming magic to give the guns unlimited ammo, because he held both triggers down, dispensing lead as if he were holding two garden hoses.

It also seemed that his aim with the stub-barreled firearms wasn't great, since instead of fleeing, the dragon turned gracefully and flew in low and close for a good look at what was making the noise.

Soon, it became painfully obvious that the bullets weren't powerful enough to deter the dragon in the least since it landed down the street, spread its wings, and roared as Gary continued to fire both guns.

"Okay," Gary shouted over the automatic gunfire. "I've got its attention. Now you do something."

Martin, still covering his ears, again triggered his macro, transformed into his thirty-foot-tall silver form, and did the first thing he could think of. He kicked Gary.

Gary stopped firing as he flew to the side of the street and hit a wall.

Martin took his hands down from his ears.

The dragon let out a large plume of fire, but Martin managed to get a force field erected in time to spare himself the pain. When the dragon had emptied its lungs, it saw Martin still standing there, unharmed. The dragon brought its head low, pointed its horns forward, and drew its body down and back, like a sprinter in the starting blocks.

Martin lifted his staff to fly, but Gary shouted, "No! Stop! Let it try! I have an idea!"

Martin moaned, but did what Gary asked. The dragon ran forward. Martin turned and ran a few steps to soften the blow. As he was still in his Giant Martin form, the dragon's horns hit him squarely in his giant rear end. Martin's real body was protected inside of the larger structure, but the sudden acceleration still jarred him quite badly. He heard Gary shout, "Tuck and roll," so he did, careening down the street like a poorly made soccer ball.

Martin came to a stop many yards away. "I thought you had an idea," he shouted as he lifted his immense form up to its hands and knees.

"I did," Gary said. "It worked! Look!"

Martin peered back and saw that the dragon had come to a stop after ramming him, but had also lined itself up to ram him again.

"Now you just play kick the can," Gary said, "only you're the can. I'll follow along and use force fields to keep you on course if I have to."

The dragon lunged forward. Martin didn't like the plan, but he didn't have time to argue, and had no better idea of his own. He stood up, turned his back, and the dragon rammed him again. He tucked and rolled again. Martin hated it, again. He had to admit, though, the plan would probably work. The street they were on led to the edge of town, and it would only take four or five more butts in the butt to get there.

The dragon made contact again, this time a bit off-center. Martin rolled to the right, toward some poor person's hut. Just before he made contact with the fragile building, he struck an invisible force field and ricocheted like a billiard ball, striking another force field on the other side of the street before stopping.

If Gary's smart, he has walls set up all the way down both sides of the street, Martin thought. *That can be a pretty big if.*

He looked down the street. At the edge of town, the road turned. A hut on the outside edge of the turn blocked his rolling path to the field beyond.

"Should I take off and fly out of town?" he asked hastily before absorbing another impact from the rear.

"No," Gary said, "Keep rolling. This is working. I'll worry about the building."

Martin came to a stop, glanced up, and saw that one more shot would send him into the hut's closest wall, and possibly through its farthest wall immediately afterward. Whatever Gary planned to do, he hoped he'd do it quickly.

The dragon hit Martin. Martin rolled forward toward the hut and hit the invisible force-field ramp.

Later, Martin would grudgingly agree that the ramp had been a good idea, and Gary would refuse to admit that it had been poorly executed.

A long, shallow ramp allows a rolling object's momentum to change direction with a minimum of violent shock, and results in a low, flat trajectory, and a less jarring impact as well.

Gary, however, made his ramp almost a perfect forty-five-degree angle. When Martin hit it, he felt like he'd hit a concrete wall. His mass flew almost straight up in the air. He untucked, centrifugal force pulled his limbs outward, and he cartwheeled gracelessly in space before landing like a sack of laundry in the hut's backyard. In his ear, he heard Roy say, "Inbound hot, one mile out."

Martin moaned and rolled over on his back. He saw the horned dragon land on the hut's roof, spread its wings, inhale, and start to cough out a blanket of fire with which to smother him. Then the dragon disappeared with a deafening crack and two streaks receding into the distance, one a dull beige and next to it a line of orange fire.

9.

The waiting room of the Atlantis medical clinic was empty. There were no sick or injured people, just one very healthy receptionist sitting behind the reception desk thumbing through a catalog. His uniform differed from the official male uniform of Atlantis in that his netting shirt and kilt were dyed the aqua color of generic hospital scrubs.

It didn't startle him when Brit the Younger and Gwen materialized in front of his desk. He'd been in Atlantis long enough to be accustomed to magic. The receptionist placed his catalog facedown on his desk, stood, smiled at Brit and Gwen, and said, "Good morning! Welcome. Please have a seat. Tell me what's wrong, and I'll see to it that the doctor is with you in a moment."

"Nothing's wrong, thanks," Brit said. "We just need to discuss some business with Louiza."

"Is the business medical in nature, or does it pertain to her role as president?"

Brit asked, "Does it really matter?"

The receptionist said, "You'll see her just as fast either way, but she likes to know what kind of unpleasant conversation she should brace for."

"It's a little bit of both, in this case."

The receptionist said, "I'm sure she'll appreciate the warning."

Gwen leaned in closer to look at the catalog the receptionist had been reading. The front cover featured a man in a puffy shirt with the collar open to the belt buckle, and the words *International Male*. The back cover offered a surprising variety of Speedo-style swimsuits.

"Interesting catalog," Gwen said. "Not many of the men in Atlantis read English."

"I don't either," the receptionist said. "The doctor got it for me, to see if there's anything I might like to wear around the office."

The receptionist pressed a button on his desk that that had been programmed to act as a buzzer and intercom. He told Louiza that there were two sorceresses here to speak with her about both medicine and city business. She sighed heavily and told him to bring them to her.

The receptionist led them to Louiza's private office. As with pretty much every room in the entire city, everything but highly specialized equipment or an imported memento from the sorceress's original time was tasteful, modern, and made from a seamless, white, crystalline material. In this case the floor, walls, desk, and chairs were clearly from Atlantis, but on the wall behind the desk, several diplomas and college degrees hung in black frames.

Louiza rummaged through the drawers of her desk. She welcomed her guests in a distracted manner. Brit and Gwen returned her greeting, smiling broadly.

The receptionist left. Louiza offered Brit and Gwen a seat while still digging through whatever clutter filled her desk. They thanked her and sat down, smiling broadly.

Brit said, "Your presidential office down in the capitol doesn't have any diplomas. You could move some of these there, for balance."

Louiza said, "No, they have to stay here. You need an education, practical experience, and certifications to practice medicine. To be president, all you need is the confidence of most of the people who bothered to vote."

Brit and Gwen sat silently for several seconds, watching Louiza continue to rifle through her own desk.

Gwen asked, "What are you looking for?"

Louiza froze and held up a single finger, communicating the idea that Gwen should wait a moment. With nobody moving or speaking in the room, they could all hear a faint but distinct beeping, like the alarm of a long forgotten digital watch going off from deep within the cushions of a couch.

"I only noticed it about a minute ago," Louiza said, "and it's already driving me crazy."

Brit the Younger said, "Oh, sorry. I can take care of that." She swiped her finger through space in front of her, looking at menus only she could see, then finally made a selection, and the noise stopped.

Gwen and Brit smiled broadly at Louiza, offering no explanation.

Louiza said, "Okay, out with it."

Gwen said, "I'm sorry?"

"I'm sure you are," Louiza said, "I just don't know about what yet. People only smile like that and don't say anything when they have something to say that's going to make someone else unhappy, so out with it."

Brit said, "Well, you know that medevac protocol we've been working on, to handle medical emergencies?"

"Yes." Louiza turned to Gwen and said, "The idea is for a sorceress or wizard to stabilize and evacuate an injured person, then treat them and replace them without them or their friends and family knowing they were ever gone."

Gwen said, "Yeah, Brit told me."

Louiza said, "Of course she did. Sorry. Force of habit. As a doctor, most of my job is to explain things in the least alarming way possible. Same goes for being president, actually."

Gwen said, "Makes sense."

"Is there some snag with writing the programming?" Louiza asked Brit. "I can get you some assistance if you need it. It's a complex job."

"No, no, the program's written, tested, and ready to go."

"Really? You tested it and it all worked?"

"Yes. We successfully transported people to the triage center, time was frozen from their point of view, and their exact time, location, and positioning at the point of extraction were recorded so that we could replace them after treatment. It's just like you requested. I also added a way for sorceresses to use the program on themselves if they get hurt."

Louiza said, "That's great! Good job! That means I can get to work on the treatment protocols."

"Yeah," Brit said. "Where are you with those?"

"I haven't started them yet. I thought we'd get phase one done, then when that worked, move on to phase two."

Brit said, "Oh." Then she and Gwen smiled broadly.

Louiza narrowed her eyes at them.

Brit said, "I also added an audible alarm to tell you when a patient arrives in the triage center. I tried to make it subtle."

"Oh, God," Louiza moaned. "You've sent me a patient already, haven't you?"

"Consider it a field test," Brit said. "A trial by fire."

Louiza said, "Fire?"

Gwen said, "And arrows. And swords."

"Where's the patient now?"

"The patients are in a facility I set up in the lower bowl to hold them so you could look them over, do some triage, and take them one at a time."

"Them? How many patients are we talking about?"

Brit said, "A few. The point is, they're in stasis, so you can take your time."

"How many is a few?"

Brit sighed and said, "Twenty-six."

"Twenty-six! You said a few! Twenty-six isn't a few! It's a few dozen."

"Oh, don't be so melodramatic. It's not a few dozen. It's just a couple dozen."

"Well that's a lot more than a few!"

Brit said, "Touché."

Louiza spent a moment glaring at Brit and Gwen, then asked, "What happened?"

Gwen said, "Well, from our point of view, it's still happening, so we really should get back to helping."

"And if it's happening in the Dark Ages, where you two spend your free time, then from my point of view it won't happen for hundreds of years, so you have time to explain."

"Louiza, we're sorry," Gwen said. "We're just both really stressed out. We just fought off a dragon attack."

"You're telling me a dragon hurt those people?"

"Five dragons. One of the wizards made some artificial dragons, and they got away from him somehow. Five of them got into a fight with a small town, but the dragons didn't really do any damage. They can't directly injure anyone."

"Then how did the twenty-six people in the triage center get hurt?"

Brit said, "They did that to each other, accidentally, trying to fight off the dragons."

Louiza said, "That sounds awful."

Gwen said, "It is."

"And you can't stay here and help because you're in a hurry to get back to it?"

"Yes."

"Fighting five dragons sounds better than staying here and helping me?"

Brit said, "When you're angry, yes."

"You can't just dump a bunch of injured people on my doorstep like this."

"That's the whole point of the medevac program," Brit said. "To deliver injured people to your doorstep."

"For that matter, that's the whole point of a clinic," Gwen said. "To create a doorstep to have the injured delivered to."

Louiza waved her hands in a motion that looked like both a signal of surrender and swatting away a bee. "Okay, yes, fine, but not yet, and not this many! I don't have any of the systems in place. I don't have all the equipment I'll need. I don't know how I'm going to treat these people without them learning things about Atlantis we don't want them to know. I only have one assistant and he's really just eye candy. I'm not prepared."

"But you have plenty of time," Brit said. "They're in stasis. Heck, you could treat one a day and just make a part-time job of it. They'll never know the difference."

"We know you can do this," Gwen said.

"In fact," Brit added, "we know you have done it. Part of the system is that we tag the patient's place and time so they can be returned seamlessly. All of the patients in the triage room right now have been returned. We saw them. They're already back, gathered in the church, sleeping while they heal, just like we talked about when we first came up with this idea. So, it worked."

"For you," Louiza said. "For me it will work, because I'm going to have to make it work."

"But you will," Gwen said.

"From our point of view, you already have," Brit added. "And we're terribly impressed, and grateful."

"Or, we will be," Gwen said. "From your point of view."

"And while I'm here, cleaning up your mess, you two run off to go dragon hunting with your boyfriends."

Brit said, "Hold on. Nobody said we wouldn't help. I'll help."

Louiza stood up. "Oh! Okay. Then let's get to it."

Brit said, "Sorry, I can't help right now, but I'll help later."

"Later?"

"Later."

"How much later?"

Brit winced. "Very much later?"

Louiza sat back down. "You're telling me to ask Brit the Elder for help, aren't you?"

Brit said, "That's one of the advantages of having a later version of myself hanging around. I can dump work off on her, and technically I'm not shirking. Just procrastinating."

10.

Brit the Younger and Gwen appeared in Martin's warehouse, looking relieved.

The warehouse had two parts: a spookily decorated vestibule for the locals to see, and a large loft-style live/work space, where the tired, bruised wizards had gathered after the battle. They had draped themselves over Martin's furniture, as limp and tired looking as the hastily removed clothes strewn around the room.

Usually they would have gathered in Phillip's rumpus room in Leadchurch, but they all agreed that once the dragons were chased off and the fires were out, hanging around to meet and greet the locals seemed like an unpleasant prospect.

Martin asked, "How'd it go?"

Gwen settled into a large leather couch next to him and said, "Louiza calmed down eventually, but for a while there she made me miss the dragons."

Phillip said, "Well, I'm glad you're both back. Now that we're all here, and we've had a chance to calm down, Jeff can explain what he's done, and make us all angry again."

Jeff said, "You all wanted the dragons to react to stuff like animals would. I tried to program that manually, but it was impossible. I had to try to guess at what you would do, and then guess how an animal would react, all in advance. I drove myself half crazy trying, then I got a little desperate."

Gwen said, "I don't know, Jeff. Seems like you were taking this all a little too seriously."

"No, I took it the right amount of seriously. The whole point of this exercise is to give us the tools to defend ourselves and the practice to know how to use those tools. I don't think there's any way to take that too seriously."

"Well there is a way," Gary said, "and you found it."

"Of course you'd think that," Jeff said. "You don't take anything seriously. You're not the one who Todd dropped off a cliff. You're not the one who fell all the way to the ground before his friends figured out a way to save him."

"No, but I am the one who got his leg cut off while you were busy falling." Gary lifted his artificial skeleton leg and wiggled his bony toes just to drive his point home.

For a long moment nobody spoke, because nobody knew what to say. Luckily, Roy had a way of dealing with awkward feelings. He ignored them. "Okay, so that's why you did it. Now tell us *what* you did."

"I isolated an animal's entry in the repository file and made a copy. I isolated the parts of the entry that seemed to relate to their fight-or-flight response. Then, I rewrote my dragons' behavioral files with hooks to those parts of the animal's original entry."

Roy nodded. "Change a few variables from manual values you chose as call outs to an existing entry and your dragons gain the natural instincts of a real animal. That's elegant."

"Thanks."

"It's also the most bone-headed, dangerous, haphazard shortcut I've ever heard of!"

"I know," Jeff said. "I knew the dangers. I took precautions. I picked the most harmless animal I could think of."

Tyler said, "No animal is harmless to an animal that's smaller than it."

Phillip asked, "What animal did you use, Jeff?"

"Sheep," Jeff said. "What's more harmless than sheep? They run from dogs, but aside from that all they do is stand around, eating grass and waiting to be fleeced."

Tyler said, "Jeff, I'm from Montana. I know a thing or two about sheep, and I can tell you that you never, ever turn your back on a ram. They're very aggressive."

Jeff shrugged. "Yeah, but sheep are docile."

"But I'm telling you, rams aren't. If rams were docile, Dodge wouldn't have named a truck after them."

"So what?" Jeff asked, raising his voice. "That has nothing to do with anything. I told you, I used sheep, not rams."

After a long silence, Roy said, "Kid, you know how a male cow is called a bull?"

"Yeah."

"And a male pig is called a boar?"

"I didn't know that, but I believe you."

"Do you know what a male sheep is called?"

Jeff cringed and thought for a long time, his cringe growing more intense as time passed. Finally, in a weak, hopeful voice, he said, "A heep?"

Tyler said, "A ram. A male sheep is called a ram. In a lot of breeds they have curved horns, and in all species they have a bad attitude."

Jeff nodded. "Yeah, okay. I see. Yes. I see the problem. Well, I gotta say, this is, by far, the dumbest thing I've ever done in my entire life."

Phillip nodded. "It is, at least, the best example I've ever seen of someone meddling with things that are beyond his comprehension."

"It's like three examples of that at once," Martin said. "It's the Neapolitan ice cream of mistakes. You didn't know enough about sheep, you didn't know how sheep behavior would translate into giant flying lizards, and you didn't know for sure what all the variables you used really controlled. We're lucky that only a few extra dragons got spawned."

"That's the thing," Brit said. "We don't know that only a few did. There could be dragons all over the world. They could even be reproducing."

"No," Jeff said. "I don't think they're reproducing."

Phillip asked, "What makes you say that?"

"They don't have genitals."

"Okay," Brit said. "I'll give that one to you. They probably aren't reproducing."

Gary said, "But they'll definitely be angry. I know I would be."

"So, I know the answer to this is probably *no*," Martin said, "but can't we just go into the file and delete them?"

"We'd have to figure out how to identify them from just their code and find all of their entries in the file. It'd be like looking for moving needles in a haystack where the pieces of hay are also moving. And if we make a mistake we could wipe all sheep from the face of the earth," Roy said.

Martin said, "Okay, also figuring this'll be a *no*, but could we just leave them be? They can't actually hurt anyone."

"No, but we saw today that people will hurt each other trying to protect themselves from the dragons," Brit added. "And we don't know what all the file is doing with them. Genitalia or no, new ones might be appearing, and if they are, even if they're only living a normal sheep's lifespan, with no natural predators, they'll just keep appearing until they eventually block out the sun."

"Nuclear winter," Phillip said, "but with dragons instead of ash."

Gary said, "At least we have the satisfaction of knowing that the end of the world will look like the cover of a Megadeth album."

"And that's the optimistic outcome," Gwen said. "It assumes the dragons won't attack people."

"They have no weapons," Jeff said. "Their flames and talons don't burn or break the skin."

Gary said, "And even without claws and fire, one could bite someone."

Jeff shook his head. "No, the teeth don't work. They're just like the claws."

"So they could gum someone," Gary said. "That sounds better, but not much better."

Phillip sighed. "I guess it's a good thing sheep are herbivores."

Again, Jeff turned to Tyler. "They are, right?"

Tyler said, "Yes, they are herbivores. In the case of rams, aggressive, violent, herbivores."

"That's good news."

"Yes," Phillip said. "The fact that the dragons aren't quite as dangerous as they could be does, in this situation, constitute good news, which might be the worst thing I've ever heard."

"Maybe we should spread the news," Gary said. "Tell everyone to keep their distance, but that the dragons aren't as dangerous as they look."

Tyler stroked his chin. "Hmm. *Attention citizens, the dragons are not as deadly as they seem. There is only some cause for alarm.* No, I think we'd be better off letting people think they're death with wings. At least they'll stay out of the way."

"Right." Roy said, "The dragons have to go, and the sooner the better. We might be able to automate a way to track them down, but we're going to have to destroy them manually, one at a time, and none of our current powers will do it."

Phillip said, "There is an option we haven't discussed, but none of you wants to hear it."

Several of the wizards groaned, knowing what Phillip intended to say, but the groans were cut short by the surprising sight of a second copy of Martin appearing directly in front of Phillip.

Second Martin waved his arms, and in a mock-spooky voice said, "Phillip, I have come from the future with a dire warning. Do not bring up the idea of Jeff going back in time to warn himself not to make sheep-dragons." Second Martin dropped the theatrics for a moment and said, "Jeff, honestly, just saying that out loud sounds like a terrible idea. What were you thinking?"

Jeff shrugged. Second Martin shook his head sadly at First Martin, who shrugged at Second Martin, who then turned back to Phillip and resumed his spooky act. "Do not suggest that Jeff go back and warn himself, Phillip. It will only start an argument you cannot win, as it has every other time you've suggested it. Heed my warning Phillip, while there's still time!"

Second Martin disappeared.

"Well, Phillip," Martin asked, "Will you heed that wise man's warning?"

Phillip said, "Mock all you want, but I don't see why it isn't worth a try."

"That's why!" Martin said. "You right now are why! It never works, Phillip! Any time any of us has tried to go back in time and warn ourselves to avoid doing something it hasn't worked. Gary, remember that time you tried to warn yourself not to time travel to 1962 and hit on Marilyn Monroe?"

"Yes."

"Did you listen to yourself, Gary?"

"No, I didn't."

"No, he didn't, Phillip. Gary, what did you say to your future self when he warned you?"

"That I would be careful, and to mind his own business, and not to ruin my fun."

"And did you go hit on Marilyn?"

Phillip said, "Martin, we all know all of this."

"Yes," Martin admitted, "but I like to hear the story. Gary, did you hit on Marilyn Monroe?"

"Yes."

"How many times?"

"Three times."

"And how'd that work out for you, Gary?"

"I got beaten up."

"All three times?"

"Yeah. Once by the Mafia, once by the Secret Service, and once by Joe DiMaggio."

"And that's why we don't go back in time to warn ourselves not to do things, Phillip. Because, of all the times we've tried, the best result any of us has achieved was getting beaten senseless by Joe DiMaggio. At least that was a good story."

"It was at a party," Gary said. "Dean Martin told him to kick me harder."

"We know," Martin said. "Several of us went to watch. Warning ourselves before a mistake just makes us feel resentful before the mistake, and feel stupid after it. The closest thing we've had to success has been with going back right after something has happened and preventing the damage. That's gotten us some limited success."

"If you call saving my life a limited success," Jeff said.

Tyler muttered, "Right now, we might."

Phillip said, "Just because something hasn't worked before doesn't mean it can't work now."

Martin said, "Let's see. I'll go back in time and warn you not to bring this topic up." Martin disappeared for less than a second, then reappeared.

"Are we still having a pointless argument?" Martin asked.

Phillip said, "Yes. And it proves nothing." Phillip turned to Brit and said, "Come on, help me out here. You have regular contact with a future version of yourself. Sometimes you listen to her. You're walking proof of my point."

Brit the Younger shook her head. "But a lot of the time I don't listen to her, dear. And when I do, she says that she remembers me listening to her, so she's walking proof of Martin's point. I'm afraid we cancel each other out."

"Well, maybe it hasn't worked yet because we almost never try it," Phillip said.

"We almost never try it because it never works," Martin countered.

Phillip said, "Maybe it does work, and we just don't know it. Maybe we only remember the times it failed, because when it succeeds it changes the timeline."

Roy said, "You're saying that reality changes, and the versions of us that have the problem just cease to be?"

"Yeah," Phillip said. "Maybe."

Roy said, "Screw that."

"Yes," Gwen said. "I'd like to keep existing, thank you very much."

"You would," Phillip said. "You'd still exist. It'd just be a different you. Or, what if reality forks? We stay in the timeline with the problem, but our warning helps another version of us avoid the whole mess?"

Tyler said, "I say let theoretical other versions of us fend for themselves. We've got our own problems, and I don't remember them ever showing up with any helpful hints for us."

Brit put a calming hand on Phillip's arm and said, "No, Phillip, I think the consensus is that we need to figure out a way to find the dragons and delete them, then jump to the moment right after we ran them out of town, and take them out before anyone else gets hurt."

Phillip sighed. "Okay. I get it. On to business, then. Anybody have any ideas?"

Jeff said, "I'll come up with something."

"And I'll help," Roy said.

"We all will," Phillip added.

"No," Jeff said. "I caused this problem. I should be the one to fix it."

"You will," Roy said. "With our help."

Jeff said, "Look, guys, this is my mess."

Martin said, "But you can share. You brought enough mess for everybody."

11.

"People of Leadchurch, thank you for coming out for this emergency town meeting. I know that we usually hold these meetings in the church, not the tavern. We chose to hold it here at the Rotted Stump because the church is full of the wounded, and given what we all went through this morning, we thought everyone would appreciate gathering someplace where they could get a stiff drink."

The man's name was Gibbons. He was one of the local merchants, a short man, but he had a larger man's voice, bearing, and belly.

"Friends, as we all know, there has been an attack on our village. Many people, including the entire militia, were injured in the act of defending our property, and now they lay, asleep and helpless in the church, leaving us, and our property, undefended. We're here to figure out what went wrong."

After a long pause, someone said, "Dragons attacked us."

"Yes," Gibbons said, "yes, that's right. Dragons attacked us. But what I'm getting at is, why? Why did dragons attack us? We need to figure out what we did to draw the dragons down on us so we can keep them from coming back because, friends, I think if we learned anything today, it is that we are not prepared to fight dragons. Everyone who tried is over in the church. Even the wizards couldn't help us much."

A horrific sound flooded the inn. Everyone who heard it cringed involuntarily. All conversation, all interactions, all rational thought came to a halt while every adult in earshot received an urgent message from their own central nervous system, a message that said, *Find the source of that noise and make it stop.* Humans are genetically tuned to abhor the sound, a sound originally meant to alert parents that their offspring were in danger, but which later got repurposed as a weapon by those offspring.

It was the shriek of an angry girl.

Everyone turned and faced Honor, and mostly saw the inside of her mouth as she persisted in screaming at the top of her lungs. She was sitting on the corner of a fully loaded bench, but all of the adults sharing the bench with her leaned away from the source of the spine-melting noise, giving her more room to flail her arms. The only one in the tavern who didn't seem bothered by the noise was Runt, who sat on the floor next to her, looking up with an air of mild curiosity.

After several seconds, Honor's angry shriek gave way to a raging torrent of words. "The wizards weren't helping us. How can you think the wizards were helping us? The wizards were helping the dragons!"

The townsfolk all looked at each other warily. None of the parents in the group had brought their children, but Honor had no adult to tell her she couldn't come, and it would be centuries before liquor laws would be invented. She was the only child in attendance and, as such, had far more control of the situation than she understood.

Gibbons said, "Now, now, dearie, that just doesn't make sense."

Like pretty much every other human being capable of understanding speech, Honor hated being told *now, now,* and despised being called *dearie.* Being told that what she knew to be true made no sense did not help.

"I know what I know, and I know what I saw," Honor said. "I saw the dragons attacking the town, and I saw the wizards protecting them while they did it. Not making sense to you doesn't mean it didn't happen."

There were a few titters from the group. Like a stream of urine, an aggressive child can be amusing when it's aimed at someone else.

Gibbons felt himself losing control of the room and asked, "Little girl, where are your parents?"

The laughter stopped. A man frowned, then stood and spoke quietly into Gibbons's ear.

Gibbons listened, bit his lip, looked at Honor, and said, "I'm very sorry. Honor, isn't it?" As much as she'd hated being called *dearie*, she hated being called by her name even more when the person speaking had a note of pity in his voice.

"I haven't seen you in quite a while," Gibbons said. "You've certainly grown."

"How would you know?" Honor asked. "I'm sitting down. In this crowd, you can only see my head."

Gibbons said, "And your head has grown," then paused and turned red while the crowd enjoyed a small laugh at his expense. "I knew your father. He was a good man. I sometimes do business with your brother. Fine boy. Where is he?"

"He's in the church, with the rest of the people the wizards cursed."

A woman seated in the middle of the throng said, "No, dear, one of the wizards told some of us they were just putting the injured to sleep."

"By cursing them," Honor said. "The wizards cursed them to sleep. I saw them do it."

"Yes," the woman said. "I suppose you could put it that way, but the wizard told me they'd done it so that they could rest and heal."

"And stop attacking the wizards' dragons. The dragons that had hurt them in the first place."

"Is that what happened to your brother?" Gibbons asked. "Was he hurt attacking a dragon?"

Honor blushed and said, "No."

Gibbons brightened slightly and opened his mouth, clearly preparing to exploit this hole in her logic.

Honor said, "He and Bishop Galbraith threw themselves over me to save me from arrows. They both got hit. One of the wizards watched it happen and did nothing to help any of us. Then another made them sleep with her magic."

Another of the local men spoke up. "I'm sorry that happened to your brother, but I saw the wizards trying to protect us and chase off the dragons."

"Then they didn't do a very good job, did they?" Honor said. "Mister Gibbons said that the entire militia is down. So are my brother and the bishop. All of the folks lying in the church right now got hurt while the wizards were *protecting* them."

"You said you know what you saw," the man said. "I know what I saw, too, and I saw the wizards trying to chase the dragons off."

Gibbons nodded. "Thank you, Seth. Very good. See, Honor? He was out there, too, and he saw the wizards helping."

Honor said, "Maybe a few of the wizards were faking. Maybe they pretended to try to help us so that we wouldn't blame them, and we wouldn't hurt their dragons."

Gibbons said, "I seriously doubt that, Honor."

"Why? Did you see them helping? Did you watch them trying their hardest? Or were you just told it and now you believe it because you want to?"

"Well, no, I didn't see them helping," Gibbons admitted. "I was in the church most of the time. I didn't really see much, but others did. Everyone, show of hands, how many of you really got a good look at what happened?"

A disappointingly small number of people raised their hands, fifteen at most. The majority of the villagers had hightailed it for cover at the first sight of dragons. Gibbons pressed on.

"Okay, and of those of you with your hands up, how many of you agree with Seth that the wizards were trying to help us?"

About a third kept their hands raised. The other two-thirds fidgeted in their chairs and made doubtful moaning noises.

"And how many think I'm right?" Honor asked.

The hands that had been up went down, and a roughly equal number came up hesitantly, accompanied by more fidgeting. All in all, five people out of well over a hundred publicly agreed with Honor, but she used child math. Having any adult agree with her meant that she was definitely 100 percent right.

Gibbons looked less convinced than ever of Honor's opinion or anyone else's, including his own. "But, Honor, why? You say that the wizards wanted the dragons to attack us. Why would the wizards want that? And if they did, why use dragons? We've seen what they're capable of. They're more than powerful enough to destroy the whole town themselves if they want."

Honor thought for a moment, then said, "I don't know."

If this gave Gibbons any satisfaction, it did not last long.

"But," Honor said, "if the wizards are as powerful as you say, why weren't they able to chase off the dragons any faster, or just kill them?"

It was a good question, and Gibbons thought about it for a bit too long. The crowd got restless and started talking among themselves. Honor heard bits and pieces of many conversations. "Just made them madder," "Called them idiots," "Turned into a dragon himself."

Gibbons said, "Okay. If we're honest, the best thing we can say for the wizards is that they helped us, but not very well."

"And that they cast a sleeping spell on anyone who tried to fight their dragons," Honor said.

"They said it's a healing spell, and we don't know that the dragons were theirs."

"The *healing spell* put them to sleep and made them stop fighting, and I know that the dragons are theirs because I've seen the pen where the wizards keep them!"

Her statement affected the crowd in ways both profound and predictable. Honor had their undivided attention, and yet she had to shout to be heard.

"In a clearing, deep in the woods, north of our pasture. I saw the dragon pen, the biggest pen I've ever seen. The fence stretched into the sky like a roof to keep the dragons from flying away."

Gibbons asked, "And how do you know the wizards built this dragon pen?"

"Because there was a wizard there."

"In the clearing, deep in the woods, next to a great big pen full of dragons."

"Yes."

"What were you doing there?"

"Tracking down one of our ewes. The wizard had stolen it."

Gibbons laughed. "One of your ewes came up missing and you assumed that an evil wizard had stolen your sheep?"

Many other adults laughed along with Gibbons. There are certain crimes that are not only wrong, but are also so ignominious that the act of accusing someone of them is laughably unrealistic and insulting. The idea that someone with magical powers would lower himself to sheep rustling didn't seem reasonable.

"How many ewes did the wizard take?" Gibbons asked.

Honor said, "One. For a while. I counted later, and it seemed like he put it back, or tricked me with his magic into thinking he did."

Gibbons laughed again. "Young lady, why would a wizard use his powers to steal one of your ewes, then give it back?"

Honor said, "I thought he meant to feed it to the dragons, but I didn't see that. I saw him with the sheep. I don't understand what he was doing. He was yelling and chasing it. It seemed like he wanted to wrestle it. He was abusing it, I guess you might say."

The laughter in the room stopped, but only after changing drastically in tone. There are certain crimes that are not only wrong, but are also so ignominious that the act of accusing someone of them makes them appear guilty, because, all joking aside, one would never accuse someone of that unless they were certain.

Gibbons said, "These are serious accusations, girl. We'll need to investigate for ourselves. Can you tell us how to get to this dragon pen you saw?"

"I'll take you there! Let's go!"

"Gracious, no, dearie. We'll get a few of the men to go. I'm sure nobody'd ask you to go along."

"You don't have to ask," Honor said, "I'll go. I can take you straight there."

"No, I'm sorry. There's no way to know what dangers we'll face."

"I know what dangers you'll face. I've faced them."

"Well, if you were able to make it on your own, a group of men should have no problem. You'll only slow us down. We won't have the time or the energy to take care of you. Do you understand?"

Honor's face turned bright red. Her knuckles went white.

"Yes," Honor said. "I understand, Mister Gibbons."

Gibbons nodded, making the common mistake of thinking that understanding and agreeing were the same thing. "Now, we'll round up a party of volunteers, and then, after you've given us directions, we'll be on our way. We'll want to enter the woods before we reach the Bastards' encampment. The dragons and the wizards are bad enough. We don't want Kludge on our hands as well."

Honor looked around the room, at the adults who had dismissed her, then listened to her, then dismissed her again. They all listened to Gibbons now, all except one. Across the inn, standing just outside an open window, Hubert, the dung sifter, stood looking at Honor.

He saw that she saw him. He smiled weakly and shook his head.

"Oh no! Kludge! Kludge!" the voice shouted.

Kludge smiled. Few things pleased him more than the sound of someone in distress, shouting his name, hoping for help that would probably not come. He stretched and yawned contentedly.

"Ahhhh! Kludge!" the voice continued.

That's right, Kludge thought. *Let everyone know that you're afraid, and who's made you that way.*

Slowly, Kludge realized that he wasn't actually threatening anyone at the moment. He was lying on the pile of cowhides he used as a bed, under another cowhide he used as a blanket. His eyes snapped open. He saw the underside of the cowhides thrown over a wooden frame that he used as a tent.

The voice called out again. "Kludge! Where's Kludge!"

Kludge sat up and pulled on the cowhide he used as a shirt. He vowed to find whoever had woken him up, and put them to sleep. He liked distressed voices, shouting his name, looking for help, but not when they were looking for help *from* him.

Kludge stepped out of the tent and nearly collided with a Bastard. He wasn't a bastard literally. Not as far as Kludge knew, or cared. Kludge led a group of young men who called themselves *the Bastards*. To become a Bastard you only had to do whatever Kludge wanted, which mostly meant calling yourself a Bastard, telling Kludge how tough he was, and playing a musical instrument.

The last part was the easiest. Making any loud noise to a predictable rhythm counted as playing, and drums qualified as an instrument. Kludge's definition of a drum included anything that made a noise when struck, including people who had gotten on Kludge's nerves.

Like any group that accepts pretty much anybody, the membership of the Bastards was made up entirely of young males who felt worthless and powerless—guys who look at the creatures wriggling around in the mud and think, *He thinks he's better than me.*

The Bastard who was risking getting "drummed out" this morning was Stretch, one of the older Bastards. Stretch hadn't gotten his nickname for being particularly tall. Kludge gave him his name in honor of something he'd done to another man's ear during a fight.

Stretch said, "Kludge! Kludge! You're up! You've gotta—"

Kludge punched Stretch in the face. Stretch flew backward and then rolled in the dirt, clutching at his nose and moaning. In truth, Kludge hadn't hit him that hard and they both knew it, but Kludge had standards, and giving him the impression that his initial attack had been anything less than devastating would be taken as an invitation to try harder.

"I'm thorry thoo dithturb you, Kludge," Stretch said through his hands, "bud you godda thee thith!"

"What is it?" Kludge asked. "I don't see anything."

Stretch pointed behind Kludge's tent.

The Bastards had claimed a broad, flat space that sat along the side of the main road through the woods as their domain. It was wide, treeless, and overgrown with tall grass, but beyond that grass were several tents, the ash pile of a near-nightly bonfire, and a barren, muddy patch the Bastards had trampled. The grass provided a buffer zone between the camp and the road and gave the Bastards something to hide in when attempting to ambush passersby.

Kludge's tent, like all of the tents, faced away from the road and toward the woods. Stretch pointed behind the tent, toward the expanse of wild grass, the road, and the rest of civilization. Kludge sneered, stepped around the tent, and froze.

Three dragons were just standing there, eating the grass, oblivious to the world around them.

When Kludge snapped out of the shock, he could see that all of the other Bastards had already noticed the dragons.

Many young men from the nearby villages would turn up each night for the bonfire and the music. They thought of themselves as members, and Kludge didn't say anything to make them think otherwise. Someday they might come in handy. But the real core of the Bastards consisted of Kludge and six other guys: Stretch, Gripper, Pounder, and Heel-Kick, all of whom were named for things they had done in fights, and L.L. (L.L. stood for Long Lobes. He'd been named in honor of something Stretch had done to *him* in a fight.) The youngest member of the group was Only Donnie. He got his name when another member named Donnie quit.

Kludge could see the guys huddled behind trees and hunched down in the mud at the edge of the tall grass. Heel-Kick shouted, "Kludge! We need Kludge! He'll know what to do!"

Kludge proved him right, by threatening Heel-Kick with grievous bodily harm if he didn't shut up. Then Kludge stared at the dragons for a good long time. Their shoulders were about half again taller than his. Their wings folded back on themselves, and their front claws pressed into the grass, supporting the front half of their bodies like legs. Their necks hung low to the ground as they ate their fill of the wild grass.

As peaceful and docile as they acted, they radiated menace. Their skin was made up of thick armored scales. Their teeth looked like ivory daggers. One of the dragons took a step forward, briefly lifting one of its rear feet above the height of the grass. It was the single most terrifying foot Kludge had ever seen. What on any other animal one might have referred to as *toes*, on these monsters looked like a mass of small, very muscular arms tipped not with hands, but with toenails that were semi-translucent short swords.

The sight of them filled Kludge's heart with fear. He had spent years trying to convince the people who knew him that he had neither a heart, nor fear to fill it with, and had nearly convinced himself. If these things had this effect on him, he could only imagine how the Bastards felt, or how ordinary villagers would react to the sight of them.

Stretch said, "They just showed up. What are we gonna do, Kludge?"

Kludge studied the look of fear on Stretch's face, looked at the dragons again, and said, "Find some rope."

12.

The rest of the wizards were taking a break when Jeff and Roy materialized in the clearing next to the cage dome. There had been seven dragons in the cage before. Now there were two. The weapons team needed to try out their prototypes on something, and creating new dragons would be far too dangerous, so Jeff's original seven got the job.

Jeff and Roy looked at the two remaining dragons, then at the wizards, sitting and lying in the grass, not talking. A new structure sat next to Jeff's original dragon pen: a large, rectangular cage, about a quarter of the size of the original dome, and a caged path large enough for a dragon led from the one cage to the other. A large stone wall blocked the dragons in the domed cage from seeing what happened in the smaller cage.

Roy said, "Simple math tells me that you've been productive."

"We've learned a lot," Phillip said.

"Yes," Martin agreed, lying on his back, staring at the sky. "For instance, I've learned that testing weapons on caged animals makes me feel like a monster, even when I know the animals aren't real, and they look like death with wings."

Brit said, "Hear, hear."

Jeff looked at the ground and said, "Sorry. Still, it looks like you came up with something."

"We came up with many things," Gwen said. "Not all of them worked the way we'd hoped."

Tyler stood and walked toward the domed cage.

Jeff said, "Anxious to show us what you've got, eh?"

"Not in the slightest," Tyler said, "yet there are some things you don't want to deal with, but you just have to grit your teeth and get through it."

Roy asked, "Learned that from working on ranches, did you?"

"No, from growing up as a black man in Butte, Montana. Hey, Gary, help me out here."

Gary shrugged, hoisted himself up off the ground, and followed Tyler.

The two wizards climbed through the fence, then managed, through a combination of running and shouting, to maneuver one of the dragons into the chute. Gary and Tyler followed, and the cage section that acted as a door rematerialized behind them.

The rest of the wizards moved behind the wall, to the second, smaller cage.

Martin said, "Force fields don't work on the dragons. Neither do missiles, direct physical force, or sarcasm. We tried Gwen's macro, with the fabric that entangled the dragons, and Gary's stupid spiderwebs, but without you there, Jeff, to deactivate the dragons when you think they've lost, the dragons just tore right through them. Same goes for Brit's asphyxiation bubble. So, we had to invent some new stuff."

"All right," Tyler said. "Shall we start with the ray?"

Gary nodded.

Tyler pointed the chrome hood ornament on the head of his staff at one of the two dragons and said, "*Radion drako unu.*"

A white bolt of light shot from Tyler's staff and hit the closest dragon in the hindquarters. The beam faded and disappeared, as did a portion of the dragon. A small portion. The specific part the beam had hit—a triangular chunk of the beast's rear flank. The rest of the dragon remained perfectly intact. The spot where the triangle had been was now an open hole, revealing the inside of the dragon to be an empty void, as if the dragon were a statue made of sheets of plywood. The dragon showed no pain, or even any sign that it had noticed a problem.

Phillip said, "As you can see, our first attempt at an anti-dragon ray didn't destroy the dragon, but only demonstrated that they are hollow, which is a nice metaphor for life's problems, but isn't particularly useful beyond that. Our theory is that the dragons are made up of polygons, and that each polygon, for whatever reason, is treated as a separate object. Then we took the obvious next step; we widened the beam and deleted more of the dragon by hitting more polygons."

Tyler nodded at Phillip, then said, "*Radion drako du.*" Instead of a thin beam, a cone of light shot from the head of Tyler's staff, bathing half of the dragon in its harsh white glare.

When the beam dissipated, half of the dragon had vanished. The remaining half was a hollow shell, like half of a broken chocolate bunny, only much larger, and dragon shaped. Instead of falling over, the half dragon remained suspended in air, as if the rest of the dragon was still there, just invisible.

Phillip said, "So, you see, it doesn't kill the dragon. It merely renders parts of it invisible. Bathing an entire dragon in the ray wouldn't destroy it. It would only make it more dangerous."

"They somehow have access to the instincts and intelligence of an animal," Brit explained, "but they still have the body of a video game character. When you damage that body, instead of killing it, it glitches out."

Gary pointed at the flailing half dragon and asked, "Are we done with this one?"

Phillip said, "Yes."

Martin said, "I'll go get the last dragon," and jogged toward the original holding pen.

Gary said, "*Krei duono ringego,*" then tilted his head back and shouted, "Gooooal!"

At the end of the rectangular pen, a metal arch, easily thirty feet tall and sixty feet across, appeared. A thin, iridescent blue membrane, like soap film, stretched across its inner circumference. Tyler and Gary spent several minutes chasing and dodging, and harassing the half dragon until it tried to escape by running through the arch, into the blue membrane. Its leg and wing continued to move under their own power right up until the second they disappeared.

Tyler said, "*Forigi duono ringego* goooooal!" The arch disappeared. Then, as if on cue, the final dragon ran into the ring, slid to a stop, and breathed fire at Gary and Tyler, both of whom yelped and hastily created force fields to keep the fire at bay.

Martin ran in behind the dragon, then made a hard right and squeezed through the fence to rejoin the group.

Brit said, "We got to thinking that if it has the instincts of an animal, maybe we should try to kill it the way we'd kill an animal, instead of trying to delete it like a computer-generated character. Gentlemen?"

Gary and Tyler nodded at Brit, turned to each other, and Tyler said, "It was your idea. You do the honors."

Gary smiled, thanked him, and then ran around so that he faced the dragon head-on. "I got the idea from a kung fu movie I once saw."

Gary hunkered down a bit, extended his left arm to his side, and curled his right arm inward, as if he intended to throw a Frisbee. He said, "*Krei* flying guillotine."

A ring about a foot in diameter appeared in his right hand. He threw the ring toward the dragon's head. It flew gracefully, growing in midair as it went. A thin line of glowing energy extended from the ring back to Gary's hand. The ring dropped over the dragon's head and slid down its neck, resting at its shoulder blades. Gary hauled back with his hand, as if pulling on the glowing line that tethered him to the ring. The glowing ring became a glowing disk, then disappeared as the dragon's head and neck fell away from its body.

The head thrashed and lolled on the ground for several seconds. Then it continued for several more seconds. When nearly thirty seconds had passed with the head and severed neck still thrashing around, Roy said, "This isn't going to stop, is it?"

"No," Phillip said.

The dragon's body continued to stand around, fidgeting in a bored sort of manner, with a large hole where its head used to be. The body took a small step forward and accidentally kicked the head, which breathed a plume of fire at its own former body. The fire washed over the body's legs and belly without it seeming to notice at all.

Phillip shouted, "All right. They get the idea."

Tyler shouted, "*Krei duono ringego* gooooal!" The arch with the semi-transparent blue membrane reappeared.

Gary grabbed the head and neck and held it close to his body, as if hugging it. The head swung wildly, like the nozzle of a fire hose at full pressure, shooting a steady stream of fire in every direction as Gary walked the head over to the arch to dispose of it. Then, he and Tyler both shoved the headless body through the arch like sumo wrestlers ganging up on a confused elephant. When they had finished, Tyler made the arch vanish, and he and Gary stood with their hands on their knees, breathing heavily.

When he'd finally caught his breath, Gary said, "Way to go, man. High-five!" He held his hand up, waiting for Tyler to slap it.

Tyler looked at Gary's hand like it was plutonium.

"Come on, man, high-five!"

"Never."

"Man, don't leave me hanging."

Tyler said, "I will always leave you hanging."

Outside the pen, Jeff closed his eyes and pinched the bridge of his nose. "So, you haven't come up with any weapon that's effective against my dragons."

"They're not really your dragons anymore," Martin said. "They belong to the world now."

"Please, don't remind me."

Phillip said, "We came up with an effective weapon. It works like a charm."

"Then why didn't you show us that?" Roy asked.

"We did. You've been looking right at it. We call it *the goal*. That glowy blue-arch thingy. It destroys the dragons instantly and completely. We figure we can just trick the dragons into going through it and that's that. We came up with the other stuff we showed you while trying to think of an alternative to using the goal."

Jeff asked, "Why would you want an alternative?"

"Because, like any really good weapon, it's nearly as dangerous to us as it is to the dragons. The goal utterly destroys anything that goes through it by automatically isolating and deleting its entry, and only its entry, in the repository file. Really, the arch and the blue glow are just markers. The macro that creates them monitors a circular plane in space, then identifies and deletes the data of that specific instance of any object, but doesn't delete or alter the object's global codebase. It cleanly eradicates anything that passes through, including us."

Jeff said, "So, if a dragon pulls us in with it . . ."

". . . or if we fall through it on our own . . ." Brit added.

". . . or just aren't watching where we're going and walk into it . . ." Gwen continued.

". . . we'd be irrevocably dead," Phillip finished.

Roy nodded. "I see why you used this delivery method. A ray would be more convenient, but if you miss, it'd be a disaster."

"Can't we put a force field up in front of the goal? Dragons go right through them, but they stop us."

"Yeah," Martin said. "That's the first thing we did."

"Oh," Roy said. "Good. And does it work?"

"Should."

"What do you mean, *should?* Haven't you tested it?"

"How would you test it? We threw rocks and sticks at it, but that only proved it works for rocks and sticks. There's no reason it shouldn't work, but that doesn't mean that it does. You know the safety on a gun should work, but would you test it by putting the gun to your head and pulling on the trigger as hard as you can?"

Phillip said, "The only way to be sure that it works for us would be for one of us to walk into it. We believe it would work, but if it doesn't, the person testing it is dead. The only sensible course of action is to assume that it works, and do everything in our power to keep from ever finding out for sure."

Brit said, "Don't trust, and never verify."

Roy said, "That doesn't fill me with confidence."

Gwen said, "It's not supposed to."

"Quite the opposite, in fact," Phillip added. "So, that's what we've come up with. How about you two?"

Roy said, "We've got some good news there. We were able to take the file entries for the dragons Jeff made and isolate certain chunks of code that are common to all of the randomly occurring dragons. Then, we did a global search of the file, and we came up with a snapshot of the rough location of all dragons, as of the moment we ran those ones out of Leadchurch."

Gwen asked, "And are there more?"

"Yes, but it could have been worse," Roy said. "Jeff used the entry of a sheep as his template. It seems that anywhere that breed of sheep lives, there was a small statistical probability of generating dragons, some of which, unfortunately, are rams. Luckily, he accidentally used a sheep from a rare breed that's only in the British Isles."

Jeff produced a small tablet computer from his robe pocket, tapped at it a few times, and turned it so the rest of the wizards could see.

"This," Jeff said, "is the mess I've made. It's a heat map of the dragon population, as of the moment we left town."

The screen showed a map of England, Ireland, Scotland, and a bit of the west coast of Europe. Dark red blobs represented places where dragons had appeared. The bad news was that there were five blobs, all fairly distant from each other. The good news was that there were only five blobs, including Leadchurch. Also, those blobs were all on the island that contained England, Scotland, and Wales. None of the dragons had spawned anywhere else, and they had not managed to fly across the Channel, or to Ireland.

Roy said, "Jeff and I figure we can split up into four teams of two. The good ol' buddy system. Leadchurch had the largest group, including Jeff's original seven, all of which have now been destroyed. That leaves the four dragons we chased off, and three strays. Jeff and I will take care of them, then move on to London, where there appear to be five dragons on the outskirts of town. There's a flock of eight in Yorkshire, four and two loners in Wales, and a big party of ten up in Scotland."

Jeff said, "Once a team has dealt with their dragons, they'll just check to see who's still working and go help. Any questions?"

Brit said, "Yeah, do we have any idea how far these things can fly? Could they make it to Ireland or France?"

Roy said, "We don't know, but I don't see any reason to assume they couldn't. That's just more reason to eradicate them as quickly as possible. Any more questions?"

Nobody said anything, but Jeff raised his hand.

"I was asking if any of them had a question for *us*," Roy explained.

"Yeah, and they don't," Jeff said. "So now I have a question for them."

"What is it, Jeff?" Phillip asked.

"Are you going to banish me?"

Phillip said, "I'm sorry, what?"

Jeff asked again, "Are you going to banish me?"

Phillip and the other wizards all looked at each other for a moment, then Phillip said, "We really haven't discussed it, Jeff. You're the first person to bring it up. I suppose now that you have, we'll have to put it to a vote. I can't speak for everyone, but I can tell you that I would vote against it. Why are you asking us this?"

Jeff said, "I just want to know where I stand. I can't believe the idea hadn't occurred to any of you. I'd be tempted to banish me, after what I've done."

Gwen said, "You made a mistake, Jeff. Everybody makes mistakes. We don't banish people for it."

Jeff said, "I'm pretty sure all three of the people we've banished would claim that we did it because they made mistakes."

Tyler said, "Jimmy tried to kill us all and didn't finish the job. That's a way bigger mistake than the one you made."

"And Todd showed us that he enjoyed torturing people," Phillip said. "That's a massive character flaw, not a mistake."

Jeff said, "What about that wizard from Paris—Mitchell? We banished him, and he didn't kill anybody. He didn't even hurt anyone."

"Mitchell," Phillip said, "was a pathological liar. We all tried to ignore it, but it just got worse and worse. Eventually we just humored him, even Jimmy. You remember what that was like. He'd tell you to your face that he'd done things you knew he hadn't, and all you could do was accept it and leave as fast as you could. We had to send him away."

"And we didn't really banish him," Gwen said. "I mean, we banished him, but we didn't *banish,* banish him. We sent him back to his time with a long, healthy lifespan and one hundred million dollars, and told him that if he ever touched his file entry, we'd take it all away and do something worse."

"How's he doing?" Tyler asked."

Phillip said, "Last time we checked on him, he was running for mayor."

13.

A group of ten able-bodied men, led by Mister Gibbons, set out on horseback immediately after the town meeting. When it became clear to Honor that she wouldn't be allowed to go along, she gave them detailed directions through the forest to the giant cage.

"The woods are tough, and you'll have to watch out for thorns, but it's the best way. The riverbank isn't trustworthy, and up north there are plants that burn if—"

Gibbons put a hand on Honor's shoulder, both to reassure her that he was listening, and to get her to stop talking. "Thank you for your help, dearie. It's much appreciated."

"But you haven't written down the directions, and with all due respect, you didn't look like you were paying attention."

Gibbons looked down at her and asked, "Honor, did anyone give you directions to this clearing?"

"No."

"Well then, if a girl like you found it without directions, ten men should have no problem."

Honor returned to the church and stayed there, at Sonny's side, until late in the afternoon, when word came that the posse was on the way back.

Honor, along with most of the other townsfolk, made it to outskirts of the village in time to witness the party's triumphant return.

Ten men sat or lay in the back of the hay cart that had gone to collect them. Their horses were nowhere to be found. Some of the men were covered with cuts, some had roughly made splints and crutches, some were soaking wet, and some had red, blotchy skin and painful-looking blisters. Most of them had more than one of these problems. Gibbons had all four.

Gibbons stood up on the cart, leaning heavily on a broken tree branch. "Friends, I am sad to report that we did not, in fact, reach the clearing, and as such we cannot directly confirm what young Honor claims to have seen. I will say, though, that I, for one, believe her, and I think all of the men who accompanied me will agree."

Some of the men groaned.

Gibbons continued, "As soon as we left the road, it was as if the forest itself rose up to impede our progress. It attacked us relentlessly and mercilessly, and when we finally reemerged from the cursed woods, our horses had vanished. It had to be the wizards, my friends. There's no other logical explanation."

A woman in the crowd asked, "So what do we do now, Mister Gibbons?"

"The only thing we can do. We wait for the wizards to make their next move. When they do, I suggest we try to find out what they want, and then we give it to them. Take it from me, their magic is too strong to fight. Now, if you'll excuse me, I must go home and rest."

Gibbons limped through the crowd. Nobody tried to stop him.

Honor watched Gibbons and the rest of his merry band of former adventurers groan and grumble their way through the crowd, then walked directly back to the church, where she sat with her brother a little while before telling the nuns that she would have to go home to tend to the sheep. "Sister Flora," Honor said. "I want to thank you for taking care of my brother, and for the food you offered me. It was very kind of you."

Sister Flora said, "It's our role to be kind, my dear. And, I'm sorry we had to make your doggie stay outside. I know it's been allowed in before, but those were exceptions. I'm running things until His Excellency wakes up, and I had to reassert the rules."

Honor said, "I understand, Sister Flora."

"Good girl. Now, will you be safe walking home alone? I'm sure I could get one of the menfolk—"

"I'll be fine on my own," Honor said.

Sister Flora said, "I see."

"Please watch my brother for me."

"We will dear, we will. And we'll get word to you as soon as he wakes up."

As Honor emerged from the church into the sunlight, Runt was right where she had left her, curled up by the church door. Honor noted that while the nuns made it very clear that the dog could not come in, Runt had received a dish of water and a bone since Honor had last seen her.

Honor walked with speed and purpose. *I'm not helping anyone sitting around waiting for something to happen,* she thought. *Anyway, I need to get out of this town. The nuns are nice but I can't bear to look at the burnt buildings, I'm sick of the people, the place even smells awful. In fact, the smell seems to be getting a lot worse.*

"Hello, young lady," Hubert the dung sifter said.

Honor returned his greeting without smiling or slowing her stride. Hubert fell in beside her, matching her pace. On her other side, Runt kept up, but drifted a few feet away, lest Hubert's aroma put her off the bone she carried in her mouth.

Hubert said, "Leaving, are you?"

Honor said, "Yes."

"To tend to your sheep, no doubt."

"Someone has to."

"That's very responsible of you. And then a good night's sleep, I'd suspect."

"I am tired."

"Yes. Understandably." They walked in silence for a moment, then Hubert said, "I was there to see the raiding party come back from the woods."

"I was there, too."

"Yes. I saw you there. Honor, I just want to talk to you for a moment. Do you know what my job is, Honor?"

"You remove the dung from privies and sift it."

"Yes. I picked up the trade from my father. He's been a dung sifter since before I was born, and I just sort of fell into it. The job, not the dung."

"Hubert, why are you telling me this?"

"Please just hear me out, and my meaning will reveal itself, like a lost coin in the sifting pan. Anyway, I picked up the trade from my father. My earliest memories are of him holding his pan with one hand, swatting away flies with the other. For years, we sifted side by side, then one day, I realized that there had to be a better way."

"A better way than sifting dung?"

"A better way *to* sift dung. I saw in my mind a series of finer and finer meshes, and a river of dung diverted through them. We could let the dung sift itself, and collect the spoils at the end of the day."

"Did you tell your father?"

"Yes, and he didn't want to hear it. He'd been sifting dung his whole life, and he didn't think someone as young and inexperienced as me might be able to improve on his techniques."

"What did you do?" Honor asked, now genuinely interested.

"I waited for him to get sick. We dung sifters are out sick a lot. Part of it's the working conditions, and part of it's that you don't have to feel very bad to justify not getting out of bed to go sift the dung. Anyway, I waited until he got sick, then I built what I'd seen in my head. It wasn't hard. It was just three screens and a ditch. When he came back to work, he found my invention already working, a larger pile of salvage than we usually found in a week, and me, sitting in the shade nearby, watching to make sure the screens held."

"What did he say then?"

"That I had the beginnings of a good idea, and that he could probably improve on it and make it work."

Honor snorted derisively.

Hubert laughed. "My point is, I know what it's like to have people not pay attention to me, because I'm younger, or they think I'm below them. Understand?"

Honor kept her eyes forward, but said, "Yes."

Hubert said, "I was paying attention at the meeting this morning, and I heard you say quite a few things that matched up pretty well with what I'd seen happen myself. I was also paying attention when Gibbons and his friends returned, and it seemed to me that all of their injuries matched the kinds of injuries overconfident townsfolk usually come out of the forest with, even without evil wizards working against them."

Honor said nothing, but she did give the faintest hint of a grin. They had passed the village limits, and were following the road into the woods.

Hubert said, "Now, this is speculation, but if I were a smart young lady who didn't feel that anyone had listened to her, I might decide that somebody has to do something."

Honor said, "You've put some thought into this."

"Yes. It's sort of a hobby, imagining myself in other people's positions. I've whiled away many an hour of dung sifting, pretending I was anyone else. As I was saying, if I was such a young lady, and I knew where the wizards kept their dragons, I might well intend to act on that knowledge, somehow."

Honor said, "If I were an adult who suspected a girl might be about to do something like that, I might be tempted to stop her, or try to come along and help."

"Again, you might, unless you had faith in the girl, and knew yourself to be a useless woodsman, an inexperienced fighter, and that you had an odor that wizards and dragons would smell from miles away. But you couldn't in good conscience send a young lady out alone, without any assistance besides her dog."

Hubert stopped walking, looked at the village now far behind them, and asked, "Say, do you like dollies?"

Honor said, "I'm sorry. What?"

"Dollies! You're a young girl. I thought you might like dollies. Here, I have something for you." Hubert reached into his bag and pulled out a small human figure. Honor could see how someone might refer to it as a doll if they didn't know better. It was the most evil thing she'd ever seen. Its gruesome armor, grim visage, and inhuman pointed tongue identified it instantly as a demon, despite the thick, dried layer of what Honor chose to call *dirt*. She recognized it as the magical item Hubert had used that morning to protect himself from dragon fire.

"Where did you get it?" Honor asked.

"Everybody uses public latrines occasionally. Even necromancers."

"Hubert, I can't take this."

"You'll have far more use for it than I do."

Honor thought for a moment and said, "Maybe I can take it."

"Please do," Hubert said, thrusting the magical item toward her.

Honor opened her bag. "Okay, thank you. Let me see if I have a rag or a cloth I can *take it* with."

'Oh," Hubert said, "If it's a rag you want, I have plenty of those as well!"

"No," Honor said. "No, thank you, Hubert. I'll use my own cloth. You've already given me quite enough."

14.

Louiza flew down from her clinic and landed outside the home of Brit the Elder: a stylish domicile, located down at the bottom of the Atlantis bowl, made of rectangular boxes carefully stacked to give the impression of haphazardness. It could have been mistaken for a late-career Frank Lloyd Wright design if not for the fact that it, like all of the buildings in Atlantis, was made from a milky, glasslike material. Also, its roof did not leak. Brit the Elder's guards, two large men with thick necks and calves larger than their brainpans, greeted Louiza.

Louiza did the guards the courtesy of telling them what they already knew: her name, and that she wanted to see Brit the Elder. They returned the courtesy by telling her what she already knew: that Brit the Elder would be out as soon as possible. They stood in silence for less than thirty seconds, then the glass doors into Brit the Elder's home slid open, and she emerged.

She looked exactly like Brit the Younger, of course. Physically, she hadn't aged a day in more than a hundred years, which was how much time had passed since she had, in fact, *been* Brit the Younger. This didn't mean she hadn't changed. She had longer hair, and her clothes tended more toward flowing dresses. The frames of Brit the Elder's glasses were thin and graceful, and she had a calmer, more confident manner. She invited Louiza inside, to the tasteful but minimal sitting room where she received most guests. She offered a glass of her favorite beverage, Hi-C, to Louiza.

Once they were both seated, and had each had a sip of their bright red sugar water, Brit the Elder said, "So, Madame President, what can I do for you?"

Louiza said, "I thought you would know. I'm afraid Brit the Younger has dropped a pretty big problem in my lap, and told me to come to you for help. I figured that since you used to be her, you might remember."

Brit the Elder nodded and frowned simultaneously. "Yes, understandable. But Louiza, I remind you, I was Brit the Younger a very long time ago."

"Okay. She and I have been working on a system for evacuating and stabilizing injured people in emergency situations so that we could treat . . . I'm sorry, are you all right?"

Brit the Elder had closed her eyes and exhaled sharply, almost as if she had experienced a terrible pain. Louiza stopped speaking, but Brit the Elder opened her eyes, smiled, and said, "Sorry. I just remembered. Instead of giving you time to prepare your part of the system, she's dropped, what was it, twenty-six injured men on your doorstep and left you to sort it all out."

"Exactly."

"So, what specifically is the issue? If it were just as simple as treating each patient and sending them back, you wouldn't need me."

"True. See, the injured men are in stasis in a holding room right now. I've done some triage. Some of them seem to have superficial wounds, some have arrows sticking out of them, and many of them will need surgery."

"Sounds straightforward."

"It is, mostly. There are three parts to a doctor's job: diagnosis, treatment, and recovery. I think I have treatment and recovery sorted out. Diagnosis is what's going to be tricky."

"Even for the ones with arrows sticking out of them?"

"Especially for the ones with arrows sticking out of them. It's a common pitfall for a doctor to see one obvious problem and assume it's the only problem. To do a thorough diagnosis, eventually you have to ask the patient how they feel."

"And that's an issue?"

"Yes. I can knock them out and treat their wounds, then send them back to their time and place as if they never left, to sleep until they're well enough to be active again."

"Yes," Brit the Elder said. "This part I remember. You send them back when they're ready, but you leave them unconscious for two more days. We didn't want the healing spell to work instantly because that would give people the idea that they can do any stupid thing they want, and we can just magic away their injuries."

Louiza nodded. "Yes, and the idea is that they'll wake up remembering nothing. If I revive them to ask them questions before I treat them, that won't happen. They'll wake up with stories about a shiny white room and a woman with an accent asking them where they hurt."

"And erasing their memories isn't an option?"

Louiza said, "I wouldn't know how, and if I did, I'd be afraid to try. We want to send the patients back healthy but confused. Healthy but with brain damage would be a bit much."

"Yes," Brit the Elder said, "I see. So the problem is, how do we wake a medieval villager up, ask them where it hurts, watch them point to where the arrow is sticking out of their torso, then send them back to home without them all telling the same strange story."

"Yup, that covers it. So, what do we do?"

"I don't know."

"How can you not know? You must remember. You've lived through all of this before."

"No, I haven't."

"What do you mean, you haven't?" Louiza sputtered. "You're Brit the Elder. You used to be Brit the Younger, and she's the one who got me into this mess."

"I used to be, but I'm not anymore. I'm me now, not her."

"But you have access to her memories."

"They're my memories, Louiza, from when I was her."

"And you remember giving me this problem."

Brit nodded. "Giving us this problem, yes. How we solved the problem, no. Look, here's what I remember. Brit the Younger dumped this problem in your and Brit the Elder's laps. Brit the Elder did help you, and together you found some solution, but Brit the Elder never told Brit the Younger what that solution was."

"Why on earth not?"

"Mostly out of spite at Brit the Younger for being so inconsiderate, and also for forcing me to resort to speaking about myself in the third person. I hate that. It's so pompous."

"Yes. But it is less confusing."

"I'll choose being confusing over being pompous any day."

"And you do. Okay. You never told you. But I must have told you at some point."

"No, you didn't."

"Why wouldn't I?"

"Because you don't."

"That's not a good enough answer."

"I know that better than anyone. But it is the answer regardless of whether or not you think it's good enough. That's what makes reality reality, the fact that it just keeps being true no matter how much you argue with it."

15.

Martin and Phillip materialized in the gray morning sky above a pasture in Wales. This was their preferred method of arrival in a new place. Appearing at ground level might alarm the locals, and you always ran the risk of materializing in the middle of someone's bedroom, campfire, or wall, all of which would alarm them even more. Of course, two men popping into existence out of thin air, then hovering in that same thin air, tended to alarm people pretty badly as well, but at least they would be alarmed at a distance.

Phillip and Martin drifted gently to the ground and looked around for a moment before Martin said, "I expected to see dragons."

"Yes," Phillip said, "that was rather the point. I'm not surprised that we didn't appear right on top of them, mind you, but I didn't expect there to be no obvious sign that they're around."

"Yeah, I figured if we didn't see the dragons, there'd be fire or shouting."

"I suppose we should be grateful that there isn't."

"Yes, but it makes our job harder." Martin switched his staff to his left hand and held his right out before him.

Phillip saw, and asked, "What are you doing?"

"Calling Jeff to complain."

Martin said, "*Komuniki kun* Jeff," and after a few rings, a flickering image of Jeff's disembodied head appeared floating in his hand.

"Oh, what now?!" Jeff cried.

"Nothing too bad," Martin assured him. "It's just that the dragons aren't exactly where you sent us."

"Sorry. There are a lot of time and distance variables. You should be pretty close."

"It might help us track them down if we had a copy of that dragon map you had."

"Of course. You're right. I'll figure out a way to make copies for all of the teams. Something you can use in front of people without having to explain what a smartphone is. I'll have it to you as soon as possible."

Martin thanked Jeff, and ended the call. He turned to Phillip and said, "Really, it seems like the kind of thing he should have thought of himself."

"Yes," Phillip said, "I suspect the stress of the situation is getting to him. Frankly, the rest of us should have thought of it as well."

"Yeah, I suspect the stress is getting to us, too. Nobody wants to be remembered as having had any part in all life on Earth being slowly smothered by artificial dragons."

"I suppose the one bright side to all life on Earth ending is that there's nobody left to remember who was responsible."

Martin asked, "Have I ever told you that you always know the perfect thing to say to cheer me up?"

"No, you haven't."

"Good."

Phillip took a few steps, planted his staff, and bent down to examine the ankle-length grass. "Coming down, I noticed a big dark streak going through the field. It's harder to see this close, but this is the edge of it. It's like a big patch of the grass has been disturbed. A group of four dragons walking through might do that."

Martin's surprisingly distant voice said, "Yeah, and it might do that, too."

Phillip looked up and saw that Martin had already walked away along the path of the dark streak, but had stopped to answer, and to point his staff at a dark hole in the tree line caused by broken branches. The streak of disturbed grass led directly to it. Martin started walking again.

"That might be the wrong way," Phillip shouted.

Martin stopped again, and turned back to Phillip. "The other direction might be the wrong way, too."

"True, so it's a fifty-fifty chance. Why pick that way over this one?"

Martin said, "Well, the dragons appeared in places there were already sheep, right? This is a pasture. There's more pasture behind you. This way leads into the woods. I don't think sheep usually live in the woods. It seems more likely that they would have appeared in the pasture and headed into the woods than the other way around."

Phillip shrugged, then walked to catch up with Martin. The two set off on foot in the direction of the gap in the trees.

Martin said, "The guys were surprised when you suggested that you and I make one team and Brit and Gwen make another."

Phillip said, "Yes, well, the guys are all single aren't they? They probably haven't learned yet that one of the secrets of getting someone to stay with you is giving them plenty of time when they're not actually *with* you."

"Yup. You've got to leave them wanting more."

"Or, at least give them enough space that they don't start wanting less. You'll notice that neither Gwen nor Brit argued with the idea."

"Yeah, I did notice that. I also noticed that Brit insisted on taking Scotland."

"Yes, not surprising. It has the largest single group of dragons. Sadly, women often have to take on the most daunting challenge merely to be seen as an equal."

"True," Martin said. "But, are you sure that's why she took Scotland?"

"Why else would she?"

"I dunno. It's just interesting. When you think of Scotland, what's the first thing that comes to your mind?"

"Bagpipes."

"Okay, then what?"

"Accents."

"Fine, what else?"

"Haggis?"

Martin rolled his eyes. Phillip asked, "Look, Martin, what are you getting at?"

Martin said, "Kilts. Most people think of kilts."

Phillip shrugged. "So??"

Martin said, "The big sweaty beefcakes who do all of the work in Atlantis, they wear kilts, don't they?"

"Yes, they do. What are you trying to say, Martin?"

"Brit the Elder designed Atlantis. Did she pick uniforms for the workers? And if so, does something happen in Scotland now that makes her want to be around men in kilts when she designs Atlantis later?"

"I suppose it's possible, *if* you believe that they're the same person."

"And you don't."

"No, I don't."

"Because you believe in free will."

"Yes, I do."

"And Brit the Elder truly being Brit the Younger from the future would mean that Brit the Younger has no free will."

"Indeed."

After a few more steps, Martin said, "Of course, if she doesn't really have free will, it would make the whole men-in-kilts question meaningless. It would mean that no matter what happened, she never *chose* to be around men in kilts."

"Perhaps not."

"She was irresistibly compelled to be around men in kilts."

Phillip shouted, "Shut up," and Martin did shut up, because it's hard to talk while laughing.

They walked through the dark hole broken into the forest's edge where they presumed the dragons had gone. They could see down the path ahead, but tree trunks and undergrowth limited their visibility. The path appeared to have existed before the dragons came along, but the dragons seemed to have widened it, roughly shoving the foliage away on all sides as they walked through. Unfortunately, much of the displaced debris had fallen directly on the path, so Martin and Phillip had to watch their step.

They didn't know if the dragons had split up, then doubled back. Without discussing it, they knew that a dragon could come crashing through the woods at them at any moment, from any direction.

Without warning, they heard a trumpet fanfare emanating from an empty spot in the air above Martin's head. The instant the fanfare ended, a rolled piece of parchment appeared in midair. Martin caught it as it fell, then unrolled it.

The map itself was useless. When zoomed down to a local level, it showed roads, rivers, and castles, all drawn in a charming style, but they did not and could not correspond to any existing landmarks in the real world. Instead of drawing a map from scratch, Jeff had just used an image of the board game Carcassonne, which looked enough like a map to fool the casual medieval observer. The important parts were a stick-figure drawing of a wizard that obviously signified their current position, and various red dots, connected to the wizard by lines, and marked with a number that appeared to be the distance between the two in meters. Two dots crowded along the border of the map, well behind the wizard figure. The numbers showed that these two dragons were thousands of meters away from Martin and

Phillip, and each other. The other four dots were all within a few meters of each other, and only a couple hundred meters away from Martin and Phillip.

"Those dragons are close," Martin said. "That's good news."

"Is it?" asked Phillip.

They continued walking, following the trail as it meandered through the woods.

"I'm glad we got this map," Martin said, rolling it up and placing it in his robe pocket. "We might have been looking all day."

They heard a rustling in the distance, coming from the trail ahead, not nearly loud or violent enough to be a dragon approaching, but loud and violent enough to give the wizards pause. They stopped in their tracks, held their staffs forward, and prepared for whatever was headed their way.

After a few tense seconds of ever-intensifying noise, a man ran around the bend. He was a short, stout, older man in new leather breeches and a woven tunic. He had fear in his eyes and a sword in his hand. He looked like he had much more experience with the fear than he did with the sword. He skidded to a stop, looked at Martin and Phillip, and asked, "Are you wizards?"

Martin tensed a bit. Phillip said, "Yes, we are wizards."

The man said, "Oh, thank the heavens!" He dropped his sword, stepped toward them, and in a beseeching voice said, "I need your help!"

Phillip asked, "What's troubling you that you need a wizard's help?"

"Dragons! I'll show you! Follow me!"

Martin said, "Maybe we didn't need the map so badly after all."

The man feared dragons, but he didn't seem concerned that the dragons would hear him. He talked the entire time he led the wizards to the problem.

"Look, gentlemen, what you're about to see, it's, um, look, it's going to surprise you. I need your help, no two ways about it, but I'm trusting you to be men of honor. I'm not averse to paying a fair wage for fair work, and greed is a sin, but I hope we can all agree that what's mine is mine, and to take it away would be stealing."

Martin and Phillip exchanged an amused but weary look. Phillip said, "My good man, I'm sorry, what's your name?"

"Kneath."

"Kneath, we are wizards. We can bend, shape, and manipulate the very fabric of reality as if it were so much . . ." Phillip trailed off, looking for the right word.

"Fabric?" Martin offered.

"Yes. I promise you, we have no interest in stealing whatever it is we're about to see."

Kneath said, "I'm glad to hear that. Because we're almost there. It's just inside this cave."

The path had led them to the side of a steep hill. Set into the hill they saw a dark, gaping hole. It resembled what Martin imagined a giant's upper lip and mouth would look like when viewed from a giant spoon. Kneath disappeared into the cave without stopping to make sure the wizards were still following, which they weren't.

Phillip and Martin looked at the cave, dubiously.

"Martin, can you think of a single example of someone finding something in a cave that they were happy about afterward?"

"No, but maybe we'll be the first."

"Martin, can you think of a single example of something pleasant happening to the two of us first?"

Phillip walked into the cave, not waiting for an answer. Martin followed.

Martin muttered a spell to turn his staff into a flashlight, then said, "That's better."

The inside of the cave looked exactly as Martin had expected it would. Rough rock walls curving seamlessly into a rock ceiling over a bed of wall-to-wall dirt, all enlivened by the decorative flourishes for which bats are well-known. The cave stretched out ahead of them, remaining surprisingly roomy as it curved out of their view.

Phillip stopped him. "That fellow, Kneath, he didn't need a torch."

"Maybe he knows the cave really well. He might spend a lot of time here."

"We've been lured into a cave by a man who spends lots of time in said cave. Splendid. I only hope we don't come to regret his home-cave advantage."

Kneath emerged from around a bend in the distance, begging them to hurry. Only when they had him as a visual reference did they realize that the cave had maintained its full height. Also, now that they looked at it critically, the cave seemed far too long and straight, and the radius of the curved ceiling was too regular for a naturally occurring geological formation. The cave appeared man-made, or more likely, wizard-made.

They followed the man around the bend and into a large chamber the size of a small basketball arena—filled with gold. Not the large, loose heaps of gold, like comic-book artists and theme-park-ride set designers are fond of creating, but countless tall, neat, orderly stacks of gold objects, carefully sorted, organized, and stored in their assigned places, with large golden signs specifying what went where. And the items were not coins, goblets, and crowns, as one might expect. The sign next to several rectangular stacks of thin gold plates said *shingles.*

Looking around the room, they saw many rectangular stacks of a variety of solid-gold slabs, marked with signs saying *tile-floor, tile-wall, tile-ceiling, siding, paneling,* and *flashing.* They also saw golden bins full of golden nuts, bolts, nails, and screws, and stacks of solid-gold I beams, railings, balusters, and posts, all of it illuminated by the kind of lights one would expect to find hanging from the ceiling of a Home Depot, only they were floating in midair, and made of gold.

Phillip said, "Jimmy!"

Martin was rendered speechless by the sheer amount and strange forms of the gold before him, and by the sight of the four sleeping dragons draping themselves over the stacks of priceless building materials like cats making themselves comfortable in a room full of cardboard boxes.

Phillip said, "We all knew that Jimmy went somewhere to make materials for Castle Camelot. It's not like you can pop down to the lumberyard for a solid-gold two-by-four."

Martin said, "Yeah. It makes sense that he'd create a stockpile so that work could go on without his supervision. He probably set up a portal into this cave for his workers."

"Yes. And when the castle was done, Jimmy wouldn't have destroyed the surplus material. It's gold. For all we know, he went looking for this cave when we exiled him."

"Nah, you're giving Jimmy too much credit."

"You don't think he'd have remembered where this cave was?"

"No, I don't think he could have ridden from Argentina to Wales on a bicycle."

"Good point." Phillip tapped Kneath on the shoulder, distracting him from staring in anguish at his gold being used as a bed by dragons.

"How long have the dragons been in here?" Phillip asked.

"A little over two days."

"How did they get here?"

"They were drawn to the gold."

"Really?" Martin asked. "Are you sure?"

"Yes. Absolutely. I was out for a walk, coming to check on my gold, and in a big clearing on the way, I saw the dragons. I thought to myself, *They're clearly after my gold.* So I tried to shoo them off, but they wouldn't leave. Then I ran all the way here to try to protect my gold from them."

"And they followed you," Phillip said.

"No, I outran them."

"All the way into the gold chamber," Martin said.

"Yes," Kneath answered, proudly.

Phillip asked, "And you say they haven't left this room once since they got here?"

"No, sir, they haven't."

Phillip turned to Martin and said, "Good. Seems these four are neutralized. We can just throw a goal up in the cave leading out, go destroy the other two dragons that've been assigned to us, and with any luck these four will have taken care of themselves by the time we return."

"Wait," Kneath said. "What do you mean, *destroy the other two dragons?* You two are here to destroy the dragons anyway?"

"Yes," Martin said.

Kneath said, "Oh. Could I trouble you to please take care of these four first, since you're here already?"

Phillip shook his head. "I really think it will be easier if we leave them for later."

"But I'd rather have them gone now. If you'll kill them first, I can make it worth your while."

Martin asked, "How?"

Kneath said, "I can pay you in gold."

"We're wizards," Phillip said. "We can make our own gold."

"But if I give you gold, you won't have to."

Martin shook his head. "But you don't have any gold. From where I'm standing, the dragons have the gold, not you."

"Yes," Kneath said brightly. "So the sooner you get rid of the dragons, the sooner I can pay you!"

16.

Somewhere in the Scottish Highlands, Brit and Gwen hovered slightly above the eye of the dragon storm. They attempted to count the dragons, which was a challenge, since they were mostly identical. Two had horns; the rest didn't. Aside from that, they were essentially ten of the same animal, flying in a circle. Just when they both thought they had a handle on the dragons' formation, and a general idea of where to start counting and where to stop, the dragons broke their pattern, diving to the ground.

They had focused so fully on the dragons that neither of them had bothered to look directly down at the ground. They finally did look, just in time to see a clump of people huddling beneath large wooden shields while being periodically doused in flames.

The dragons couldn't turn quite sharply enough to stay permanently within fire-breath range of the poor people on the ground, so instead they each chose an orbit that brought them in close enough to attack, then took them far enough afield to be out of the path of the next dragon. Each dragon could muster about three good puffs of flame, and between them they kept the poor saps with the shields under constant assault for nearly fifteen seconds, which might not sound like a long time, but to someone attempting to fight back fire with a piece of wood, fifteen seconds is an eternity. The intricate, looping pattern the dragons traced as they wove in and out of range while staying out of each other's way seemed almost mathematically perfect.

Brit and Gwen knew that the people under the shields had to be terrified and in agony, but were not in any direct danger from the dragons. Also, the realization that the dragons were attacking something, then the shock at what they were attacking, then the surprise at how they were attacking, all came in such quick succession that it would have left any witness momentarily stunned.

"Such an interesting mix of animal instinct and computer precision," Brit the Younger said. "It would be fascinating to keep a few to study, if it didn't mean risking all life on Earth."

"The age-old lament of the scientist," Gwen said.

The dragons had done their worst, and ascended to regroup for another run. As the dragons flew back to a safe altitude, Brit and Gwen noted that the lead dragon and the last dragon were the two with horns.

The mound of shields rose as if a single piece of wood, then the individual shields tilted, lowered, and virtually disappeared, revealing four large men. They all looked like variations on the same theme, as if they had been assembled at random from the same assortment of available parts: long hair, trim beards, thick muscles, and kilts.

They stood back-to-back, unaware of the sorceresses directly above them, instead focusing on the dragons. A man with flowing blond hair lifted his sword, looked at the surface of his shield, and shouted, "The shields held again, my friends! I doubt they can withstand another pass, but take heart, for we shall die protecting those we love! I regret that I'll never see my beloved Coira, nor little Effie and Nessa again, but knowing that they will live is enough!"

A man with dark red hair and a bright red face hoisted his sword and bellowed, "Aye, Jock! I, too, take great solace in knowing that my sacrifice has made possible the escape of my dear wife and our wee baby daughter, for I love them far more than I love life itself! I only hope they know it!"

A noticeably stouter man with brighter red hair and a darker red face switched his battle-axe to his shield hand, and used his now-free hand to grasp the other man's shoulder. "Morag knows, Kyle. Morag knows. And when Rut is old enough, Morag will tell her. That woman adores you beyond the ability for words to express it. I know this, because while I am here fighting for my betrothed, the lovely Donalda, a good, good woman, far better than I deserve, the truth is that I, too, love Morag, and have since we were all wee. I would never act on it, for I love you like a brother, but I cannot help how I feel, and now that we face certain death, I want you to know the truth."

Kyle put his hand on the other man's as it clutched his shoulder and said, "Leslie, I know. I've always known. Everybody's seen the way you look at Morag, even Morag. But we knew you were far too good a man to ever say a word, no matter how painful it was, and we respect you all the more for it!"

Jock laughed, "Truth be told, all of the men in the village have been in love with Morag at one time or another!"

Kyle shouted, "Don't I know it!"

All of the men laughed, save for one, a black-haired hulking figure clutching a battle-axe with both hands as he surveyed the sky with murder in his eyes. "I've never loved Morag," he said, in a somber, determined tone. "Bonnie though she is. No offense, Kyle."

Kyle said, "None taken, Mungo."

Mungo shook his head. "Before I knew what marriage, or love, or even my own name was, I've known who I wanted. She was skinny, and pale, and had hair like a thicket bush, but the first time I laid eyes on her, I knew she was for me. The five greatest days of my life are the day Grizel agreed to be mine, the days that Seonag, Jinny, and my boy Torquil were born, and today." The man turned to face the others, and held his battle-axe high above his head. "For today," he nearly screamed, "I die! I die, fighting! I die fighting for a good cause, with good men by my side! Today we give our last, here on the ground our fathers left us, to defend the lives of those we hold most dear! It's a good death! The best death possible! I'm proud, so proud to share it with you, men I love like brothers! The dragons may kill us, and burn us, and eat us, but we will fight back their fire, and we will dodge their teeth and wrestle with their tongues, and kick them in the tonsils on our way past. And if they swallow us, by God, we will do our best to give them indigestion while we're in 'em, and the trots on our way out!"

The men all shook their weapons in the air and let out a blood-curdling shriek that echoed across the landscape.

Gwen said, "Yeesh! After all that, it almost seems like a shame to save them."

The dragons had circled several times during the men's heartfelt pre-martyrdom chat, and were just starting to descend for another coordinated attack. Gwen threw herself wand first into a steep dive, got just ahead of the lead dragon, and created the destructive portal they'd taken to calling *the goal* directly in its path.

The first dragon never had the time to even try to avoid the goal, and sailed through it like a perfectly executed free throw. The second dragon attempted to pull up far too late, and only managed to run headfirst into the rim, then flop limply through the goal, carried by its own momentum.

The third dragon spread its wings wide and flapped them furiously in a desperate effort to keep from flying into the goal. Of course, it didn't know that the goal would kill it. The dragon had no idea what the goal even was, but that alone was a good enough reason for any creature with an instinct for self-preservation to want to avoid flying into it. It flailed in the air, attempting to maintain its altitude, like the world's largest hummingbird. The seven dragons behind it all had time to simply adjust their dive paths to avoid both the goal and the panicked dragon, which they did, neatly zipping past on every side.

Because the dragons had been in a dive when Gwen placed the goal, instead of being in front of the third dragon, or even beside it, the goal was actually beneath it, canted at an angle like a ramp. The dragon managed to avoid it, arresting all of its momentum, and actually started to inch away, before Brit flew directly in front of its face and emanated a blinding flash of light that stunned the dragon just long enough for it to lose altitude and fall through the goal.

Brit said, "Three down."

Gwen started to respond, but got distracted by the sound of the men below cheering. She looked down at them and managed to smile for nearly a full second before shouting, "Crap!"

The destruction of three of their number had thrown the dragons into disarray. They reacted by each flying in a graceful arc, redirecting their momentum into paths that all converged back on the men on the ground.

Gwen and Brit knew that the dragon's false fire would hurt, but couldn't kill the men directly. Indeed, the men had survived a direct assault while they watched, but the men had anticipated that attack and braced themselves. This time, they had their shields down, and didn't seem aware that the dragons were converging on them with intent to try to turn them into brisket. When the fire hit, the men would probably panic, and Brit and Gwen knew from recent experience what could happen when armed men in tight quarters panic.

Gwen dove toward the men. She watched as the looks on their faces transitioned in quick succession from elation, that two sorceresses were helping them; to fear, when one of the sorceresses shot toward them without warning; to confusion, when they felt their weapons strike the inner wall of the invisible force field she had created. Then she couldn't see them at all, because of all the fire and dragons in the way.

Gwen prayed she'd made the force bubble small enough. During the fruitless hours the wizards had spent attempting to craft anti-dragon weapons, they had discussed the uses and limitations of force fields. Gwen knew that she had probably saved the men quite a bit of pain, but there was a small chance, depending on how low the dragons had flown by, that she had trapped several armed men in a confined space, where they would be blind and in excruciating agony.

She placed a second force field around herself just in time to avoid a light roasting. She couldn't see anything beyond the fire, but she heard the sound of the men screaming at the tops of their lungs.

Normally, I'd take that as a bad sign, she thought. *But with these guys, I can't be sure.*

The fire surrounding Gwen subsided. She saw the underbelly of the dragon that had attacked her as it streaked past. It flew away from Gwen and gave no indication that it ever intended to turn back.

Below, another dragon flew over the men, raining fire down upon them for as long as it could before also gaining altitude and flying away as fast as its wings could manage.

The men's shrieking and shouting had continued unabated through the attack. Now they looked up at Gwen, and continued yelling, their mouths open wide, their eyes bulging. She still couldn't tell if she'd helped them or made their situation much worse. It wasn't until the one called Jock cried, "Gods be praised! We're saved, lads! Her magic has saved us!"

Their shouting got even louder as Gwen dropped to the ground in front of them.

As the cheering died, Kyle said, "Praise be, I may yet live to once more see my beloved Morag!"

Leslie said, "Aye, and, if fate allows it, I, too, may live to once more see your beloved Morag!"

Kyle snarled, "Come here, you wee bastard!" and tackled Leslie. The two rolled, grunting, on the ground. The other two men watched and laughed instead of trying to break them up.

After a spirited tussle, the fighting men started laughing and let go of each other, then sat up in the grass. Kyle said, "You're a true friend, Leslie. I could never hurt you."

Leslie said, "You're a true friend, Kyle, and you're right. You could never hurt me. I'd wallop you if you tried, and we both know it!"

"You think so? Then let's see, you arrogant bastard!" Kyle dove at Leslie, and the two rolled on the ground, fighting again, accompanied by a fresh hail of laughter from their friends.

Brit the Younger landed next to Gwen and said, "I managed to take out another dragon, then they all scattered. We have six left to get."

Gwen said, "Cool."

They watched and listened to the fight for a moment. Brit asked, "They okay?"

Gwen shook her head, chuckled, and threw her hands up to signal her uncertainty. "I guess. They seem to be trying to determine exactly what kind of bastard Leslie is, arrogant or wee."

Brit said, "I see."

Gwen and Brit stood and watched the two men struggle, the sounds of their grunting and cursing almost drowned out by their friends' laughter and cheers.

Brit said, "Those kilts really allow for a lot of mobility for the, uh, lower extremities, don't they?"

Gwen winced. "Yes. Mobility, and visibility."

"Unfortunate angle though."

"Agreed."

Gwen could barely discern a high-pitched warbling sort of sound over the fighting and the laughing. She lifted her hand, saw that the call was from Jeff, then turned to Brit and said, "I'm getting a call. You want in on this?"

"No, I think I'll watch the fight. I'll let you know if you miss anything."

Gwen took to the air and put fifty yards or so between herself and the fight so she'd be able to hear and speak in a normal tone. She answered the call.

"Hello, Jeff. What's up?"

The hazy image of Jeff's head floating in her palm said, "Hey, Gwen. I'm sending you something. Please look up."

Above, just in front of Gwen, a rolled piece of parchment appeared. She caught it easily.

"It's a map," Jeff explained. "It's useless for finding your way to the nearest town or anything, but it will tell you where the dragons you're after are. Some of the teams had a hard time finding them."

"Really? I wouldn't think it'd be hard to spot a dragon."

"I know, right? I don't get it either, but apparently some of the dragons were hiding."

"They're as big as a house and shoot fire. Where did they hide, inside a volcano?"

"I don't know. They asked for a map, and I made them one."

"Who, specifically, asked for the map?"

"I shouldn't tell you that."

"Meaning it was Martin."

"I didn't tell you that."

"No, you didn't."

17.

Leadchurch looked deserted. All of the citizens were hiding in the church. If Jeff and Roy had listened carefully, they might have heard their former selves still arguing with the other wizards about what Jeff had done.

Jeff said, "Well, let's go unmake my mistake."

Roy shook his head. "Kid, the only one who's still mad at you is you."

"I hope that's true, but I don't know. I mean, you acted pretty mad before."

"Yeah, before. Back when we were armpit deep in dragons and you were acting evasive. It looked like you didn't want to tell us what you did because you didn't want to admit you'd made a mistake. Now I see that you didn't want to say anything until you were sure what mistake you'd made. That's understandable."

"So you'd have done the same thing?"

"No, Jeff, I didn't say that. I don't think I'd have ever pulled this particular boner, but I understand how you did. Kid, I worked in the aerospace industry on military projects. You don't do that for long without becoming real comfortable with the idea of unintended consequences. Nobody sits at a desk drafting plans for a wing spar, hoping that someday it will lead to a firebomb landing on a grass hut somewhere on the other side of the globe."

"I suppose not."

"You don't have to suppose. I told you. Now let's get a move on. There are still dragons to kill."

"There is one thing I should mention though, Roy."

"What's that, kid?"

"You're from the seventies, so I get it, but you should know that people don't say *boner*. Any more."

"What?"

"Boner. People don't say it. I mean, they do say it, but not to mean *mistake*. When most people hear it they think you mean—"

Roy waved his hands. "Yeah, I know what they probably think. We used it that way, too."

"It's weird that we use the same word to describe that and to refer to making a mistake."

"Not really. I've made some of my worst mistakes while I had one."

Each team of wizards had certain dragons assigned to them. Jeff and Roy got the four that attacked Leadchurch, the random stragglers wandering around the wilderness nearby, and the pod of five massed on the outskirts of London, which the locals and a few of the wizards still habitually referred to as *Camelot*.

Roy and Jeff made the Leadchurch dragons their priority, and dispatched them with little difficulty. Having a fixed moment in time when they knew the dragons were far from any person, and from each other, flying at high speed in separate directions, made it fairly straightforward to coax them through the goal one at a time. Jeff noted with some satisfaction that if the wizards had just looked around right after the attack while they were berating him for his mistake, they would have seen him in the distance, taking an active role in fixing it.

Jeff looked at his map and said, "I think the next logical move is to go take out the cluster in London. A bunch of dragons working together near a city is far more dangerous than a few wandering around the wilderness. Besides, they won't be wandering around for long. We pretty much have the hang of this."

Roy agreed.

Jeff and Roy teleported to a spot two hundred feet above a field just outside the walls of Camelot. After several seconds of scanning the skies, searching for signs of dragons, Roy finally looked down. Five dragons stood around grazing on some poor farmer's crop. Jeff searched the area, hoping he wouldn't find any people in peril. He was happy to see nobody anywhere near the dragons. He was unhappy to see that the top edge of the city's nearest wall was filled to capacity with citizens who had gathered to watch the dragons.

Jeff said, "Great. We have an audience."

"Yup, and I don't expect them to go away anytime soon," Roy said. "We're doing something interesting. If you had a choice between doing your work or watching two wizards fight five dragons, what would you pick?"

The two wizards lowered silently to the ground, a safe distance from the dragons, and discussed their options.

"They aren't moving," Jeff said. "We can't trick them to go through the goal unless they're moving."

Roy said, "I guess we gotta flush 'em out."

"What?"

"Flush 'em. It's a bird-hunting term. It means to startle them so that they take off flying. That way, shooting them is more sporting."

"Or it just guarantees that they die terrified and fleeing."

"Maybe, kid, but we aren't gonna be shooting them, are we? Besides, look at yourself, then look at them. Do you really think they're going to be terrified?

"Yeah, I guess not."

"Then get to it."

Jeff glared at Roy, but he glared while walking toward the dragons, intent on doing as Roy suggested.

Jeff took a second to consider how he would frighten the dragons. Two had horns; three did not. They had deduced that, though all of the dragons lacked any genitalia, the horns signified a male. Since many of the dragons' instincts came from sheep, this meant that the males were more aggressive, and that once one dragon started running, male or female, odds were good that the others would follow. Jeff figured that the horned males would be the easiest to goad into action, and once the dragons were in flight, they could just apply the same system they'd used in Leadchurch.

Jeff triggered a macro he'd been playing with that combined elements invented by Gwen and Gary. After uttering a few words of Esperanto, he radiated waves of dark energy, and his voice was amplified to ear-splitting volume. He ran toward the nearest male, and in his deepest, scariest voice shouted, "Hey! You! Dragon! Get outta here! Scram!"

The horned dragon didn't run, but instead reared back and lowered its head, threatening to ram Jeff. The other dragons all turned to look, but none flew away. Clearly, as in humans, their urge to avoid danger didn't stand a chance against their competing urge to watch someone get their butt kicked.

Jeff stumbled to a stop, still visibly radiating energy. He kept his eyes on the dragon, but tilted his head back over his shoulder to Roy, and in his still-amplified voice said, "I think it's going to ram me."

Roy, his voice faint due to the distance, shouted, "Good! I'll throw up a goal right in front of you!"

"No!" Jeff shouted. "Don't! Don't do that!"

"Why not?"

"Because if you time it wrong, I get rammed. If you place it wrong, I get cut in half lengthwise! Or the dragon gets cut in half, and its front half still rams me!"

"Fine," Roy shouted, sounding more than a little disappointed. "I guess you're right."

"So what do I do?"

"Brace yourself!"

Then the dragon rammed Jeff.

Jeff picked himself up off of the ground and flew back to Roy's side, disabling the macro as he went.

Roy asked, "So, what do we do now?"

Jeff said, "We tried scaring them off with something we thought they wouldn't like. What if we lure them off with something they would like?"

"Okay? What do dragons like?"

"I dunno. Eating people?"

"No. If that were it, they would be chasing you right now."

"Yeah. True. Okay, they're dragons, but they're also kinda sheep, right? What do sheep like?"

"I don't know."

"Neither do I. One second, I'll look it up." Jeff looked around to make sure nobody was too close. He reached into his pocket and pulled out his smartphone. All of the wizards had tampered with their smartphones' entries in the file to allow them to work any place, in any time, without draining their batteries. No amount of magic could prevent them from incurring Roy's scorn.

"You kids," Roy sneered. Being the wizard from the earliest original date, he tended to view the other wizards as kids, and their technological advancements as toys. "That's your answer to everything. *I'll look it up on my phone.*"

"What would you have me do," Jeff asked, scrolling through pages on his screen, "stay ignorant?"

"It just seems to me that having all of that information available makes you complacent and lazy, and it keeps you from ever having to admit you don't know anything."

Jeff shook his head. "I admitted I didn't know, right before I said that I would look it up. And I don't understand how I'm being lazy when I'm the one going to the trouble of tracking down the information, instead of just shrugging and saying *I don't know.*"

Roy shook his head and looked away, the closest thing to an admission of defeat he was ever going to commit. Jeff poked a few more links and scrolled through a few more screens, then said, "Apples. Some people who raise sheep give them apples as treats."

Jeff continued navigating through his phone.

"What are you doing now?" Roy asked.

"I probably shouldn't say. Learning new information might make you lazy."

"Telling you I wasn't mad at you anymore was a mistake."

Jeff smiled. "I'm looking up a 3D rendering of an apple that I can project to lure the dragons." He tapped at his phone and said, "Okay, I've got one." He tapped a few more times, turned the phone sideways, did a few seconds worth of thumb typing, then looked toward the dragons and said, "Here we go."

Jeff aimed his wand toward a point a hundred feet or so away from the dragons and pressed his right thumb to the screen. An apple appeared. It didn't look quite real. It appeared to be a solid object in the real world, but its color was too uniform, and its shape was too perfect. Also, it was flying, and measured ten feet across.

The dragons all snapped to attention, turning to look at the hovering uber-apple. They stared, alarmed, for half a second, and then shrunk back from it, cringing, but not actually stepping or flying further away.

"Fantastic," Roy said. "Your *treat* has given them the creeps. This whole dragon thing has been a textbook lesson for you in why you don't mess with things you don't understand."

Jeff said, "I know."

"Why'd you make the apple bigger than their head? Were you counting on the dragons being greedy?"

"I wanted to make it big enough for all of them."

"But if they can't get their jaws around it—"

"I know," Jeff interrupted, neither needing nor wanting Roy to finish the sentence. "Let me try something else."

Jeff monkeyed with his phone. The giant apple disappeared. After a few more seconds of tapping and wand pointing, a large pile of normal-sized apples appeared in its place. Again, it didn't look like a real stack of apples in that the apples were all utterly unblemished, perfectly uniform, oriented identically, straight up and down with their stems tilted in the same direction, and positioned in a perfect four-sided pyramid, which floated two feet above the ground.

The dragons looked puzzled, but that was a step up from looking vaguely uneasy.

The dragons looked at the apples. Then looked at each other. Then looked at the apples again. Finally, one of the horned dragons started slowly crawling closer, as if attempting to sneak up on the apples. The other dragons cautiously followed suit.

Jeff said, "Okay, quick, throw the goal up in front of it."

"Will do."

Roy took a moment to judge the distance, pointed his staff at the space in front of the dragons, and whispered, "*Krei duono ringego, goal.*" The goal appeared—a large, translucent blue half disk rooted to the ground between the dragons and the apples. The horned dragon stopped walking, as did the other dragons.

Jeff sighed. "Let's try something. Please take the goal away."

Roy made the goal disappear, and the dragons resumed slowly advancing toward the apples. Roy made the goal reappear, and they stopped again.

Roy said, "The goal's blocking them from the apples."

"Yup," Jeff agreed. "If this is going to work, we need to get them moving fast enough that they won't have time to stop before they hit the goal."

"Here's an idea. We wait 'til the lead dragon almost gets to the apples, then you take off flying, trailing the apples behind you. If they follow, you slowly gain speed until they're moving fast enough, and I'll throw the goal up behind you."

"You said that I take off flying," Jeff said. "Why do I have to be the dragon lure?"

"What happened to all of that *this is my mess, I should be the one to fix it* crap?"

"There has to be a better way than this."

"If there is, we haven't thought of it."

18.

It was a pleasant day in Yorkshire. A cool breeze blew the tall, soft grass in graceful waves around the legs of the seven dragons that stood, grazing peacefully in the sunlight, atop one of the gently rolling hills that stretched off to the horizon in every direction.

The sound of birds singing and trees rustling was interrupted by the sound of Tyler materializing twenty feet above the ground, directly in front of the dragons, then shouting, "Hey, look at me!"

The dragons all looked up at Tyler, mildly interested. In that instant, Gary materialized silently behind the dragons. He held his staff high over his head by its narrow tip. The large, glowing blue disc of a goal was affixed to the head of his staff, and Gary wielded it like a gigantic butterfly net, swinging it downward over the top of the dragon farthest away from Tyler. Because all of the other dragons were looking at Tyler, none of them saw Gary take the rear dragon out. Gary disappeared, leaving the herd one dragon smaller, and a disk of grass the exact circumference of the goal trimmed to a uniform height.

Tyler disappeared. The dragons looked at the empty space he left behind for a moment, then went back to their grazing, unaware that one of their fellow dragons was no more.

After a moment or two's worth of peaceful grazing, Tyler reappeared, again floating twenty feet above the ground, but facing the dragons from a different direction.

"This," he shouted in an oddly conversational (if loud) tone, "is what's called a *diversion*."

Again, the dragons looked up from their grass to face him. Again, one dragon stood alone at the back of the group. Again, Gary appeared, swung the goal down over the top of the hapless dragon, and disappeared. Tyler disappeared as well. The dragons went about their business.

Tyler reappeared on the opposite side of the group and said, "It's also sometimes called a *distraction.*"

The dragons turned to face Tyler. Yet again, Gary materialized and swooped the goal down over the dragon at the back of the pack. This time, however, he let out a little giggle at how well the plan was working. The dragons all turned to see what had made the noise, but he had vanished mid-giggle, and was long gone by the time the dragons looked his direction. They turned back to where Tyler had been, but found him gone as well.

Tyler reappeared. "But a diversion won't work if your partner screws up and draws attention away from it. That's why you never hear about a *double distraction.*"

The dragons heard nothing behind them this time, but when Tyler disappeared, there was, again, one fewer dragon to not hear it. Soon only one dragon remained, which Gary neutralized from behind without bothering with a distraction or a diversion.

Tyler appeared, and the two of them surveyed the scene of their triumph. An empty field with a large patch of perfectly mowed grass.

Gary put up a hand and said, "All right! High-five!"

Tyler looked at Gary's palm as if it were radioactive. He pulled out the dragon map.

"Come on," Gary said. "Don't leave me hanging!"

Tyler said, "Your life will get a lot more pleasant if you learn to enjoy hanging."

Gary put his hand down.

"Okay," Tyler said, "That's seven down, which leaves one that must have wandered away from the pack."

"I didn't see it when we materialized," Gary said.

"Neither did I," Tyler said, "but we weren't looking for it. We were told to look for a bunch of dragons, and we found a bunch of dragons, so we stopped looking. According to the map, it's hiding somewhere over there, behind that hill." Tyler pointed toward a large hill covered with grass and a lush stand of trees.

The two of them flew only a few feet above the treetops, hoping to maintain the element of surprise. They reached the hill's crest, where they landed, walked to the edge of the trees, and got down on the ground to observe the vista beneath them without being seen themselves.

The whole side of the hill had eroded away long ago, creating a small, crumbly cliff. At the base of the cliff, nestled in the valleys between the many hills of the northern English countryside, there was a large path, or a small road. It wound out of a grove of trees, past a glassy pond, and around a bend out of sight.

At the edge of the road, a little girl no more than six years old sat by the side of the pond with her bare feet submerged. She sat bent forward in concentration, manipulating something with both hands, her golden-blonde ringlets falling down in front of her face.

"There!" she exclaimed, in the kind of slow, high-pitched voice that is adorable when it comes out of a child and creepy when it comes out of an adult. "It's done!" She lifted up a piece of bark with a straight stick protruding from it. Several large leaves hung from the stick, forming a sail.

"It's a boat, Kelly! I made a boat!"

The dragon poked its nose forward, as if sniffing the boat, but made no other move or sound.

The girl giggled. "Now to see if it floats."

She placed the boat in the water, then nudged it out into the pond with her foot.

"It works, Kelly! It works!"

Gary whispered, "She made friends with a dragon?"

Tyler said, "Yeah, and named it Kelly, for some reason."

The dragon blew a jet of flame. The boat shot out of the fireball and rocketed across the width of the pond with great speed, only stopping when it hit the far shore.

The girl squealed and clapped her hands. "You made my boat go! Oh, Kelly, you're my best friend. I love you." She hugged the dragon's ankle, the closest part to her. The dragon looked down and made a terrifyingly deep grunt, but made no move against the girl.

Gary said, "Okay, here's the plan. You grab the kid and drag her away. Her kicking and screaming will distract the dragon, and I'll pop up behind it and kill it."

"While the little girl watches?" Tyler asked.

"Unless you cover her eyes."

Tyler pictured it and shuddered. "I don't think I could do that."

Gary thought for a moment and said, "Yeah, I understand."

Tyler said, "Good."

Gary said, "You kill the dragon. I'll grab the girl."

"No. We have to make her choose to leave the dragon. Then we can take it out."

"We could wait until her back is turned, than zap her with some fire. Make her think Kelly did it."

Tyler pinched the bridge of his nose. "I have more than one problem with that idea. The first I'll bring up is that you shouldn't call it Kelly. Destroying a dragon is much, much easier emotionally than *killing Kelly*. The second is that we're trying to keep from upsetting the little girl, and setting her on fire is probably going to upset her."

Gary rolled his eyes. "It wouldn't be real fire. I'm not a monster! She'd just think she was burning, and feel like she was burning. You know what, forget I brought it up."

"Gary. There has to be a simpler way to get the girl away from the dragon than to frame the dragon for a crime it didn't commit."

"It always works in the movies."

"No, it never works in the movies. The person who gets framed is always vindicated, and the person who did the framing ends up dead or in jail, because they're the bad guys. We aren't bad guys. I don't care how much black you wear."

"Okay, okay. Fine. How would good guys handle this, Tyler?"

"They might actually go talk to the girl. Introduce themselves. Explain that it isn't safe to have the dragon here, and that we can take it somewhere it will be safer for everyone."

"So, good guys lie to children?"

"Everybody lies to children, even their parents. The day a child realizes that is the day they start becoming an adult."

"Fair enough." Gary got up to his hands and knees. "Better get to it, then. The girl's not going to lie to herself."

Gary stood up, thought for a second, and then changed his artificial skeleton leg to look fully intact. Then he scrambled over the crest of the hill and carefully stepped down a part of the eroded-dirt cliff face that wasn't quite as steep. After two steps, the ground gave way beneath him. The girl and her dragon watched silently as Gary slid down the remaining ten feet on his rear.

Gary smiled and said, "Hello, little girl."

The dragon watched. The girl said nothing.

Gary stood up, beat the dust out of his robe as best he could with one hand, and said, "Uh, sorry to sneak up on you like that."

The girl said, "You're not a very good sneaker."

"No," Gary chuckled. "I guess not. Anyway, I wanted to talk to you about your dragon."

"I'm not supposed to talk to strange men."

"Ah. Very good. You shouldn't talk to strange men. I'll introduce myself. I'm Gary."

"You're strange, Gary."

The girl looked up, obviously noticing the sound of muffled laugher coming from the crest of the hill. Gary pretended not to hear it.

Gary forced a smile. "I couldn't help but notice your dragon."

"His name is Kelly. He's my best friend." She hugged the dragon's scaly leg. Gary noticed that her eyes moistened slightly as she looked up at him and said, "I love Kelly, and he loves me. He'll cook you alive if you try to hurt me."

Gary said, "I would never hurt a sweet little girl like you."

"Kelly'll cook you even faster if you try to hurt him."

Gary could see that the girl was getting upset. He remembered from his childhood that a kid's emotions have a kind of momentum. When a child starts working themselves up, you have to make them as calm as possible, as fast as possible, or else they will whip themselves into a day-ruining frenzy that will remain long after the actual cause of their unhappiness is gone.

An object in motion stays in motion. A child who's upset stays upset.

"I'm not here to hurt Kelly," Gary lied. "I'm here to help. See, I'm from a town far away that was   attacked by dragons."

"Kelly didn't do it!" the girl said, tears now rolling down her face. "Why are you blaming Kelly? He hasn't hurt anyone, much."

"I . . . much? Um, I know Kelly didn't do it. I was there—I saw it. Kelly wasn't there. I'm sorry. Come on. Don't cry. I hate to see a little girl cry."

"Then go away," the girl sniffed.

Gary said, "I'm here to help Kelly. I see I've made you unhappy. I'm sorry. I'm going to sit here, and shut up until you calm down."

The girl instantly started crying, shouting, and advancing on Gary. "Don't tell me to calm down! I don't gotta do what you say! You're not my dad! You're just some dumb guy who fell down the hill!"

She stood a few feet away now, and because Gary was seated on the ground, he had to look up at her.

"I know I'm not your father. Please don't cry. I know Kelly's your friend, and I know he didn't attack that town. But some people are mad because other dragons did, and they blame all dragons."

"Why? Why would they blame all of the dragons?"

"They don't know dragons as well as you or I do."

The girl was still crying, but she seemed at least willing to listen. "What do we do? How can we protect Kelly?"

"That's why I'm here. I'm looking for . . ." Gary paused and looked up at the dragon, "gentle, friendly dragons, like Kelly."

"Why?" the girl sobbed. "What are you gonna do to him?"

"I'm not going to do anything to him. I just want to take him somewhere safe. That's all."

The girl's sobbing slowed. She looked at Gary and said, "Really?"

"Yes."

"You just want to take him somewhere safe?"

"Yes."

"And you won't hurt him?"

"I won't hurt him."

"Where is this place? What's it like?"

Gary said, "Oh, it's . . . it's wonderful! It's a big farm, on an island, far away, with fields, and grass, and wide-open patches of sky for Kelly to play in, and other gentle dragons for Kelly to make friends with, and he'll be fed and looked after for the rest of his life."

"That sounds lovely."

"It does. It is!"

The girl smiled. "When can we go?"

Gary said, "I'm sorry, but you can't come. It's only for dragons."

The girl exploded into loud wailing sobs. Gary looked at her, then turned, and, at the crest of the hill, saw Tyler smiling broadly and giving a double thumbs-up.

19.

Honor walked the winding forest road home, only slowing slightly as darkness began to fall. Runt trotted along beside her, perfectly matching Honor's speed.

"I see you slowing down, Runt," Honor said. "That's all right, but we're safe. Safer than we were in town, at least. Remember what father always said: *It's wise to fear animals, but animals fear you back. People won't always show you that courtesy.*"

Their pace slowed further when they approached Kludge's camp. It was getting late. The sun had not fully set, but with the tall tree coverage, it might as well have. Honor had expected to hear the awful, tortured sounds and blood-curdling shrieks that Kludge and the Bastards generated when they had finished doing violence for the day and turned their attention to making their music, but the woods were strangely quiet. This scared her more than the terrible music would have, because if the Bastards weren't making music, then they were doing something else, and she didn't think she wanted to know what.

Only as she drew alarmingly close to the camp did she start to see or hear anything. She heard grunts of exertion, occasional shouts of encouragement, and far more frequent cries of fear. She saw the trees painted with staccato bursts of orange light that she now recognized all too well as coming from dragon fire.

Honor hunched over to make herself even smaller. She and Runt kept to the far edge of the road, ready to dart into the woods at a moment's notice if they thought they were being pursued. She always worried when she passed Kludge's camp, but at least it was dark, just dark enough that she thought she might not be spotted.

As they rounded the corner, she could see that she probably wouldn't have to put quite as much energy into sneaking as she'd feared. Kludge and the Bastards' attention was fully occupied.

Several of them were pulling mightily on ropes, leaning far over, putting all of their weight into simply standing their ground. The other ends of the ropes were tied around various parts of a horned dragon.

The dragon was certainly stronger than any one man, probably stronger than all of the Bastards put together. The fact that the Bastards had enjoyed any success in subduing the beast at all would have been a testament to the power of coordination and teamwork—if the Bastards had worked as a coordinated team. Instead, their ropes looped around whatever part of the dragon they'd been able to lasso, and they each pulled in opposite directions, accidentally leaving the dragon no efficient means of pulling away, as no one direction was "away."

The whole chaotic mess probably still wouldn't have worked if Kludge himself hadn't managed to get his rope looped and cinched tight around the dragon's mouth. The dragon couldn't open its jaws. That meant it couldn't bite, and when it tried to breathe fire, two intense jets of flame shot out of its nostrils at forty-five-degree angles, illuminating the forest and confusing the dragon, but missing the rope and its attackers entirely.

Honor crept along the edge of the woods, as far from the action as she could, but she never fully took her eyes off the fight. She had no love for Kludge and his stooges. She wasn't fond of dragons either. Being a decent person, she had a natural tendency to feel sympathy for any dumb animal caught in a bad situation, but that described all of the participants in this conflict.

One of the men was shouting, "Oh, no. This is bad! It's stronger than us! What'll we do!?"

Kludge bellowed, "Shut up, Heel-Kick! We'll take this critter down yet! Stretch, Gripper, make sure you're pulling opposite directions. Pounder, L.L., you do the same."

One of the men shouted, "Why don't you pull opposite to Pounder? Why do I have to?"

Kludge said, "Because I'm going to be too busy punching you in the face for questioning me if you don't shut up, Long Lobes! Only Donnie, you'll . . . whoa!"

The Bastards pulled the horned dragon in six different directions, using six different ropes, but only one of those ropes was looped around its head. While six of the Bastards all teamed up against the dragon's lower body, Kludge fought its head and neck alone.

The dragon whipped its head around at the end of its powerful serpentine neck. Kludge lifted off the ground and swung back and forth like a pendulum but kept his grip, even as he bashed sideways into Pounder.

The two of them lay groaning for a second, then Pounder gasped, "Sorry I got in your way, boss."

Kludge just had time to grunt, "Watch it next time," then he was yanked away again. The dragon threw Kludge as far as he could in one direction and watched him slam to the ground, then threw him the other direction, just to watch him come crashing down again.

"Everybody, pull as hard as you can," Kludge shouted. "Only Donnie, you let go of your rope and climb up on its neck. Try to weigh it down."

Only Donnie, the smallest of the Bastards, said, "Yes, Boss!" He turned to Gripper, the largest Bastard aside from Kludge, and said, "You heard Kludge. Climb up on its neck!"

Gripper said, "Done," and started pulling himself hand over hand toward the struggling dragon.

Kludge shouted, "That's not what I said to—" then got yanked through the air again.

Gripper reached the dragon's leg and climbed on, leaving his rope unmanned. This caused an imbalance in the forces pulling on the dragon, which in turn caused the dragon to spin. It rotated slowly at first, allowing Gripper the time needed to make his way to the dragon's neck, but the other Bastards all ran in orbit of the dragon, trying to get it under control.

Heel-Kick shouted, "Oh no! We're losing it! We're losing it!"

Their running caused them to exert less force on the ropes, which allowed the dragon to speed up. Soon, the dragon spun quickly in place, the Bastards ran around it as fast as they could, Gripper had his arms wrapped around the dragon's neck, trying desperately not to lose his grip, and Kludge hung from the end of the rope and swung around in a circle like he was riding a deranged carnival ride.

Heel-Kick shrieked, "Oh no! I'm going to be sick!"

Gripper slid up the dragon's neck, onto its head. His feet swung outward, and his body lay between the dragon's horns, over its eyes, and onto its nose. "I ain't letting go."

The dragon let out a burst of fire through its nostrils, which hit Gripper in the pelvic region. Gripper let go.

As he flew outward, Gripper managed to grab Kludge's rope. He slid down the rope and into Kludge.

As in any group, some of the Bastards were faster runners than others. As they were running in a circle, this meant that after only two revolutions the men running around the dragon were bunched up in a group. It only took a few more steps before they tripped each other and fell over, but they kept their grips on the ropes.

Their ropes wrapped around the dragon's legs, and the resistance of the men sliding across the ground stopped the dragon's rotation and brought Gripper and Kludge to the ground in a heap. The Bastards rose woozily to their feet and started pulling on their ropes again.

Kludge left his rope to Gripper, walked over to Only Donnie, and punched him in the side of the head. Only Donnie fell to the ground. Kludge picked up Only Donnie's rope and started pulling.

"What was that for?" Only Donnie asked. "I didn't do it!"

"That's right," Kludge said. "I told you to do something, and you didn't do it."

Honor was so intent on watching the fight that she nearly tripped over Runt, who had stopped walking and faced away from the battle, staring into the woods, quietly growling. Honor crouched and petted Runt, trying to calm her into silence, but Runt's growling continued, and the little dog's attention remained locked on a specific patch of darkness beyond the tree line. Honor tried to pick Runt up, but she squirmed and dodged, making it clear that if she had her way, all four of her paws would stay on the ground, and that dark void in the woods would continue to get growled at.

Honor squinted into the woods but she couldn't see a thing, until the dragon fighting the Bastards made another attempt to breathe fire. The twin fireballs ascended quickly, briefly bathing the woods in an orange glow, creating two sets of quickly shifting shadows behind every branch and leaf, illuminating the dragon hiding among the trees less than ten feet from where Honor stood.

Of course, the instant Honor saw the dragon, she moved. She leapt several feet back, stumbled, and fell on her rear in the middle of the road. The dragon stuck its head out of the trees. Honor silently thanked Hubert for giving her his magical idol. Runt got between Honor and the dragon, growling louder than ever.

The dragon looked down at Runt and Honor, then looked up, toward the other dragon, still struggling with Kludge and his friends, and quickly withdrew its head back into the cover of the woods. Runt's growling grew a bit more confident.

The dragon's scared, she thought. *Not of Runt, but I won't tell Runt that. If the dragon is scared, that means that dragons can be hurt, and if they can be hurt, they can be beaten. Beaten as in defeated, not beaten as in mistreated, though that's probably possible, too. And if they can be mistreated, they can be treated well. If you treat a dragon well, could you tame it? Maybe even train it? If animals as fierce as bears and bulls can be trained, why not a dragon?*

Of course, Honor didn't know that the training often starts when the animal is young, not fully grown. She also didn't know that Jeff conjured the dragons into existence less than a week before, so they were, in effect, still quite young.

Occasionally, ignorance works in one's favor.

Honor reached into her bag and pulled out one of the scones she had packed that morning for when she and Sonny got hungry. As it happened, Sonny ended up in no condition to eat, and seeing him get that way had caused Honor to lose her appetite.

She broke off a large piece of scone and held it out in front of her. She waited, motionless, for another plume of fire, just to make sure the hiding dragon saw her and the food she offered. After a burst of flame, Honor placed the scone on the ground and stepped away.

Runt started to go for the piece of scone herself, but Honor held her back, lest the dragon get the wrong idea about what was being offered as a snack. Runt whined and squirmed, but stopped when the dragon again extended its head from the tree line. The dragon sniffed at the scone, ate it, and receded back into the dark.

Honor placed another piece of the scone in the same spot, but this time only backed about half as far away as she had before. She didn't have to restrain Runt to keep her from making an attempt at the scone herself.

The dragon stuck its head out, more slowly this time, eyeing Honor warily. It ate the scone, then kept its head out in the open. Honor rewarded its bravery with more scone. She considered trying to pet it, but then both she and the dragon were startled by Kludge shouting, "You there! Girl!"

The dragon disappeared back into the brush. Honor turned around to face Kludge.

"What did you do?" Kludge shouted, still pulling on his rope with all of his might. It was said in an angry, accusatory tone, because it was said by Kludge, but Honor also heard a hint of awe and confusion in among the normal baseline hostility.

Honor said, "What?"

"How did you get that dragon to come out like that?" Kludge asked, between grunts of exertion.

"I work with animals."

Kludge screwed his face up in intense effort. He seemed to be having some sort of internal struggle. Finally, he asked, "Could you help us with this?"

After a moment, he added, "Please?"

After another moment, in a wrong-headed effort to further ingratiate himself, he added, "Girl?"

Honor said, "Maybe, but first, I have two questions. What are you going to do with the dragon once you have it calmed?"

Kludge said, "I plan to use it to make the wizards sorry they were ever born."

Honor smiled. "Second question. Do any of you Bastards know anything about baking?"

20.

At first, the man knew only one thing: his back hurt.

He flexed his shoulders, and in doing so, learned two other things: that he was lying on his belly, and that his back hurt worse when he flexed his shoulders.

He remembered a dragon threatening his town. He remembered he and his friends using their bows and fire-tipped arrows to threaten it right back. He remembered a wizard, floating in air, telling them to stop. The wizard used his magic to make their arrows fly back over their own heads and hit them in the back. After that, all he could recall was a blur of pain and panic, ending with another wizard, a lady wizard, flying in and casting some sort of spell that made the world go dark.

And now he was here.

He opened his eyes and instantly became disoriented. His brain struggled to make sense of what he saw. When it did, it struggled to convince itself that it was mistaken.

He was lying on some sort of table with his head turned to the side, in a room filled with flames. His only company was two demons, both unmistakably female, and just as unmistakably evil. They were clad in a red, shiny material, as if instead of clothing, they wore a glossy layer of liquid blood. Both wore red masks that covered the area around their eyes. Long, pointed red horns protruded from their hair, and long whip-like tails waved and swirled in the air behind them hypnotically.

"He's waking up," one of the she-demons said.

The other hissed, "Yessssss. Sssplendid."

The demons crept in closer.

"Tell us your name."

"Richard. My name is Richard!"

One of the she-demons barked, "Correct! We are tesssssssting you, *Richard*, to ssssee if you are an honesssst man."

Both of the demons spoke strangely. One elongated all of her S sounds into hissing noises. The other spoke slowly, in a deep voice, and with an accent Richard had never heard before.

"I am," Richard cried. "I try to be!"

One demon said, "Exssssellent!"

"Good, very good," the other agreed. "So tell us honestly, *Richard*, do you have any allergies?"

"Allergies?" Richard didn't know how to answer. He had never heard the word.

"Do any plants or animals make you feel sick, or make you sneeze?"

"No."

"Okay. Good. Thank you."

The other demon cackled and said, "You have been ssssent here for your ssssinssss, *Richard*. Thissss issss your reward for a life missssspent."

The other demon moved in even closer, and used some satanic device to peer into Richard's eyes. She asked, "Have you been sick recently?"

"Is it a sin to be sick?"

"No, but lying to me about it would be."

"A sssssin mosssst heinousssss!" the second demon agreed.

"No, I haven't been sick in a long time! I'm healthy as an ox! I swear it!"

The demon peering into his eyes said, "Good."

The other said, "We are not assssking you about your ssssinssss out of ignoranccccce. We know your ssssinssss already. The lisssst issss far to long for me to . . . lisssst."

The other demon smirked, and said, "Sssssmooth."

"SSSShut up."

"Tell us, *Richard,* do you have any other pain, besides your back?"

"No."

The hissing demon said, "Not yet, at leassssssst."

The other said, "Only a couple more questions. Have you chewed on any willow bark recently?"

"No."

"Do you have any loose teeth?"

The hissing demon asked, "What doesssss that have to do with anything?"

"They can be a choking hazard during the procedure."

"No," Richard wailed. "Please don't choke me with my own teeth!"

The demon with the accent said, "We won't! We won't. We're giving you a second chance. We won't hurt you."

The other demon cackled. "But we might, ssssomeday. If you don't change your wayssss, we will bring you right back here and choke you with your teeth, then ssssstrangle you with your own tongue . . . ssssomehow!"

"Yes, like my friend said, *somehow.* But you can prevent that. Go back to your life. Be a good man. Treat others well. Take it easy for a while. No heavy lifting for at least three weeks. And avoid tobacco products. Do all that, and we shouldn't see you here again."

"He'ssss from a time hundredssss of yearssss before tobacco issss introducccced from the New World."

"Oh," the non-hissing demon said, "that should make that easier then. Any questions, Richard?"

Richard shook his head.

The demon said, "All right then," put her hand on his head, and swiped her finger in the empty air, a streamer of light trailing from her fingertip. Richard fell into a deep sleep.

Louiza removed her hand from the patient's head and tapped at a couple more selections in the Atlantis interface. The light in the room went from red to white, and the projected flames faded away. Their tails continued whipping and swirling behind them, as they were controlled by a separate algorithm. She pulled off her mask and said, "One down, twenty-five to go. Laid it on a bit thick, didn't you?"

Brit the Elder removed her own mask. "We're supposed to be demons, and this is supposed to be hell. The whole point is to make it unpleasant for them. That way we can ask them your questions, their pain will make sense to them, and we can maybe con them into being better people when they get back. The last thing we want is for any of these guys to go back to their normal lives thinking, *Hell wasn't so bad. Sure it was hot, but the people were nice. It's like a subterranean Orlando, Florida.*"

"But strangling him with his own tongue?"

"Yeah," Brit the Elder admitted. "That got a bit dark, but I was just trying to compensate for these ridiculous demon costumes."

Louiza glanced at Brit the Elder and said, "What's wrong with them? I think you look good."

"I do look good. So do you."

"Thank you."

"You're welcome, but that's not the point. We're sorceresses. We could make ourselves look like actual demons."

"Actual demons," Louiza said. "What do *actual demons* look like, Brit?"

"Okay, yes, you're right. There are no *actual* demons, but if there were they wouldn't dress like . . ." Her voice trailed off as she looked down at her tight red pleather catsuit and matching patent-leather pumps, then sighed, "I'm trying hard not to make a Bananarama reference here."

"You dated Phillip for a long time, didn't you?"

"Depending on how you look at it, I'm still dating him."

"That's true," Louiza said. "I never thought about that. You can't just put the relationship behind you. You have to watch your younger self date him. That's gotta be bad."

"Not as bad as you think. Sometimes watching them reminds me why we were together in the first place. Other times watching them reminds me why we aren't together right now. And when I'm mad at Brit the Younger I can always torture her by bringing up some of my juicier memories about their love life."

"Ooh! Like what?"

"I'm not going to tell you. They're juicy memories about my love life, too. I do have some sense of propriety, which brings us back to these ridiculous sexy demon costumes, which I'll remind you, is what was written on the packages. *Sexy Demon Costume.* We're two intelligent women. Why are we dressing like this?"

"Because we were in a hurry, and I didn't see the point in wasting time reinventing the wheel when demon costumes for adult women were easy to find. Also, because it's fun."

21.

Martin and Phillip sat in the cave, using a chunk of golden I beam as a bench. They watched the dragons and discussed their poor decisions.

"Pressuring Jeff to make the dragons better without offering to help was wrong," Martin said.

"Giving him the job of creating the dragons in the first place was a bad move," Phillip said. "Sure, he had the expertise, but he was also the one who had to be rescued after Todd dropped him off of a cliff. He was bound to take training for self-defense too seriously."

"Yeah, we should've just fought each other for practice. Just, you know, we all get together, pick teams, and fight, like a magical version of flag football. Say, do kids in Europe and England play flag soccer?"

"No. We just played what you call soccer. You don't need body armor and a trauma specialist on hand to play the full version of our game. That's why we love it."

Martin said, "I think that's also the reason Americans don't. Anyway, that's how we should've handled the self-defense training. The dragons were an unnecessary complication."

Phillip nodded. "Agreed. And, now that I think about it, splitting up to get rid of the dragons wasn't necessary either. We're time travelers. We could have all just swarmed the dragons in each location, then traveled back in time to the same moment at the next place where dragons had appeared. In essence, we all would have taken out all of the dragons at the same time, everywhere. No matter how comfortable we get with the idea that we can travel through time, our brains just aren't designed to work that way. It runs counter to our instincts."

The two looked off into the middle distance for a moment. Then Martin said, "Also, assuming that the dragons needed food was wrong. Sure, we'd seen them eating, but they aren't biological. There's no reason to believe that they'll eventually have to go outside to eat. Sure, they *should* need food, but they should also die when their heads are cut off. I guess they just eat when they're bored and there's food handy. I've certainly been guilty of that."

"Yes, you're right, of course. And creating that massive pile of hay just outside the door was folly as well. They already knew that all of the food in the world was outside. Putting another pile of food outside with it wasn't much of an added inducement. And even if it had been, the goal looks like a big blue disk, so putting it up over the cave exit was never going to make the dragons walk through. It just looked to them like we'd sealed them in with a big blue window."

"Yeah, I think the key is to get them moving so fast that they can't stop before they go through the goal."

Phillip screwed his face up in deep concentration. After several seconds of intense thought, he said, "They probably eat grass not because they need it, but because sheep eat grass and they have some sheep instincts, yes?"

Martin said, "Yes. We think."

Phillip smiled. "Okay. What else do sheep want? More to the point, what do they want badly enough to run to get it?"

"I dunno, what?"

Phillip sat a little taller, proud of the insight he was about to share. "They want to not get eaten."

"You're saying that sheep will run to *not* get *eaten*."

"Well, I wouldn't put it that way."

"Yes you would. You would and you did. You put it exactly that way. *What will sheep run to get? To get not eaten!*"

"Okay, fine, but you see what I mean?"

"Yes," Martin said, "Once I deciphered your sentence structure."

"The point is, if we can trigger the sheep-like fear instincts in the dragons—"

"The point," Martin interrupted, "is that you are an Englishman. Your people invented English! And here you are, being corrected by an American. A less-educated American! How will you ever face your fellow Englishmen again?"

"The same way we always face each other, with a hint of embarrassment."

Martin said, "Okay. So what do we do?"

"We put something in here with them. Something that will cause them to flee at great speed out into the tunnel, where a goal is waiting in the dark for them."

Phillip walked out into the tunnel and put up an opaque force field to keep light out, and to keep Kneath from accidentally entering the cave and walking into the goal, which he placed a bit deeper into the cave. Phillip returned to the cave's main chamber. He found Martin, still sitting on the I beam, fiddling with his smartphone.

Martin said, "It's just about ready." He placed his phone back into the silver-painted, wooden box he carried it in. "The animation's going to be pretty rough, and the sound is just what I could find on short notice, but if the dragons have the intelligence of sheep, it should do the job. You ready?"

"Very much so," Phillip said.

Martin pressed a finger to the screen of his phone. In the distance, behind the dragons, beyond the stacks of solid gold tiles, shingles, planks, and I beams, at the very back of the chamber, opposite the entrance, a giant wolf materialized.

The wolf stood thirty feet tall at the shoulder, with matted gray fur and beady gray eyes. It snarled, revealing fearsome gray teeth.

Martin said, "I didn't have time to paint it."

The wolf looked hunkered down, as if ready to pounce. At first it didn't move. After several seconds, it still hadn't moved.

Phillip asked, "Is it going to move?"

"Yeah. I hoped the sight of it would freak the dragons out, but they haven't noticed it yet. I guess we'll have to get their attention."

"Yes," Phillip agreed.

"But before we do, I want to remind you, I didn't have a lot of time."

Phillip nodded impatiently. "Yes, I understand. Just do it."

Martin poked at his smartphone again. At the far side of the chamber, the wolf's mouth opened. It didn't hinge down from the back, like a real wolf's jaw would. Instead, the entire lower mandible slid straight down in one piece, like the chin of an old-fashioned ventriloquist's dummy. The jaw lurched up and down in time with a loud, regular, rhythmic barking sound that seemed more appropriate to a small terrier than an immense wolf.

As pathetic as the animation and sound were, they succeeded in drawing the attention of the dragons. All four of them jumped, startled from their slumber by the ridiculous barking. They turned and saw the artificial wolf. For a moment, save for the barking and the badly animated jaw movements, the world was all silence and stillness. Then for quite some time, the opposite was true.

Four full-sized dragons panicking in an enclosed space, flying at top speed in a tight, tangled mess while roaring at the top of their lungs and breathing fire at the same time, would have been quite chaotic enough on its own. Adding in tons of solid-gold building materials flying in every direction, the sounds of Martin and Phillip shouting in surprise and alarm, and the rhythmic barking of the fake wolf resulted in a feast for the senses that left said senses feeling overstuffed, and fearing they may soon be sick.

Martin and Phillip dove to the ground behind the I beam they had earlier used as a bench. Martin hastily threw up a force field just in time to deflect a shower of glittering gold doorknobs, knocked their way accidentally by some passing dragon's tail.

Phillip huddled in a fetal position with his arms covering his head and his eyes squeezed shut. He lay that way for a moment, his only information from the outside world coming in through his ears. He listened, then asked, "Martin, is that 'Jingle Bells'?"

"What?" Martin shouted, trying to be heard over the roaring, and the crackling of fire, and the crash of precious metal being thrown against the walls.

Phillip crawled closer to Martin, and as loud as he could, asked, "Is that wolf singing 'Jingle Bells'?"

Martin smiled and shouted, "Yes. I thought you'd find it amusing."

"I might," Phillip admitted, "if I weren't terrified."

"Yeah. Timing is everything."

Martin and Phillip carefully peered over the edge of the I beam. The force field would protect them from flying gold, and from the dragons' fire, but the dragons themselves would sail right through it. Besides, just like some movies are scary enough that they're best viewed through a protective screen of fingers, the sight Martin and Phillip were witnessing was best viewed while peeking out from behind something heavy.

One of the dragons started at the far end of the cavern and flew directly at the wolf in as menacing a manner as it could muster, blowing a huge ball of fire before it. As large as the cave was, the dragon could only get in three good flaps before it came very close to the wolf and lost all of its nerve. The dragon turned, swooping away, putting as much distance as it could between itself and the wolf without actually leaving the chamber. The dragon stopped short of striking the wall. Its wing clipped a shelf, sending several thousand solid-gold plumbing elbows flying. The dragon turned away from the wall, looked at its surroundings, saw the wolf at the far end of the cavern, and decided to attack, starting the whole cycle over again. All this happened while the three other dragons went through the exact same series of steps at their own differing paces, from different angles, while the wolf stood motionless and barked the tune of "Jingle Bells."

Phillip said, "I thought they'd want to escape."

"I think they do," Martin said, straining to be heard.

"What?" Phillip said, straining to hear.

"I said, I think they do want to escape."

"Then why don't they? The tunnel out is right there."

Martin said, "I think it's like a fish trap. Fish swim in through a hole, find themselves in an enclosed space, freak out, and can't find the hole to swim out again. Fish aren't very smart."

"So how do we stop this?"

"Show 'em the exit."

Martin activated the voice amplification spell, flew over to hover next to the tunnel opening, motioned toward it like a magician displaying the spot where his assistant had just been, and said, "Ahem!"

All four dragons took notice, altered their course, and within seconds had settled into a new cycle of attacking the wolf, then flying across the cavern to breathe fire at Martin before repeating the process again.

22.

The fight left both Scotsmen exhausted. Kyle's burly frame heaved with each breath. His flaming red hair was matted with sweat. Leslie seemed to be in as bad or worse shape. His slightly smaller frame heaved every bit as violently as Kyle's, and his slightly less red hair was just as matted.

The fight was over, but the hostility was not. The two men stood, grasping each other's shoulders, supporting one another, but whenever one of them managed to regain some strength, they would use it to shove, insult, or, on one occasion, pinch the other.

"Enough," Jock, their leader, an imposing mass of blond hair, thick muscle, and woolen clothing shouted. "This was good fun at first, but it's gone on far too long. After you volunteered so bravely, and fought side by side so valiantly, it makes me sick to see the way you've embarrassed yourselves and your families by not only fighting each other in front of these ladies who have saved us, but by doing it so badly!"

Kyle and Leslie turned to face Brit and Gwen but still kept an arm around each other's shoulders for support.

"He's right," Kyle said. "We've behaved shamefully. I hope you can forgive us."

"Agreed," Leslie said. "It's been a pitiful display, and one of which we are not proud."

Gwen said, "It's all right."

Leslie said, "You're kind. Far too kind, but the idea that you had to witness us grappling in the dirt grieves me to no end."

"And the language we used," Kyle said. "Words that should never be said in the vicinity of any lady, let alone two ladies to whom we owe our lives. It will pain me to my dying day."

Brit said, "The important thing is that it's over now."

Kyle said, "True, good woman, true. It's for the best that you'll no longer be subjected to the undignified spectacle of me losing my temper over my supposed friend's unfaithful nature."

"Aye," Leslie said, "And we can all be happy that your delicate, ladylike ears will no longer be sullied by my lifelong mate's pitiful squealing as I grind his face into the dirt."

And with that, the fight began anew.

Jock said, "Come, Mungo. Let us break the lads up. This serves no purpose."

"Indeed."

Mungo reached down with one of his immense man paws and grabbed Leslie by the scruff of the neck, then pulled him away from Kyle. Jock placed himself between the fighting men and pushed Kyle back, away from Leslie.

"Stop this," Jock grunted. "This is folly. Can you not see that?"

Kyle struggled and strained to break free of Jock's grip, reaching out toward Leslie. "Then let me go, Jock, and I promise to end it quickly."

The two of them grappled with each other for several seconds, but Kyle seemed to lose enthusiasm, and soon stopped.

Mungo laughed as he stood, still holding Leslie by the back of the neck. Leslie did not fight back. Instead he seemed to simply hang from the larger man's grip in a sort of mellow stupor.

"Finally got him under control, Jock?" Mungo asked. "I was afraid I might have to step in and scruff Kyle as well, but I chose to give you a chance, and in time you finally accomplished what I was able to do with one hand."

Jock said, "You're by far the largest of us, Mungo, and you chose to restrain the smallest of us. Don't act surprised that it required less effort when that was clearly your intention from the start."

"Are you doubting my courage, Jock?"

"Let's just say that I'm not doubting your craftiness, Mungo."

Mungo let go of Leslie and advanced on Jock. "Perhaps I can think of something equally crafty to do with your vertebrae, Jock. Perhaps I'll tie your spine into a necklace for Coira to wear to your funeral."

Leslie quickly snapped out of his stupor and tried to hold Mungo back, but only got dragged behind the larger man. Jock turned and reached for Mungo, despite Kyle's attempts to restrain him.

Brit shouted, "Stop it! If we'd known you idiots were going to try to kill each other, we'd have just let the dragons do it instead of saving you."

"Totally," Gwen said. "It would have been faster, easier, and less embarrassing for your wives."

All four of the men turned toward Brit and Gwen with hurt and anger in their eyes, but stopped, looked at each other, and relaxed.

The men all apologized, both to Gwen and Brit, and to each other.

Gwen said, "Before you start fighting over which of you is most sorry for fighting, why don't you tell us how you ended up out here by yourselves, fighting so many dragons."

Jock said, "We all hail from the same village. A lovely wee place called Cryb. This morning, Lagan, another of the village folk, came into town telling stories about seeing dragons. Lagan is a mate, and a good enough man, but he has the gift of gab and a taste for the drink."

"He gets drunk and makes stuff up," Gwen said.

"Aye," Jock said. "But he doesn't usually lie about anything dangerous, just his hunting skills and how far he can toss a caber. We decided to send a scout to confirm his story before we did anything drastic."

"And the scout confirmed his story?" asked Brit.

"Aye."

Gwen said, "So you did something drastic."

"Aye. The four of us volunteered to hunt and kill the dragons. It only made sense. We're young, brave, able-bodied, and we're experienced fighters who have each squared off many times against equally experienced foes."

"Each other," Brit said.

"Aye," Jock said. "We set out straightaway, and found the dragons with little trouble. But we were not prepared for the dragons' ferocity, and things were looking quite grim indeed until the two of you saved us."

Jock dropped to one knee and held his sword in front of him, with the point set in the ground so that the hilt formed a cross.

"I thank you for saving my life, and my friends' lives. I thank you not only for us, but for my beloved Coira, and my daughters Effie and Nessa. May they grow to be half the women you are."

Mungo, the largest of the men, followed suit, also dropping to one knee, though doing so merely lowered him to being just slightly below Gwen's and Brit's standing height. "Aye, and I thank you for my darling Grizel, and for my girls Jinny and Seonag, and my boy Torquil, who will all be told many times of your bravery and strength this day."

Kyle also knelt and said, "And for Morag and Rut."

Finally, Leslie said, "And for my betrothed, the lovely Donalda, whom I cherish more than my own life."

"But not more than Morag, it would seem," Kyle said.

Leslie remained on bended knee, but turned looked to Kyle, his long red curls whipping around his angry red face. "I'm beginning to regret I ever said a word to you about Morag."

"I regret that you ever said any word to me about Morag, or anything else!"

Leslie smiled, bitterly. "Well then, perhaps I should let my fists do the talking from now on!"

Brit said, "Thank you," in the tone of voice she usually employed to stop Phillip when he'd try to explain the plot of *Zardoz*. "We were happy to help."

Her intervention had the desired effect, temporarily ending the men's back-and-forth.

Gwen recognized what Brit had done. She'd had to perform a similar maneuver more than once when Martin started discussing the career of Bruce Campbell. She continued the diversion, saying, "Yes. And as much as we hate to leave your charming company, we have to go deal with those dragons before they try to roast someone else."

Jock rose to his feet and asked, "By *deal with*, do you mean kill? Is it your intention to hunt down and kill the dragons?"

Gwen said, "That's the plan."

Jock said, "If we may ask you to wait just a moment, my friends and I need to talk."

The four men huddled up and engaged in a great deal of impassioned mumbling. Gwen thought she could pick out the names of more than one of the Highlanders' wives and children. This did not surprise her.

The men separated. Jock bowed to Gwen and Brit and said, "We have discussed it, and we all agree that we cannot allow you to face the dragons alone."

Gwen said, "We didn't ask for your permission. We told you what's going to happen."

"Of course. We didn't mean to suggest otherwise. Another moment please?"

The Highlanders huddled and muttered again. This time the muttering took on a much more concerned tone. Among the mumbling, Gwen picked out different voices saying short sentences containing the name Morag at increasing volume until Jock said, "Enough!"

The huddle broke up. Jock said, "I apologize. I put that quite badly. You do not need our permission to do anything, and we wouldn't suggest otherwise. We not only respect women who are independent, some of us greatly prefer it."

Kyle and Leslie both nodded.

"Of course," Jock continued, "you are perfectly capable of hunting and killing the dragons, but you will find that trying to do it without us will be more difficult than you think."

"Why is that?" Brit asked.

"Because we're coming with you."

"And that'll make killing the dragons more difficult?" Gwen asked.

"No, the *killing the dragons* part should be easier with our help, but the *doing it without us* part will be well near impossible."

Gwen shook her head. "I'm sorry, but we can't let you come along."

Jock said, "We weren't asking for your permission."

Brit chuckled, and muttered, "Touché."

Jock stepped forward. "You see, ladies, you don't need our help, but I'm afraid that we need to help you. We swore an oath—"

"A sacred oath, sworn to God himself!" Mungo interrupted.

Jock continued, "To slay the dragons and keep our families safe. It is our duty—"

"Our sacred duty, conferred upon us by God himself!" Mungo interrupted.

"—to see it through to the end, no matter how difficult it is," Jock said, seeing his sentence through to the end, no matter how difficult it was. "It doesn't matter how valiant you two are, or how powerful with magic you may be, it would be a terrible disgrace on all of us to return, saying that we left you to do the dirty work for us. I could never face my sweet Coira again, nor look into the eyes of Effie or Nessa without feeling the shame of it."

Mungo said, "Nay, nor could I ever look at Grizel, or Seonag—"

"All right, fine," Brit said. "We get that this is important to you and all of your relatives. But why would you be so ashamed if we did this for you? Is it because we're women?"

The men blanched, looking genuinely hurt. Jock said, "I'm sorry, but you don't understand. It's not at all because you're women. It's because you're not us. We have to see this through. We all promised—"

Mungo shouted, "Promised God himself!"

"Okay! Yes! All right," Brit said. "You promised many people and supernatural entities that we need not list that you would kill the dragons, and you don't want to go back and tell them that you let someone else handle it. Is that right?"

Jock smiled and bowed. "That is correct."

Leslie said, "And the fact that you're ladies would be a tad embarrassing."

Jock gritted his teeth, bowed more deeply, and said, "Would you mind excusing us again?"

Brit and Gwen nodded.

The Highlanders huddled up again, but instead of talking, they all took turns slapping Leslie on the back of the head. Kyle took several turns.

23.

Gary lay on the crest of the hill, flushed and panting.

It was not a particularly tall hill, but it was steep, and it had put up a good fight.

The loose dirt had given way more than once during his climb. On one occasion, he grasped at a large weed sprouting out of the side of the hill, hoping to pull himself up Indiana Jones style. Then the weed tore loose from the soil, just like the weed had for Indy. Gary's arm shot backward until his clenched fist slammed into his forehead. His weight pitched backward, and he only managed to keep from falling by turning and sprinting all the way down the hill.

He went more slowly and carefully on his next try, and made it to the top. Then he lay on the ground panting while Tyler laughed.

"You think it's real funny," Gary said between breaths. "Don't you?"

"I do. I really do."

"You think you coulda done better?"

"At climbing, probably not. But I like to think that I would have remembered that we can fly. At least the girl isn't crying anymore. Watching you cheered her right up."

"Good. She'll be crying again soon enough. So, back to Plan A. You go grab her and run clear; I'll appear behind the dragon and take it out."

"No, Gary. I told you—we aren't going to do that."

"Do you have a better idea?"

"Yes," Tyler said. "I'll go reason with her."

"I already tried reasoning with her."

"Yes, and having me do it is a better idea."

Tyler stood up and looked down at the little girl and the dragon she'd named Kelly. They hadn't moved a muscle since Gary left them.

Tyler looked down at Gary and muttered, "Here's how a wizard does it." He raised his staff and floated forward silently, landing on the ground a nonthreatening ten feet in front of the girl.

Tyler smiled at the girl. She frowned at him.

Tyler smiled up at the dragon. It looked down at Tyler with an expression that seemed familiar, and definitely hostile, but hard for Tyler to place.

It's like it thinks I'm beneath contempt, and it really wants to eat me. Like I'm both food and garbage. Then it struck Tyler. *That's probably the expression I have on my face when I look at a Big Mac.*

Tyler said, "Hello. My name's Tyler. What's your name?"

The girl said, "I told your friend that I don't talk to strange men."

"Yes. That's very wise, but you see—"

"Yeah, your friend kept talking when I told him that, too. Your friend seemed really dumb, mister. My daddy says I shouldn't be friends with dumb people. He says that if your friends are dumb, you get dumb."

"There's probably some wisdom in that."

"How long have you been friends with him? A long time, I bet."

Five minutes later, Tyler stood up straight and tall, turned his back on the little girl and her dragon, and flew back to Gary's position with a look of dignified stoicism on his face. Gary had heard the entire conversation, and enjoyed every second of it.

As Tyler landed, Gary asked, "When she called you *Butt Brain,* do you think she meant that your brain is in your butt, or that your brain *is* a butt?"

"I hadn't given it much thought," Tyler said, through gritted teeth.

"But if you were to give it some thought, would you do it in your b—"

Tyler pointed his staff at Gary. The silver hood ornament wobbled in the air inches from Gary's face.

"Keep talking," Tyler said. "Say one more word. That's all the excuse I need."

Gary carefully pushed the hood ornament away from his face and smiled up at Tyler. "She's harder to deal with than we expected."

Tyler deflated. "Yeah. She's . . . she's a real pill. I had to leave before I did something I'd be ashamed of."

"And you're not ashamed of letting a little girl talk to you like that?"

"No. I'm not particularly proud of it either. We have to figure out how to get her away from that dragon."

Gary said, "I have an idea."

Tyler looked up hopefully and said, "Shoot."

"You go down there, grab the girl by the arm, and drag her away from the dragon."

Tyler looked away from Gary, disgusted, and mumbled, "Shoot."

"How much time are we going to waste getting rid of this dragon?"

"As much time as it takes to figure out a way that doesn't involve manhandling a child."

Gary shook his head. "So instead you're trying to think of a way to trick her."

"I'd like to walk away from this not feeling like a monster." Tyler stood up, beat the dust out of his red-and-purple-striped robe, straightened the matching hat, and said, "I'm going back in."

"What are you going to do?"

"I'm going to go lure her away from the dragon."

"How?"

"Somehow. I don't know. Just wait here and be ready to transport in behind that dragon as soon as she's far enough away."

Tyler pointed his staff and glided down the cliff face to a patch of ground near the pond's edge that he figured was far enough away to be safe for him and the girl when Gary lowered the boom.

Tyler forced a cheery look onto his face, and in a bright, friendly voice said, "Hello again."

The girl turned at the waist and craned her neck to glare sidelong at Tyler, and said, "Go away!"

"Now, now, there's no need to be rude."

"You're the one being rude," the girl shouted, "by bothering me when you know I don't want to talk to you, because you're stupid!"

Tyler dropped the cheery facade, but managed to maintain his temper. "There's no need for insults either."

"That's right! You should say you're sorry!"

"What for?"

"Insulting me! You called me rude, Butt Brain."

In his ear, Tyler heard Gary, talking to him through the battle comm. "She actually has a point, Tyler. Maybe you should apologize."

Tyler shook his head.

"Come on, Tyler. You know you've gotta."

Tyler shook his head again.

"What's the goal here?" Gary asked. "To make the girl admit she's wrong, or to get her away from the dragon so we can take it out and never see her again?"

Tyler clenched his jaw so hard he feared his teeth would crack. He parted his lips and grunted, "I'm sorry."

The girl smiled beatifically and said, "Apology accepted."

Tyler closed his eyes. *Gotta calm down. Gotta think rationally. Remember what the goal is here, just like Gary said. Wait, I'm following Gary's advice now? Is that really thinking rationally? Eh, first time for everything. Gotta get her away from the dragon. What can I use to draw her over? What does she like? Dragons! Making a second dragon seems counterproductive. She likes insulting me. Making me feel bad. Maybe I can use that.*

Tyler said, "I challenge you to a game."

The girl sighed heavily but asked, "What kind of game?"

"It's like Follow the Leader, but in reverse."

The girl thought a moment. "So, I don't follow the leader?"

"That's not what I mean."

"That'd just be me standing here watching you act like a fool."

"Yeah, that's not the game."

"Good, 'cause I'm already doing that."

Tyler said, "The way the game works is, whatever I do, you do the opposite. If I raise my left arm, you raise your right. If I take a step forward, you take a step back. We do that until you mess up, then you lead, and I follow, and we see who can go longest without making a mistake."

The girl said, "That's a dumb game. I don't wanna play."

"You're afraid you'll lose."

The girl looked disgusted, but said, "Fine." She stood and faced Tyler.

Tyler put down his staff, stood with his arms at his sides, and said, "Okay, starting now," and lifted his right arm. The girl lifted her left.

Tyler lifted his left arm. The girl lifted her right.

Tyler took a small step to the left. She took a small step to the right.

Tyler took a giant step backward. The girl took a giant step forward. The dragon stayed put.

Tyler took another giant step backward. She took another forward while the dragon didn't move.

Tyler lowered his right arm, and whispered, "How much farther?"

Gary said, "One more big step ought to do it."

Tyler took a large step backward. He felt the panicky sensation of his foot not finding ground where it thought it would. Then he felt his foot plunge into cold water, followed by soft mud. He waved his arms in an effort to stay upright, but in the end it only made a larger, more interesting splash as he fell backward into the pond.

He thrashed around for a few seconds, then stood up, still knee-deep in the cold, muddy water.

Tyler muttered, "She's far enough away. Make your move!"

Gary said, "Actually, she's still too close. When I said one more big step would do it, I meant it would drop you in the pond, and I was right!"

24.

Jeff and Roy watched the dragons creep toward the pile of apples. When the lead dragon looked ready to venture its first exploratory bite, Jeff took to the sky, pulling the apples along in his wake. He flew barely faster than a walking pace at first, watching as the horned dragon snapped its jaws at the empty space where the apples had been. The dragon stepped forward, then leapt forward, then ran, and finally took to the air. Soon, Jeff was flying backward, pointing his wand behind him at the flying pile of apples. Beyond it, he saw a parade of five dragons, flying in a loose single file line, slowly gaining on him.

Jeff needed to gauge his speed carefully, making sure that he kept the dragons close enough to not lose interest in the apples, but not so close that they ever caught up and discovered that the apples were an illusion. He also had to steer the whole processional in a large turn and then come back past Roy so he could place the goal, and do all of this while flying backward.

He managed the turn, and dropped altitude so that he passed Roy at a distance of about two hundred feet and a height of one hundred. He risked glancing away from the dragons long enough to see Roy standing with his staff at his side, making no effort to create a goal.

"What the hell?" Jeff yelled.

Roy shouted back, "I'm just enjoying the show."

Jeff led the dragons away, through a wide radius turn, and back past Roy, who still did nothing.

"Come on, man!" Jeff shouted.

Roy said, "Maybe next time!"

"Any time now, Roy," Jeff shouted as he passed his compatriot, still standing on the ground, refusing to create a goal in front of the lead dragon.

"I have an idea, kid. Back at Leadchurch, we beat the dragons eventually, but not until all the civilians had hidden indoors, right? So all any of them saw was us pretty much getting our butts handed to us."

"So?"

"So, we looked like a bunch of idiots. We can't just leave it like that. Word will get around. It's bad for business. We need to save face, do something to show we're in control so that when people hear about how we screwed up in Leadchurch they won't buy it. Right now, all of those people standing on the city wall are watching you lead these dragons around like a herd of baby ducks. It's impressive. So why end it?"

"You want me to showboat for the crowd?"

"Think of it as PR. The military has air shows. Why not us? My boy, you and those dragons are the wizards' Blue Angels."

"Okay, I get it. I guess there's no harm in putting on a little show before we take the dragons out. What should I do?"

Roy said, "I don't know. I'm not a dragon choreographer. Make something up. Just make sure it's fancy. And get in close to the crowd. Buzz them a couple times."

Jeff aimed himself in a direction parallel to the wall, at an altitude where he would not hit anything, and looked back over his shoulder so he could watch the dragons. He wasn't directly controlling the dragons, just the apples they chased, but he could use that to his advantage. He spun the tip of his wand in a slow, clockwise circle. The apples moved in proportion to the wand. The lead dragon followed the apples. The second dragon followed the first. The pattern continued through all five dragons, resulting in a graceful spiral.

Jeff spun the wand the other direction. The spiral reversed direction.

Jeff moved the wand up and down, and watched as a wave propagated through the tail of the last dragon, like a whip cracking.

Jeff stopped, hovering stationary above the ground and slowly spun, holding his wand out to the side. The apples and the dragons flew around him in a wide circle.

"Roy, are you seeing this?"

"Yeah, it's real impressive."

"I know, it's kinda like rhythmic gymnastics. You know, like in the Olympics."

Jeff experimented with making the dragons double back, trying to see how tight a turn they could manage. When he thought he had a good idea of their capabilities, he flew toward the wall.

As part of Jimmy's "civic renewal" program, back when he went mad with power, he put a protective wall around the entire city. He built it in solid gold, of course, because that way it matched the immense castle he also built. Anything else would have been gauche. Or, at least, more gauche.

The wall stood three stories tall and at least ten feet wide. The top of the wall teemed with people who had heard about the wizards and the dragons doing something and wanted to see for themselves.

Jeff flew straight toward the spectators, trailing the dragons behind him. He stopped, then brought the dragons around so that the far end of their circular course took them directly over the people's heads. The dragons were easily twenty feet above them, but the people still ducked and shrieked as they passed by.

Jeff turned around, swinging the dragons in a wide arc. He made the dragons fly in a loop, then nearly hit the wall before doubling back, then fly in an inverted loop, then over the wall and the crowd again.

Jeff brought the dragons to the point of the circle farthest from the wall and the crowd, then swung the wand and the apples up over his head. The apples traced a curved path over him and down toward the ground just inside the city wall. The dragons obediently followed.

As he turned back to execute the apples' recovery from the dive, he noticed that he had drifted a bit closer than he'd thought, but he wasn't worried about it. He made the apples pull up over the wall, back out into the open. The dragons followed the apples into the dive, but dropped behind the wall and did not come back out.

Jeff heard yelling. He quickly flew over the wall and looked down at the spot beneath where he'd last seen the dragons.

"Oh, fantastic," Jeff moaned. "Of all the places to put on our little air show, we pick a spot right next to the farmers' market."

Roy said, "I didn't know that Camelot has a farmers' market!"

"*Had,* Roy. Had."

25.

Bishop Galbraith slowly opened his eyes. At first he thought he was staring directly into the sun, flooding his eyes with blindingly powerful light. Then he feared that he had gone blind, and that his damaged eyes would only show him an unbroken field of white for the rest of his life.

He blinked several times, and saw the world go dark for a microsecond each time. He strained to roll his eyes downward and saw a blurry view of the side of his own nose. He puckered his mouth to the very limits of his strength in an attempt to see his lips until he heard a female voice say, "Okay, he's awake." He immediately relaxed his face muscles. He had established that he could see. Now he didn't want to look ridiculous.

Galbraith realized that the unbroken field of white light was actually an unbroken surface as white as milk, hanging above him. He could see a dim reflection of himself, a dark mass of leather and wool and hair with a wooden cross around his neck and an arrow sticking out of his leg. He puzzled over what this miracle material could possibly be until he saw the faces of two women, who approached either side of his bed and looked down at him.

Brit the Elder said, "Hello, Bishop Galbraith. Welcome."

Louiza asked, "How are you feeling?"

Galbraith asked, "Am I in heaven?"

Brit the Elder said, "No, Father, I'm sorry, but this isn't heaven."

Bishop Galbraith let out a long breath, then laughed. The two women looked at each other, confused.

Brit the Elder smiled at the incongruity of it. "You seem relieved."

Galbraith said, "Young lady, if heaven let someone like me in without asking some serious questions, then frankly I'd have to worry that it wasn't as hard to get in as I've been telling people."

"But how could you not be allowed into heaven? You're a bishop."

Galbraith laughed. "I wasn't born a bishop. A man can get into a lot of mischief before he joins the clergy. Sometimes, the night before he joins."

Brit said, "I see."

"Also, I didn't want to spend eternity in heaven with a burnt leg that has an arrow sticking out of it."

"Yes, about that. Does it hurt?" Louiza asked.

"It's burnt, and it has an arrow sticking out of it."

"Do you have pain anywhere else?"

"Not nearly as bad, but yes, my hands hurt."

Louiza took his hand in hers. "Do you have any idea why?"

"Yes," Galbraith said. "It's probably from slapping Sonny, one of the boys from my flock."

"With both hands?"

"Yes."

Brit asked, "Why were you slapping him?"

"He was on fire, and I wanted him to stop being on fire. I take a dim view of burning to death, as per the scriptures. Look, you're Brit, that wizard woman who is good friends with Phillip, aren't you?"

Brit the Elder winced, and said, "We prefer to be called sorceresses, or just wizards."

"And I prefer to be called either Bishop Galbraith or Your Excellency, but I didn't bother you about it when you called me Father, did I."

Brit blushed. "Of course, Your Excellency. Please forgive me."

"I might, after you tell me what this is all about."

"Dragons attacked Leadchurch. You got hurt. My friend's name is Louiza. She's a healer. She's going to tend to your wounds while you and I have a little talk."

Louiza shifted her gaze from the bishop's hands to his face, and said, "Good to meet you, Your Excellency. You have second-degree burns and some pretty bad bruises on your hands. You must have really been trying to put that fire out."

"He's a fine young man. There are others I might not have gone to that much effort for. Do you know how he is?"

Brit the Elder said, "If he was injured in the dragon attack, he should be all right. Nobody was killed. We've brought all of the injured here for healing. That's what I want to talk to you about."

"But first," Louiza said, "I'll need to cut your pants leg to get access to your wound. I hope that's not a problem, Your Excellency. We'll supply you with a new pair of pants before we send you back to your ti—" Louiza and Brit exchanged a look. Louiza said, "Town."

The bishop nodded. "That's fine, of course. Just don't make the new pants too nice. A clergyman shouldn't be dressed better than his flock."

Louiza nodded and got to work. Brit said, "About your flock, Your Excellency. We've been misleading some of them. The ones who got injured. We don't want them learning things that will needlessly confuse them. When we found you among the wounded, I decided it would be best to tell you the truth."

"Why?"

"Because you're a good man, and I didn't want to lie to you. Also, we thought you'd see through our lie anyway."

"How would you know? We've only met a few times, and Phillip did more talking than both of us put together."

Brit the Elder said, "I don't know you well yet, but in time I'll get to know you quite well, and we will be friends."

"How do you know that?"

Brit had a hard enough time discussing time travel with other wizards who had used it themselves. She didn't even want to try to explain it to a medieval clergyman. "I really can't say."

Louiza said, "Your Excellency, I'm going to numb your leg, then pull the arrow out now." She swiped her finger in the air, stabbed it forward a few times, then grasped the arrow and pulled it out of his leg wound with little resistance.

Galbraith said, "That didn't hurt at all. My burn doesn't hurt either, now that I think about it. How did you do that?"

Brit the Elder knew that simply saying *magic* wouldn't satisfy him, so she said, "I'm sorry, but we really can't tell you."

Galbraith looked at Louiza. "Well, no matter how you did it, I'm grateful. I don't recognize your accent. Where are you from?"

Brit the Elder knew that the answer was Brazil, which wouldn't exist as a nation-state until hundreds of years after Galbraith's death, and was on a continent Galbraith didn't know existed, so she said, "I'm sorry, Your Excellency, but we can't tell you that either."

"I thought you said you were going to tell me the truth," Galbraith snapped.

"Yes," Brit said, "But I didn't promise the whole truth."

Galbraith said, "You might think you're clever, but being tricky with your words just irritates people."

Louiza said, "I know, right? I've tried to tell her that. So has Brit."

"Wait," Galbraith said. "She's Brit, isn't she?"

"Yes, she is."

"So there's another wizard named Brit."

Brit the Elder said, "No. There isn't."

Brit cut in before Galbraith could react. "The point is, Your Excellency, the dragons that attacked Leadchurch were our fault. We wizards, that is. We didn't want them to attack, but it was our fault that they could. Thankfully, nobody died. We brought the wounded here so Louiza can tend to them. Right now, every wizard you know is out rounding up and dealing with the remaining dragons."

"Every wizard except you two," Galbraith said.

"Except Louiza," Brit the Elder said.

"Seriously. Don't ask," Louiza said, not looking up from her task of cleaning the bishop's burn.

Brit said, "Your Excellency, we needed to wake your people up to heal them, but we didn't want them to ask a lot of questions about where they are, or go back to Leadchurch with a lot of confusing stories they wouldn't understand. So, we've been pretending that this place is somewhere else. Somewhere they've heard of."

"Where?" Galbraith asked.

"Hell. We've been dressing up as demons and pretending that this place is hell. It gives us an excuse to ask them questions, explains why they're still in pain, and telling them how they can avoid returning gives us a chance to send them back to Leadchurch a little better than they left. We wanted you to know because when they all wake up, a lot of them will be claiming to have gone to hell, and you'll have to deal with the theological fallout."

Galbraith lay quietly on his back, thinking about what Brit had just told him. After several seconds' thought, he said, "So you've been using people's fears and beliefs to fool them into being honest with you, and to motivate them into resisting all of their baser instincts and lazy, selfish habits so that they'll do what they know in their hearts is the right thing to begin with."

Brit nodded solemnly. "That's a fair description, yes. I'm not proud to be telling you this. I know as a man of the cloth you won't approve."

"As a man of the cloth, I'm not proud to tell you that you might be surprised just how much I do approve."

Me, helping Kludge and the Bastards, Honor thought. *Nobody would have guessed it. I wouldn't have, but then Kludge said the magic words:* Make the wizards sorry. *And* please. *Saying please didn't hurt.*

Once she decided to help, things moved pretty quickly. The boys hauling on the dragon with ropes all watched, amazed, as Honor slowly walked up to it with a scone in her outstretched hand, Runt following behind her.

The dragon kept struggling with the Bastards at first, but when it saw Honor and Runt, it calmed down a bit. Whether it smelled the scone, was somehow soothed by Honor's demeanor, or was simply confused that these two tiny creatures weren't terrified, she'd never know. The Bastards knew that they'd spent the better part of the day avoiding getting in front of the dragon out of pure fear of being burned alive, and now this little girl just walked up to the dragon as if there was nothing to fear at all. They didn't know about the magical doll Hubert gave her, and she didn't plan to tell them.

She broke off a hunk of the scone and tossed it at the dragon's feet. The dragon sniffed it a few times, then ate it.

She broke off and threw another piece, which met the same end as the first. The dragon looked at Honor expectantly, and slowly lay down on the ground.

The Bastards relaxed and allowed the ropes to go slack.

"How long have you been fighting it?" Honor asked.

Kludge said, "Since dawn."

"It's exhausted. You all must be."

Honor broke off another hunk of scone, and said, in a quiet, soothing tone, "If one of you were to tie the longest of those ropes to a big tree, we might have him."

Kludge himself took a rope cinched around the dragon's right rear leg and tied it quickly around a large tree trunk, using a hastily improvised knot that would either fall apart at the first tug, or be absolutely impossible to ever untie.

She broke the scone into many pieces and tossed them onto the ground in front of the dragon. For a moment, Runt looked as if she might run forward to claim her share of the scone, but Honor looked down at Runt and the dog stopped cold. Kludge and the Bastards were smart enough to keep quiet and back away. Within a few minutes the dragon had fallen asleep, not even realizing it was tied to a tree.

Honor took the last scone in her bag and used it to lead the other dragon out of the woods. While Honor kept it captivated with food and gentle talk, Kludge snuck up behind it and looped a rope around its back left leg, so gently that the dragon barely noticed. Of course *barely noticed* means *noticed,* and the dragon did turn, snap at Kludge, and panic for a moment, but Honor got the dragon's attention back and managed to calm it down. Soon it was lying in the grass with the horned dragon and seemed well on the way to unconsciousness itself.

The dragons looked peaceful, but Honor knew better. Besides, her father had lectured her many times about the difference between a friend and a resource. People could be friends. Dogs could be friends. Sheep were food and clothing waiting to be made. They were raw material. Looking at them that way made lambing and herding them less enjoyable, but it made shearing and slaughtering them without feeling like a monster possible.

Honor looked at the dragons and thought, *They're weapons. Weapons made by the wizards to be used against us normal folk, obviously, because who else is there to use them against? That's all right. We have two of them now, and we will use them against the wizards.*

Honor looked at Kludge. *I helped him get the dragons, but now he's got them. He still needs my help to train them, but I don't know that he knows that, and I don't think he'd like being told by a girl.*

Kludge sat down on the ground. He seemed as tired as the dragon. He looked at her and tried to smile, but he was badly out of practice. In the end, he gave the impression of a frightened man trying to ingratiate himself to the person frightening him. Kludge had seen this expression many times. It was easy for him to imitate.

"Your name's Honor, right?"

"How did you know that?"

"Everybody knows that. You and your brother raise sheep down the road, don't you?"

She nodded.

Kludge looked at the dragons, then looked at her and said, "You asked if any of us were able to bake. Is that so you can show us how to make those things you were feeding the dragons?"

"They're scones," Honor said.

"Call 'em what you want. The dragons had to work to chew them, but seemed to like them enough."

Honor said, "Yes, I'll show you how to make them, and I'll give you the ones I already have, tomorrow."

"Why not now?" That question coming from that man in that tone of voice might well have made most people start to sweat and gibber, but Honor had seen much worse things than Kludge that day.

"Because it's very late, and the scones are at my cabin. I have to go there to get them, and I might as well sleep and bring them in the morning. That's where my kitchen is, too, and my ingredients. If I'm going to teach you to makes scones, it'll have to be there."

While the villagers saw Kludge as a dumb brute, he was the chief dumb brute. One rarely manages to rise to leadership, even among

Neanderthals, without some intelligence. He recognized that Honor was telling him the facts, and he was impressed that someone so small was looking him in the eye while doing so.

Kludge said, "I'll send someone home with you to get the scones. Then, first thing in the morning, I'll have someone there to learn to make more."

Honor said, "Not first thing. I have to tend to the sheep."

"Why can't your brother?"

Honor looked down at Runt, took a moment to stifle the urge to cry, looked back to Kludge, and said, "The wizards bewitched him, and a lot of other people. They're asleep in the church. Nobody can wake them up."

Kludge stared at her for several seconds.

He's waiting, hoping I'll cry, Honor thought. *He's going to be disappointed.*

Honor didn't cry.

Kludge smiled, turned slightly to shout over his shoulder without taking his eyes off Honor, and hollered, "Stretch! Come here!"

Stretch was Kludge's second in command, which seemed like a good job to the other members of the gang, none of whom understood that being second in command just meant being first to do whatever Kludge wanted done.

Despite looking utterly exhausted, Stretch ran to Kludge and asked, "What do you need?"

"Seems the wizards put spells on a bunch of people in town. Put 'em to sleep."

"Is that right? Spineless snobs. If you're gonna knock someone out you should have the decency to punch 'em in the face like a man."

"I agree. Our new friend's brother was one of the victims."

"Oh. I see. That's not good."

"No, it is not. Since she helped us, and has promised to help us further, you are going to take Long Lobes and accompany her home."

"Why do I have to take Long Lobes?" Stretch asked. "I can't stand that guy."

"That's why," Kludge said. "He knows not to step out of line because you'd love an excuse to make his lobes even longer, maybe even tie them in a bow for him. You're going to have Long Lobes stick around and make sure she's safe while she sleeps, and you will bring every scone she has back here so we can use them to keep those monsters from cating us."

He looked at Honor, expectantly. She realized he was waiting for her to either agree or disagree. She nodded.

"Then," Kludge continued, "in the morning, you're going to return to her house, and the two of you are going to help her get her flock squared away, and learn how to bake."

27.

When Gwen and Brit the Younger agreed to allow the Highlanders to join them on their quest to rid Scotland of its six remaining dragons, they did so on the condition that the Highlanders wouldn't slow them down. The Highlanders assured them that it would not be a problem, and proposed several means by which they could travel along the rugged landscape just as fast as two flying sorceresses. In the end, everyone agreed that one of the proposals was far more practical than the others.

The sorceresses would carry them.

Brit crafted a transparent half sphere of pure diamond with a flat floor inserted for the Highlanders to stand or sit on. The men greeted it with enthusiasm, got in with enthusiasm, and enthusiastically shouted their lungs out the entire time they were in flight.

Brit the Younger flew behind, carrying the bowl of Scotsmen with her magic. Gwen flew in the lead, consulting Jeff's interactive map to find the dragons.

It did not take long.

The dragons were resting around the shores of a lake. Gwen, Brit, and their passengers landed in some hills about a half mile away to discuss their options.

"The way I see it, there are two possible ways to do this," Jock said. "One is that I charge with my bow. I stop well shy of the dragons, and soften them up with arrows while Kyle, Leslie, and Mungo run in and finish them off with our swords and axes. You two will fly in behind to back us up and take care of any dragons that try to escape."

The other Highlanders all nodded in agreement, obviously approving of this plan. Brit and Gwen considered this plan for several seconds before Brit asked, "What's the other way?"

Jock said, "I lead the charge with my bow, stop shy of the dragons, soften them up with arrows, and Kyle, Leslie, and Mungo finish them off with our swords and axes while you two watch from a safe distance."

Again, the other men all seemed to agree with Jock's plan.

Brit said, "The whole point of bringing you here was for us to all kill the dragons together."

Jock said, "That's right. And you two have already more than done your parts by finding the dragons so quickly, and bringing us to them."

"You don't think we can take on the dragons ourselves?" Brit asked.

"On the contrary. We know you can."

"But you think you men can do it better," Brit said.

"No, I'm not saying that we can do it better," Jock said. "Just that we should be the ones to do it."

Gwen said, "One moment, please. My associate and I would like to have a word in private." She put her hand on Brit's shoulder and flew them straight up, several hundred feet onto the air, well out of the men's hearing range.

The two women floated just below the cloud cover. The Scottish Highlands sprawled out in all directions like someone had taken an immense sheet of dark green paper, crumpled it up, then attempted to smooth it out again.

"It's just so typical," Brit said, fuming.

"Yes," Gwen agreed. "It is."

"They always think women are useless."

Gwen suspected the conversation would go in this direction and intended to head it off at the pass. She nodded, as if agreeing, and said, "Yes. Yes. Except, when you think about it, that's not actually what he said, is it?"

"Isn't it?"

"Well, no. If you look at what he said, he told us we'd done more than our part, and, from his point of view, we have. I mean, they already think we saved their lives and killed three dragons when they haven't killed even one. Then we carried them over a distance that would have been more than a day's hike for them in about a half hour. And we led them directly to the dragons, so they didn't have to spend any time or energy searching themselves. Look at all the things we've done for them, balance it with the fact that we are two people and they are four, and you'll see, we have done way more than our share of the work."

"Yes, we have! Of course we have! But do they see that?"

"Brit, they're the ones who mentioned it."

Brit seethed at Gwen, but said nothing.

Gwen said, "I know."

Brit continued seething.

Gwen said, "Yeah, yeah, I get it."

Brit looked away in disgust.

Gwen said, "Yes, I understand. But I need you to calm down. Please? You're right that men in general don't give women the respect we deserve, and don't value us as highly as they should, but we aren't dealing with men in general here. We're dealing with those four guys. We've known them less than an hour and we can already recite the names of all of their wives and children, and most of those children are daughters."

Brit said, "Okay, great, they love their wives and daughters. That doesn't mean they respect them at all."

Gwen said, "I dare you to go down there and say something bad about Morag."

Brit snorted, which signaled that Gwen had won the argument.

"We brought them because they feel that they need to kill the dragons to save face," Gwen said. "They don't want to spend the rest of their lives having little Rut ask them to tell the story of how they valiantly allowed us to carry them, then they bravely stood by and watched while we did all the work."

Brit said, "But we both know they can't actually hurt the dragons."

"And they don't have to. They'll run in, fire some arrows, and wave their giant knives."

"Swords."

"Same thing. Anyway, we let them do their best, then swoop in, get rid of the dragons, thank them for loosening the pickle jar lid for us, and we all get on with our lives."

Brit and Gwen landed. Brit said to the Highlanders, "We've discussed it, and we think your first plan is the way to go. We'll provide backup. I have a question. Last time you attacked the dragons it didn't go well. What are you going to do differently this time?"

Jock said, "Last time, we stumbled upon the dragons with no warning. We didn't have time to prepare properly. This time, we'll be fully prepared and ready."

Gwen said, "Then I guess you'd better start preparing."

In the end, Brit felt grateful to Gwen for talking her down from her anger cliff. If Gwen hadn't, Brit would not have gotten to watch the men's battle preparations, a fascinating spectacle that she and Gwen would remember fondly for the rest of their days.

First, each man proclaimed their willingness to die in battle, for the honor and safety of their wives, children, girlfriends, parents, and dead ancestors, most of whom they listed by name.

Then the men took turns praising the other men in the group, boasting of their skills, remembering their past triumphs, and saying what an honor it would be to die by their side in the coming battle. The last one to speak, Mungo, said in a voice choked with emotion,

"It would be worth dying, and I'd do so with a smile on my face, if I knew any of you, you who fought and risked death beside me, would live to carry my bones, or as many them as you can find, back to my beloved Grizel, so that she can divide them amongst Seonag, Jinny, and Torquil, my firstborn son, who is entitled to a double share of my carcass."

After that, the men hugged, cried, and removed their shirts.

Brit said, "Oh! I didn't know it was this kind of party!"

Gwen shushed her harshly, then whispered, "Don't remind them we're here. They might stop!"

When all of the men had stripped to the waist, they smeared each other with blue paint, all the while boasting of their courage, their skill in battle, and the quality of the paint patterns they were creating.

Each of the men had a unique paint pattern, with differing parts of their faces and torsos left bare. They looked quite fearsome, except for Kyle who had a bare patch in the shape of a curved line on his belly, and circles around his nipples, causing Gwen to tell Brit, "I'll never look at a frowny-face the same way again."

Each man took one more turn speaking, though by now they were so keyed up it was more yelling than talking. They all bellowed poems about battle or delivered a litany of threats until the last man, Jock, their leader, shouted out a poem that was made up mostly of threats. Then all of the men turned their faces to the sky and screamed for all they were worth.

Brit said, "They're pretty much the opposite of Phillip and Martin, aren't they?"

The communal scream ended. Jock grabbed his bow and ran over the crest of the hill in the direction of where the dragons were still resting by the lakeside. He shouted, "In we go, men, to fight, and most likely die!"

All of the men cheered and followed him.

Gwen said, "They're the opposite of Phillip. They've got a little in common with Martin."

Brit and Gwen flew straight up and hovered, ready to move in and take over when the Highlanders got tired.

"They really are very brave," Gwen said.

Brit nodded. "They fully expect for at least some of them to die, but they're still running into battle."

"They aren't running very fast."

"Well, the ground's wet and uneven. And the yelling is slowing them down. There's a reason Olympic sprinters don't scream through the entire race."

"Good point," Gwen said. "Although that would be fun for the spectators. It's really touching, how devoted they are to their families."

"It goes without saying that we can't let any of them die."

Gwen said, "The way I see it, the question isn't: *Will we have to save them?* it's: *Which one of them will we have to save first?*"

The sorceresses watched as the four bare-chested, blue-painted men ran in a clump across the rugged landscape toward the now perplexed-looking dragons.

True to the plan, Jock stopped while his friends continued. He nocked an arrow into his bow and fired it in a graceful arc that sailed over the men. The distance was so great, and the trajectory so high, that by the time his arrow had bounced uselessly off one of the dragons, he had already fired a second, and was reaching for a third.

The dragon that the arrow hit shuddered and looked at the oncoming men, still screaming bloody murder, waving their weapons and shields as they approached. The dragon watched them for a few seconds, then took to the sky. All five of the other dragons followed, the last one lifting off the ground just as the men reached the spot where it had been lying only seconds before.

Mungo shook his sword at the retreating dragons and shouted,

"That's right! Run away!" He probably meant to say more, but his concentration got broken by an arrow that zipped past his head and stuck in the ground. Mungo turned and shouted, "Jock!"

Mungo saw that the dragons were headed back over the attacking party's heads, straight for the lone man firing arrows at them.

Again, Mungo shouted, "Jock!" Like the dragons, he made a beeline for his lone, vulnerable friend, which unfortunately meant charging straight through his other two friends, who had followed him into battle. He shoved Kyle and knocked Leslie over, all the while shouting, "Jock! Jock! Jock!"

Mungo realized that Kyle and Leslie were not following him. He turned and ran backward for several steps, to look at Kyle helping Leslie up. "Jock!" Mungo yelled.

Kyle asked, "Jock?" while hauling Leslie up by one arm. There was a blue smear on the grass where Leslie had fallen.

"Jock," Leslie gasped, and with that all of the men sprinted back to help their friend.

Still hovering a half mile away, watching events transpire, Brit sighed and said, "Jock?"

Gwen nodded and said, "Jock." Then they flew.

The dragons followed a low, slow flight path, looming over the ground with their wings spread wide, casting large, dark shadows on the ground and oozing menace. The sight of them approaching only sped Jock's bow, unleashing arrow after arrow as quickly as he could while still bothering to aim. He had focused his attention so exclusively on the dragons that he didn't even realize that the arrows were bouncing off of them and falling straight down into the path of his friends, who were risking their lives, sprinting directly beneath the dragons, trying to reach him in time to help.

The dragons reached Jock before his friends, of course. At the last possible second, he withdrew his bow and crouched behind his shield.

He held out no hope that a single wooden shield could hold off the fire from the first dragon, let alone the five more that followed it, but one does what one can.

He looked at the back of his shield, and the grass beneath him, and he thought of his wife Coira holding their girls, Effie and Nessa. Then the world seemed to turn bright orange. The dragons were upon him, and the fire had begun. Next, he could expect a quick but painful end.

The orange light intensified, then lessened, then went away, but the pain never started. Jock looked up over the top of his shield and saw that the first dragon had passed, but the second opened its mouth to take its turn. Again, the world turned orange, but Jock quickly realized that he was unharmed inside what appeared to be a perfect dome made of fire. He lowered his shield, stood, and spun around to find Brit the Younger standing behind him.

"Hey, Jock. You're pretty good with that bow. Coira would be proud."

He hugged her with all of his might, lifting her feet off the ground and smearing the front of her clothing and her face with blue paint. Luckily the force field didn't need her continued efforts to remain in place. After the hug, they laughed in an uncomfortable, flustered kind of way.

As the last dragon in line passed overhead, they saw the others running through the grass, followed by Gwen flying behind, keeping them as safe as she could. Brit managed to drop the force field just in time to keep Mungo from running face first into it, then managed to re-create the force field, despite being trapped in the center of the loudest, most violent group hug of her life. Through a small hole she could see a patch of sky. Gwen flew by, looking down at her, smiling, then flew off after the dragons.

Brit began to fear she might suffocate, but then one of the men shouted, "They're on us again!" It hadn't taken long for the dragons to circle back. The lead dragon opened its mouth for a fresh blast of fire. The men transitioned from joyful-group-hug mode into fight-fiercely-for-survival mode. They released each other and turned so quickly that Brit fell to the ground, no longer supported by the men's grateful arms.

None of them but Jock knew about the force field. From the rest of the men's point of view, he and Brit had merely withstood the fire without harm. And they had all been too preoccupied to notice when Brit put the force field back up. The men all rushed to raise their shields in hopes of fending off the flames long enough for Brit to work whatever magic she had used to save Jock, not knowing she'd already done it. Kyle discovered the force field first. He stood farthest from Brit, and thus closest to the force field, so close that when he raised his shield, its top edge hit the inside of the force field and bounced back, hitting him just above the eyebrows, giving him a nasty cut and knocking him unconscious.

The dragons soared overhead in single file, expending their entire lung capacity as they passed. Brit looked at the men hiding beneath their shields, then looked at the blue-smeared mess they'd made of her robe and shook her head.

"Relax guys, we're safe."

Jock lowered his shield first and shouted, "She's done it! Brit the sorceress has saved us all!"

Brit saved herself from another round of aggressive gratitude by asking, "Is Kyle hurt?"

The men turned, stricken, and regarded their friend, lying unconscious and bleeding on the ground. They converged on him just as the final dragon flew past. As soon as she knew Kyle was breathing, Brit said, "Okay, you guys stay here. You'll be safe. I'm going to go help Gwen."

She left the Scotsmen tending to Kyle and flew to join Gwen. It looked as if the dragons had been lining up for another run at the men, but Gwen got out in front of them, deliberately making herself their primary objective.

Gwen triggered the weaponized macro she'd been working on back before the dragons posed a real threat. Her robe got longer and billowed out behind her. It grew, rippling and waving, and utterly enveloping the lead dragon in thousands of yards of gray fabric. The five remaining dragons peeled away, abandoning the lead dragon and flying past it and Gwen on all sides.

Gwen disconnected from the mass of cloth and it began to constrict, blocking the view and binding the wings of the dragon. Every time she'd done this before, the entangled dragons had fallen to the ground, helpless. Of course, Jeff had manipulated the dragon's actions in real time to make them seem natural. These dragons had nobody manipulating their actions. It turned out that the dragons weren't actually held aloft by aerodynamic forces. The fabric-covered wings moved in stunted, flailing jerks that apparently counted as *flapping*, but the dragon remained aloft and continued moving forward, its claws tearing at the fabric.

Gwen created a goal in front of the dragon. It staggered blindly through of its own accord.

She heard Brit say, "Let's get after the rest of them!"

Gwen turned to find sixteen Brits floating behind her. She looked at the retreating dragons. The five of them had re-formed and fled toward the horizon. "I dunno. I think we're going to have to think of a better plan. They seem to be learning. They flew slower this time, so they could dodge." She turned and addressed Brit, disregarding the decoys. "I only got one of them by using my macro, and it didn't work like I expected it to."

"How did you know which one was me?" Brit asked.

"The others aren't smeared with blue paint."

She looked at herself and let out a disgusted "*Eugh*." She deactivated her decoys and said, "Don't go away. I'll be right back."

Brit disappeared. Gwen hung alone in the air for a moment, then Brit reappeared, squeaky clean in fresh clothes, with her hair still slightly damp.

She said, "While I was in the shower, I got to thinking. Maybe we aren't using our friends down there to our greatest advantage."

Gwen arched an eyebrow. "You were in the shower, thinking about how to use four burly men?"

"Shut up. I'm just saying, this is Scotland. The dragons are essentially flying sheep."

"Flying sheep. It's strange. Real sheep don't fly. I wonder how these dragons with the instincts of sheep got the hang of it so fast."

Brit waved a hand at their surroundings, pointing out the fact that the two of them were hovering high above the ground. "People don't fly, but we seemed to take to it pretty fast."

Gwen said, "Good point."

"Anyway," Brit continued, "one or two of the guys might have been a shepherd at some point. They may know things we can use."

Mungo and Jock stood, shoulders slumped, heads bowed, while Leslie sat on the ground, cradling Kyle's blood-covered head and shoulders in his lap. Gwen and Brit landed next to the three standing men. Before either of them could ask, Leslie looked up at them, his face a mask of grief, and said, "He's dead! My friend Kyle is dead!"

Gwen watched Kyle for only a few seconds and said, "He's breathing!" She said it cheerfully, passing on what surely would be seen as happy news.

Kyle said, "Breathing his last!"

"I dunno," Brit said. "He's breathing steadily."

"He's strong," Leslie lamented, "always has been, but there's only so long even a man like Kyle can last with such grievous wounds. Oh, I don't look forward to telling poor Morag that her Kyle is gone. She's likely to be inconsolable."

Jock said, "I could tell her. It might be better actually."

Mungo said, "Really, I think we should all be there. We were all his friends."

"We should all take an interest in Rut's well-being also. She'll be needing a father's hand. Between the three of us, we might almost equal Kyle."

"It's kind of you to offer," Leslie said, "but I feel personally responsible for making sure that Morag has help and comfort in her time of grief."

Gwen said, "Guys, I'm pretty sure Kyle isn't hurt that bad."

"I know, he looks strong as an ox," Leslie said, "but he's at death's door, I tell you."

Gwen said, "Tell Kyle, because he's waking up."

Kyle's eyelids fluttered, then popped open. He took looked up at the faces of Jock and Mungo, who had dropped to their knees and crowded to see for themselves if their friend would in fact live. Kyle lifted his gaze from the three men around him to the one supporting his head and looking down at him from above.

"Leslie," Kyle whispered. He reached up with his right hand and grabbed Leslie's hand. "I heard you, Leslie. I heard all of what you said about me."

"I meant every word of it Kyle."

"I know you did, Leslie. I mean it just as much when I say, you stay away from Morag, you back-biting bastard!" Then Kyle used his free hand to punch Leslie in the face.

Kyle and Leslie wrestled on the ground while Jock and Mungo whooped and cheered. Brit and Gwen watched for a couple of minutes, then grew bored.

Gwen said, "Excuse me."

The men didn't hear her.

She cleared her throat, and in a louder voice repeated, "Excuse me." The men still didn't hear.

Gwen shrugged at Brit. Brit shrugged back. Gwen stuck out her wand, mumbled some Esperanto, and both Kyle and Leslie flew ten feet into the air and hung there. They continued to try to trade blows at first, but Gwen separated them, and they reverted to hanging in the air sullenly.

"Sorry, guys," Gwen said, "but time is short. We still have five dragons to kill, so as much fun as it would be to stand here and watch you two beat each other senseless in the name of manly friendship, we really should get to work. Agreed?"

The men mumbled sounds of apologetic agreement.

"Good," Brit said. "Now, Gwen and I were talking, and we have a question to ask you. It may seem strange, but we were wondering if any of you had ever done any sheepherding."

All four of the men raised their hands.

28.

He woke to the sound of a man moaning. He was groggy, so groggy that it took a while to realize that he was the one moaning. He opened his eyes, looked around, then quickly squeezed his eyes shut, praying that he had imagined what he saw.

One of the demons said, "We know you're awake."

He opened his eyes. He was lying prone on some sort of altar, in a room bathed in red light, being watched by three demons. One demon stood close by, looking up and down his body in a way that made him profoundly uncomfortable. The demon looked female, with glossy red skin, horns, a tail, and a mask to hide her soulless eyes. Behind her stood two more demons: another female, and a male in flowing red robes, a similar set of horns and tail, and a pointed black beard.

"Yes," the closer demon said, looking into his eyes. "That's better. How do you feel?"

"I hurt," the man blurted. "I'm in pain."

The demon looked down at his body again and said, "I bet you are. What's your name?"

The male demon, speaking in a deep, gravelly voice, said, "Sylvester! This sinner's name is Sylvester."

The other female, who stood beside the male demon cackled. "Sssssylvesssster! The ssssinner'ssss name isss Sssssylvesssster! Sssssplendid!"

The closer demon shook her head.

"He was a candle maker's apprentice," the male demon said, dismissively.

"Oh, an apprenticcccce," the second female said, clapping with glee.

"Yes," the male continued. "His father is dead. His mother still lives, but he didn't go see her nearly as often as he should have. He had two younger brothers, at least one of whom is on a bad path and could have done with some brotherly guidance, but Sylvester here seemed more interested in candles."

"I work to make money," Sylvester whined. "Money I can use to help my family!"

"You could have," the male demon said, sneering, "but did you?"

"If they ever asked—"

"They shouldn't have had to ask! They're your family. And if I were a betting man—"

The she-demon next to the male coughed and elbowed him.

"Uh, which I'm not. A man, I mean. I'm a demon. But if I were a betting demon, I'd wager that your mother and brothers would have gladly done with less money to see you more, not that you shared your money with them anyway."

Sylvester sobbed. "Yes, you're right. I was a terrible person. They deserved better."

The closer demon examined the right side of Sylvester's body in great detail during all this, then said, "Well, now that that's all taken care of, let's get down to business. Tell me, Sylvester, does it hurt when I press here?" The she-demon pressed gently but firmly into the right side of Sylvester's belly.

"Yes! Ow! Yes, that hurts a lot."

"That'ssss good to know," the second female said. "Are you ready, Ssssylvesssster, for a thoussssand yearssss of ussss pressssssssing there?"

The closer demon turned around to the others and said, "That's not helpful," then turned back to Sylvester and asked, "Do any plants or animals make you feel sick, or make it hard for you to breathe?"

"No."

The male demon said, "More's the pity."

"Have you been ill recently?" the closer female asked.

"No."

"Have you chewed any willow bark recently?"

"No."

"Do you have any loose teeth?"

"No."

The demon nodded, gently prodded him in a couple more sensitive regions of his torso, then said, "I have good news for you, Sylvester. You aren't dead. Not fully. Not yet. You're going to close your eyes and go to sleep, and when you wake up, you'll be alive again."

The other female said, "You're getting a ssssecond chancccce. Try to be a better man."

The male said, "Pay more attention to your family. Spend less time at work."

The closer female said, "Stay off your feet for a few days, and when you do go back to work, take it slow."

The other female said, "Find a nicccce girl, ssssettle down, and treat her with kindnesssssss and ressssspect."

The male nodded emphatically, then said, "And be sure to tithe generously to your local church."

Both of the female demons stiffened, as if they'd both smelled something they didn't like. They turned in unison and stared at the male demon.

"What?" the male asked. "It's a reasonable request."

29.

Tyler and Gary hid behind a large tree. Gary laughed at his own cleverness. "This is going to be great!"

Tyler shook his head, but said, "Yup."

"Oh, changed your mind, have you? Now you think it'll work?"

"No," Tyler said, "It's never going to work, but it's going to be great watching it not work."

"It's a really good plan! It's so simple it can't not work! See, when the girl comes—"

Tyler put up a hand. "You don't have to explain it to me. Believe me, I understand how it's supposed to work. I just don't think it's gonna."

After his unintentional fully clothed swim, Tyler had briefly considered simply grabbing the girl by the arm and dragging her away from the dragon kicking and screaming. He was still too angry to come up with a better plan, so Gary stepped up with an idea, and Tyler felt too contemptuous of the idea to dignify it by arguing, or helping.

He watched while Gary followed the path that the girl and the dragon had obviously used to get to the pond. When they were around a bend, out of the girl's field of vision, Gary used various spells to excavate a huge pit, fifteen feet deep, completely blocking the path. Then he created a goal and placed it facing upward in the bottom of the pit. He used magic to create a patch of false ground that would break under excessive weight. It would hold a small person, but would certainly not support a large animal, like an elephant or a dragon.

"It's foolproof," Gary said. "The girl will walk right over, because she's light, but the dragon will fall through, because it's heavy, and it'll be so surprised it won't think to fly until it's already going into the goal."

"Maybe," Tyler said, "you could take the goal out of the pit and just let the girl and the dragon fall in. Then you put the goal over the top of the hole and when the dragon flies out, we've got him."

Gary arched an eyebrow. "You really want to make that little girl fall into that hole?"

Tyler shrugged. "Sometimes there's a big difference between what I know I should do and what I want to do."

"My plan's still the best one we've got."

"But Gary, what if it doesn't fall through? The dragons aren't natural. They're still partly CG. It might not weigh much at all."

"We've seen them fall."

"But that doesn't mean that they're heavy. Light objects fall just as fast as heavy ones."

Gary shrugged. "Well, if it stands on the trap and doesn't fall through, I'll just magic the ground out from under it."

"Well then why bother with having the ground break under the dragon's weight at all? Why not just put up a force field across the hole? The girl would walk on it, no problem, but the dragon would fall right through."

Gary thought about it for a second and said, "No, I'll stick to covering the trap with a big chunk of fake ground. Sometimes the old ways are best."

Tyler asked, "The old ways of what? Destroying spontaneously generated CGI dragons?"

Gary said, "Exactly! High-five!"

Tyler held up a clenched fist.

Gary said, "You're saying you'd rather fist bump?"

"No," Tyler said, "I'm saying that if you ask me to high-five you again, I'm going to punch you. Look, how do we know she'll even come this way?"

"It's the only path to the pond."

"But what if she didn't take the path here?"

"Why wouldn't she? Why walk over the hills and stuff when there's a perfectly good path? Now you're just looking for problems."

"And I'm finding them. Say you're right, and she did follow this path here, and she will take it when she leaves. When will that be? Are we going to hide behind this tree until dark?"

"I have a plan for that as well. Observe!" Gary stood up from behind the tree, pointed his staff with its three remaining members of KISS at a spot far down the path, and said, *"Ventriloquia!"* He sat back down behind the rock and smiled at Tyler, looking maddeningly pleased with himself.

Tyler waited, but noticed no change whatsoever in Gary or their surroundings. Finally, he gave up and asked, "What was supposed to happen?"

Gary smiled and said, "This." His mouth moved, and his tone of voice sounded perfectly normal, but the actual sound came from the spot farther down the path, where Gary had pointed with his staff when he said the magic word.

"A ventriloquism spell. Why would you even make such a thing?"

Gary said, "For fun." Even over this short distance, the sound took just long enough to reach Tyler that Gary's lips and his distant voice seemed minutely out of sync. Gary continued, "That's the same reason I made this spell, too. *Sono impostor Tyler!*"

Tyler knew Esperanto as well as Gary did, and couldn't help but recognize his own name, so he wasn't surprised when Gary said, "There, now we're ready to begin," and instead of Gary's voice, he heard a fair approximation of his own voice drift to them from the distant spot Gary had chosen. Gary continued in his fake Tyler voice, "And don't even try to say that you don't really sound like this, because you totally do."

"How long have you been able to imitate my voice?" Tyler asked.

"Remember that time we went to Norway to visit the Magnuses, and that blonde girl slapped you for no reason?" the distant voice said.

"They were all blonde girls, but yeah, I remember."

"Since just before that. And she had a reason. A pretty good one."

"So you can imitate my voice and throw it somewhere else. How's that supposed to get the dragon in the trap?"

Gary held up a single finger, looked in the general direction of the dragon and the little girl, and shouted, "Aw! Ow! Oh no! This is so embarrassing! I am humiliated! I'm just glad that that little girl and her dragon aren't here to see me embarrassed and humiliated, right now!"

Tyler said, "That's never going to work."

Gary shushed him and pointed up the path, where he saw the little girl tentatively peeking around the corner.

Tyler sighed heavily, but said nothing.

Gary, using Tyler's voice, said, "Ngaaah! This is even worse! I must look so silly! Yes, quite silly indeed! I'm so glad nobody's here, as they would find my predicament quite laughable!"

The girl made a quick beckoning motion to the dragon, which still hadn't entered the wizard's field of view, then ran down the path, directly onto the dragon trap. Tyler held his breath. He intended to intervene to make sure the girl didn't fall through and into the goal if he had to. He might not like the girl, but he didn't want her dead.

She didn't seem to notice any difference between the cover over Gary's trap and solid ground. She made it to the far end of the trap and kept running, not stopping until she reached the far bend of the path that would again take her out of the wizard's sight. There, she stopped, turned, and looked at the dragon, which had taken a step or two forward, but remained pretty much where the girl had left it, nowhere near stepping on the trap.

The girl said, "Kelly? Aren't you coming?"

The dragon didn't move.

"Come here, Kelly. Come here!"

Tyler whispered, "She's far enough away! I could just appear behind it and take it out butterfly-net style!" He grabbed his staff and started to say the teleportation spell, but Gary put a hand on his shoulder and said, "No, don't." Then he realized that his voice was still Tyler's, and was coming from around the corner, and also that the little girl had heard them. "Uh, erm, no, don't get worse," he said, covering for his mistake. "Oh, it is getting worse! Much worse! I look even more foolish now than I did before!"

The girl craned her neck to look as far down the path as she could, then turned one last time and said, "Come on, Kelly! This is gonna be great!"

The girl ran down the path and out of sight.

The dragon watched her go, waited five seconds, then followed her by flying over the trap, rejoining the girl much faster than it would have on foot.

Gary ran out from behind the rock, into the middle of the path, looking in the direction the girl and the dragon had gone.

He shouted, "Damn!" Of course, his mouth made no discernable sound, and in the distance, Tyler's voice cursed instead, causing the girl to shout, "Where is he Kelly? We have to find him, and laugh at him."

Tyler stood up from behind the rock and said, "You forgot that the dragon could fly, didn't you?"

Gary stomped his foot in frustration, then flailed his arms in panic as the false surface beneath him gave way. The leg he'd stomped with dropped right through fake ground. He fell smoothly until he reached his pelvis. His crotch and other leg stopped the fall briefly and painfully, creating a radiating pattern of jagged cracks and fissures around the site of impact. He rolled on his side, mouth open, contorted in pain. In the distance, Tyler's voice let out a squeal, then a moan. Gary's torso rolled to the side, the ground supporting his weight shattered, and he fell into his own dragon trap.

Tyler quickly flew over the trap and looked straight down the hole.

Happily, Gary had not fallen into the goal and been killed. Instead, he had managed to hold on to his staff, which was longer than the hole was wide, and stretched across the opening like a bridge. He hung, dangling by his hands over the deadly blue field of the goal.

Gary's mouth moved, and in the distance, Tyler's voice said, "Help me up?"

Barely audible, the little girl said, "No. Where are you?"

Tyler looked down at Gary, smiled, and said, "And, once again, you forgot that you can fly, too, didn't you?"

30.

They hadn't taken the time to discuss it. They didn't have to. Roy and Jeff knew each other well enough to know that they were in complete agreement: things were not going well.

Jeff's effort to implement Roy's idea of impressing the locals by leading the dragons around with fake apples had fallen apart as soon as the dragons saw real apples. Now, instead of demonstrating their total control of the animals, they instead demonstrated their total lack of control.

All of the fruit, vegetables, and gourds had been neatly displayed in piles on carts or tables before the dragons came, but now the dragons had reduced the apple stand to a splintered wreck, and the apples themselves rolled around on the ground. The dragons hungrily scarfed as many as they could, as quickly as they could, but they were having some difficulty. Their mouths seemed better adapted for pushing the apples around the ground than for actually picking them up.

Roy flew up to join Jeff as he hovered above the market and tried to use his virtual apples to get the dragons' attention. Nothing he did, including hitting the horned dragon on the side of the head with them, did any good. He had managed to attract and hold the interest of the citizens who still lined the top of the city wall, watching events unfold. They were joined by countless people silently peeking from around various huts and buildings, and from behind the other produce stands. Only one person made any noise—a very angry man hiding behind a well, shouting curses either at the dragons, or at the wizards about the dragons.

"It's no good, kid," Roy said. "Those dragons aren't budging until the real fruit's all gone."

"You're right." Jeff looked down at the chaos they'd helped create and sighed. He made the useless fake fruit vanish, then shouted to the merchants, "Our apologies. Look, you should all get out of here. Go somewhere safe while we deal with this."

Some of the merchants looked up and nodded. Most didn't. But all of those whose wares were already loaded started slowly pushing their carts away from the dragons. The others carefully loaded their arms with as much of their merchandise as possible before making a very cautious break for it.

Roy looked down at one remaining fruit seller, the man hiding behind a stone well, peering around its side at the dragons eating his apples out of the wreckage of his destroyed stand. Roy said, "We're sorry about this. We're going to try to get these dragons out of here as soon as we can."

The man shouted back, "Great! Thank you! When I go home to my wife and children, and tell them that all of the apples are gone and we have no money to show for it, we'll all feel much better knowing that at least the wizards who brought the dragons raining down on us *tried* to get them to leave *as soon as they could.*"

Roy said, "All right, calm down. They haven't eaten all of your apples yet. You may get some of them back."

"Well, that is fortunate, isn't it? What luck!!! Oh, how I look forward to telling my wife and children the great news, that only most of our apples got eaten by a bloody damned dragon! I'm sure my babies won't mind going to bed hungry because I have no money for food, they'll be so entertained by the story. *Tell me again about how you feared for your life, Daddy! What did the customers say when you tried to sell them bruised apples that the dragons didn't want? I like the part when you tell us how much of your hard work went wasted, Daddy!"*

Jeff and Roy looked at each other, then at the dragons. The dragons weren't going anywhere. That was the problem. The two of them, however, would have to go down there and talk to the angry apple salesman, which was also a problem.

They didn't land so much as they sunk, touching down directly in front of the merchant, who remained cowering behind the well.

Jeff said, "First of all, please know that we'll keep you safe from the dragons."

"That's kind of you," the man said. "Offering to protect me from the dragons you brought while we discuss the damage the dragons have already done."

Roy said, "Look, we want to make this right. Once the dragons are gone, we'll use our magic to replace your apples. How's that?"

"Wonderful. Then, instead of having to tell my wife and children that we have no money because the apples were all eaten by dragons, I can tell them we have no money because my apples didn't sell, what with everyone knowing that they were a wizard's unnatural guilt apples. Do you really think anyone will want to buy apples that are literally the uncanny fruit of dark magic?"

Jeff said, "Not if you describe them that way."

"Well, what do you want us to do then?" Roy asked.

The vendor leaned out from behind the well and pointed at the apples rolling on the ground as the dragons chomped on them, oblivious to the drama they were causing.

"I sell fruit. That's my fruit. I can't sell it now, and that's your fault. If you want to make this right, buy my fruit!"

Oh," Jeff said, disgusted. "You want money."

"Yes! I want money! I sell my fruit, to get money, which is what I want!"

"Okay," Roy said, pulling off his hat. "Fine. How many apples did you have?"

"Three hundred."

"You did not," Roy growled.

"Did."

Roy pointed at the apples rolling around on the ground beneath the dragons' feet and mouths. "There's no way that's three hundred apples."

"The dragons ate most of them already."

"That's such a load of—"

"Just pay him," Jeff said.

"He's ripping us off," Roy snarled.

"What do we care? We just need to make him go away so we can concentrate on the dragons."

Roy shook his head, turned back to the merchant, and asked, "Okay then, how much do three hundred of your apples cost?"

"How much do you have?"

Roy muttered expletives under his breath as he reached into his hat. He pulled out a sack of gold coins and handed it to the merchant, who said, "That's a start. How much more have you got?"

Roy shook his head at the merchant, the turned to Jeff. Jeff shrugged, and motioned for Roy to continue. Roy shook his head at Jeff and turned back to the merchant. He reached back into his hat and pulled out a second sack of gold, but held it back for a moment, squinting into the merchant's eyes. "This is it, understand? It's all you get."

The merchant nodded, and once Roy had handed the sack over, the merchant opened the tops of both bags, examining the contents and doing math as quickly as he could without moving his lips.

Roy said, "I trust that will be sufficient."

"Yes, thank you! It's a pleasure doing business with you. The next time your dragons are hungry, I hope you'll think of me."

Jeff said, "They aren't our dragons." Jeff didn't know if the merchant heard, because he was already gone. There's no word for how the merchant ran. It was a cross between a dead sprint and a happy dance.

"He knew he had two suckers," Roy said.

Jeff said, "Doesn't matter. The point is that now we can concentrate on the dragons."

Jeff and Roy heard a sound, a soft, chaotic sound, like many irregularly shaped objects all falling a short distance then bouncing off the ground and each other, almost like a table covered with pears being knocked over. They turned, and saw the man who had been selling pears nearby, but who now stood behind an empty table, pointing in horror at the ground, where a great many pears were now mixing with the apples that were already there.

"Oh no," the man cried, "my pears! My three hundred . . . and . . . fifty pears! The dragons have them! How will I feed my family now?"

They heard another muffled crash, and another voice calling out, "My carrots! My entire crop of carrots for the year, taken by dragons."

Another impact followed, and a voice saying, "I needed the income from that rhubarb to get my sick daughter leeched!"

"Bring her here," Roy mumbled. "We have plenty of leeches."

31.

The interior of the cave remained utter bedlam until Martin and Phillip removed the false wolf. Dragons swirled, billowing plumes of fire erupted almost constantly, and solid-gold lag bolts and sheet metal screws were thrown around the room like waves on a rocky shore.

But when they made the wolf go away, the chaos didn't fully stop. The dragons had a head of steam up, and they couldn't just turn it off like a light switch; so while the fire stopped, the speed of the swirling and the frequency of the golden hardware showers only lessened.

Martin and Phillip huddled behind a large gold I beam for refuge and had to shout to converse.

"Well," Martin said, "That worked less well than we hoped. We took away the things that were scaring them. What can we do to calm them down?"

They heard a particularly loud crash, then a large wave of solid-gold hex nuts broke over them. When the onslaught had subsided, Martin grabbed a handful off the ground, looked at them in his palm, and said "Nuts!"

"Yes," Phillip said. "I know. Anyway, if we put something down the dragons like—"

"No," Martin said. "I meant *nuts* like an exclamation, like *damn*, or *drat*."

Phillip said, "Yes, I know."

"It was a kind of joke."

"The kind I don't laugh at. Now If I may continue, if we create something the dragons like, maybe they'll calm down."

"Yeah, okay. I'll be right back." Martin pulled out the wooden box he used to conceal his smartphone. He swiped a few times, tapped a few times, then disappeared.

Less than a second later, he reappeared, apparently unchanged.

"Where did you go?" Phillip asked.

"Home Depot. It's a store from my time. I needed to get something." He pointed his staff at the floor. A large roll of pre-grown sod appeared, lying over on its side like a Swiss roll made of grass and dirt.

Martin flew sneakily (since flying made no sound, *flying sneakily* mainly meant flying slowly, with his shoulders hunched, as if tiptoeing) over to the passageway, levitating the turf roll along in front of him. He placed it on the floor in front of the passage that led outside, then reached down with the end of his staff and nudged the cylinder. It unrolled like a carpet, into a strip of lush, green grass. He darted back behind the I beam with Phillip to await the results.

The four dragons still looped and banked around the interior of the cave, but they had slowed considerably over time. Now, one of them slowed even more.

It banked a little tighter, then hovered, flapping mightily in the center of the chamber, the other three dragons still whizzing around it like protons. The dragon looked at the green rectangle on the floor, then advanced, landing next to it. It looked closer, sniffed, and started eating.

The other three dragons hadn't noticed the grass on their own, but the sight of a dragon eating grass got their attention. Soon, all three of them hovered, flapping like swimmers treading water, watching the fourth dragon enjoying its snack.

"The patch is too small for more than one dragon," Phillip said.

"Agreed. I'm on it." Martin pointed his staff and created three more rolls on the ground in front of the opening. "Now that I've got the sod rolls in the system I can make as many as we need. When this is all done, I think I might redo the floor in Gary's cave."

Phillip said, "A nice, green lawn. He'd hate that. I'll help."

Martin flew toward the opening and unrolled the bundles of sod, then circled around the back of the chamber. He noted that what had been an immense but orderly storeroom full of itemized golden building materials was now a random field of mixed objects, all blending together to form an indeterminably deep pool full of items made of solid gold.

By the time he had circumnavigated the room and rejoined Phillip, the three dragons had landed, and were enjoying the grass as much as the first dragon had.

Martin said, "That seemed to work."

"Yes," Phillip agreed, "but what will happen when they run out of grass, like that one's about to do?" The first dragon had reduced his patch of lawn to little more than crumbling dirt, and now looked to the other dragons' grass with jealous eyes.

The placement of the three other dragons gave Martin little room to work with, so he carefully aimed his staff, rifle-style, at a spot behind the dragons, further down the passage to the outside world, said the secret phrase, and created another roll.

The dragon went for it immediately. It muscled its way past the other dragons, nudged the roll of turf open with its nose, and started chowing down.

"Huh," Martin said. "That is interesting."

"Indeed," Phillip agreed.

They both flew sneakily past the eating dragons, landed in the passageway, and looked at the light coming from the outside world, off in the far distance.

"I bet if we could get them out in the open," Phillip said, "we could get them going fast enough to fly through the goal. Or, we could get them all into the passage, then put a goal at each end. Eventually they'd have to go through one or the other."

Martin said, "Yeah, I'm not sure I want to wait for *eventually*. They've shown us that they're perfectly willing to sit around waiting for something to happen. What if once they're out in the open we just somehow drop the goal down over the top of them, kind of like a net?"

"I doubt that would work."

"Whatever. Either way, we agree that it would be good to get the dragons outside."

Phillip nodded, then pointed to the empty floor between them and the cave entrance and said, "Sod it."

Martin stared at him.

Phillip said, "It's a joke, because that kind of grass is called sod, and in England—"

Martin said, "I get it. It's a joke. Not the kind of joke I laugh at. One side, please." Martin pointed his staff rifle-style again, and in a few seconds had created a line of sod rolls, as neat as Pac-Man pellets, down the center of the passage all the way to the cave entrance.

The dragons at the rear crowded past the lead dragon to get to the fresh rolls of turf. After a few minutes, an organized system emerged where the last dragon in line would finish its tiny bit of lawn, then squeeze around the other three dragons to get to fresh grass, and take up the lead position. Progress came slowly, but the trend seemed to be leading inexorably outside.

Martin and Phillip walked ahead of the dragons, keeping their distance and watching the giant creatures at all times. Aside from glancing at the light coming from the end of the tunnel at the very beginning of their trip to the surface, neither of them had really bothered to look outside, or even behind them as they carefully backed out of the cave, leading the dragon parade. The farther down the tunnel they progressed, the brighter the distant light behind them got. Eventually, tiny pinpricks of light started to dance on the dark walls around them as faint traces of daylight reflected off Martin's sequined robe and hat. As such, they were surprised when Kneath came sprinting into the tunnel behind them.

"Oh, good, I thought I saw your robe," he said to Martin. "I need your help."

"With what now?" Phillip asked.

Kneath squinted in Phillip's general direction. His eyes had not yet fully adjusted to the dark, a problem that Martin's shiny robe did not help. He finally got a lock on Phillip's general position and said, "Dragons!"

"You need our help with dragons?" Martin asked.

"Yes."

"We know that. We're helping you with dragons. Look." Martin muttered the spell that turned the head of his staff into a lantern. White light streamed out of the eyes of the bust of Santo that topped his staff, illuminating the dragons. One ate while a second crowded past. They both looked up at the light. The two dragons behind them peeked through wherever they could find a gap to see the source of the sudden bright light. The sight of them gave the impression of a massive army of dragons, but Martin knew there were only four.

Kneath didn't know that, or at least had forgotten, and let out a yelp.

"Yeah," Martin said. "Dragons. We're helping you with your dragons."

"Martin," Phillip said, "I don't think those are the dragons he's referring to. Look outside."

Martin turned. They were near the cave opening now, and through it they could see the pile of hay they'd created earlier in a misguided attempt to lure the dragons out. While that had not worked, the hay had somehow caught the attention of the other two dragons in the area, and drawn them in. They had eaten nearly all of the hay; one of the two dragons nosed through what remained. The other peered down the tunnel at them.

"They flew over a while ago and saw the straw," Kneath said. "They were between me and the cave. I didn't dare risk running in to get you until I saw that you were close, and could protect me."

Martin said, "This could be good."

Phillip said, "Move back!"

The three of them had been distracted and were standing between one of the dragons and the next roll of grass. They skedaddled with great efficiency past several rolls before skidding to a stop. They were now close enough to the opening to feel a faint breeze, smell the scent of the hay, and see the light filtering around the two new dragons. One grazed on the last roll of sod, just inside the tunnel entrance. The other crowded its way in to see what was so interesting.

Phillip said, "I'm sorry Martin, I believe you were saying something about how this situation was a good thing?"

Martin looked at the four dragons advancing slowly from one direction, blocking access to the deeper cave. Then he looked at the two dragons opposite them, blocking their only means of escape. Martin counted the meager five rolls of turf now between them and mentally estimated the rate at which the dragons were closing in. "I was saying that, yes," Martin admitted. "But the situation is fluid."

Kneath whined, "We're gonna die."

Phillip put a reassuring hand on his shoulder and said, "No, Kneath, the dragons are scary, but they can't kill a wizard."

Kneath whined, "I'm gonna die!"

"No," Phillip said. "We're not going to let you die. We are going to get out of this."

"Yeah, good," Martin said. "What's the plan?"

Phillip said, "I suppose step one would be to ask you if you have any ideas."

The four dragons continued to advance.

"Maybe we should stop actively luring them towards us?" Martin said.

Phillip said, "Sensible."

Martin made the three remaining rolls disappear, leaving him, Phillip, and Kneath alone between the dragons.

"Now they have nothing to eat but us," Kneath cried.

"It was Phillip's idea," Martin said.

Phillip said, "Be quiet."

Martin said, "Don't try to deny it."

"Quiet, Martin," Phillip whispered. "Kneath, my associate and I can just magic ourselves out of here if need be, and I promise, we'll take you with us. But I don't think that will be necessary. It's dark. They can't see us well. I don't want them to hear us either, because they won't try to eat what they don't know is here."

The three tried to be silent, looking at the shadowy forms of the dragons. Time seemed to stand still. They heard shuffling sounds deeper within the cave, like something very large moving slowly. The sound continued and grew until the closest of the four dragons from the cave, and the only one they could see with any real clarity, turned around and shuffled back in the direction it had come.

The forms of the four dragons mostly eclipsed the light from the main chamber. The men watched the indistinct mass recede into the dark.

Martin whispered, "Four down, two to—" then shoved Phillip and Kneath backward until they all pressed up against the wall of the cavern. Neither of them had to ask why. Phillip had seen it first, but now that they were looking somewhere other than toward the gold vault, they could see the two dragons from the outside were following the others. Martin, Phillip, and Kneath pressed themselves hard against the wall and scarcely breathed as the behemoths ambled by. When they passed completely, Kneath staggered out into the middle of the passage and watched the dragons go. Martin and Phillip sat down on the ground and enjoyed the sensation of not being completely bottled in by dragons.

As the last dragon rounded the corner and disappeared into the main chamber, Kneath said, "Well that's just great. Now there are even more dragons in there with my gold."

Martin said, "Look at the bright side. Now all of the dragons are in one place."

32.

Honor and Stretch arrived at the Bastards' camp carrying two large baskets full of fresh scones. Honor had expected to find most of the Bastards still asleep, as it was well before midday, but instead found them all awake and huddled together, discussing the dragons. More surprising than the Bastards' wakefulness was the fact that they now had three dragons, as they had only possessed two when Honor left the night before.

Heel-Kick whined, "Why do I have to?"

Kludge said, "We have to figure out how to ride these things if we're going to use them against the wizards, and that won't happen if we don't start now."

"Yeah, but why's it gotta be me?"

"Because I've decided that you're the best man for the job."

"But you're much stronger than I am, and much smarter."

"That's all true, Heel-Kick. And I would never ask you to do something that I wasn't willing to do myself."

"I'm glad to hear it."

"That's why I'm not asking. I'm telling you, Heel-Kick, ride that dragon. Now."

"But what if it takes off?"

"We'll be happy. We want it to take off."

"But how will I stay on it?"

Only Donnie said, "It looks like if you sit on its shoulder blades you might be able to hook your legs under its wings."

Pounder said, "Yeah, and the scales on the neck look big enough that you could get a handhold there. If you pull on one side or the other, it might even make the dragon fly that direction."

Heel-Kick gave them a look that said, *You're not helping.* "How am I supposed to get all the way up there on its shoulders? And once I'm up there, how am I gonna get back down?"

"You'll think of a way, because if you don't, I'll help you."

"You will?"

Yeah, I'll just throw you up there, and then when you're done I'll grab your leg and yank you back down."

Heel-Kick looked at Kludge and pleaded, "But what if I get tired while I'm riding it?"

Kludge said, "Don't be a baby. It can't fly forever."

"I can't hold on forever."

"Then think of it as a contest between you and the dragon. You win by not falling off. Falling off would be very dangerous, because you'd land back down here, where you'll have to talk to me about why you let our very valuable dragon escape."

Heel-Kick swallowed again, even harder. "But, Kludge, what if I can't steer it? What if it just flies away and takes me with it?"

Kludge said, "I'll have someone else get on one of the other dragons and chase you."

Gripper stepped forward. "Enough of this stalling. Kludge, let me do it! I'm ready."

"No," Kludge said. "I told Heel-Kick to do it."

"No you didn't," Heel-Kick whined. "You told Only Donnie to do it, and he said, *I have a better idea, let's have Heel-Kick do it.*"

Kludge said, "And I agreed with him. Now on you go!"

The Bastards set about trying to keep the nearest dragon calm while Heel-Kick figured out how to climb on without dying in the attempt. Kludge noticed Honor, and left them to it. Honor sat down in the grass to watch, with Runt lying beside her.

"Did you sleep well?" Kludge asked.

Honor said, "Yes. Thank you for sending L.L. to watch over me."

"Lots of bad people in the world. Wouldn't do to have them find you out there all alone."

"I'd always thought you and your gang were some of those bad people."

"Glad to hear it. We've worked hard to create a certain reputation. It's nice to hear that it hasn't gone to waste. How was Stretch's baking lesson?"

"It was good," Honor said. "He knows nothing about cooking, but he's good at following orders."

"Yeah," Kludge said. "That's why he's my best guy. He's smart enough to shut up and do as he's told without wasting a lot of time thinking about it."

"How did you catch the third dragon?"

Kludge smiled an actual, genuine smile. "When we woke up, we found it here, sleeping like a baby next to the other two. All we had to do was tie it to a tree without waking it up."

They watched in silence as Heel-Kick ran up the dragon's tail and back, leapt, and landed, straddling the dragon's neck. He shouted, not in triumph, but in pain, then fell to the ground beneath the surprised dragon and crawled away as fast as he could.

Kludge and the rest of the Bastards all laughed, and when Heel-Kick was safely away from the dragon he laughed as well, though obviously still in pain. Honor even managed a small chuckle, then asked, "Do you really think he'll be able to ride it?"

"If he can't then it's all pointless. I think what'll happen is that the dragons will spend the morning bucking him off, and I'll spend the morning threatening him back on. Later, when the dragon's tired and sees it's not gonna stop, we might start to get somewhere." He glanced at Runt, who had followed Honor, of course, and sat obediently staring up at her. "You know animals. What do you think?"

She watched as Heel-Kick again ran up the dragon's back and again leapt onto its shoulders. This time he leaned farther back, and landed with an impact that looked painful, instead of excruciating. The dragon panicked and bucked, but Heel-Kick managed to get a hold of the dragon's scales, as they'd discussed. The other Bastards cheered while he hung on for dear life.

Honor said, "They're animals. Animals can be trained. But I don't know if you'll be able to beat wizards with them."

"I don't know either," Kludge said, "But they're the best chance I'll ever get."

"Why do you hate them so bad?"

"They think they're better than everyone."

"That's not a reason to hate. To dislike, yes. But not to hate."

"They attacked your brother."

"That's why I hate them. You hated them before."

A wizard named Todd had created a macro, the main purpose of which was to trap and force Kludge to do whatever Todd wanted, no matter how much pain it inflicted. The wizards who witnessed it working didn't like talking about it. Kludge didn't talk about it at all. Not directly. Instead, he said, "I don't like feeling powerless," and left it at that.

It seemed to be a good enough answer for Honor.

Kludge asked her, "Where's L.L.? Did he stay at your farm?"

"Yes. He's watching the sheep."

"He should be here sleeping. He has to be beat. He didn't sleep last night when he was supposed to be guarding you, did he?"

"I don't think so. When Stretch and I left, he was sleeping in the pasture. That's fine. The sheepdogs really do all of the work anyway."

Heel-Kick still clung to the dragon's neck. The other Bastards untied the dragon's rope from the tree while Heel-Kick begged them not to. The dragon started walking slowly around the field, Heel-Kick wailing with fear the entire time.

"Good," Pounder shouted. "Now try pulling on one side of its neck or the other. See if it'll turn."

Heel-Kick shouted, "Can't!"

"Why not?"

"Already pulling back on both sides, hard as I can. Can't pull harder on either side."

Only Donnie said, "Stop pulling back. That'll make the dragon stop."

Heel-Kick cried, "When?!"

Kludge shouted, "Heel-Kick, you stop pulling back on that dragon or I'm gonna pull back on you!"

He turned to Honor and said, "When you're threatening people, the words aren't nearly as important as the tone of voice."

Heel-Kick stopped pulling, and the dragon started walking around the field faster. Then it ran two steps and took flight. The Bastards shouted in triumph, almost loud enough to drown out Heel-Kick's terrified screaming.

The dragon slowly circled the field, the loose rope dangling from its foot. Heel-Kick continued screaming the entire time. After a few moments, Heel-Kick pulled hard on the dragon's neck. The dragon slowed to a hover, flapped its mighty wings twice to tread air, and landed. Heel-Kick went limp and fell to the ground, exhausted and sobbing.

Kludge ran forward, along with the rest of the Bastards. Pounder retied the dragon to the tree while the rest of the Bastards hoisted Heel-Kick's limp body above their heads and carried him around the field cheering while he quietly begged them to put him down.

33.

"You idiots," Kneath yelled.

"We're not idiots," Martin countered. The entrance of two new dragons into the treasure chamber had seemed like a sign that the three of them should leave the cave altogether. Martin and Phillip had hoped that some fresh air and quiet would help them think of a new plan, but Kneath started shouting at them as soon as they emerged.

"I was better off before you showed up!"

"That's true," Martin allowed, "but that doesn't mean we're idiots."

"There're more dragons in there with my gold than there were before," Kneath shrieked, pointing at the cave opening behind him.

"Yes, I know. That's what I meant when I agreed that you were better off before we showed up."

Phillip said, "Pointless."

Martin said, "Don't you start in on me, too."

"No," Phillip said. "I mean this conversation—it isn't doing anything to get those dragons away from your gold, Kneath."

"But it's making me feel a lot better," Kneath said, nastily.

Phillip said, "I suppose so. But it's making my associate and me feel much worse, and if we start to feel too bad, we might just leave you to remove the dragons on your own. Do you really think you can do a better job than we can?"

"So far it looks like it."

"All right then. We'll leave you to it. Come on, Martin."

"Gladly." The two of them started walking down the dragon-widened path that led out of the woods. Kneath followed and continued his tirade.

"Oh, fine, then leave. Cowards. Run for it."

They kept walking. Kneath kept following.

"Yeah, just go. Just walk away."

After a few more steps he said, "You're really going to do it, aren't you? You're really going to abandon me here."

After a long silence, Kneath said, "You can't just go."

The wizards didn't slow their pace, or even turn their heads back to look at Kneath, but Martin said, "You told us to."

"But I never thought you'd actually do it."

"Why wouldn't we?" Phillip asked.

"Decency! Simple human decency! You can't just leave me here to deal with a problem you created."

"And what problem is it you think we created, Kneath?"

"I can't get to my gold because there are dragons on it that'll kill me if I try!"

Martin said, "You couldn't get to your gold because there were dragons on it who would kill you if you tried when we got here."

"Yeah," Kneath said, "but thanks to you there are more dragons now."

Phillip said, "Being killed by six dragons isn't much worse than being killed by four. It's a minor change at best."

"Come on, guys, you can't leave!"

Martin glanced back and asked, "Why not? You haven't given us a good reason to stay."

"I'm paying you!"

Phillip laughed, then said, "We don't care about your gold. It's not even your gold, really. The wizard you knew as Merlin created it, and hid it here until the day comes that he needs it. What makes you think it's yours? Because the cave's on your land?"

The walked in silence for several steps before it registered to Martin and Phillip that the question had shut Kneath up. Now they stopped walking and turned to look at him.

"Do you own the land the cave's on?" Martin asked, quietly.

Kneath looked at the ground, and said, "It depends on what you mean by *own*."

Martin said, "By *own*, I mean *own*."

"If that's what you mean, then no, I must admit that technically I don't *own* the land. But it is mine."

"Are you saying that the king leased you the land?" Phillip asked.

"No."

"Then how is the land yours?" Martin asked, his voice growing slower and quieter with each word.

Kneath stood tall and puffed out his chest. "It's mine because this is Wales, and I am a Welshman. Wales is the land of my father, and my father's father. And that cave is set into the land of Wales, so that is the cave of my father, and my father's father."

Phillip put a steadying hand on Martin's shoulder, but Martin brushed it off and said, "Every person in Wales can make that same argument."

"And if that many people agree, it can't be wrong," Kneath said.

"Do you intend to share the gold in that cave with every other person from Wales?"

"Yes," Kneath said. "Of course."

Martin stared at him.

Kneath added, "A bit at a time."

Martin growled, "By buying things with the gold?"

Kneath said. "That way only people who make things of value or provide a service I want get a share. It's merit based."

Martin stared. Phillip shook his head. Kneath said, "You're so smart, how would you do it?"

Martin continued staring, but his face cracked into a wide smile. Then he muttered some Esperanto under his breath and disappeared.

Kneath asked, "What's he doing?"

Phillip said, "Something rash." A few long seconds ticked by, then a tiny point of silver light appeared where Martin had stood, barely two feet in front of Kneath. The silver dot quickly expanded into a large circle of silver light, surrounding what appeared to be some sort of magical passage to another place. Kneath saw many huts and a building he instantly recognized as Cardiff Castle. In front of the huts he saw a crowd, hundreds of people strong, all looking in amazement toward the portal, toward him. He also saw Martin, standing on the other side of the portal with his arms spread wide, his staff held high, and his back to Kneath, addressing the crowd.

"Gold," Martin said. "A cave full of it! More than all of you combined could carry. Each person here could walk out with their arms full, and there'd still be enough to make it worth going back for more."

Martin definitely had the crowd's interest. One young man in tattered clothes peered around Martin and said, "I don't see no cave."

"It's at the end of this path. Only a short distance, then the cave itself is long and dark, but at the end, there is a large chamber that contains an unimaginably vast quantity of gold."

"How much gold?"

"I just told you, an unimaginably vast quantity."

"But how much is that?"

Martin said, "I can't give you an exact figure. It's unimaginably vast. Imagine the largest vastest amount of gold you can. More gold than that."

A wave of excitement shot through the crowd. The young man in the tattered clothes stepped purposefully toward the portal, saying, "Well then, what are we waiting for?"

Martin said, "I need to warn you. There's danger."

The man said, "I'll be careful," as he walked past Martin through the portal. He eyed Kneath, but didn't stop or even slow down to do it. Once he passed Kneath, he broke into a run.

"That gold is mine!" Kneath shouted at the man's back.

"Not if I get to it first!"

Martin pointed his free, non-staff-holding hand at the man and said, "*Radion de ruĝa lumo.*" A ray of silver light shot from Martin's hand, hitting the man just before he disappeared around a bend.

Martin turned back to the crowd and slowly painted them all with the same ray of light he'd used to shoot the man.

"This is a protection spell," Martin said. "It will keep you safe from the terrors of the cave." Actually, it was little more than a flashlight. A harmless bit of showmanship that helped make a wizard's more-useful spells look interesting. In this case, since the dragons had been deliberately designed to not actually be able to hurt anybody anyway, the little bit of showmanship was all that Martin actually needed.

A woman in the crowd asked, "What are the terrors of the cave?"

"Dragons," Martian said, turning his light show on the crowd. "Six full-grown, fire-breathing dragons, but take heart. Thanks to my magic, they cannot harm you. Their fire and their claws will cause you great pain, but no actual injury. Now, follow me!"

Martin deactivated the magical ray and spun on his heels, finding himself face-to-face with Kneath.

"That's my gold," Kneath said.

Martin pointed back over his shoulder and said, "Explain that to them. I think they'll find your plan to share it with them by buying stuff most interesting." Martin stepped around Kneath, as did what appeared to be most of the population of Cardiff. Kneath stood silently as they flowed around him. Some motion above him caught his eye. He looked up and saw Phillip, floating over the crowd, looking down at him.

Kneath yelled, "It was my gold!"

Phillip said, "Some of it still can be. *Radion de ruĝa lumo.*" He hit Kneath with a beam of light similar to the one Martin had used on the crowd.

Martin walked briskly. The crowd kept pace with him, but they seemed to do so reluctantly.

Phillip glided forward and landed next to Martin, matching his pace.

"How do you expect this to play out?"

"We'll see."

"That's your plan? We'll see? That's not a plan."

"Sure it is. I plan to see."

"A plan is a set of steps that lead to a goal. *We'll see* is not a plan."

Martin said, "The steps were to go to the nearest town, set up a portal back here, tell people about the gold, and tell them the dragons couldn't hurt them. That's four steps. The goal is to see what happens next."

"That's not much of a goal."

"Really? You can't tell me you don't want to see what happens."

They didn't have to wait much longer. They had walked through the forest far enough that they saw the mouth of the cave in the distance. Martin and Phillip maintained their pace all the way to the cave's entrance, but the throng of people that had followed them slowed to a crawl. Everyone wanted to go into the cave, but nobody wanted to go in first, in case Martin's magic proved too weak to protect them. The result looked similar to when children have a *going-slow* race, only in this case the competitors were adults, and they suspected that it might be a going-slow race to the death. Forward progress had nearly ground to a halt when the people at the front of the crowd started shouting that they heard something coming from the cave; then all progress did truly stop as everyone strained to hear.

It sounded like footsteps, fast footsteps. One person running, but not well. The sound had a heaviness about it, like the person might be hindered somehow, possibly very tired, or injured. Then they heard the panting. Long, ragged breaths that grew louder along with the footfalls. The woods were silent. Most of the people in the crowd held their breath. Everyone who could see the cave entrance peered in, dreading the sight of the injured wretch they were certain would soon emerge, but not daring to look away for fear that they might not get to see him.

Then, after what felt like an eternity, he emerged, the man who had left the crowd early, rushing in and ignoring all warnings in his haste. He had reaped the reward of his hasty actions. He seemed perfectly healthy, and he was carrying a small stack of solid-gold floor tiles. Gold is very heavy, so the bundle was a bit smaller than a cinder block, and was really more than he could carry, but gold is also very valuable, so despite the less-than-impressive size of his haul, it was more than enough to rivet everyone's attention.

"It's true," he wheezed. "What the wizard said is true! It's more gold than I thought existed in the world, all right there for the taking!"

"And what of the dragons?" an old man in the crowd shouted. "Did you see them?"

The man carefully placed his load of gold on the ground, then sat on it, both to rest and to protect it from theft. He took a couple of heavy breaths and said, "Yeah, a bunch of them. I thought I was done for. Two got on either side of me and they both blew fire on me at once. It hurt like hell, but when they were done, I was fine."

The crowd ran into the cave.

Martin and Phillip moved to the side and watched as the swift torrent of people flowed past them, disappearing into the dark. The sound of the crowd reverberated off the walls into a deafening roar. The pace slowed as the people at the front of the line felt their way through the dark. The sound seemed to agitate the dragons, which slowed the pace further, and flooded the cave and the treasure chamber with orange light. The entire crowd had gone in now, including Kneath. Martin and Phillip heard shouting, and roaring, and screaming, and more roaring, and then, in the end, cheering.

They saw a dark silhouette of many flapping wings and flailing claws illuminated from behind by one last spiteful fireball. Martin created a goal hovering six feet above the ground, covering most of the cave exit. He and Phillip counted as all six dragons flew at top speed into it.

Martin clapped his hands and said, "Just as I'd planned."

Phillip said, "You didn't plan that."

Martin said, "We've already established that my plan was to see what happened. That just happened, and I saw it."

34.

When Gwen and Brit the Younger remembered that Jeff borrowed large portions of the dragons' code from sheep, they had asked the four experienced shepherds they'd been hanging around with how they herded sheep. It just seemed like the obvious solution.

They learned that herding sheep was challenging out in the open, but could be made much easier using pens, gates, and trained dogs. Applying this knowledge to their current problem seemed, again, like the obvious solution.

The dragons were much larger than sheep, so the pen needed to be that much larger as well. The dragons could fly, so the pens needed to be three-dimensional. Those parameters, combined with Brit's love of crafting large structures out of molecularly perfect diamond, led to the sight of five dragons swirling around chaotically inside a mammoth crystalline cube, which itself hovered motionless above the Scottish Highlands. It perfectly illustrated the idea that a long series of obvious solutions can lead to an improbable result.

Trained dogs were indispensable to the process, but they posed two problems: dogs were quite small, and couldn't fly.

While Brit worked on the diamond cube, Gwen set about solving the dog problem. The Scotsmen happily agreed to lend Gwen the use of their dogs, on the condition that no harm would come to them. She selected the four best and got to work.

Gwen pieced the macro together using bits of existing macros, assets from old video games, and a rough flight-steering mechanic controlled by measurements of how fast the dog ran and what direction it pointed its nose. When she finished, she applied the macro to the dogs. The results were not promising. The four mixed-breed sheepdogs instantly disappeared, replaced by four identical winged horses, all of which appeared to be wading chest deep through the solid ground while flapping their wings.

She made the Pegasus shells transparent when viewed from the inside, so the dogs were oblivious to their own appearance. They each ran around, chasing the strange flapping-winged creatures that they didn't realize were their fellow dogs. They scooted around on the ground like bumper cars, emitting barking and growling noises. Gwen worried that they would never discover that they could fly, but then one of the dogs looked up, for whatever reason, and rose into the air.

Of course, it stopped dead in its tracks as soon as it realized what it had done. The animated Pegasus hovered two feet above the ground, looking noble, but emitting a frightened whining noise. All of the other dogs looked up at it, and they all rose above the ground as well, also screeching to a halt and whining pitifully.

She was just about to pull the plug on the experiment and try to think of something else when one of the winged horses slowly inched forward. It angled down, back into the ground. Ran a few steps, then lifted back into the air. It repeated these touch-and-go maneuvers several times, with increasing speed and confidence. The other dogs followed suit, and less than a half hour after discovering that they could fly, the dogs were playing with each other in the air every bit as gracefully as they had on the ground.

A quick transportation spell later, the crystalline cube full of flying dragons was a crystalline cube full of dragons and winged horses. It would have looked like a poster on a bookish girl's bedroom wall if not for the four screaming Scotsmen standing beneath the cube, shouting orders and encouragement that their dogs could not hear and did not need.

Despite the complete unreality of the situation, the dogs' herding instincts kicked in just as firmly as the sheep-dragons' grass-eating instincts. The flying horses flanked and outmaneuvered the dragons easily, and soon they had the dragons flying laps of the sphere's interior as if it had all been choreographed in advance. As the dragons gathered toward one end of the cube, Brit made a diamond wall slide forward, trapping the dragons in a smaller space, much as a gate would in a pen.

Brit conjured up a goal, and decorated it with an immense wooden gate in hopes that the sheep dogs piloting the winged horses would recognize it as a good place to herd the dragons. She held one end of the gate and flew in a quarter circle, swinging the gate open. She noted with satisfaction that the giant hinge even squeaked convincingly.

The dogs took notice, directing the dragons directly toward the goal. The dragons no longer seemed afraid of it, as they had when it appeared directly in front of them while they were flying full speed.

Then again, Brit thought, *pretty much anything appearing out of thin air right in front of your face when you're flying full speed is bound to scare the crap out of you.*

The dragons flew through the goal, probably expecting to come out the other side like they would have any other gate. Instead, they were obliterated. Each Pegasus peeled off well before reaching the gate, but Brit had been ready with a force field if they hadn't. As soon as the final dragon sailed through the goal into nothingness, she quickly eradicated the goal as well, just to prevent any accidents.

The men far below cheered themselves hoarse. Gwen drifted over to Brit.

Brit said, "I must say, your Peg—Hmm. What's the plural of Pegasus?"

"Winged horses." Gwen said, "Unless you want to sound silly."

"Fair enough. They did a great job."

"I know, right?!"

"Of course, watching them work, it did occur to me that they weren't really necessary. Once we had the dragons trapped in the cube, we could have just put the goal at one end and made the walls close in until the dragons had nowhere else to go."

Gwen thought about this for a moment, then said, "Yeah, well, this way looked a lot cooler."

The two sorceresses landed in front of the cheering men. Brit erased the diamond sphere while Gwen brought the winged horses back down to earth, then deactivated the macro, turning them back into earthbound dogs. The dogs received a hearty round of pets, rubs, ear scritches, and attaboys, but they still looked severely put out that they could no longer fly.

Brit checked the dragon map, which confirmed that Scotland was free of dragons. As a courtesy, they flew the men to a spot about a one-hour walk from their village. There, they said their goodbyes.

"Jock," Brit said, "you're a strong man, and a good leader. Coira is a lucky woman, and little Effie and Nessa are fortunate to have you for a father."

Gwen continued, "And Kyle, you're a stalwart friend and a fearsome warrior. We were all worried when you fell injured, but we should have known it would take more than dragons to tear you away from your Morag. Keep watch over little Rut. If she grows to be half as lovely as her mother, you'll be fighting off boys with a stick."

Kyle blushed slightly, and said, "One day mayhap, but it will be quite a while before I face those kinds of problems."

Mungo said, "I'm not so sure. I think my Torquil may have designs on young Rut."

Kyle said, "Torquil's a fine lad."

Mungo said, "Thank you."

Kyle said, "Keep him away from my little girl."

Mungo laughed.

Brit interrupted the decidedly downhill flow of the conversation, quickly saying, "Mungo! Dear Mungo. In many ways, I may miss you most of all. Please know that you have both Gwen's and my respect and friendship."

Mungo nodded. Gwen cleared her throat. Brit looked at Gwen, who tilted her head toward Mungo and widened her eyes. Brit spent half a second seething at Gwen, then continued, "And do give our best to your little ones, Jinny, Seonag, and Torquil, and your wife, Grizel."

Mungo smiled, as did Gwen as she looked at the last man remaining.

"Leslie, you're the youngest man here, but you're as brave and capable as any of your friends. Go home and make a good life for yourself with Donalda." She paused, then stuck a finger in his face. "And for everybody's sake, especially your own, you stay away from Morag!"

35.

"There," Gary said, taking a deep, satisfied breath. "I think that looks pretty good."

"No, it doesn't." Tyler stifled the urge to laugh while looking utterly disgusted, which is a difficult trick to pull off.

"Whatever. The point is, it'll work."

"No, it won't."

"What are you talking about? You agreed that this is a good plan."

"I most certainly did not. I never said that this was a good plan. I said it was a ridiculous plan, but that you should go ahead and do it anyway, and I only said that because I wanted to see what your idea of a *fake sexy lady dragon* would look like."

Gary looked back up at his handiwork. "And I think it looks pretty good. What's wrong with it?"

"What's wrong with it? Everything about it is wrong. It's an exercise in pure wrongness. It's wrong that you thought of it. It's wrong that you had such specific ideas about how it should look. It's wrong that it's wearing makeup. It's wrong to give a reptile mammary glands. And worst of all, it's wrong that you got all the way through making it without once looking at what you were doing and thinking, *This is wrong.*"

Gary said, "It's a first attempt—I was bound to make a few mistakes. I'll admit, it could be better."

Tyler said, "Could be better? I don't know how it could be worse."

As they looked at Gary's creation, behind them they heard Phillip say, "Oh no. Oh no, no, no."

Tyler cringed.

Martin just laughed, and kept laughing.

Gary said, "Guys! What brings you here?"

Phillip tried to explain, but he couldn't really concentrate while standing anywhere near Gary's fake sexy lady dragon. It looked like the standard model of nonhorned dragon, except for the modifications Tyler mentioned, plus a narrower waist, fuller hips, and eyelashes as long and thick as unsharpened pencils. "We got done with our dragons," Phillip said, weakly. "We saw you chaps still had one, so we thought we'd come help."

"You're beyond help," Martin gasped, doubled over with laughter. "Nobody can . . . fix . . . what's wrong . . . with you." He glanced back up at the sexy lady dragon and gave up talking, letting the laughs take over completely.

Phillip looked at Tyler and Gary and said, "Please say something that will make this better."

Gary said, "We were desperate."

Martin kept laughing. Phillip muttered, "I did ask."

Gary said, "Oh come on guys, it's not what you're thinking."

Phillip said, "I was thinking that you intended to try to lure the last remaining dragon in your area with this awful thing you've made. Are you telling me that's not what's going on here?"

"No," Gary said. "You're right. It's that."

For the first time since he was a very small child, Martin literally fell down laughing.

Tyler said, "This last dragon's been a real problem."

"So you've resorted to using ideas you've stolen from Wile E. Coyote?"

Gary said, "A good idea's a good idea, no matter where it comes from."

Martin sat on the ground and whined, "Oh God! No air! Can't breathe!"

Phillip said, "Did it never occur to you that Mister Coyote wasn't famous because he caught Road Runner so many times?"

Tyler waved his arms, as if trying to erase the last several seconds much like one would erase a chalkboard. "Okay, look, you're right. This thing here is Gary's doing. I was just a spectator. But you've gotta understand, he was driven to this. We got it down to one dragon right away, but this last dragon, it's been complicated."

Phillip said, "We came to assist you. I'm sure once Martin has recovered, we can help."

Martin laid back in the grass, breathing heavily, and occasionally giggling. "Yeah," he gasped. "Help."

"What seems to be the problem?" Phillip asked.

Tyler said, "The dragon's made friends with a little girl, and she won't let us . . . uh . . . I'm gonna wait until Martin stops laughing."

Martin looked like he might take quite a while to stop, so Tyler and Gary led Phillip through the small stand of trees they'd been using as camouflage, to where he could see the little girl and her dragon, still playing by the pond.

Phillip whispered, "She looks darling."

Gary, speaking in hushed, covert tones said, "She's tough, man."

Phillip said, "She's a child."

"Yeah," Tyler said, "but she's clever."

"A clever child."

Martin walked up beside them, looked at the little girl and the dragon, and at full speaking volume asked, "That her?"

"Yes," Gary said. "Be quiet. She'll hear you."

"So what if she does? She's a little girl."

"Don't underestimate her," Tyler said quietly. "She's beaten us so far."

"Does she have super hearing or something?" Martin asked.

Phillip asked, "What have you tried so far?"

Gary said, "Everything."

"Fair enough," Phillip said. "What did her parents say when you talked to them?"

Gary and Tyler looked at each other and said nothing.

"You didn't talk to her parents?"

"Should we have?" Gary asked.

Phillip said, "When you have a problem with someone else's children, the first thing you should always do is talk to the parents. That's the first rule of dealing with kids."

Martin said, "It's the first rule of not being a creep."

Gary said, "Her parents aren't around."

"So find them," Phillip scolded. "I'm sure they're probably at the nearest farmhouse. If not, the people there'll probably know her and be able to direct you to them."

"But who knows how far away the nearest farmhouse is?"

"It can't be farther than a little girl can easily walk, and besides, even if it is miles away, you're a wizard! You can fly! Have you forgotten that, Gary?"

Gary chose not to respond.

Martin said, "Okay, I'll get some altitude, find the nearest farmhouse, and ask around. Phillip, I think since our friends here have been harassing her all day, it might be good if you went and tried to keep her calm and get her to stay put until I get back with the parents. I'd do it myself, but you look . . . I dunno, *kindly*."

Phillip stood up and dusted off his robe. "Yes, Martin, thank you. Lord knows what kind of trauma these two have put the poor dear through."

Gary started to say something, but Tyler stopped him. "No, you know what, I think this is a good plan. Let's let them handle it, Gary. We can watch them and see how well they do."

Martin flew straight up through a hole in the tree cover. Phillip walked out of the woods at a casual pace and approached the girl. Moving quickly, hoping to be in position before she noticed Phillip, Tyler and Gary scurried like poorly coordinated commandos, hiding behind and then peeking out around a large tree trunk.

The girl and the dragon both saw Phillip coming. They watched silently as he approached, then sat down, cross-legged on the ground.

Tyler and Gary were behind Phillip. They couldn't see his face, but they could hear the smile in his voice. "Hello, young lady. My name is Phillip. I'm here to apologize. I understand these two have been bothering you." Much to Gary and Tyler's chagrin, Phillip pointed back at the tree they were hiding behind as he said it.

"Yes. They have. It was awful."

"I'm sorry about that. They will be talked to about how to treat a young lady who's out with her pet, minding her own business."

"Thanks. They're dumb."

"They can be, yes."

"Are they friends of yours?"

Behind the tree, Gary said, "Here it comes."

Phillip said, "More colleagues, really. People I'm forced to put up with."

The girl smiled.

Tyler said, "Yup. There it is," and sat down behind the tree. He no longer had the stomach to watch or actively listen to the conversation between Phillip and the girl. He tried very hard to think of something else, but occasionally Phillip said things that got his attention.

"Yes, quite silly."

"*Butt Brain!* No, I suppose he didn't like being called that."

"He fell off of the hill, then part of the hill fell on him? I'm sure that was very funny."

"He stepped backwards into the water all on his own, you say. I do wish I could have seen that."

The conversation felt endless to Tyler, but in truth, it only took five minutes, then a portal materialized about fifty feet away from where the girl and her dragon stood. Through the portal, Tyler could see Martin standing in front of a small but very tidy farmhouse, with a man and a woman who looked confused at first, then alarmed when they saw their little girl standing next to a dragon. The woman shouted, "Chelsea!" Martin put a calming hand on her shoulder.

The girl smiled and waved, and shouted, "Momma! Poppa!"

Phillip twisted his neck and back around to look at Chelsea's parents. He smiled, reassuringly, and said, "Hello. Delightful young lady you have here. I've just been talking to her, making sure nothing bad happened while my friend found you."

Chelsea's father said, "Thank you," looking meaningfully at both Martin and Phillip. He glanced over and saw Tyler and Gary hiding behind a tree. Gary waved. Chelsea's father did not wave back. He said, "All right, Chelsea girl. It's time for you to come home now."

"Yes, Poppa. Can I bring Kelly with me? Please?"

Chelsea's parents were terrified at the sight of their little girl that close to the vicious-looking dragon, but they both put on a brave face and fought through it. Chelsea's mother said, "No dear. That thi— *Kelly* has to stay, and I think you know it."

"Aw, but he's very nice, and I love him an awful lot."

"The answer's no, Chelsea. Now come here."

"But I want to bring Kelly. You're not being fair."

Chelsea's father said, "Don't argue with your mother. Do you think she likes not letting you have things you want?"

The girl looked at the ground and said, "No."

"That's right. She'd like nothing more than to be able to say yes. We both would. But we can't, because Kelly is a wild animal. He needs to be free. He wouldn't be happy on our farm, would he?"

"I suppose not."

"Right. So tomorrow, when you come out to play, if Kelly's still here, then the two of you can have a good time. But if he isn't, you can't be sad, because it means he's off being happy, doing what dragons do. Understand?"

"Yes, Poppa. I understand."

Her mother said, "Good girl. That all depends on if you're allowed to come out and play tomorrow, and you won't be if you don't do as you're told and come home now."

"Of course, Momma. I'm sorry." Chelsea looked up at Kelly, then hugged him which, given their size discrepancy, meant putting her arms around Kelly's wrist. The dragon looked down at her, but made no move to show whether it liked, disliked, or even understood the gesture.

Chelsea walked away from Kelly. As she passed close to Phillip, she stopped and hugged him, too. When she finally reached her parents, standing next to Martin and his portal back to their home, she asked, "Did you mean it, Poppa? If Kelly's still here tomorrow, I can play with him again?"

Her father hoisted her up in his arms and said, "Of course. He's your friend. Now let's get you inside." He carried Chelsea off through the portal and toward the farmhouse.

Chelsea's mother lingered behind a moment, and as soon as Chelsea was out of earshot, she turned to Martin and said, "But it won't be here tomorrow, will it?"

Martin smiled, shaking his head, and said, "Definitely not."

"Good. Thank you for protecting our girl, and for coming to get us." She hugged Martin, gave Phillip a look of deep gratitude, glared at Tyler and Gary still hiding behind the tree, and walked through the portal herself.

Martin collapsed the portal, clapped his hands, and said, "Okay. Phillip and I did the hard part, apparently. Now get to work."

"What?" Tyler asked. "You two call her parents to do all the work, take all of the glory for yourselves, and now you want us to destroy the dragon?"

"Yeah," Martin said. "This is your area. That's your dragon. We're happy to help, but we aren't going to do everything for you."

Phillip said, "I agree. It's time for you two to do your part. But, I know it's been a hard day for you, so if it makes you feel better, feel free to give the dragon a makeover first."

36.

Martin, Phillip, Gary, and a still-sulking Tyler appeared in the sky above and just outside Camelot.

When Martin and Phillip had eradicated their dragons, they looked at the map, at first planning to go help Brit and Gwen, because they had the most dragons to deal with. When they saw that Tyler and Gary only had one left, they decided to go help them knock that one out, then the four of them could go help the women. When Gary and Tyler's final remaining dragon was gone, and Tyler gave up trying in vain to explain their embarrassment away, they checked the map again and found that Gwen and Brit had defeated all of the Scottish dragons. The logical move was to make for Camelot, where Jeff and Roy still had five, then they could tend to the three remaining strays which, according to the map, were still loitering harmlessly in the woods outside Leadchurch.

Phillip consulted the map and pointed in the supposed direction of Camelot's dragons, but it wasn't necessary. They didn't see any fire, or hear any screaming, but the black tendrils of smoke drifting up into the sky seemed like a good indication of the dragons' location. Once the smoke told them where to look, the wizards could also see two human figures floating just above the rooftops, looking down.

The wizards flew to the figures, who turned out to be Brit and Gwen. They all said their hellos, then Phillip looked down at the scene below and asked, "What happened here?"

Brit the Younger smiled, and said, "Gwen and I got done with our dragons, came here, found what you see below, had about enough time to wonder what happened, then you showed up."

"Ah. Thank you for that most comprehensive report."

Below them, they saw a scene of utter chaos, made all the more chaotic by the fact that it wasn't the sort of chaos they'd expected.

The dragons, which they'd feared would be in the middle of some sort of rampage, seemed perfectly sedate and happy. All five of them stood around, peacefully munching on a surprising abundance of produce, strewn through a seemingly random pile of debris and old wheeled conveyances.

Jeff and Roy, who they'd expected to find either locked in combat with the dragons or hunkered to the side planning their next move, seemed instead to be engaged in some sort of heated negotiation.

The citizens, who they'd have thought would be taking cover or hiding from the dragons, instead filled most of the square, forming the other side of whatever argument Roy and Jeff were in. The citizens seemed to be winning, primarily by all yelling at once so that nobody but the people right at the center of the action could hear anything Roy and Jeff said. The wizards watched as a citizen wheeled a large wheelbarrow full of cabbages right up to the dragons, dumped the cabbages where the dragons were sure to be able to eat them, then parked his wheelbarrow and joined the crowd shouting at the two wizards.

The local constabulary, whom they might have hoped would be fighting to keep the peace, seemed to have given up on peace as a concept and were instead trying to keep the conflict orderly. They escorted pedestrians around the disturbance, and made sure that the angry citizens formed something resembling a line while they waited for their chance to accost Jeff and Roy.

The smoke seemed to be coming from a single medium-sized building on the outskirts of the market square, which looked almost entirely intact except for one charred corner on the back of the building, away from the dragons.

Phillip activated the battle comm so that Jeff and Roy would hear him. Unfortunately, the communication went both ways. When Jeff answered, they heard the roaring crowd, Jeff pleading with people to calm down and speak one at a time, and Roy refusing to pay someone for their pumpkins. Jeff took a moment to say, "Hello?"

Phillip cleared his throat and said, "What's all this then?"

Martin muttered, "He's always wanted to say that."

Gwen countered, "If you had an English accent, wouldn't you?"

They all saw Jeff look up to see them hovering high above the city. He leaned over and shouted something in Roy's ear, but Roy was still too busy yelling about produce to respond. Jeff took flight and approached the rest of the wizards. He looked simultaneously tired and full of restless stress energy. He also looked several years older than he had when the groups split up.

Phillip asked him, "What's going on?"

"Disaster," Jeff moaned. "It's a total disaster."

Brit asked, "Why haven't you destroyed any of the dragons?"

"Because they're the least of our problems."

Jeff explained how, while following Roy's advice, he had accidentally led the dragons directly to one of Camelot's largest produce markets, and how they had made the mistake of publicly reimbursing the first merchant whose stock got destroyed. A second merchant claimed that the dragons bankrupted him, then a third. Soon, word spread, and merchants who weren't located in the square the dragons had staked out, and who didn't sell food, turned up.

Jeff and Roy stopped giving anyone money pretty quickly, but by then the snowball was already headed down the hill. While they were tied up with trying to talk sense into the merchants they already had on their hands, a steady stream of more kept arriving. Soon the two wizards found themselves completely swamped, and had spent the time since just fighting to be heard.

While Jeff explained, the wizards watched a man with a wheelbarrow full of what appeared to be beaded necklaces and bracelets run into the square and dump his whole load, then join the mob of people crowding around Roy, demanding to be compensated for their losses.

"He didn't even ask to see if Roy was still paying out," Brit said.

"He knows he's up to no good," Gary said. "When you're gonna do some shoplifting, you don't ask the cashier if they still aren't looking."

"Yeah," Brit said. "I suppose him walking up to Roy before dumping his stuff and asking, *Are you still falling for it?* would be a dead giveaway."

"Why didn't you just fly away?" Gary asked.

"After what happened in Leadchurch, we wizards look bad enough. That's why I paraded the dragons around in the first place. Just leaving Camelot with five dragons and a bunch of loud, angry, liars in our wake didn't seem like a great PR move either."

Brit said, "You could have called for help."

"We did. Not to any of you guys. You had your hands full with all the other dragons. We called Eddie."

Eddie was the wizards' liaison to the royal family, and he lived in Camelot. He came from New Jersey originally, but because his family was Asian, the locals knew him as *Wing Po, the mysterious wizard from the East.* He had been Jimmy's right-hand man back when Jimmy called himself *Merlin.* Jimmy fed both Eddie and the royals a steady diet of lies and manipulation right up until the moment the whole Camelot thing hit the fan. In the aftermath, Eddie could relate to the king far better than any of the other wizards, and already knew the ins and outs of the kingdom's workings. In the time since Jimmy's banishment, he had grown into the position quite nicely, and Phillip thought he was starting to show the keen instincts and pragmatic attitude of a born politician.

Phillip asked, "What did Eddie do?"

"He listened to our problem, said, *My name's Paul, and this is between y'all,* and left."

"Yeah," Phillip said. "That sounds like him."

Gary looked down at the crowd surrounding the still-shouting Roy and said, "I think he had the right idea."

Martin said, "No, don't say that. We can help. Look, I live in this town. I know these people, and they know me. I'm sure I can talk to them."

Martin ascended silently to a position about ten yards directly above Roy. Normally, the sight of a flying man in a silver sequined robe would have drawn some attention, but everyone in the market was focused like a laser on Roy, who shouted at the top of his lungs, but his voice couldn't be heard over the hundreds of people shouting so that he could hear them. Martin hovered there for a few seconds, tapping at the screen of his smartphone, still concealed in its silver box, setting up a string of spells, effects, and macros too complex to be triggered by speaking Esperanto.

He activated the program, took advantage of the five-second delay he'd included to put his phone away, stretch, and wink at Gwen, who smiled and rolled her eyes. Then the five seconds were up.

Martin exploded with a deafening boom that people a half mile away could feel in their chests. It overpowered the sound of the combined shouting, rendering the crowd silent with shock. A visible shockwave also radiated out from Martin, moving at well below the speed of sound. He had spent a lot of time on it, modeling it on the expanding ring of fire George Lucas had added to the Death Star explosion for the *Star Wars Special Edition*, and he didn't want all of his work to go unnoticed because it moved too fast.

Martin still hovered above the crowd, but now energy seamed to radiate from him in thick, fast, dangerous-looking waves. A pentagram drawn in silver flames floated in the space behind him. His eyes, mouth, ears, and nostrils emitted silver light as if his skull had been hollowed out and his brain replaced with a halogen bulb. He spoke in a voice not only tremendously amplified but deeper, and made to reverberate as if he were singing in the world's largest bathroom.

"All right, you primitive screw heads, listen up!"

The crowd had fallen silent as soon as the explosion fired, and they stayed silent. Even the dragons lifted their heads from their feast to look.

Martin spread his hands with a flourish, like a casino hotel owner in a bad in-room video, showing guests how large the pool is. A glimmering wall appeared, forming a large circle, blocking all of the streets and paths leading to or from the marketplace and cutting through buildings and objects in its path.

"We will finish this now. Nobody comes or goes until this dispute is settled. Nobody speaks until I tell them to. There will be order. Is that understood?"

Nobody said a word.

"You may speak to answer."

Martin couldn't make out any one person's voice, but the crowd's general murmuring sounded positive.

Watching from well above and far away, Jeff said, "This is exactly the kind of thing Roy and I were trying to avoid."

Brit said, "Yeah, but do you really prefer what you got instead?"

A single voice in the crowd called out, "Hello Martin. I'm glad to see you."

Martin peered into the crowd, trying to locate the person talking, then said, "Oh, hey, Pat." He turned back to look at the other wizards, still floating a good distance away, watching. "It's Pat. I buy cheese from him." Martin never ate the cheese, or any of the food from the Middle Ages, because of their less-advanced ideas about refrigeration, cross-contamination, and whether it was necessary to wash the manure off of a piece of food before you ate it. Nonetheless, he made a point of purchasing things from the local merchants just to be a good neighbor.

"What are you doing way over here on this side of town, Pat? Kinda far from your usual territory, aren't you?"

"One must go where the business is," Pat said.

Martin smiled. "Yeah, I suppose so. About that . . . You know what? One moment, please." Martin had realized that the tone of the conversation had turned cordial enough that it no longer felt appropriate to speak in a terrifying voice with light radiating from every hole in his head while floating in front of a pentagram. He pulled out his phone, poked at it a few times, and one by one the light, pentagram, waves of energy, and reverb went away. The silver walls and the amplification stayed, for now.

"Okay," Martin said. "My friends, the wizards Jeff and Roy, don't own these dragons. Nobody owns these dragons. These are dangerous wild animals that my friends came here to get rid of before they hurt anybody. The first vendor's cart got destroyed, they felt bad about it, and reimbursed him. Then things got out of hand. I'm sure you can all understand that."

A plaintive voice from the crowd cried, "But I'm out all my stock of gourds! It's not fair that that other guy got paid for his stuff and I get nothing."

Roy, still angry and full of adrenaline, bellowed, "Life isn't fair! I never told you to feed your damn gourds to the dragons!"

"What about my building?" another voice cried. "The dragons burned my building down!"

"Your building didn't burn down," Roy said. "It's still standing right over there. It's singed at worst, and I know for a fact that you set that fire yourself."

"Are you calling me a liar, sir?"

"I didn't call you a liar, I just pointed out that you're lying."

Martin said, "Okay, enough, shut up the both of you." And, because his voice was still the loudest thing in the city, they both did.

"We can stand here and argue all day, but it won't solve anything. Here's what we're going to do instead. Roy, you're going to get out of here for a while. I think everyone can agree that you've been through, and caused, a lot of stress. You could do with a little time to calm down. All of you who have lost your belongings to the dragons will form a single-file line around the outside of the market. One by one, me and some of my wizard friends will hear your complaints and compensate you in gold. You all know that you were trying to take advantage of the situation. We could just leave you with nothing, but we aren't. We'll try to be fair, but we also aren't going to put up with any argument. Understood?"

Martin believed that the crowd understood. He also believed that there would still be more than a few arguments, but they'd take that on a case-by-case basis.

Roy and Jeff watched, disgusted, while Martin, Gwen, Brit, and Phillip worked their way through the line. The wizards erred on the side of generosity, and most of the merchants were grateful to be getting anything by that point, so there was little argument and the line moved fast.

Tyler and Gary took care of the dragons in the same manner they'd taken out the majority of the dragons in Wales, by distracting them, eradicating the dragon at the rear of the group butterfly-net style, then disappearing. It didn't take long, and the crowd found it quite entertaining. Tyler and Gary fed off of the crowd's energy, and did a little showboating. Tyler appeared before the dragons floating upside down, or wearing a different robe and asked the dragons if it made him look fat. Gary swung his staff, and the goal attached to it, with all of the grace and subtlety of a twelve-year-old using a wrapping-paper tube as a sword.

As Gary lowered the goal over the last remaining dragon, a cheer went up from the citizens still watching from the wall and the merchants standing in line. Tyler and Gary took a bow, then Tyler turned to Gary, held a palm up at face level and said, "High-five!"

Gary said, "You had plenty of chances," and walked away.

When all of the merchants had been paid off, Martin removed the walls he had created, and the crowd dispersed. Many of them traded disdainful glares with Roy on the way. Once they were all out of earshot, Roy said, "I hate the idea that all these frauds managed to turn a profit off of this."

Phillip patted him on the back. "Oh, I wouldn't worry too much about that, Roy. I think that unless they spend that gold pretty fast, they'll find that it has been significantly devalued in the British Isles."

"Why?"

"We'll tell you later."

"Yeah," Martin said. "Over dinner. I say we all celebrate. Those were the last of the dragons, right?"

Jeff had his dragon map out, and said, "Eh, almost. There are still those three stragglers in the woods outside Leadchurch. They weren't in as dangerous a spot as these in Camelot, so we left them for last. Looks like they haven't moved much at all, so that's good. Roy and I'll just go get them and then it's all done."

Phillip said, "You know what? You and Roy have had it pretty hard today, and frankly, I think of Leadchurch as my territory. I'll go get them. Brit explained her method to me. It seems pretty straightforward."

The rest of the wizards sort of communally shrugged.

Martin said, "Okay, then. Everyone else come to my place. Phillip, you meet up with us later. Promise you'll call if you need some help."

Phillip agreed, and a few seconds later, every wizard but Phillip appeared in the living quarters and workshop at the rear of Martin's warehouse. A quick, informal game of musical chairs ensued as everyone tried to find a seat. They all sagged for a second, exhausted, before Martin, playing the good host, said, "Okay, let's talk dinner. Pizza or Chinese?"

They all lay motionless for a moment, trying to summon the will to answer, but before they could, the peace was shattered by the high-pitched warbling noise that signified a call coming in from another wizard. Martin lifted his hand and saw an image of Phillip floating in his palm.

Phillip's voice said, "On second thought, I could use some help. From all of you. Now."

37.

Honor woke up to find Kludge kneeling over her, holding her tiny shoulder in his huge, meaty hand. Runt sat next to her, whining a bit. When Honor looked at Runt, the dog stopped whining and rested her head on Honor's thigh.

Honor pushed Kludge's hands away and sat up, rubbing her eyes. She had fallen asleep watching the Bastards practice flying the dragons. She looked up and saw that they were still up there, steering their dragons in long, relaxed curves, or the occasional banking slalom.

"Hmmm. I'm a bit hungry. Think I could get a scone?"

"Stretch has been making them dragon sized, but I'll have him break a corner off of one for you," Kludge said.

"I hope you haven't used up all of my flour and butter. Sonny and I traded a lot of mutton for that."

"We did use up what you had, but I sent Gripper into town to replace all of it and get enough to make scones ourselves."

"Oh," Honor said. "Good. What did you trade for it?"

Kludge laughed, looked at Honor for a long moment, then decided to change the subject. "Your brother's name is Sonny." He said it like a statement, but he had meant it as a question.

"Yes. I just had a dream about him."

"From the way you were shouting *Sonny*, I figured it was either that or you were dreaming that you were a deaf old lady."

"Wow! They're getting pretty good at that." Honor pointed at the other gang members drifting around the sky on the backs of dragons. Now it was her turn to change the subject.

"Better than I ever expected," Kludge said. "The dragons seem to like being ridden. It's like they go into a kind of trance. I wish horses were as easy to ride."

"The boys seem sure of themselves. Seems brave of them to be going so high."

"What's the point of riding a flying dragon if you stay close to the ground? Besides, it ain't an accident that gangs are made up of young men who have nothing. We value our lives little enough to risk them for a little money or a lot of fun."

"Still only three dragons? We haven't found more?"

"No, but that's fine. Might be better. We can double up this way. We could patrol the skies and attack any wizard we see. We'll take it in shifts until we actually find one of them, then I figure one guy can fly the dragon and a second will ride behind him, tied together at the waist. They're practicing it right now. The one in back can throw rocks or shoot arrows. Maybe taunt the wizards. Anything that makes 'em unhappy. They're practicing with the rocks right now."

"Why start with rocks? Arrows seem like a better weapon."

"Yeah, but before we can get any archery practice we'll need to steal some bows."

Honor looked past the dragons at the sky itself. It was late enough that she wouldn't be quite comfortable calling it late afternoon, but she also couldn't quite call it early evening. "So, what do you think? Are you planning to go after the wizards tomorrow?"

"Yeah. We could be in Leadchurch by nightfall, but it's been a big day. I figure the lads'll be more dangerous after a good night's sleep."

"Kludge, do you think you can really beat the wizards?"

"The dragons are the break I've been waiting for. I'll never get a better chance."

"But can you really do it?"

"Yes. I believe I can."

"Why?"

"Because I have to believe I can, or believe that I can't. Those are the only two options. And I don't want to believe that I can't."

Honor said, "I guess we'll find out for sure at dawn."

"Yeah," Kludge agreed. "Unless something happens that makes us attack sooner."

They both saw movement in a part of the sky where there were no dragons. It was Phillip, flying into view.

"Something like that," Kludge said.

Phillip stopped all forward flight and looked at the dragons, clearly stunned to see people riding them.

Kludge pointed up at Phillip and shouted, "Attack! Attack! It's a wizard! Get him!"

The three dragons turned sharply in the air, making tight spirals until their riders caught sight of Phillip, then all three started to converge on his location.

On the ground, Stretch came running from the spot next to the fire he'd been occupying most of the day. "Do you want I should attack, too, Kludge? I only ask because I have a batch of scones baking. They aren't quite ready yet, but they're due to come out soon. It's really easy to burn them if—"

Kludge shouted, "Stretch, stay with the scones." Then he shouted toward the dragons, "Pounder, get down here, now!"

Pounder was the one Bastard riding solo. He peeled off from the other two and descended back to the ground. Gripper and L.L. guided their dragons into a swooping dive to intercept Phillip. They flew in rings around him while Only Donnie and Heel-Kick rode behind them, each carrying a large sack full of rocks.

Phillip recognized the Bastards, of course. Anyone who lived in Leadchurch and wanted to keep all of their teeth knew how to recognize and avoid the gang. Phillip, as a wizard, was invulnerable to physical attacks. As long as he had his powers, the only nonmagical ways to kill him were to starve him, smother him, or deny him water until he died of dehydration, none of which were part of the standard street-tough repertoire. They couldn't hurt him, but they could easily hurt other people, or themselves, so Phillip decided to try starting with diplomacy.

"Gentlemen! Good to see you. I must say, I'm impressed that you've managed to learn to ride dragons. You seem quite adept, and I know you haven't had much time to learn. Congratulations! If I might inquire, what's in those bags? The ones the passengers are carrying. Yes, what is that?"

A small rock bounced off of Phillip's head.

"I see. They're rocks," he said, shielding his head with his arms as best he could. "Yes. Both of you have rocks. Look, there's no need to keep throwing them. I'm fully aware that you have rocks. Aren't you better than this? Riding dragons and using them as a platform for rock throwing? Really? I mean they aren't even hurting me. You can see that. They bounce ri—oof. Okay, very good. You got one in my mouth. It was blind luck, but still, bravo."

The dragon riders kept circling Phillip, pelting him with rocks. Phillip said, "*Persona ŝildo.*" The rocks stopped hitting him, instead bouncing off of an invisible force-field cylinder that surrounded him.

"There, see, your rocks can't hit me anymore. Now, if you'll excuse me, I have to make a quick call."

Pounder brought his dragon, the only one with those tough-looking horns, down next to Kludge. One of the primary skills that all of the Bastards had mastered was the ability to anticipate what Kludge wanted.

It went without saying that you gave Kludge whatever he wanted, but the Bastards who managed to stay in the gang *and* remain healthy tended to try to give him what he wanted before he requested it, as Kludge's requests usually came with some form of physical abuse.

Pounder pushed himself farther back on the dragon so that Kludge could take control and said, "Come on, Boss. Let's go!"

Kludge hoisted himself onto the dragon's shoulders, then shoved Pounder off of the beast's back. Pounder landed on his side and rolled, trying to get wind back in his lungs.

Kludge said, "You stay here and watch the girl."

Honor said, "Yeah, watch me go with Kludge to fight the wizards."

"No," Kludge said, "you aren't coming with me."

Honor had already shoved Runt in her carry bag and was pulling herself with great difficulty up onto the dragon's back behind Kludge. "Fine," she said, "If you don't want to go with me, stay here, but I'm going after the wizards!"

Kludge bared his teeth at her and growled. When that had no effect, he bared his teeth again and growled, "All right, hang on then."

Pounder lay there, dumbfounded by what he'd seen. Not the sight of a man, a girl, and a dog flying away on the back of a dragon, but the sight of Honor standing up to Kludge and getting her way.

The rest of the wizards appeared, suspended in midair around Phillip.

"Okay," Martin asked, "What's going on?"

Phillip said, "Kludge and the Bastards found the dragons and figured out how to ride them."

Jeff spun around. "Hey, the dragon-riding algorithm seems to work great, doesn't it?"

"That's really not the point," Phillip said.

Gwen cried out, more in surprise than pain, "What was that?"

"Probably a rock," Phillip said. "They're also throwing rocks."

Gwen rubbed the back of her head and said, "That's just petty." She quickly created a force field around herself to repel the rocks. The other wizards followed suit, showing Gwen that she'd had a good idea without lowering themselves to actually telling her. The onslaught continued but now, instead of hitting the wizards and causing them to flinch involuntarily, the rocks bounced off their invisible barriers, causing them to flinch involuntarily.

Tyler said, "This isn't good."

Roy countered, "No, it's great. Phil wanted to put on a bit of a show for the people in town to rehabilitate our image. What'll look better: getting rid of three dragons, or defeating the town's most feared hoodlums while they're riding dragons with intent to harm us?"

"Again with the air-show concept," Jeff said. "We tried to grandstand earlier and you saw where that got us."

"Yeah," Roy said, "But we learned from our mistake."

"Did we? I know I did, but you? I'm not so sure."

"Kid, what are the odds of things going south on us twice in one day?"

"Given that it's us, pretty good."

Roy turned away from Jeff and toward Phillip. "Look, they're trying to hurt us, right? We'll keep them focused on us, lead them around the outside of town or very high over it, not down in the streets. Then, after we've put on a little bit of a show, we separate the guys from the dragons somehow and take the dragons out. It's a good plan."

Jeff said, "Good plans almost never contain the word *somehow*."

Phillip bit his lip, thought a second, and said, "Yeah, okay, but we try to keep them from going over the town itself, and we only play with them for a minute—two tops—before we get rid of them. Got it?"

A few of the wizards said yes as if this was the best idea they'd ever heard. The rest said yes as if it was the worst.

Gary pointed off into the distance. "Leadchurch is that way. I guess we should get a move on." He set out first, but all of the wizards followed very close behind. Phillip left last, partly because of his lack of enthusiasm for the plan, but mostly because he was distracted and confused by something he had seen as the group left.

Brit noticed that Phillip seemed preoccupied, flying forward, but continually looking back. She decreased speed slightly to draw even with him.

"What?" she asked.

Phillip shook his head, looked at her, and asked, "What?"

"That's what I'm asking. What's bothering you, Phillip? I can tell something's up."

"Oh, it's probably nothing. Just something weird I thought I saw."

"Given the current situation, I'd be curious to hear what struck you as being particularly weird."

Phillip chuckled, then said, "For just a moment, I could have sworn that one of the dragons is being piloted by one person who has three heads."

Kludge, Honor, and Runt hadn't quite reached the group when the wizards flew away. The other two dragons continued to circle around an empty chunk of sky while the riders and rock throwers decided how to react, and dodged rocks that had been thrown while there were still intended targets in the crossfire.

Any doubt about how to proceed evaporated the instant they saw Kludge fly past, yelling "After them, fools!"

The wizards flew well below their top speed, but took great care to almost exactly match the dragons' top speed. They flew in a loose clump, mostly looking to the rear, instead of where they were going. Behind them, the three dragons flew in a V formation, with the horned dragon ridden by Kludge and his passengers in the lead.

Kludge sat across the dragon's shoulders with his legs hooked under its wings. He had a death grip on the edges of two of the scales on either side of the dragon's neck. He concentrated on catching up to the wizards while trying not to think about what would happen if he lost his grip.

Honor would have said she was standing behind Kludge, and her feet were resting on the dragon's back, but it would be more accurate to say that she was lying on Kludge's back with her upper body slewed far to the left so she could see around his head. She had her arms wrapped tight around his torso, and was concentrating on catching up to the wizards while trying not to think about what would happen if she lost her grip on Kludge.

Most of Runt's body was in Honor's sack, which was slung around her right side and lay on Kludge's back, a smallish mass of warm, dead weight. Runt's head protruded out into the open, and stuck up and to the right so she could see around the other side of Kludge's head. She was concentrating only on how good the wind felt rushing over her tongue, because it was simply unthinkable to her that Honor would ever let her fall.

Kludge looked at the makeup of the two sides and did the math. He counted eight wizards. On his side, he had three dragons, two of which held two men each, the third of which carried himself, Honor, and Runt. Add all of them together, including the dragons and Runt, that made ten fighting on his side, which was more than eight, so the very laws of mathematics stated that Kludge would be victorious.

He knew that this was terrible reasoning, but these dragons were the best chance he might ever get to show the wizards that he wouldn't be pushed around, and he didn't intend to let it slip through his fingers just because it was a terrible idea.

The trickiest part would be finding a way to get the girl safely on the ground before things turned violent. He'd let her tag along because he hadn't had time to argue, and she had as much reason to want to see the wizards go down as anyone, but he had no intention of letting her be anywhere nearby when things turned ugly.

One of the wizards, the older one in a light blue robe, kept looking back at him.

The wizard slowed slightly, drawing in closer to Kludge's dragon. Kludge cursed the fact that they hadn't found a way to make the dragons breathe fire on command. If he had, he could have roasted the wizard like a big light blue squab.

The wizard got close enough to get a good look at Kludge and Honor, and seemed horrified. The wizard flew through the air only feet in front of Kludge's dragon. He turned, and in a voice full of anger and reproach said, "Kludge, on the ground now!"

Town was pretty far from the Bastards' camp and Honor's farm beyond it, as judged by people who had to ride horses along the winding, muddy road, walk along the same road, or push their way through the woods to get there. For wizards and dragons flying in a straight line at a little under thirty-five miles per hour, the trip took less than a minute.

By the time Phillip recognized what and who he was looking at, the town was close enough to see people walking around the buildings.

Kludge scowled at Phillip, but silently thanked him for the excuse to drop Honor off. He landed in the street outside the Rotted Stump.

Phillip landed in front of the dragon. He said something, but Kludge didn't hear. He listened instead to Honor, who squeezed him slightly tighter and whispered in his ear, "This one's their leader. I'll handle him. You go back up and help the others."

Kludge looked at her, incredulously, then turned to Phillip and said, "What did you say?"

Phillip said, "Let the girl go."

Kludge's first impulse was to do anything but what the wizard had told him to, but Honor was already scrambling down off the dragon, and she seemed at least marginally safer on solid ground with one wizard than up in the sky, clinging to a dragon, surrounded by the other seven wizards.

Kludge gave Phillip a look he hoped communicated the idea that if any harm came to Honor, he would kill Phillip. He figured Phillip probably misinterpreted it as a threat to kill him in any case, but Kludge didn't mind so much.

Honor hit the ground. She pulled Runt out of her bag and put her down. Then Honor reached into the bag and locked eyes on Phillip, but spoke to Kludge. "Go!"

Phillip shouted, "Yeah, go, Kludge! Run! I knew you were a coward, but I didn't think you'd use a little orphan girl as a human shield."

Kludge reluctantly dug his heels into the dragon's ribs. As the great beast took off, he saw Honor start running toward Phillip, and heard her shout, "I'm not a shield! I'm a sword!"

The remainder of the wizards were still flying high above the outskirts of town, and they found themselves in a situation familiar to anyone who has ever been attacked by a kitten. They were the target of an irritating and embarrassing assault by an obviously inferior force, and they had to find a way to end the fight without harming the opponent, who seemed intent on murdering them. They flew in a tight group, followed by two dragons, the riders of which were still peppering them with rocks.

"Okay," Brit said, as a rock bounced harmlessly off the force field behind her. "Ideas, anyone?"

Gary twitched as a rock hit the force field near his head, and said, "How about we just yank them off the dragons one at a time, then take out the dragons when we're done?"

Gwen said, "We'd have to be careful. Grabbing them by an arm or a leg with a force field at the speeds we're moving could easily break bones. Even if we got them around the torso, if we pull too hard there could be internal injuries."

Brit asked, "Do you have an answer to that, Gary?"

Gary said, "No. I hadn't thought it through. Heck, I didn't even think of using magic. I meant just flying up and, like, grabbing them by the collar or something."

"And you expected to carry them all the way to the ground like that?" Brit asked.

"I already said I hadn't thought it through."

Tyler said, "The point is, we have to get the Bastards off the dragons gently, in a way that they know they're supported. We don't want them to think they're falling and die of a heart attack."

"Yes. Good point," Brit said. "The most important thing is to get this done without any nonwizards getting hurt, even the ones attacking us."

A rock nearly, but didn't quite, hit Brit in the face, causing her to cringe and mutter a string of obscenities.

Gary asked, "Are you sure we can't hurt them at all?"

Brit chose not to answer.

Roy said, "I have an idea. The dragons sail right through our force fields, but the people riding them wouldn't."

Martin said, "Yeah, we can screen them off."

"Yeah," Roy said. "But, if we just throw one up in front of them it'll be like running full speed into a brick wall, and the dragons' wings would crush their legs. I think though, if it was a spherical force field that appeared around them, then moved forward clear of the wings, then straight up, it'd pull them off with nothing worse than a few scrapes."

Tyler added, "And if you make the bubble glow, they'll know they're held up by something."

"Yeah, but it'll take me a few minutes to program."

Brit said, "I'm sure it will. In the meantime, we get to try out our anti-dragon macros on live targets. Just remember, keep it strictly kid gloves."

Gary pumped his fist and said, "Woooohoooo!"

Martin said, "I think *kid gloves* means no Uzi, Gary."

"Maybe. Or maybe it means I only fire my Uzi over their heads."

Phillip was in a similar predicament. An opponent who couldn't possibly hope to defeat him was attacking him nonetheless. But his friends faced an at least formidable-looking force in the sky fairly distant from the citizens of Leadchurch. Phillip faced the town's favorite orphan girl in the middle of the street. The locals hadn't come out to gawk yet, but the sight of a dragon ridden by the town's top bully, landing in the street followed closely by the town's top wizard, had drawn everybody to the windows. Especially in the tavern, where watching people fight was one of the primary pastimes.

Phillip hadn't fully processed this, or much of anything. Having the girl he thought he'd rescued prove just as hostile as the man Phillip had rescued her from, then start frantically rushing him while screaming bloody murder, caused his entire nervous system to freeze.

Honor suffered no such paralysis. Her mind and body were both working far faster than normal. She closed the distance between herself and Phillip in no time at all, then used her momentum to give her attack more power.

Honor was a girl, but she had a brother, and had had a father, both of whom wanted her to be able to protect herself. They had each, at one point or another, explained to her the best, and by *best* they meant *worst,* place to kick a man. That is where she attacked Phillip, but instead of kicking, because of her shorter stature and running start, she chose to punch instead.

Phillip was a wizard. This meant that he was impervious to physical damage, but this was not the same as being immune to pain. Impacts could still hurt, and impacts to the area Honor had targeted still hurt quite a bit.

This was a substantial weakness for the male wizards, but nobody had thought of a permanent solution to resolve it. In the end, the wizards decided that the best way to protect that area was to act in such a manner as to keep people from wanting to hurt that area in the first place.

It was a good plan, which hadn't worked in this case.

Phillip doubled over in pain and dropped to his knees.

Honor stepped back and said, "That was for my brother."

Phillip knew Honor's situation, including the fact that her older brother, barely more than a boy himself, was raising her. Hearing her mention him triggered the memory of how he and Martin had taken care of Tyler and Gary's problem involving a child.

"Where is your brother?" Phillip asked. "I'd like to talk to him."

"You don't even know?" she shouted. "That's how little you lot care? You don't even bother to find out which of us you've hurt?"

"What?"

"You heard me! You wizards play your silly tricks and lord your power over the rest of us, and when we get hurt, you can't bother yourself to find out who we even are. You just hit us with a sleep spell so we won't complain and go on about your merry way!"

Phillip searched his memory like a criminal tossing a room in an old detective movie, eventually coming up with the name, "Sonny." He looked at Honor. Hearing her brother's name had silenced her for the moment. Phillip glanced around and saw that people had started filtering out of the tavern, and the various other huts and hovels that lined the streets, drawn out by the sounds of a fight, the promise of possible magic, and the absence of Kludge riding a dragon.

"Your brother's name is Sonny, right?" Phillip asked. "Was he hurt in the dragon attack? Is that what you're saying?"

"Yes," Honor shrieked. "That's what I'm saying! Your dragons attacked our town. You tried to keep us from hurting your dragons. Sonny got hurt. You put him under some sort of evil sleeping spell and left without even saying you were sorry!"

"He's not under an *evil sleeping spell*."

"Then why won't he wake up?"

"Because of magic," Phillip said, wincing at how bad it sounded, even to him. "Okay, it's a spell, but it isn't evil. It's just to give him time to rest and recuperate from his wounds. It's meant to assist people who are hurt."

"People you hurt!"

"We didn't hurt your brother," Phillip said, trying out his *being firm* voice. "Some people were injured running from the dragons and some were injured fighting the dragons, but nobody was attacked by a wizard."

Honor, being a child, had the innate ability to tell when an adult was simply trying out their *being firm* voice, and as such, pressed her attack. "And I know that you wizards were keeping the dragons like livestock. I saw the pen you kept them in. You trained them to attack. You might have even created them."

Phillip realized instantly that everything Honor had said was true. He also recognized that admitting any part of it would be disastrous. He had no children, so he didn't feel comfortable just deliberately lying to a child. He looked around to the people watching, people he considered friends and neighbors. He shrugged and made a facial expression that said, *Kids—am I right?*

More than one of the spectators replied with an expression that seemed to say, *The kid's got a point.*

In the air high above Leadchurch, seven wizards did their best to confuse five men riding on three dragons.

Gripper and Heel-Kick were chasing Brit to pelt her with rocks, when suddenly there were many of her, all identical, all laughing at them. Heel-Kick wound up to throw a rock and froze, suddenly seized with a crippling case of option paralysis.

"Oh no," Heel-Kick shouted. "Oh no no no!"

"Throw," Gripper shouted into the wind.

"There's too many of her," Heel-Kick cried.

Gripper shouted, "That'll just make her easier to hit!"

Gripper did his best to maneuver the dragon through the Brit cloud, but he had difficulties because the Brits kept moving.

When he finally managed to find his way to clear sky, he immediately had to make a tight turn that devolved into a dive in order to avoid hitting another dragon. He feared it was Kludge, but as the dragon gave chase, Heel-Kick said, "Oh God! There's nobody riding it!"

Gripper worried that one of the gang members had fallen from their dragon. He couldn't help imagining their terror at falling, and only snapped back to reality when a voice called out, "Hey, you two, up there on the dragon I'm chasing. I don't want to see you get hurt. Land and get off of the dragon now, before things get ugly."

Gripper asked, "Who said that?"

Heel-Kick answered, "The dragon! The dragon chasing us said it!"

Elsewhere, Kludge fended off an attack from Gwen's clothing. He hadn't even been chasing her. She flew down in front of his dragon, then her robe grew to fill his field of vision, slapping him lightly in the face as it rippled in the wind.

Kludge had plenty of experience as a fighter and knew how to use an opponent's attack against them. He grabbed a handful of the fabric and yanked back as hard as he could, intent on stopping Gwen's forward motion, but the fabric went completely slack, stretching and expanding faster than he could pull on it. He grabbed another handful and pulled, then another, then another, hauling back like a magician pulling an endless rope of knotted scarves out of a hat.

Only Donnie and L.L.'s dragon flew a serpentine path, twisting and turning in a vain attempt to lose Martin, whose immense silver glowing form dangled from their dragon's tail.

Only Donnie shrieked, "Get rid of him!"

L.L. had a death grip on the scales of the dragon's neck. He pulled and twisted with all of his might. "I'm trying, but he won't let go. How about you do something, instead of panicking?"

"What can I do?" Only Donnie said, "I've already thrown all my rocks at him. I dumped the whole bag! Then I threw the bag at him! Nothing!"

"Well then find something else to throw!"

"How about you, L.L.? I could just grab you by the earlobes and whip you around my head a few times to build up speed."

Martin shouted, "Don't feel bad, guys. At least you both know you've done your best."

In his peripheral vision, Martin saw a dark object, roughly the size of a person, falling. He assumed it was one of the Bastards, and prepared to intercept and rescue them before they hit the ground, but then a straight, white line shot from the falling person and hit the dragon's right wing with an audible *thwip*. The line tightened into a cord and the person falling swung into Martin with great force.

Martin managed to keep his grip on the dragon's tail despite the impact. He looked over and saw Gary, hanging on to one of his Spider-Man webs. The dragon's tail and torso stayed relatively steady in flight. Gary's web was attached to the dragon's wing, which did not. While Martin's enlarged form only bobbed up and down slightly in the air, Jeff bucked up and down as violently as a roller coaster, and he whooped and cheered accordingly. After several seconds of this, Gary reached into his robe with one hand, pulled out his Uzi, and fired a burst into the air.

Martin yelled, "Gary, what did we say about the gun?"

Gary said, "Relax! It's blanks," then fired another burst.

Martin said, "That's not the point. It's the principle of—"

"Hold that thought," Gary said. "I see Kludge!" Gary let go of his web and fell away.

Martin looked toward the two men on the dragon's back, both of whom had their necks craned around to look at him. Martin said, "Sorry, guys, I gotta go have a talk with my friend," and let go of their dragon as well.

"Well, how do you like that?" L.L. said. "They're just ignoring us, like we aren't even a threat."

Only Donnie said, "We aren't a threat. I'm out of rocks and they know it. Besides, are you really going to complain because two wizards aren't attacking us?"

L.L. said, "It's nice to feel wanted is all."

Now far behind them, Kludge still circled high above Leadchurch on the horned dragon, but he no longer flew alone. He had finally given up on defeating the multiple Brits and Gwen's robe. He disengaged, and only managed to fly a few precious moments unharassed before a white, stringy substance shot into his field of view from above and struck the head of his dragon. The material seemed to be many long, straight strands of a ropelike fiber, held together by smaller threads to form a cable about as big around as a man's thumb. The cable thickened as its elasticity drew whatever hung from the other end closer to him, until finally Gary dropped into view, landing very fast, straddling the dragon's neck just behind its head.

Kludge was very close to Gary, but he couldn't just reach out and grab him. Kludge only felt confident in his ability to stay on the dragon as long as he used both hands to do it.

Gary saw that all of Kludge's limbs were occupied. He reached into his robe and pulled out his Uzi, which he held in Kludge's face and said, "Land this dragon now."

Kludge went cross-eyed looking at the Uzi, then leaned to one side and asked Gary, "What's this thing?"

Gary said, "What do you mean, *What's this thing?* It's a gun."

Kludge nodded and looked at the Uzi again, then asked, "What's it do?"

"What do you mean, what's it do? It's a gun! How ignorant are you?"

Behind Kludge, a voice said, "How ignorant are *you*, Gary?"

Kludge looked back and saw Brit the Younger flying up fast.

She made contact with Kludge's dragon, and flew along, carefully matching the dragon's speed and direction so that she appeared to be standing casually on the dragon's back.

Brit said, "Guns aren't even invented until, like, over a hundred years from now."

Gary said, "What about cannons?"

"A cannon is a kind of gun. I think they might have them in China, but not around here for a long time."

"But we've screwed up the timeline so much, I'm sure a violent guy like Kludge has heard of them. How about it, Kludge, ever heard of a cannon?"

"No."

"How about gunpowder? It's this black powder you can make that burns violently when you light it?"

"I may have heard of something like that."

"Well that can be used to make a weapon."

"Yeah?"

Gary said, "Oh yeah!" He fired a burst into the air to demonstrate his point. "If you put enough of it into a really strong tube, and put a ball of like, rock or lead in there you—"

Brit hit Gary with a blast of energy that knocked him off the dragon. Gary fell out of view, then a line of webbing streaked through the sky, barely missing the dragon's wing, then falling, slack, pulled down by Gary's weight.

Brit leaned over the side of the dragon and shouted, "Remember, you can fly!"

Brit and Kludge made eye contact, sharing a brief chuckle at Gary's expense. Then, while Brit was distracted, Kludge threw the dragon into a sharp banking turn, followed by an equally violent turn in the opposite direction. He glanced back again, and Brit wasn't there. He had successfully shaken her off. He turned forward again and saw Brit slowly rise in front of him.

Brit said, "Remember, I can fly, too."

While the other wizards enjoyed their participation in a one-sided contest they knew they couldn't lose, Phillip was stuck in a battle he knew he couldn't win. An ever-increasing number of his friends and neighbors had gathered to watch him get shouted at by a young girl, which is always damaging to an adult's dignity, even if the adult is in the right. The constant angry yapping of her little dog certainly didn't help.

Phillip said, "Listen, I need to go help my friends. Please stay right here, and I promise you won't be harmed. When I get—"

Honor said, "Don't threaten me."

Phillip sputtered for a moment before finally spitting out, "I didn't! I said you wouldn't be harmed! What kind of threat is that? And can you please do something to calm your dog down?"

Honor said, "You said I wouldn't be harmed *if* I do what you say. *If* I stay here, and don't help my friends, while you go fight them."

"All I meant was that you'd be safe here. As for helping your friends," Phillip pointed straight up into the sky, "the fight is up there! I can go there because I can fly. You can't."

"Don't tell me what I can't do!"

"I'm not trying to tell you what you can't do! I'm just telling you that you can't . . . Look, I'm not ordering you not to fly. I'm pointing out that you're not able to. Can you please make the dog stop barking?"

"You think wizards are the only ones who can do magic? Well, you're wrong!" She reached into her bag and pulled out a small bundle wrapped in cloth. She shook the bundle. The fabric loosened and fell away, revealing the muck-encrusted idol Hubert had given her.

One of the town folk watching said, "I've seen that before. It belongs to the necromancer. He sings to it in an unnatural voice while twisting and manipulating its limbs."

Phillip rubbed his eyes wearily and said, "One moment, please." He activated the battle comm and said, "Hey, Gary?"

Phillip heard Gary say, "Sorry Phil, can't talk. I'm busy webbing up a dragon so it can't fly."

Tyler's voice said, "No, you're busy webbing *me* up so I can't fly!"

Gary said, "Oh. Okay. Yeah, Phillip. I've got a minute. What do you want?"

Phillip asked, "Did you lose one of your KISS dolls?" He did it in a hushed tone. The people watching knew he was communicating with someone, but none of them knew who, or what he said. They all recognized his expression of displeasure when Jeff told him not only that he'd misplaced the doll, but where and how.

He deactivated the comm, looked at Honor, and said, "I really don't think you want to be touching that thing. Why don't you just put it down?"

Honor shouted, "Never!" She and Runt both rushed Phillip. Their sudden advance, and the object that led the advance, startled and horrified him so badly that he stepped backward, stumbled, and fell flat on his back.

Honor stood over Phillip, straddling his chest. Runt danced around his head, still yapping and snarling. Phillip started to push her off, but Honor held the doll inches from his face. He turned his head away and grimaced, but he stopped resisting out of fear she might touch him with it.

"There," Honor said. "You're afraid of it, aren't you? I knew it had power. It's not so much fun to have magic used against you, is it?"

"I'll admit, I'm not enjoying this," he said, keeping his head turned to the side and pressed onto the dirt to gain as much distance as he could from the doll. Phillip knew the doll had no magic. All of its power was biological and olfactory in nature, but he feared that any disagreement with the girl would only result in her pressing it to his face, an outcome he wanted to avoid at all costs.

In his ear, Phillip heard Roy through the battle comm say, "Okay, the macro's almost done."

Phillip decided to buy some time. If he could hold out, hopefully Roy's macro would distract Honor and all of the spectators long enough for him to gently remove her and the doll from his personal space.

"Fine," Phillip said. "You've got me. What is it you want?"

Instead of showing signs of relief or triumph that she might get her way, Honor seemed livid that he even had to ask. "I want my brother back!"

Phillip said, "We didn't take your brother. He's still here, somewhere. Where is he?"

"He's in the church, with everyone else you hexed."

"Well, there you go. He's in the church, and I don't like the word hexed. It suggests—" Phillip stopped talking abruptly as the doll got closer to his face.

"His body is in the church, but he isn't. He's gone. I want him back."

"He'll wake up soon."

"I don't want him back soon! I want him back now! You think you can just tell us how it's going to be and we have to take it because you have magic and we don't."

Roy's voice in Phillip's ear said, "There. It's done."

Honor said, "You do what you want, when you want, and you don't care what anyone thinks, or what it does to anybody's lives but yours!"

Phillip heard Gwen ask, "It won't hurt them, will it?"

Roy answered, "Who, the Bastards? It shouldn't. I've tried to make it as gentle as possible, but if there are some bumps or bruises, hey, they attacked us, right?"

Honor continued, "And why do you do it? To rub our faces in the fact that you're wizards and we're not."

In Phillip's ear, Martin asked, "So the macro will pull them off of the dragons?"

"Yup," Roy said. "And it'll make a nice show of it, too. Glowing bubbles of energy, lots of light and sound effects. Should make quite an impression."

Honor drew Phillip's attention back to the conversation at hand by shaking the doll over his face and shouting, "You're not even listening!"

"I am," Phillip said as articulately as he could while keeping his lips pressed mostly shut, lest something should be shaken loose of the doll and fall toward his mouth. "I'm sorry."

"Sure, you're sorry now that I have magic, too. You're not sorry for what you did to Sonny. We're just bugs to you, aren't we? We can't do anything to you, so why worry about us, right? And if someone comes even close to being a threat, you make them sorry. I don't know what you did to poor Kludge, but he won't discuss it, and fighting and pain are his favorite things to talk about."

"Look, I'm not happy about what happened to Kludge, but, I mean, he is Kludge. You can't say he's an innocent victim."

"Kludge and his friends have been kind to me and Runt! None of them has hurt us. You wizards have."

Phillip rolled his eyes to look at the people watching. At first he'd assumed that nobody came to his aid because he didn't seem to need help. Then he assumed that they saw he was in a mess and didn't want to get into the mess with him. Looking at them now, he saw that at least some of them weren't interfering because they wanted to hear what the girl had to say. Maybe some of the things she was saying were things they had thought before.

The conversation in Phillip's ear had continued, but he'd been concentrating on Honor and had lost the thread. Now he picked it up again, and heard Martin ask, "—it'll keep the Bastards neutralized?"

Roy said, "Completely. They'll be stuck in energy bubbles, floating around in the sky for everyone to look at until we decide they're ready to come down."

Phillip pictured it in his head. Then, he pictured how it would look to the girl using his sternum as a stool, and all the people standing around, watching. He activated the battle comm and said, "Everyone, disengage with the Bastards and medevac yourselves now, before doing anything else. Now!"

38.

Louiza slumped in her desk chair. Her back curved in a way that she knew was terrible for her lumbar region, but it was the only way to get her body low enough for the back of the chair to support her head.

She shifted her eyes to look at the ice-cold bottle of beer sweating on her desk. She wanted it very badly, but she hadn't wanted to expend the energy to turn her head to look at it. The much-greater effort it would take to reach out for the bottle and bring it to her face just didn't seem feasible. She considered creating a spell that would deposit a small amount of beer directly into her mouth. It would have been very handy in this situation, but also sounded like a good way to choke to death.

It said something about her level of fatigue that the idea of drowning in beer didn't sound bad.

Her thirst finally overcame her lethargy. She took a long drink from the bottle and savored it, holding the bottle on her belly with both hands. Feeling a bit rejuvenated, she looked across her desk at Brit the Elder.

She had to be tired, too, but she wasn't giving in to it, at least not as obviously as Louiza was. Brit the Elder sat with perfect posture, and her hair and clothes were as impeccable as ever, but she stared into the middle distance with no light in her eyes, even as she enjoyed a sip of ice-cold Hi-C.

Louiza said, "Would you like me to get you something stronger?"

"No, thank you."

"We could pour a jigger of vodka in that or something."

Brit the Elder smirked and asked, "Isn't it a bit unusual for a doctor to recommend liquor to her patients?"

Louiza said, "It depends on the doctor. The whole reason I got into this racket is that I grew up watching reruns of M*A*S*H. It holds up surprisingly well when translated into Portuguese. We just spent a whole day treating battle injuries. After a day like that, Hawkeye and B.J. would always have a stiff drink."

Brit said, "I always preferred Trapper."

Louiza said, "Old-school. Nice."

The two sat in silence for a moment, each enjoying her drink.

Louiza said, "I liked Bishop Galbraith. He really got into the spirit of the thing."

Brit the Elder nodded. "I think you'll probably see him again. Now that he's gotten a glimpse of modern medicine, I suspect he'll ask Phillip to get you if a member of his flock gets terribly injured."

"You suspect he will, or you remember that he does?"

"I don't think I should tell you."

"Don't think you should, or remember that you don't?"

"Louiza, I haven't lived this conversation before. I don't have any idea what you or I are going to say next."

Louiza considered Brit's statement for a few seconds, until her train of thought got derailed by a sound similar to a digital watch chime. Louiza knew instantly what it meant. A fresh patient had materialized in the medevac triage room.

"And I suppose you don't remember this either."

Brit sighed. "I remember that it happened at some point, because I was involved when I was Brit the Younger, but I didn't know when we . . . ugh, I don't have the energy to get into it. Just go. It's not as bad as you think."

Louiza teleported to the triage room, which was empty save for Phillip, who lay on his back on the floor, knees bent, head twisted to the side, and both hands raised as if fending off an attack.

"Hello, Madame President," Phillip said without moving.

"Hello, Phillip. Please call me Louiza."

"Thanks. Louiza, please take a good look at me, and try to help me remember what position I'm in later."

"I'm not sure I'll ever forget."

Brit the Elder appeared, still holding her glass of Hi-C. "Hello, Phillip."

Phillip sat up, dusted himself off, and said, "Hello." He avoided calling Brit the Elder by any name, because he was in a relationship with Brit the Younger, and she understandably didn't like it when he called Brit the Elder *Brit*. Just as understandably, Brit the Elder didn't really enjoy being addressed directly as *Brit the Elder,* so it was safer just to keep names out of it.

Phillip asked, "How'd it go with the injured from the dragon attack?"

Louiza said, "Mostly superficial wounds and minor—" She stopped midsentence when Martin appeared out of thin air.

"What is it, Phillip? Oh, hi, Louiza." Martin turned to Brit the Elder and said, "Hello . . . ma'am."

Louiza and Brit the Elder both said hello.

"How'd it go with the injured?" Martin asked.

Louiza said, "I was just telling Phillip. It was—"

Gwen appeared. "What's wrong, Phillip? Oh, hi, Louiza. Brit."

Louiza said, "Hello."

Brit the Younger appeared. "Yes, Phil? What can . . . Oh! Hello, Louiza." She nodded at Brit the Elder, who nodded back.

Gwen asked, "Say, how'd it go with—"

Louiza blurted, "Mostly superficial wounds and minor—"

Gary appeared. "What's up? Oh! Hello *ladies!*" He bowed toward Louiza and Brit the Elder.

Louiza let out a frustrated grunt, but Brit the Elder smiled and said, "Hello, Gary. Good to see you." She always made a point of being extra friendly to Gary when Brit the Younger was around because she knew that Brit the Younger was horrified at the idea that her future self might be attracted to him.

Gary asked, "How'd it go with the hurt?"

Martin said, "He means the people who were hurt."

Gary said, "Yeah, the hurt."

Louiza started to speak, but Brit the Elder placed a hand on her shoulder to stop her.

Jeff appeared. "What do you want, Phillip? Oh, hello—"

Brit the Elder held up a finger to silence him.

Tyler appeared, partially covered with Gary's webbing. "Okay, Phillip—"

Brit the Elder said, "One moment please."

Roy materialized and immediately asked, "What is it, Phil?" He didn't bother to look around to see who else was present.

Brit the Elder nodded to Louiza.

"Now that everyone's here," Louiza said, "the injuries to the men you sent us were mostly superficial wounds and minor burns. A few people needed stitches. Nothing I couldn't handle. I just wish there hadn't been so many of them at once."

Roy said, "Good. Thanks for handling the injured and all, but we have important business to discuss. Why'd you put the kibosh on my macro, Phil? We could have this whole thing done by now."

Phillip said, "Please tell me you didn't trigger your macro before you came here."

"I didn't. I wanted to. I'm still not sure I shouldn't have. But you said not to do anything, and it seemed important to you. Now what's the problem?"

"Yes," Louiza said. "Who's hurt?"

Phillip said, "Nobody. Sorry for the false alarm. We needed to go away and talk without anybody realizing we'd left, and this was the only way I could think of to do it on short notice."

Luckily for Phillip, Louiza was more relieved than irritated.

Roy said, "Yeah, yeah, okay. What's the problem?"

Phillip said, "It's about this fight we're in the middle of."

Martin said, "If you want to call it that. It's not really much of a fight."

Phillip said, "That's the problem. We need to lose it."

Tyler said, "And by *lose,* you mean?"

"Lose," Phillip said. "The opposite of win. We need for the other side to defeat us."

Brit the Younger asked, "Why on earth would we need that?"

Phillip said, "Because we have a much more serious image problem than I thought."

Tyler said, "And that's why we're making a show out of beating Kludge and his boys."

"Yes," Phillip said, "but publicly defeating some locals, even the Bastards, won't help the problem we have. We've been thinking that we look incompetent, but the real problem is that we look too competent."

Gwen said, "I'm sorry, but have they been watching us? Have they not seen the mess we've made?"

"They saw it, but to them all magic is impressive, even when it's done badly. When something we do turns out wrong, they assume that was our plan, because we're wizards and we must know what we're doing."

Martin said, "They give us the benefit of the doubt."

"Yes," Phillip agreed. "In the most negative sense possible. The locals see us as invincible, infallible, and, probably insufferable."

Roy said, "So after all the crap we've all put up with, you want to throw a fight so that everyone can see us get our butts handed to us?"

"I feel we have to. Roy, we know that we're all borderline incompetent, but nobody else knows it. They think we're almost unbeatable, and that we think we're totally unbeatable. In order to demonstrate to everyone else that we're fallible, we need to have it demonstrated to us, in as public a manner as possible."

Roy said, "That's nonsense."

"No," Brit the Elder said. "Phillip's right. I usually wouldn't say anything. I make a point of not interfering in your lives."

Brit the Younger said, "Since when?"

Brit the Elder said, "I wasn't speaking to you, dear. You're me. Your life is my life. Everything I do interferes with it."

"So it would seem," Brit the Younger said.

Brit the Elder said, "Roy, everyone: I know that what Phillip is saying sounds crazy to you, but I remember the situation well, and he is exactly right. There are people who suspect that you created the dragons. People don't just forget that sort of thing. They need to see you suffer or they'll never rest until they make it happen themselves."

Tyler said, "But that's just a few people. What about the hundreds we've helped?"

"You've made a lasting impression on them, too, and not an entirely positive one." Brit the Elder pointed at Roy and Jeff. "You've caused rampant inflation in London. The merchants have fewer goods to sell, and more money in their pockets thanks to the settlements you all gave them, so they're less inclined to haggle. It takes months for prices to come back down to normal, and by the time they do, most people are poorer than when they started."

She looked to Martin and Phillip. "And you two are even worse. Your actions destabilize the price of gold throughout Europe for generations to come. The entire economy of the known world has been thrown off."

Roy said, "Lord. This is terrible. Who knows what kind of effect this will have on the future?"

"None," Martin said. "You know that. It'll have no effect on the future. We know that because every time we've done anything, we've gone back to the future to check, and nothing's ever different, which just raises more questions, and that's why we don't talk about it, okay?"

Roy said, "Yeah. But still."

"NO," Martin said. "No *but still*."

Brit the Elder said, "Martin's right that it has no effect on the distant future, but it has a huge effect on the near future. Tyler, Gary: that little girl you encountered grows up to be a mean, unpleasant, angry woman who nobody likes and who likes nobody but her pets."

"Yeah," Tyler said. "I'm not so sure that's anything we did."

"And Gwen," Brit the Elder said, "while the Scottish dragons never attacked any populated areas, I can tell you for a fact that our interference destabilized at least one marriage."

"How do you know this?" Brit the Younger asked.

Brit the Elder shrugged. "I remember it happening."

Brit the Younger asked, "Which marriage?"

Phillip asked, "And when do you remember this happening?"

Brit the Elder smiled at Phillip, then said, "The point is that hundreds of people have seen you meddle to some degree in the affairs of man, but none of them have seen you suffer for it. If we wizards don't get taken down a peg, there's a good chance they'll turn against us."

Phillip nodded. "We need some humility knocked into us, but nobody else can do it, so we'll have to knock it into ourselves."

39.

The wizards spent two hours plotting, planning, comparing notes, writing macros, and raiding Louiza's beer fridge. When they were ready, Phillip assumed the position, Louiza triggered the medevac macro's now-modified return protocol, and the wizards teleported back to their exact former locations, milliseconds after they'd left.

Phillip squirmed and cringed beneath Honor, but the cringing was now an acting exercise. He had taken the time to create a force field that would prevent anything, including the doll, or any detritus that might fall off of the doll, from touching his face.

Phillip looked up at Honor, and in a voice dripping with fear and contempt in equal measure, said, "Foolish child! Where did you get the Mego Demon Figure?"

"From a friend."

"You have no clue as to the powers you are meddling with."

Honor said, "Good."

Phillip said, "Just, for your own safety, do not repeat the phrase *Detroit rokenrolo vilaĝon* while you hold the Mego Demon Figure."

Honor gave Phillip a shrewd look, but said nothing.

"Yes, the consequences would be quite dire, if you were to say *Detroit rokenrolo vilaĝon* at this time."

Honor continued to stare, but her mouth moved silently, as if working through how to create unfamiliar sounds.

Phillip pushed himself up on his elbows, looked her in the eye, and in a slow, deliberate voice, said, "Indeed, I, your enemy, would be particularly displeased if you were to say the words *Detroit rokenrolo vilaĝon* now. Right now."

Honor said, "*Detroit rokenrolo vilaĝon?*"

For an instant, Phillip smiled before remembering himself and contorting his face into a cartoonish approximation of utter horror. "You said it! Oh no! You were clever to see through my ruse! This is terrible!"

The Gene Simmons doll pulsed red with arcane energy and rose free of Honor's hand. The doll stopped when it reached an altitude of ten feet and started spewing waves of blood-red radiation.

Phillip let out a high, unearthly scream. Then the doll seemed to burst with a tremendous amount of energy, but instead of the energy distributing evenly in every direction, it flew with great precision in eight directions, striking each of the wizards, no matter how far away they were, or how fast they were moving. Phillip instantly collapsed into unconsciousness, as did all of the others. Phillip slumped back onto the ground, but the others, who were all airborne, went limp, and started slowly descending to the ground. A red mist rose from all of the wizards, coalesced into a vaguely humanoid form, then dissolved, except for Phillip's, which solidified into Louiza in her she-devil costume. The area around Louiza suddenly seemed filled with a thin white smoke. Behind her, a line of six pyrotechnic fountains spewed multicolored sparks ten feet into the air.

They had considered having both Louiza and Brit the Elder participate, but they chose not to for three reasons: It would have seemed odd to have two demons come from one wizard; someone would probably have recognized her as being physically identical to Brit the Younger; and the most compelling reason—Brit the Elder said she didn't want to.

Honor asked, "Who are you?"

Louiza said, "I am the demon."

"What are you?"

"I am a demon."

Honor had gone through a lot, and the stress showed. Louiza led her through the rest of the conversation, in much the same way a pediatrician has to talk a frightened child through a procedure.

Louiza asked, "How did you know that the Mego Demon Figure could break my control over these wizards?"

Honor said, "Your control? So it wasn't them, it was you all along?"

Louiza looked around and noted with satisfaction that she had the undivided attention of everyone present. Even the men riding the dragons had circled in close, since the wizards they'd been intent on fighting had seemingly fallen of their own accord.

"Yes, of course it was me. You don't think these so-called *wizards* could have done any of this? They're fools! Foolish fools who behave foolishly. They're far too foolish to ever . . ." Louiza trailed off, seeing that Phillip had cracked an eye open and was using it to glare at her.

"They're far too decent to have done any of this, not unless someone evil pulled their strings. They have no vision, no drive. These wizards only want to live in peace and occasionally help people. They never would have created the dragons on their own, and certainly wouldn't have unleashed them on your miserable little town."

Phillip smiled at her, faintly.

Louiza shouted, "The weak-minded fools! They tried to resist. They even tried to use the Mego Demon Figure against me themselves. They said the incantation once, which drove me from the host I had inhabited and gave me physical form, but I stopped them before they could say the incantation a second time, banishing me for all eternity. I cast the Mego Demon Figure away, where I thought nobody would ever look for it, lest someone else say the incantation twice, and banish me themselves."

Honor's eyes grew wide with realization, then even wider with fear, then she looked up and to the right, screwing up her face as if trying desperately to remember something. Louiza looked down at Phillip, who had cracked both eyes, and very slightly shrugged.

Louiza said, "But now I will destroy the Mego Demon Figure before anyone can say the incantation: *Detroit rokenrolo vilaĝon.*"

Honor laughed in triumph and shouted, "*Detroit rokenrolo vilaĝon!*"

Louiza screamed. A deafening screech, which only time travelers could identify as an electric guitar, played throughout the town. The Gene Simmons doll disappeared in a pulsating mass of pitch-black energy that exploded outward, enveloping Leadchurch and a several-hundred-yard radius of the woods and farmland outside town.

The black energy hid another force bubble, this one made to deform and wobble according to a complex algorithm. Matter could get through its boundary with no resistance, but light could not. Since night had not quite fallen, precious few fires were burning in Leadchurch, and even where there was a light source, the sudden plunge into darkness prevented anyone's eyes from adjusting until just before the darkness field disappeared on its own. Light came flooding back in, seeming that much brighter in relation to the blackness they had just experienced.

Darkness only enveloped the town for a short time, but it was long enough for Roy's macro to remove Kludge and the Bastards from their dragons, and for each dragon to find itself surrounded by a crystalline cube with a single, sliding wall that forced them through a goal and out of existence.

When the darkness dissipated, the doll, the demon, and the dragons were all gone. Honor, Runt, and Phillip's supine form were all in a round section of discolored ground. Kludge and the Bastards descended slowly, safely ensconced in glowing spheres that popped like soap bubbles when they touched the ground.

All of the wizards got up groggily from the places where they had landed. Most were on the ground. A few were on top of buildings. Gary hadn't been paying attention to his descent and had landed draped over a fence. He had to lie there, all of his weight resting painfully on his belly. Now that he could extricate himself, he teetered awkwardly for a moment, then cartwheeled headfirst to the ground.

Phillip sat up. He made a show of rubbing his eyes and looking disoriented. He saw Honor, who still stood where she'd been before the darkness, looking both overwhelmed and weary. Runt stood beside and behind her. The dog bared her teeth, but tucked her tail between her legs.

Phillip rose to his feet, staggered forward, knelt in front of Honor, and took her hand. "Thank you, Honor. Thank you for saving us. All of us." As he kissed her hand, he did a frantic mental check to see if he had any memory of her having held the Gene Simmons doll with that hand.

He looked up, alarmed at having remembered something. "Your brother! Your brother and the other injured. Where are they?"

Honor said, "In the church."

Phillip walked back to where he'd fallen and picked up his staff. He pointed it at the church and said, "*Tempo veki!*" A beam of blue light extended from the head of his staff to the point of the church's steeple, the only part of it visible from where they stood. The entire church glowed with blue light for several seconds before Phillip ended the spell. He turned to Honor, smiled, and said, "You should probably go talk to your brother. He's going to be very interested in what you've been up to."

Honor was too grateful to be bothered with thanking him. She sprinted toward the church, using stores of energy she hadn't known she possessed.

Before, the church had been bathed in the eerie quiet of more than two dozen people lying unconscious. Now it hummed with the dull murmur and lethargic motion of more than two-dozen people moaning, sitting up, and asking for a glass of water.

The wizards chose to cut short the post-treatment sleep portion of the medevac protocol. It was an unnecessary piece of stagecraft for most of the patients, as they had only superficial wounds. For those who had required more extreme intervention, the residual pain from their stitches and the admonitions of the demons they'd encountered would probably be enough to make them take it easy for a while.

Honor darted past the pews and nearly leapt at Sonny, who had barely lifted himself off of his belly and into a sitting position when she barreled into him, nearly knocking him down again. She threw her arms around his midsection and squeezed him hard. "Sonny! Are you all right?"

"Yes, Honor. I'm fine. But my back does hurt quite a lot."

Honor quickly stopped hugging Sonny, muttered, "Sorry," then threw her arms around his neck and squeezed just as hard as she had before. "I was so worried about you."

"I can tell," Sonny croaked, fighting for breath.

They spent a while hugging and crying, Honor out of relief that her brother was back, and Sonny because tears are contagious, and he was touched to see how much his sister cared for him. Finally, Sonny said, "I died, Honor."

Honor said, "You were asleep. The wizards did it. I'll explain later."

Sonny shook his head. "No," he said, quietly, "I know what I saw Honor, and for at least a little while, I was dead. I saw the afterlife."

Honor asked, "What was it like?"

"Yes," Bishop Galbraith asked, "what was it like?" He'd woken up at the same time as Sonny, and now sat on the pew behind Sonny, trying to fend off the two nuns aggressively fussing over him.

Sonny painfully twisted in his seat to look at the bishop, and said, "Well, I didn't see heaven. I saw the other place."

Galbraith raised his eyebrows and said, "Really?"

"Yes. There were three devils. Two were female. I think they were there to tempt me. The third was male. I think he was in charge."

Galbraith nodded sagely. "He had a forceful manner, did he? The bearing of a natural leader?"

"No. He was just older than the other two."

"Oh."

"Much older. Maybe hundreds of years."

"I see."

"And the other two moved around and did things while he just stood in one place and talked, like he was used to having others do things for him."

From several pews over, Sister Flora said, "Typical."

Bishop Galbraith said, "I understand. What did these devils say to you, Sonny?"

Sonny looked at the bishop, then at Honor, and said, "That's the strange thing. The very old one said that I was a good boy, and that I was on the right path. They said that if I keep going exactly as I am, that I wouldn't ever have to go back, or see them again. Father, what does it mean?"

"Probably exactly what it sounds like. Did they say anything else?"

"They said to keep my back wounds clean and dry, and to wear loose-fitting, light shirts until my burns have healed. And the very old one said that it's perfectly acceptable to pay my church tithes in meat or wool instead of coin, but to bear in mind that lamb would be preferable to mutton."

Galbraith said, "He sounds very wise."

40.

When Honor and Runt streaked off into the distance to their reunion with Sonny and, to a lesser extent, Bishop Galbraith, Phillip remained, standing alone in the middle of the road, surrounded by people he thought of as his friends and neighbors.

Before they'd played their ruse on the girl, she seemed to be the only one ready to accuse him of anything. Now they all seemed to be silently accusing him of terrible misdeeds with their eyes.

He'd already claimed at least partial responsibility for the dragon problem, though he'd done so through an elaborate lie. To accuse someone of wrongdoing after they'd already confessed seemed unfair, even cowardly. The fact that Phillip knew that he and the wizards were responsible only made the silent accusations sting more.

The other wizards joined Phillip. Predictably, Brit the Younger reached him first, followed closely by Martin, Gwen, and then the rest. Phillip addressed the citizens.

"We're sorry for the trouble. We regret any unpleasantness we may have caused. None of us ever meant any of you any harm." He turned to his fellow wizards and said, "Let's all go to my shop."

Phillip started walking down the street, his eyes locked firmly on the ground directly in front of him.

Gary said, "Why don't we fly there, or teleport?"

Martin said, "Because this situation calls for slinking."

The wizards slunk down the street, feeling the eyes of the citizens follow them, the eight floats that made up the First Annual Leadchurch Parade of Shame.

Phillip noticed Kludge, standing straight and tall, watching the wizards with open satisfaction. When he drew close to Kludge, Phillip told Brit to let everyone upstairs, and that he'd be right behind them. He stopped next to Kludge as the rest of wizards walked on.

"Kludge," Phillip said, "I don't think we wizards ever properly apologized for what Todd did to you."

"No," Kludge said. "You didn't."

"We were never on friendly terms, the wizards and the Bastards, but that can't justify what happened to you."

"No, it can't."

"Well, I am sorry. We all are. It should have never happened. I know that doesn't make up for anything."

"No, it doesn't."

"If it makes you feel any better, we punished Todd, rather harshly, for what he did to you."

"Yeah," Kludge said, "where is he now?"

Phillip said, "Dead."

Kludge said, "I suppose that's a start."

By the time Phillip reached his rec room, everyone was already seated, including Louiza, who'd arrived first and waited for them. She had removed her mask, but still wore the remainder of her sexy devil costume. She tried to act as if she didn't notice Gary staring at her.

Phillip leaned against his bar and said, "That was a right mess, wasn't it?"

Roy muttered, "We went through all that just to end up exactly like we started, only now everyone respects us less."

Gwen said, "Yeah, but maybe we deserve to be respected less, or we didn't deserve some of the respect we were getting."

Brit said, "And it was a learning experience."

"Yeah? What did we learn, exactly?" Roy asked.

"Not to play God?" Jeff said.

Martin said, "I dunno. Seems to me it depends on what you mean by *playing God*. I mean, creating the dragons in the first place wasn't a great move, but since then, all of us have done a lot of messing with people's lives, and made a lot of big messes. In the end, we had lie to an entire town to make it all right. I think at most we can say we learned to be very careful when we play God."

Tyler said, "That's a stupid lesson."

Gary said, "We paid off all those merchants in Camelot, and you two drove those dragons out of that cave by triggering a gold rush. Maybe the lesson is that bribes work."

Tyler said, "That's a stupid lesson, too, and we already knew it anyway."

Phillip said, "How about this, Tyler? Martin and I took care of your last dragon by getting that little girl's parents involved. Brit and Gwen got rid of their dragons when they asked those shepherds for advice. I realize now that the little girl who just exorcized us is a shepherd herself, and probably could have been a helpful ally instead of an enemy if we'd only gone to her and her brother for advice to begin with. I think the lesson is that just because we know about magic doesn't mean we know everything, and that we aren't just here to help the locals, they're here to help us as well."

They all thought about that for a moment, before Gary said, "I don't like that at all."

Phillip said, "Which is how you know it's true."

Brit the Younger said, "Louiza, one thing I'd like to know is why you and Brit the Elder had those skintight devil costumes just sitting around ready. You didn't have to magic them up or anything. They were just draped over a chair in your office."

Louiza said, "I can't tell you that."

Brit asked, "Why not?"

"Because Brit the Elder doesn't want me to tell you."

"But she's just my future self, supposedly. I want you to tell me. Surely that must cancel her wishes out. It's like I've changed my mind retroactively."

Louiza thought for a moment, and said, "You want me to tell you. She doesn't want me to tell you. I'm still not happy that you dragged me into this with no warning, so I don't want to tell you either. That's two votes to one. You and I have you outvoted."

Epilogue

The next day, Bishop Galbraith walked around the church grounds as usual. Only his slower pace gave any indication that anything out of the ordinary had happened.

The bishop stopped when he heard a voice behind him call out, "Your Excellency!" He turned to see Phillip walking quickly to catch up.

"How's your leg, Your Excellency?"

"Sore, but nothing I can't handle."

"And how's the church doing, after everything that happened?"

"Well, I think. It wasn't damaged in any of the fighting. In fact, I strongly suspect attendance will be way up for a while."

"Yes, experiences like these tend to bring people to religion."

Bishop Galbraith smiled, and said, "Some of them much more than others. I see some of your friends are flying around the rooftops this morning. They seem awfully busy."

"Yeah, they're trying to repair the damage."

"Making everything as good as if nothing had happened, eh?"

"Better, hopefully. We plan to leave the roofs less leaky and the walls less drafty than they were before. The hope is that, in the end, people will feel like they were lucky that their house got broken by a fire-breathing dragon."

"But it doesn't look like you're fixing any carpentry."

"No, I got the hard job. I've spent the last two hours talking to Kludge."

"Never a pleasant prospect."

"No, and that's part of why we wizards never properly apologized to him for what happened to him. You remember what I'm talking about."

"All too well. Did he accept your apology?"

"No, but he is accepting our help. We spoke to the king. The chunk of land where they camp is now deeded to Kludge, and we're going to help them build a house to live in."

"Help them build it? You're not building it for them with your magic?"

"No. We're giving them the materials, the tools, and paying two carpenters to supervise them, but they have to build the thing themselves. The thinking is that they'll respect the house more if they have to put some effort into it, and maybe one or two of them will learn a real trade. At the very least, for a little while they might be too tired to bother menacing anyone."

Galbraith said, "And perhaps they'll be friendlier once they start sleeping indoors."

Phillip said, "Indeed. They seemed pretty happy about the idea. One of them, *Stretch* I think they called him, already has ideas for his dream kitchen."

Bishop Galbraith squinted up into the sky and said, "Here come some of your friends."

Martin, Gwen, and Brit the Younger soared gracefully through the air and landed in front of Phillip and the bishop. Martin asked, "How'd it go with Kludge?"

Phillip said, "It went well. I just finished telling His Excellency about it. We can discuss the particulars later." The others took the subtle hint from Phillip not to ask any further questions about the Kludge conversation, because he hadn't quite told the bishop the whole story.

"The fact that you're all three here leads me to believe that you're ready to go make our final stop," Phillip continued.

The bishop said, "And I must get back to the church. Phillip, it's always a pleasure to talk to you. Gwen, good to see you. Martin, good day. Brit, it's wonderful to see you. I do hope you'll stop by the church occasionally. You'll always be welcome."

"I, uh, thank you, Your Excellency. I'm sorry, I just haven't talked to you that often. I didn't think you really knew my name."

"I didn't," the bishop said, "but I do now. A woman I'm told is you in the distant future and I have become very well acquainted, and I hope that you and I can be good friends as well."

As Bishop Galbraith walked away, back toward the lead church, Brit said, "I'm not sure I like the sound of that."

Phillip said, "I know I don't."

"So," Martin asked, "Kludge went for it?"

"Yes," Phillip said. "Starting next week, instead of training by fighting fake dragons, we train by fighting Kludge and the Bastards. They were dubious at first, but they came around when I told them that we would promise to never hurt them, and that they'd be required to do their absolute best to hurt us any way they could. Is Jeff working on his end?"

Gwen said, "He and Roy are already done. They just took the original, dumb, fake dragons, made 'em look like they're made of metal, stripped out all of the behavior algorithms, and figured out a firing system for the fire breath. They just stand there like a statue unless someone rides them."

Phillip said, "Good. Telling them they'd get to use dragons to try to hurt us with was a big part of my sales pitch."

Martin said, "I wonder if the Bastards will be disappointed."

"In what?" Brit asked.

"The dragons," Martin said. "Because they aren't like real dragons."

"There are no real dragons," Brit said. "There never were. They were all fake, Martin."

"I know that. It's just, these dragons are going to be even faker than the ones they're used to. Really, they're little more than mean-looking flying motorcycles that shoot fire."

"Mean-looking flying motorcycles that shoot fire," Phillip said. "Yes, I can see how a gang of toughs would be disappointed in that."

In Honor and Sonny's pasture, the sheep grazed under the watchful eyes of Blackie and Harry. Honor sat, leaned back against a tree with her eyes closed, her left hand in her lap and her right hand listlessly scratching Runt, until a soft male voice said, "Pardon me," at which point Honor's eyes popped open and she let out a panicked yelp.

Phillip, Brit, Gwen, and Martin were all standing in the grass in front of her. Phillip said, "I'm sorry. I was specifically trying not to startle you."

Honor glared at him and said, "You didn't do very well, did you?"

"No. I didn't. We stopped by your house looking for you. Your brother told us you were out here."

"I am."

"Yes. Honor, we are all grateful to you, and quite impressed with what you accomplished. You suffered a terrible loss, stood up for what you knew to be true when all of the adults seemed to be against you, befriended people of whom even we wizards chose to steer clear, and confronted an adversary you had every reason to believe was far more powerful than you."

"I wanted my brother back."

"Well, we're all very impressed, and grateful."

"So you say."

"Exactly. We've said it, and now we're here to show it with our actions. But first, we do have one question. We're curious how you came to possess the Mego Demon Figure."

"Hubert gave it to me."

"Yes, the dung sifter. I thought that might be the case. We must reward him."

Brit said, "We could set him up in another line of work. Any other line of work."

"No," Martin said. "He wouldn't go for it. That business is in his blood."

Gwen said, "Then maybe a course of antibiotics. And a case of rubber gloves."

Phillip cut in, "We can discuss that with Hubert. We're here to reward Honor." Phillip knelt down and pulled out a small leather pouch. He opened the drawstring and showed Honor that it was full of silver coins.

"This pouch will refill itself with silver coins once a month, rain or shine, for the rest of your life. You could use it to buy food. There's enough for you and Sonny to just get by, or you could use it to buy more sheep, and pay for hands to help you tend them. Play your cards right, and this silver can help you make even more silver on your own, and if it doesn't work out, you still have next month's silver to count on. Also, if you're ever in trouble, stick your hand in the pouch and snap your fingers twice. One of us will show up as soon as possible to help in any way we can."

Honor took the pouch. It felt heavy in her hands. She looked inside, rattled the coins around a bit, then looked at Phillip and said, "Thank you."

"You're most welcome."

"It's very nice."

"You deserve no less."

They lapsed into a long silence, during which everyone fidgeted uneasily. Finally, Phillip asked, "Do you have any questions, Honor?"

Honor thought for a moment, then asked, "Why silver? Why not gold?"

"I know that right now gold is the more standard currency," Phillip said, "but in the coming years, silver will be much preferable, trust me."

Honor's expression darkened as Phillip said this, then said, "I suppose that's the problem. This is all very nice, but I just don't trust you wizards."

Phillip smiled and said, "And until we earn your trust, you shouldn't."

Later that night, 1,500 years earlier, Brit the Younger sat in her living room back in Atlantis, watching a school of fish swim by the window when the doorbell rang.

Nik shouted from the kitchen, "I'll be right there."

Brit hoisted herself up out of her chair. "Don't worry about it. I'll get it."

She looked through the peephole and sagged visibly when she saw Brit the Elder waiting on the doorstep. She opened the door, but said nothing.

Brit the Elder walked in. "You don't have to act so unhappy to see me. I'm making an effort here. I've started knocking like you asked instead of just coming in."

"That's your idea of some great concession to my feelings? Knocking? That's just common courtesy when you visit someone in their home."

Brit the Elder sat down in the chair Brit the Younger had just vacated. "You forget, this is my home, too. I lived here longer than you have, then saved it so it would be waiting for you when you showed up."

Brit the Elder looked around the room. "Phillip's not here."

"No. He's not."

"That wasn't a question. I know he's not here because I remember that he wasn't here when Brit the Elder came by to see me the day after the big dragon battle. I wasn't happy to see her."

"I bet you weren't. Anyway, Phillip's at his place, right through one of those doors." She pointed at the two rustic wooden doors set into the pristine glass wall of her living room.

"I know. I'm not here for him. I'm here for you."

"Okay, what do you want?"

"To give you the opportunity to ask any questions you might have."

"Will you answer them?" Brit the Younger asked.

"You won't know until you ask."

"Okay. First question. Why did you and Louiza have devil costumes on hand?"

"I can't tell you. Louiza already explained that."

"She said that you didn't want to tell me, not that you couldn't."

"Yes, well, when I was Brit the Younger, Brit the Elder didn't want to tell me, so now that I'm Brit the Elder, I can't, even if I wanted to. Which I don't. Next question?"

"How did you and Louiza deal with all of those injured people we sent you? I figure it'll be handy to know when I'm you."

"Yes, it would be. Sadly, I can't tell you that either."

Brit the Younger closed her eyes and let out a long, slow grunt. "If you knew that you weren't going to answer my questions, why did you bother coming over in the first place?"

"Because that's what Brit the Elder did when I was Brit the Younger, damn her. This isn't fun for me either you know, playing the villain in reenactments of all of my most aggravating memories."

"It's not like I enjoy getting aggravated to create those memories in the first place."

"Yes, I know, but we each have our cross to bear. Speaking of which, the Leadchurch apology tour went well for the most part."

Brit the Younger said, "Yes."

Brit the Elder said, "Again, that wasn't a question."

"Of course it wasn't."

"My memory is that it all went pretty well. Most people were fairly forgiving and many of the ones who weren't come around eventually. Shame about Kludge though."

Brit the Younger said, "Yeah well, that's . . . wait a second. What do you mean, *Shame about Kludge*?"

"Just that it's a pity he chose not to cooperate."

Brit the Younger said, "But he did. He agreed to the proposal."

Brit the Elder said, "What?"

"Yeah. Does he go back on it later?"

"No. He turned it down at first. It took a year to win him over."

"No. He's on board. You remember it differently?"

Brit the Elder's eyes widened, but she said nothing.

"You do! You remember it differently!" Brit the Younger laughed, then paused, then laughed again, then looked very nervous. "What does this mean?"

Brit the Elder stood up and smiled. "It means that I'm messing with you, just like Brit the Elder messed with me when I was you."

Brit the Younger said, "Get out."

"That's what I said."

"Out! Now!"

Brit the Elder stepped out of Brit the Younger's quarters. The instant she heard the door shut, her expression changed from her customary look of smug amusement to a most unusual one of alarmed confusion. She teleported back to her home, as walking or flying would have taken too long.

Because for once, Brit the Elder had no time to waste.

ALSO BY SCOTT MEYER

Basic Instructions Collections:
Help Is on the Way
Made with 90% Recycled Art
The Curse of the Masking Tape Mummy
Dignified Hedonism

Magic 2.0:
Off to Be the Wizard
Spell or High Water
An Unwelcome Quest

Master of Formalities

The Authorities

Run Program

ACKNOWLEDGEMENTS

As usual, this book would not exist without the people who assist, support, and put up with me. I'd like to thank Rodney Sherwood; Mike Dunnigan; Steven Carlson; Ric Schrader; my wife, Missy; the readers of my comic strip, *Basic Instructions*; and everyone who has read my previous books.

I'm also grateful to Joshua Bilmes, Eddie Schneider, Steve Feldberg, Matt Sugarman, and the whole team at Audible.

ABOUT THE AUTHOR

 After an unsuccessful career as a radio DJ, and a so-so career as a stand-up comic, Scott Meyer found himself middle-aged, working as a ride operator at Walt Disney World, and in his spare time producing the web comic *Basic Instructions*. He slowly built a following, which allowed him to self-publish his first novel, *Off to Be the Wizard*. The book's success brought him a publishing deal.

Scott is the bestselling author of seven novels. He lives in Arizona with his wife, their cats, and his most important possession: a functioning air conditioner.

Printed in Great Britain
by Amazon